WHERE DANGER HIDES

A BLACKTHORNE, INC. NOVEL

WHERE DANGER HIDES

TERRY ODELL

FIVE STAR
A part of Gale, Cengage Learning

Detroit • New York • San Francisco • New Haven, Conn • Waterville, Maine • London

GALE
CENGAGE Learning·

LIBRARY OF CONGRESS CATALOGING-IN-PUBLICATION DATA

Odell, Terry.
  Where danger hides : a Blackthorne, Inc. novel / Terry Odell.
  — 1st ed.
    p. cm.
  ISBN-13: 978-1-4328-2512-6 (hardcover)
  ISBN-10: 1-4328-2512-7 (hardcover)
  1. Missing persons—Fiction. 2. California—Fiction. I. Title.
PS3615.D456W49 2011
813'.6—dc22   2011004259

First Edition. First Printing: May 2011.
Published in 2011 in conjunction with Tekno Books.

Printed in the United States of America
1 2 3 4 5 6 7 15 14 13 12 11

To the family—Dan, Jason, Jessica, Nicole: near or far, you're always there, and always special.

ACKNOWLEDGMENTS

I might sit at the computer alone, but I owe the words on the page to so many people around me.

To Sandra McDonald for being there from the beginning, and always finding time to give me advice.

To Tom Fuller for telling me how Dalton would react under fire, and all things combat-related. Any errors are mine.

To Wally Lind and the gang at Crimescenewriters, and the folks at Clues & News for answering so many questions.

To the Florida chapter of MWA for putting on SleuthFest, where everyone is willing to help writers at all levels.

To Tammy Strickland for what goes on in hospitals, and C.J. Lyons for medical advice.

To Tony Cartledge for his critiquing and helping Fozzie sound more Aussie.

To Karla, Dara, Julie & Steve for their critical comments. To Kelly for her review of the draft manuscript. It's stronger for your help.

To Jess for reading and brainstorming.

Acknowledgments

Thanks to those people on airplanes who are willing to tell me all about explosives, tunnel systems, and drug-smuggling. Flying out of military towns provides amazing help, even if it remains anonymous.

And, of course, to Brittiany Koren, editor extraordinaire, and every one at Five Star for turning the manuscript into a finished product.

CHAPTER 1

Jungle noises filled Dalton's ears. Monkeys chattered; birds sang; insects buzzed. Familiar sounds. Good sounds. Sounds that meant nothing was amiss in this Colombian hellhole. Yet.

He shifted his weight, taking some of the pressure off his injured arm, which didn't hurt nearly as much as his ass would when his boss found out he'd finagled his way into a detour from the team's mission.

But it would be worth it once he found Rafael.

Another lead on a client's long-missing daughter meant Blackthorne, Inc. deployed a team within spitting distance of one of Rafael's drug plantations, and he'd convinced Blackie to include him.

"You're forgetting you're supposed to be dead," Blackie had said. "When you fake your own death, you need to stay off the radar awhile."

"No reason to rub elbows with anyone who'd recognize me," Dalton had argued. "Cali's not the jungle. Rafael doesn't hang there. We insert, find the target, and we're out. You're short-handed, and I'm available."

When the lead turned out to be a dead-end, he'd convinced the team to delay their return long enough to check out a trusted source who said Rafael would be inspecting his domain today.

Heat and humidity enveloped him. Sweat dripped from his forehead, down his nose and onto the rotting vegetation where he'd dug in, watching and waiting. He blinked but made no move to wipe his face. Sooner or later, the drug lord would appear.

Show yourself, scumbag. You'll pay for all the lives you've ruined.

To his left, bushes rustled. A flock of birds screeched, and as one, flapped out of the trees. Barely breathing, Dalton waited. Strained to hear what caused the birds to scatter. He heard nothing but insects. Then more rustling, getting closer.

"Fozzie?" he said into his lip mic, knowing his teammate had the entire area under surveillance.

"Hold tight, mate. Targets approaching. Below you, coming from the east."

Dalton used the scope on his assault rifle, trying to pinpoint who Fozzie had seen from his perch in the blind on the hill above. Dense vegetation made it almost impossible to spot anything but more dense vegetation. He'd wait until the targets hit the small clearing directly in front of him.

One shot. That's all he needed. One clear shot and Rafael would be dead. Dalton waited. His finger inched toward the trigger of his rifle.

"Abort. Abort," resounded from his headset. "Primary target is not, repeat, *not* present. Targets are *not*, repeat, *not* hostiles."

The *whup whup* of an approaching helo drowned out the jungle sounds. A hand yanked on his belt. "Intel was compromised. Those are innocents. We're outa here, Cowboy."

Dalton scrambled to his feet and raced through the jungle, following Cooper to the waiting helo. His ass was fried. He'd be lucky to get anything but a desk jockey assignment if Blackie didn't outright fire him.

"I might as well walk in there naked." Dalton patted his jacket where his semi-automatic Glock 17 should have been. He raised his eyebrows as his partner, Foster Mayhew, gave him an exaggerated once-over.

"Sorry, mate. I think wearing the tux is a smarter move."

Dalton quelled his rising impatience as Fozzie pulled the Blackthorne Ford Town Car into the line of luxury cars and limousines heading up the hill into one of San Francisco's wealthiest neighborhoods. They entered the driveway, nearing the valet checkpoint, and a red-liveried kid with spiked hair jogged toward them.

Dalton twisted the rearview mirror and straightened his bow tie. "Whoever invented these monkey suits should be strangled with a cummerbund."

"You're the only bloke I know who'd rather hang out in some godforsaken jungle instead of enjoying caviar and champagne while women drool over you."

"I'm not after drooling women, Fozzie. Rafael's still out there."

"Can you quit jonesing for that drug lord for one bloody night? He's in Colombia. We're here. We'll get him another time. Relax. We're on a civilized assignment for a change. We go in, do what Blackthorne sent us to do, and have some fun."

Dalton would rather be up to his eyeballs in rattlesnakes than at a fundraising gala. Gala. Why not call the thing a party? "Right."

"Lose the scowl. You know the drill. Play nice." Fozzie laughed. "Think of it as another night of torture, and you'll survive." He caught Dalton's gaze with his own. "You do have the goods, right?"

Dalton slapped his pocket. "Yes, sir." He gave a fleeting nod to the young valet who opened the door as soon as Dalton unlocked it.

"Enjoy your evening, gentlemen," the valet said.

Dalton paused at the base of the sweeping marble staircase and absorbed the imposing edifice Andrew Patterson, patron of the arts, called home. In the perfectly manicured hedges, tiny lights flickered like the fireflies he remembered from Texas summers. At the top of the stairs, a pair of double doors stood open. Classical music drifted down. Two men in black trousers, white shirts, and red jackets greeted guests.

Too bad there was a metal detector at the door. Kind of spoiled the image.

Fozzie adjusted his jacket and made a futile attempt to tame his unruly mop of brown hair. "You heard the valet. It's Saturday night. I, for one, intend to take his advice and have a good time. And find someone to have it with."

Dalton grunted. He shot his cuffs and followed the flow of guests up the stairs. "We look like the damn marching penguins."

"Ah, but elegant and well-hung penguins."

The two men smiled at the greeters, exchanged gold-edged invitations for dinner seating assignments, then passed through the metal detectors. Engulfed by a fog of expensive perfumes, Dalton waved off a waiter offering flutes of champagne from a silver tray.

The beginnings of a headache pinched the base of his neck. He stopped and eyed his partner. "Let's get it over with. I'll go left, you go right."

Fozzie snagged a canapé from a buffet table. "No worries, mate. I've already spotted my target for some post-party R and R."

"Let me guess. The woman in black."

"Not fair. Even odds at a black-and-white ball."

Dalton scanned the crowd for Fozzie's likely target. Red fingernails and lipstick on the women, red jackets on the wait staff spattered the room with relief from an endless sea of black and white. "The redhead, right?" Dalton motioned with his chin.

"You know my weakness."

"Yeah, well once in a while you might try to find one with an IQ bigger than her bra size."

Fozzie punched his arm. Dalton grimaced and sidestepped.

"Sorry, mate. Arm still sore?"

"Only when some idiot punches it." He dodged another hit.

"I'll meet you on the west balcony in fifteen minutes."

Fozzie wrinkled his nose. "With the smokers? Don't you know secondhand smoke can kill you?" The twinkle in his eyes belied his dead serious expression.

Dalton rubbed his arm. "As opposed to bullets, right?"

Fozzie joined the crowd. Dalton moved in the opposite direction, searching for a glimpse of their host. It didn't take long. Andrew Patterson commanded an immediate presence. He stood well under Dalton's six-two, but he projected the illusion of a much taller man. His hair hung in glossy black waves, with the exception of a snowy white streak in front. The ideal showcase for his black-and-white affair. Patterson whisked from group to group, a wide smile revealing perfect teeth. Rarely did the smile reach his pale blue eyes.

Although he considered tonight's assignment trivial, Dalton regarded the room as if it were any other covert operation, noting entrances, exits, places affording cover. A waiter offered a tray of canapés. As Dalton reached for a sliver of toast topped with smoked salmon, he imagined one of Rafael's henchmen in the man's Hispanic features. The waiter smiled, and the image disappeared. Dalton chided himself for being so eager to get back in the field that he saw hostiles everywhere. He counted his blessings that Blackie hadn't suspended him after what he'd done in Colombia. He popped the morsel into his mouth and continued his surveillance.

At the fifteen-minute mark, he worked his way to the balcony.

An elderly couple sat on a polished wooden bench, more intent on their cigarettes than each other. Fozzie stood at the balcony's edge, gazing into the distance. An infinitesimal shoulder twitch told Dalton his partner noted his arrival. He stepped beside Fozzie and rested his hands on the stone railing. Below them, the city lights sparkled like the jewels in the room behind them.

"Great view, isn't it, love," Fozzie said. He put his arm around Dalton's shoulders, leaned his head into his chest. "I'm so glad we came."

The couple stubbed their cigarettes into the sand-filled container and hastened inside through the open French doors.

"It's okay, Fozz. They're gone. No need to kiss me."

"Thank God for that. What did you find?"

"Nothing unexpected. Blackthorne's floor plans are reliable. Everything's happening on this floor. I counted six guards dressed like the caterers, but they're more like traffic cops, keeping people where they belong. Patterson obviously doesn't want his guests to feel there could be a security problem."

"Well, that's one thing in our favor," Fozzie said.

"What's bugging me is that the guard at the stairs let one of the waitresses go up with a tray. Means someone's probably up there."

"Also means if we have a tray, we might get up there, too."

"Means scamming a red jacket."

"You're the pro scammer, mate. Think we should try that route? Kitchen access seems liberal, and no guards in there."

"As a last resort." Dalton cocked an eyebrow. "You know—you don't look so hot."

Fozzie flashed a cockeyed grin in return. He clutched his stomach. "Yep. Must have eaten a bad shrimp."

A fanfare blared from inside. The background undercurrent of voices quieted. Dalton and Fozzie hovered in the doorway as people gravitated toward the center of the floor. Andrew Patterson's voice resonated over the sound system. "Ladies and gentlemen, if I may direct your attention to the far side of the ballroom, please."

Fozzie and Dalton exchanged glances. Dalton nodded. Without a word, they inched inside, staying close to the walls, skirting the outside of the crowd. The lights dimmed, and a large screen descended from the ceiling.

Satisfied that Red Jacket from the stairs was focused on Patterson's speech, Dalton snaked his arm under Fozzie's. "Show time."

Fozzie put his hand on Dalton's shoulder, and they staggered toward the staircase.

At the bottom step, Red Jacket put out his hand. "Sorry. The party's restricted to the first floor."

Fozzie lurched and groaned. "Oh, man, I'm sick." He clapped a hand over his mouth. His shoulders heaved.

Dalton put one foot on the first step. "No way to the downstairs johns through the crowd. Mr. Patterson won't appreciate a guest puking all over his floor."

The guard shrugged. "Second door on the left."

Dalton thanked the man as he hurried Fozzie upstairs. Once out of sight, Dalton released his hold on his partner and found the bathroom. He darted inside to turn on the water. When he came out and closed the door behind him, Fozzie waited down the hall, poised at what the floor plan indicated was Patterson's study. Dalton joined him, and they slipped inside.

Dalton locked the door. "I figure we've got until Patterson stops talking before the guard notices we haven't come back. Let's hope Patterson's typical of the fundraising breed—give 'em a microphone and time loses all meaning." He clicked on a small penlight.

Fozzie pulled out a pair of latex gloves from his pocket. Snapping his fingers into them, he muttered, "This isn't the kind of glove I wanted to be wearing tonight. Did you see the hooters on that redhead?"

"Shut up and get going. You might salvage your date yet."

Fozzie clicked on his penlight and slid into the chair behind the desk while Dalton moved toward the file cabinets on the adjacent wall.

"Um . . . mate?"

Dalton froze at Fozzie's whisper. He jerked his head around.

"The chair's warm. I'm thinking we're not alone in here."

Miri Chambers huddled under the antique mahogany desk, her heart thudding against her ribs like a snare drum. She'd barely managed to shut off the computer and grab her jump drive when she heard voices in the hall. Something about a date. God, with the kazillion bedrooms in this mansion, why would someone sneak in *here* for a quickie?

"You sure?" another voice whispered.

Even in a whisper, there was no mistaking the gender of the second voice. Male, like the first. Miri closed her eyes and magnified her prayers tenfold. She did *not* want to think about what might go on while she pretended to be invisible.

Blood drummed in her ears. Footsteps approached. Too late, she realized that when she'd ducked for cover, she'd gone in headfirst, which meant that her butt would be the first thing anyone saw if they checked under the desk. She squished herself into as tiny a package as she could, silently cursing the short skirt the caterer demanded its female staff wear. She wasn't exactly displaying her greatest asset.

Oh God, a warm hand touched that asset. She jerked away.

"Well, what do we have here? You want to come on out, darlin'?" The voice was deep, warm, and decidedly Texan.

"Stop. Please. I won't say anything. I'll stay right here and you can go find a bedroom, and I'll count to ten, or a hundred, or a thousand, before I come out, so I won't know who you are. Please?"

The hand withdrew. "What do you think?" the Texan said. "Do you think a bedroom's a good idea?"

Miri thought he was trying not to laugh.

"Might be interesting, but you're not my type, mate," the other man said. "Maybe whoever's under here is more to my liking. Come on out."

That voice was definitely Aussie, and definitely meant business.

"Okay," Miri said. "Please turn off your flashlights." She slid the tiny jump drive with the computer files she'd copied into her bra. The beams of light disappeared, leaving the green readout on the desk clock the only illumination in the room.

Her brain kicked into gear. Whoever these guys were, they had no business in here either, or they'd have turned the room lights on. Maybe they'd be willing to deal. Footsteps shuffled on the thick carpet, and she thought she heard the door open and close. Had they left?

She scooted back from her hiding place, trying to keep her skirt over her hips. Once she cleared the desk, she scrambled to her feet. The glow from the clock cast the room in shadows. Tugging her jacket back into place, Miri mustered as much dignity as she could and faced the shadowed man perched on the edge of the desk. He was peeking under the plate covers on the tray she'd brought up. She glanced around the room. There was no sign of the second man.

"What do you think you're doing in here?" she said. "Upstairs is off-limits to guests."

"My friend wasn't feeling well. The guard let us up."

So, Texas was in the room. Aussie must have left. "Yeah, and if you expect me to believe that, I've got a winning Internet lottery ticket. Where's your friend?"

"In the john. I'm sure he'll return shortly."

A resounding burst of applause came from below, followed by the opening strains of Mozart's *Marriage of Figaro*.

Miri moved toward the door. "I have to go. They'll be serving dinner."

Texas blocked her path. "Not so fast, little lady. What are *you* doing here?"

She planted her feet and put her hands on her hips. "Delivering food to Mr. Patterson's aunt."

"Oh, now who's got the lottery ticket? I suppose dear Auntie hangs around under desks?"

"Please. Let me get downstairs. I won't say anything about you being up here." She sidestepped and he grabbed her shoulders. He was tall, broad, and smelled like sandalwood. She struggled, but he held her at bay. She went limp in his grasp, put her arms around his waist and he relaxed his grip. With a quick jerk and a brisk heel to his instep, she wriggled away and dashed for the door.

Head high, she strode through the hall. Peering down the stairs, she noticed the guard wasn't at his post. She trotted down and meandered through the guests into the chaos of the kitchen. With everyone scrambling to get dinner plates to the tables, nobody would notice if she was coming or going. She worked her way through the lines of wait staff and through a side door into a storage closet.

She locked the door and bent over, hands on her thighs and took several deep breaths. She had what she came for, and those two men no longer concerned her. The LED on the clock had given off only enough light to navigate the darkened room. From her brief encounter with Texas, she was certain he'd be dressed like every other man here—in a tuxedo. She'd never pick him out in the crowd. Unless, of course, he opened his mouth, and that slow, honey-rich drawl flowed out. Or he stood close enough for a whiff of his delicious sandalwood scent.

Time for part two. She stripped off the caterer's uniform and changed into the black ball gown she'd hung in the closet when she arrived. She yanked off the short black wig and fluffed out her light brunette hair so it cascaded to her shoulders. From her evening bag, she retrieved her makeup kit and mimicked the society image, although she felt more like a clown than a woman when she was done. A spritz of perfume, and Miri took comfort knowing Texas wouldn't recognize her, either.

She slipped the treasure she'd retrieved into the beaded purse and snapped it shut. After exchanging her sensible waitress shoes for strappy stilettos, she took one more deep breath, fixed a smile to her face and stepped out to join the party.

CHAPTER 2

Round dining tables covered in crisp white linen filled four rooms surrounding the ballroom. Dalton found his assigned table and seated himself across from Fozzie. Patterson glided from one room to another, the consummate host. Although others ate with gusto, Dalton had no appetite. Three tables away, Fozzie's redhead seemed engrossed in animated conversation. Fozzie, undaunted by what would no doubt be a temporary separation, entertained their dowager seating companions with tales from the Australian outback.

Dalton sipped his wine and broke his roll into pieces on his bread plate, all the while eyeing the waitresses, trying to determine which one they'd encountered in Patterson's study. From their brief contact, he estimated her height at about five-six. A well-rounded rump, he recalled with a faint smile. Feisty. Husky voice, unaccented English. Short hair. Black, or dark brown. He couldn't rule out Hispanic heritage, which included a fair number of the staff. He eliminated about half the waitresses, but the puzzle of why she was hiding in the study nagged at him. A week's rations said there was no Auntie Patterson upstairs.

Dismissing the thought as irrelevant to the night's task, a success even with their minor setback, Dalton resigned himself to getting through the evening until it was safe to leave without calling attention to himself and Fozzie. Yet despite his best efforts, he couldn't get the mystery woman out of his mind.

She'd nearly squelched the assignment, and he cringed when he thought what his boss, Horace Blackthorne, would have to say about it if she had. He reminded himself she was an impediment, not a warm female who smelled like a spring breeze, with a voice like she'd spent the night making passionate love. After yet another fruitless scouring of the room, he returned to picking at his meal.

Unable to settle, he excused himself to use the men's room, taking a roundabout route through the other dining rooms in search of his mystery waitress. No luck. Maybe she worked in the kitchen. If not for Blackthorne's strict admonition to blend in, he would have checked. Dalton returned to his seat and a waiter set a meringue swan filled with chocolate mousse in front of him. Dalton snapped the swan's neck and popped it into his mouth. The cloying sweetness half-sickened him.

Fozzie raised his bushy eyebrows. Dalton shook his head. Fozzie shrugged, apparently unconcerned about what happened upstairs, as long as they'd done what they'd come to do.

By nine-thirty, the staff had cleared the dessert plates and refilled coffee cups. Vaguely aware of someone speaking, Dalton faced the source of the voice. The silver-haired woman seated beside him tapped a glossy brochure with an age-spotted hand.

"I'm sorry," Dalton said. He gave her a polite smile. "My mind drifted. I'm afraid I didn't hear you."

"I said, what did you think of Andrew Patterson's announcement? Did it surprise you as well?"

Dalton threw Fozzie a silent plea for help. The man merely sipped his coffee. The twitch of his eyebrows told Dalton his partner was having too much fun watching him squirm.

"Um . . . yes, I have to say it did."

"This seems to be such a departure for him. It's very noble, but also out of character. I'm going to have to think about it a while before I commit."

"Always a smart thing to do. I agree, it requires some thought." Dalton reached for one of the fanned brochures in the center of the table, then slipped it into his breast pocket, nodding. "Definitely going to study this some more."

The woman extended her hand. "I'm Grace Ellsworth."

"Pleased to meet you, Ms. Ellsworth. I'm Dalton."

Penciled eyebrows lifted. "Dalton Something or Something Dalton?"

"Just Dalton. I find *Mr.* Dalton's too formal," he said and smiled.

"Oh, you are a rascal. Well, *Dalton,* I don't suppose you'd do me the honor of a dance?"

Why the hell not? He figured at least another hour before they could leave. "My pleasure, ma'am."

"Grace."

"Grace." He pushed his chair back, stood, and held out his hand.

Fozzie winked at him and got up, no doubt seeking his redhead. Grace placed her hand in Dalton's and he guided her through the groups of people heading for the ballroom. Her movements personified her name, carrying him back to those Sunday afternoons in Texas when his grandmother insisted on teaching him and his brothers to dance.

"A man has to be able to do more than ride and rope," Grandma had said. "You'll impress many more women on the dance floor than in the rodeo ring." Dancing with Grace was a trip back to Grandma's parlor with her scratchy records. Except for the ball gown and diamonds.

Grace tilted her head up at him. "Have you found her yet?"

Dalton's grip tightened on hers, and he quickly loosened it. "What do you mean?"

"I couldn't help but notice the way you were searching around during dinner. I can't believe a handsome man such as yourself would be here alone. Not like me—an old widow with too much time and enough money to be hit for every so-called worthy cause in town."

So, he'd been that obvious. Dalton cursed inwardly for relaxing his guard. The way to stay sharp was to be on duty no matter what. "No, not really," he said. "I thought I saw someone I knew when I arrived. I must have been mistaken."

"You don't strike me as the type to make those kinds of mistakes," she said. "When you look at something, you *see* it, if you know what I mean." Her eyes narrowed ever so slightly. Was she more than a rich woman at a fundraiser?

"Tell me why you're really here," she said. "You might be wearing a designer tuxedo, but you aren't like the rest of the guests. And I've never seen you at any of these silly functions."

Dalton kept a smile on his face. "I'm new in town, ma'am, and you're right. My cousin couldn't make it tonight, and I'm here in his place." Not a total lie. Horace Blackthorne *was* his cousin, a few times removed.

Before she dug any deeper, the music shifted tempo. Grace's eyes lit up. "I hope you can waltz, young man. It's my favorite, although nobody's been able to match my Edgar, bless his soul. The man could float me around the floor like I was an angel on a cloud."

"I'll do my best."

As they danced, her expression turned dreamy. He hoped she was with Edgar in her thoughts.

When the dance ended, her eyes glistened. "Thank you," she whispered.

"My pleasure. Would you like another?"

She gave a rueful smile. "I think I'd like to remember this one. Thank you, Dalton. I sincerely hope you find whomever you're searching for."

"I intend to." If nothing else, Grace had dumped a bucket of ice water into his pity party. As an operative for Blackthorne, Inc., no matter how stupid he thought the assignment, he was on a job. After escorting Grace back to her seat, he scanned the room for Fozzie. Sure enough, he spotted him, entwined with the redhead on the dance floor.

Dalton gazed toward the front door. Only one or two guests were leaving. At the moment, most of the crowd was in the ballroom. He wandered through the main dining room. A few couples sat lingering over coffee and conversation.

Blend in. Mix, mingle, and don't stay too long with anyone. Be forgettable. His headache settled behind his eyes.

A woman with flowing light brown hair sat by herself at a table nearby. Unlike the majority of the women, she wore a high-necked gown, and she didn't seem as overburdened with jewelry as so many of the other guests. She also appeared to be several decades younger than most of them. He ambled over and stood beside her chair. "I don't mean to intrude," he said, "but if you're not with someone, would you like to dance? Or can I get you a drink?"

Her eyes widened at his questions.

As soon as he opened his mouth, Miri knew it was Texas. Had he recognized her? Afraid to study his face, she ducked her head, painfully aware she was blushing. Where was his Aussie boyfriend? Right. As if she really believed the two men were a couple. They'd been up to something in the study, and it wasn't sex.

He leaned on the back of the chair next to hers. The essence of sandalwood removed any doubt of his identity.

"We're both a little out of place here, aren't we?" he said. "Age-wise, I mean."

She shrugged, trying to ignore the way his drawl heated her insides.

"You didn't answer my question. Would you like a drink? Or a dance?"

If she recognized his voice, he'd know hers. She shook her head and pointed to her throat. "Laryngitis," she whispered.

"Ah," he said. "I have just the thing." He reached into his jacket pocket and handed her a wrapped yellow candy. "Have a butterscotch. Should soothe the throat."

Reluctantly, she accepted the sweet. It provided some moisture for her rapidly drying mouth. Hoping she wouldn't choke on it, she mouthed a thank you.

He flashed a lazy grin. "So, what'll it be? Drink or dance? You can move your head, right?"

She lifted her chin.

"I take it that's a 'yes.' "

His eyes were gunmetal gray, the color of the sky right before it rained. Creases at the corners deepened when he smiled, as he did now, and she couldn't help but return it. What the hell? She held out her hand. Although his touch was gentle, she felt an underlying strength. And calluses. Which didn't quite jibe with his tailored tuxedo. Thick, dark brown hair curled over the tops of his ears. Her guess was he preferred it short and was ready for a trim. That he hadn't bothered before coming to the event added to her curiosity. Why had he been invited? Had he been invited? She hadn't.

She stood and led the way to a corner of the dance floor. When she turned to face him, he cocked his head, and those gray eyes seemed to see her thoughts. She hoped not, because her thinking about him naked would embarrass both of them.

Unlike the last few guys she'd dated, this one knew what to do on a dance floor, and she followed his lead without any trouble. He held her close. Caught up in the music, or maybe because of the second glass of wine she'd drunk with dinner, her mind drifted and she savored the sensation. He made no attempts to talk, apparently accepting her laryngitis excuse. Two dances later, the orchestra took a break.

"Thanks," he said. "Would you like that drink?"

Common sense prevailed. She shook her head and moved toward the table. She mouthed an "excuse me" and wove her way in the direction of a restroom, afraid to glance back to see if he followed. A set of French doors opened onto a flagstone patio. She stepped into the chill night air, found a path toward the front of the house and asked the parking valet at the top of the driveway if he'd call a cab.

"We have a service, ma'am," he said. "Will you need someone to deliver your car tomorrow?"

She smiled. "No, that won't be necessary."

He gave her a nod and waved a car from a line of black sedans. When it halted at the pickup point, the valet opened the door for her. "Have a good night," he said. "And there's no charge." He stared at the driver as he spoke, as if to make sure he wouldn't pull a fast one.

"Thank you." She gave the driver an address and clutched her purse on her lap, wondering how much to tip him. Too little, or too much, and he might remember her. When the car approached the apartment building, Miri gave him a folded ten-dollar bill and slipped out the door as soon as he stopped at the curb. She watched from the lobby until he drove away, then called a cab to take her home.

Half an hour later, in her bedroom in a neighborhood the driver would most definitely remember as totally inappropriate for one of Andrew Patterson's guests, Miri placed her gown carefully on a padded hanger. Her gown for the night, anyway. Tomorrow it would go back to her sister where it could hang in the spacious walk-in closet with lots of other fancy gowns for company. Tonight it would go slumming with its poor relations in Miri's cramped reach-in with the warped louver doors that were forever coming off their tracks.

Miri scrubbed off her makeup. She donned an oversized T-shirt, pulled on some thick wool socks, and wrapped herself in an old terrycloth robe. After capturing her hair at her neck with an elastic band, she powered up her laptop and fetched the jump drive from her purse. While everything booted, she fixed a mug of hot chocolate and started a jazz playlist on her iPod.

To the driving rhythm of Dave Brubeck's *Take Five*, Miri transferred the files to her hard drive and password protected the folders, mentally thumbing her nose at Patterson for his arrogance in assuming his personal home computer was safe from intruders. Not that she'd noticed an abundance of files in her quick peek. She surmised he kept his work at the office—if he even did that work himself. Probably had a staff of secretaries, assistants, and accountants to do it while he spent his days on the golf course or tennis court.

Nancy'd known about his habit of background checks on people up for positions like Hunter's. Hell, the investigator's report was right there in his desk drawer in a yellow file folder clearly labeled *Hunter Sanderson*.

Cold air found its way through gaps in ill-fitting windows, but with the robe warming her outside and the cocoa warming her inside, Miri relaxed for the first time in the two weeks since her sister had called, panic-stricken.

"I can't risk it, Miri. You've got to help me. Hunt's up for a fantastic job, working for Andrew Patterson, but they're going to do a complete background search. On me, too."

"Why is that a problem? You've buried the past long ago. Your identity is secure. You've got all the right credentials. College degree, job history, the works."

"If Hunt finds out I was a resident of Galloway House—"

"After all these years, don't you think it's you *he loves, not your past."*

27

"I'm not worried about that. It's that he won't get the job, and who knows what else might happen. If we didn't have this damn anniversary cruise with his family, we'd be there, and I could get a better feel for things."

"Right."

Miri hadn't considered the stratosphere of society Hunter and Nancy inhabited, where it was borderline acceptable to marry a woman who actually *worked* for a living. But finding out she'd come from lower than middle-class stock, often dodging the law to put food on the table for herself and her little sister, would never fly with Andrew Patterson. Or the rest of Hunter Sanderson's clan. Which pissed the hell out of Miri. What was wrong with rising above your beginnings?

So, she'd spent tonight playing waitress and socialite. To deny her sister would be like not breathing.

Miri opened her e-mail program and clicked her sister's address, choosing her words with care.

Welcome home! How was the cruise? Hope you and Hunt had time to enjoy the sunshine—and some moonlight? <g> And thanks for the tip. You were right. Shopping was great. Found exactly what I was looking for. TTYL.

She hit "Send." That should cover it in case Nancy's husband read her e-mails.

Sipping the last of her cocoa, she stared at the screen and the icons for the folders she'd downloaded. She wasn't sure what triggered the impulse to copy them from Patterson's computer, other than old instincts that said it was always a good thing to have some extra insurance, even if you didn't know it was insurance when you took it.

Curious, she double-clicked one of the icons and waited for it to open. What would a man with more money than God keep in his computer? Apparently not a list of his investments or a draft of a memoir with instructions for making more money than God. It appeared to be a remodeling job. Basement renovations, it said. A few schematics, something about an air-conditioning system. Updating his servants' quarters, perhaps. She closed the file.

Sudden exhaustion blanketing her, Miri powered down the laptop and went to turn off the lamp by the couch. The beaded evening bag lay there, open. It would have to go back with the dress. Miri unzipped the interior compartment and dumped everything onto the couch. She sank to the cushion and stared at another reminder of her past, of survival skills she apparently hadn't left behind. She traced her finger along the smooth leather billfold she'd lifted without thinking.

CHAPTER 3

Dalton and Fozzie stood in a crowd of departing guests waiting for the valets to ferry their cars back.

"I'll send the 'mission accomplished' e-mail," Fozzie said. "My money says the boss isn't going to want the face-to-face until Monday." He grinned and flashed a scrap of paper with a phone number scribbled on it. "And I'm spending the rest of the weekend with a glorious redhead named Clarissa. I saw you with a classy brunette. You going to be seeing her again?"

Dalton shook his head. "Nope. We never even exchanged names, much less phone numbers."

"Losing your touch?"

"I told you. I'm not interested. I danced with half a dozen women to pass the time. We're supposed to blend in, remember. Not be memorable. Besides, I've got bigger things on my mind."

Dalton mulled over finding leads on Rafael while they waited. In twos and threes, expensive cars—predominantly black or silver—hummed to the apex of the driveway, and hard-breathing, red jacketed youths exchanged vehicles for gratuities.

"Pay the man, mate," Fozzie said when their car arrived.

Dalton reached into his hip pocket. His empty hip pocket. Puzzled, he patted his breast pocket, then the front. Nothing but his butterscotch stash. "Dammit!"

"What?"

"My wallet's gone."

"You lost it? You want to go back?"

Dalton replayed the evening, freeze-framing on the short scuffle with the waitress in Andrew Patterson's study. "That little—" He shook his head. "No. Drive."

Fozzie slipped a bill into the valet's hand and levered himself into the car. Dalton slid into the passenger seat, and they followed the curved driveway to the street. Two blocks away, Fozzie pulled over. "You sure you didn't drop it? Maybe someone picked it up and turned it in."

"Oh, someone picked it, all right. Right out of my pants while I was in the study and you were turning off the water in the bathroom. The waitress."

"Well, shouldn't we go find her?"

"That would violate the 'blend in' rule. Besides, the caterers are gone. I'll call them tomorrow and find our little wench." Irritated as he was, Dalton admired her for pulling that stunt—and getting away with it. He *was* really off his game.

"Suit yourself." Fozzie pulled away from the curb and headed down the hillside. "She get much?"

"Not much cash. Mainly hassle." He slapped the dashboard. "Shit. Double shit."

"What now? You said you didn't have much cash. What else did you have?"

"About the most top secret piece of information out there. I'll have to kill her."

Fozzie swiveled his head and glanced at Dalton. "What the hell were you carrying?"

"My HLB cover ID."

"So? What can she possibly find out from that? It's got less information on it than a business card. Unless . . ."

"Right. She'll know my first name."

Fozzie's laughter exploded through the car.

By nine-thirty Monday morning, Dalton sat at a computer

terminal in one of the back offices at the headquarters of Blackthorne, Inc., taking advantage of the access to the Department of Motor Vehicles databases. That Horace Blackthorne hadn't given up any of his weekend for a formal report reinforced Dalton's conviction that Saturday night's assignment was trivial. He struck the keys with unnecessary vehemence.

He'd blown a good hour this morning laying on the charm with the owner of Taste of Heaven, Patterson's caterer, finally scoring the names of possible employees meeting his vague description. The woman also added it was equally likely she'd hired his mystery woman through a temp agency she used when she needed extra staff.

He sucked on a butterscotch candy as he worked through the catering list, eliminating possibilities, hitting dead ends, noting potential matches. With only names to work from, nothing to narrow the search, it was slow going. Hell, for all he knew, his mystery woman didn't drive, so searching the DMV lists was a waste of time.

Dalton's missing ID said he worked for a company called HLB Imports and Exports. Anyone searching would find a tiny office, open "by appointment only," located alongside a dozen legitimate businesses in a fifteen-story office building. The same building that housed the swank, ultra-modern offices where Blackthorne, Inc. received ultra-rich clients seeking ultra-discreet private investigators and almost-invisible bodyguards. Blackthorne, Inc.'s not-so-public operations, where Dalton actually worked, were headquartered in a field station miles from the city.

Although Dalton wasn't worried about the waitress discovering his identity from his ID card, he'd rather not have to ask for a replacement. That would entail a report ending up on the boss's desk, and quite likely an up close and personal ass-chewing.

Dalton had eliminated half the list when his cell phone signaled a text message.

Blackthorne with a 9-1-1.

He grabbed his sports jacket and hustled toward the elevator, shoving his notes in the pocket on the way. The boss was ready for the face-to-face report on the gala's dog and pony show. Maybe he'd tell Dalton what the crazy assignment was all about. Dalton didn't care. It was over, and it was time to get back into the field to hunt for Rafael and his drug smuggling ring.

Anticipation rippled through him. He tapped his foot while the elevator numbers lit up in slow motion as he ascended to Blackthorne's inner sanctum. When he exited the car and strode to the end of the hall, it was like moving through time. Nothing swank and ultra-modern here. The scratches and gouges in the wainscoting had darkened over the decades, in contrast to the brown and green striped wallpaper, which had faded.

Lingering smells of tobacco and floor wax teased Dalton's nostrils, and he inhaled deeply, the familiar scents both calming and invigorating. He opened the door to Blackthorne's outer office and glanced around for Fozzie but didn't see him. Confident his partner wouldn't have exposed his gaffe, Dalton smiled for Madeline Scott, Blackthorne's assistant. As always, she wore a tailored suit. Navy blue pinstripe today, with a pale blue blouse, and the inevitable strand of pearls. A throwback, like this office, although today her silver hair was shorter, in a style much softer than her usual tightly twisted knot.

"Good mornin', Maddie darlin'. You're exceptionally lovely today. I like the new look."

She touched her hair, her eyes widening when her fingers contacted unfamiliar territory. A faint blush tinged her cheeks, and she smiled. "Thank you. My daughter dragged me to a makeover session Saturday."

"Not much of a challenge, seeing how they had near-perfection to begin with." Dalton tilted his head to the closed door behind Madeline's desk. "Is he ready for me?"

"He certainly is." She pressed a button on the phone and announced Dalton's arrival. Without waiting for the response, he stepped behind her desk and tapped on the door.

"Enter."

He twisted the knob and pushed the door open.

Horace Blackthorne sat behind his battered steel desk, poring over the contents of a manila file folder. Dalton took two paces into the room and waited for the ritual to play out.

Blackthorne closed the file folder, gave it a tap, then placed it in the wire box on the corner of his desk. Without raising his head, he removed his half-frame reading glasses, snapped them into a leather case, and slipped them inside his jacket.

"Sit."

Dalton knew it was an acoustical quirk, but Horace Blackthorne's deep voice filled the space like a ten-speaker stereo system. He pulled out one of the utilitarian chairs and complied. The man wore an unreadable expression.

"Saturday night?" Blackthorne said.

Dalton plucked a folded piece of paper from his jacket and dropped it in front of his boss. "As ordered. One letter from a Mr. William Bingham, regarding an insurance rider for an emerald bracelet. And in its place, the envelope you gave us." Fed up with the formalities, he raked his fingers through his hair. "Shit, Blackie. What's this all about?"

The use of the familiar name sent one of Blackthorne's eyebrows up a few millimeters. Normally, Dalton reserved the childhood nickname for his distant cousin to non-work-related venues.

Blackthorne fixed his gaze beyond Dalton. "A small wager with Andrew Patterson, pointing out he would benefit from a better security arrangement."

Dalton bit back the curse. "You mean that whole thing was nothing but grandstanding?"

"I prefer to think of it as demonstrating the superior abilities of Blackthorne personnel. Out-of-the-country undercover work incurs significant expenditures. It's not as if we can hold our own gala to raise funds, considering nobody is supposed to know about that part of the company." Blackthorne tapped a file folder with his index finger. "I seem to recall numerous requests for upgraded surveillance equipment. Andrew Patterson's museum contract alone would supplement the budget considerably."

"Great. We've demonstrated our superiority. Good for Blackthorne." He gave an abbreviated fist pump. "Now, I'm ready to put together a team and get back to Colombia. Rafael's setting up a new string of drug-processing plants. We wipe them out, we make a huge dent in the influx into the States. Don't you care that people die because of him? And our people have been dying trying to stop him?"

Dalton detected a fleeting twitch of a vein at Blackthorn's neck. He'd punched a button. Probably the wrong one. He set his back teeth to keep from saying more.

"Loss of life is part of the business, regardless of our personal feelings. We don't simply chase drug lords on your whim." Blackthorne's eyes narrowed. "Or is there a client I'm unaware of?"

Dalton slumped. "No, sir. But damn, we could sneak in and do some serious damage to their drug train. Can't you tie it to a legitimate op?"

Horace Blackthorne leaned forward and placed his palms on the desk, half-rising. "The way you took it upon yourself to do last week? When you're sitting on this side of the desk, young man, you can make those calls."

"Come on, Blackie. You know I can blend in anywhere.

There's got to be a way."

Dalton waited. Blackthorne's nostrils flared before he continued.

"For your own good, and the good of Blackthorne, Inc., there will be no OCONUS assignments for you for at least three months. You're becoming fixated and it's affecting your work."

The thought of three months inside the continental US jabbed like a knife in Dalton's belly. He clenched his jaw.

Blackthorne lowered himself into his chair. "I had half a mind to send you on enforced R&R, but Mr. Harper needed it more. Consider yourself on domestic investigative detail until further notice."

Dalton nearly groaned out loud. He knew his frustration flashed on his face like a neon sign. But lying on some beach definitely wasn't for him. Work was his answer. At least private investigation wasn't as big a slap as personal security detail, which meant babysitting for spoiled offspring of the too-rich and too-famous.

"Yes, sir." Dalton stood, prepared to leave before he dug his hole any deeper. "I'll be waiting to hear from you," he added, anxious to get back to his search for his mystery waitress.

"You can wait right there." Blackthorne opened a side drawer and tossed something on the desk. A wallet. A very familiar wallet. The scowl that crossed Blackthorn's face was definitely not unreadable.

Dalton tried for a smile. "Thanks. I dropped it last night."

Dalton reached for his billfold, but Blackthorne's palm slammed on it first. His gaze burned through Dalton like a laser.

"You want to try that one again?"

Dalton kept his spine straight, his chin lifted, even as he wished Scotty would beam him up. He swallowed. "Someone took it, sir."

"Stop with the 'sir' crap. And sit down. Mistakes are one thing, honesty's another. I won't tolerate less, and you know it."

Fire burned Dalton's neck. He managed to keep his eyes level with Blackthorne's as he sank into the chair.

"Do you know who took it?" Blackthorne asked.

"Sort of."

"Elaborate, please."

Dalton sighed. "A waitress from the catering company. She was in the study when Fozzie and I went to exchange papers. But the lights were off, and I didn't get a good look at her. I've already got a list of personnel from the caterer, and I'll find her soon."

Blackthorne picked up a pen and tapped a slow cadence on the desk. "You're telling me you were in a situation where I expect my people to be diligent and cautious, and you allowed a *waitress* to pick your pocket? Are you sure you weren't engaged in some other activity at the time?" He lifted an eyebrow. "I *am* aware of your reputation, and of Mr. Mayhew's."

"Dammit, I'm sorry. You knew I didn't want to be there, I knew it was some sort of bullshit assignment—and okay, I wasn't in it one hundred per cent. But when the stakes are for real, I stand by my record. You know how I operate. I'm good. Damn good, but let me do what I'm good at, not this games-manship crap." He'd overstepped the limits, but he didn't care anymore. "Some little gal lifted my wallet. She got some cash, and my cover ID. It didn't affect the op. And since it's been returned, no harm, no foul."

For an instant, Blackthorne's eyes softened. "I know this time of the year is hard for you. I don't want you distracted and get-ting yourself—or anyone else—killed."

"I can handle it," Dalton insisted.

"Saturday night's slip says otherwise."

Dalton's jaw ached from all the clenching. "I need to keep busy, sir."

"And you will be. But stateside, on investigative assignments. You've already missed the important question about your pick-pocket."

Dalton stood there, puzzled, until the answer—or, the question—dawned on him. Shit. Maybe Blackie was right. "How did she connect me to you?"

Blackthorne nodded, obviously satisfied he'd made his point. "Indeed. But I'd like you to meet your next assignment." He pressed a button on his phone. "Mrs. Scott, we're ready."

The door opened. When a woman entered, Dalton stood. If Madeline Scott had spent Saturday having a makeover, this woman must have had a makeunder. No makeup, brown hair pulled back at the nape of her neck. A shapeless sweater a size too big and loose-fitting khaki trousers revealed little of the woman inside. Nondescript with a capital N. His mind whirled through possible reasons she would be hiring a private investigator. Cheating husband? Blackthorne didn't do that kind of work. And considering Blackthorne's rates, she didn't seem the typical well-heeled client.

The woman crossed the room and sat in the second visitor's chair, the scent of a fresh spring breeze cutting through everything else. Dalton eyed her more carefully.

"Good morning," she said.

He froze.

CHAPTER 4

Miri watched Texas go from puzzled to slack-jawed when she sat down. He'd connected the dots. A touch of embarrassment, then full-blown irritation.

She smiled. "I'm Miri Chambers. I believe we've met."

He gave her a long, hard stare, all expression erased from his face. "Twice, apparently." He shoved the wallet in his hip pocket. "Excuse me if I have mixed feelings about the return of my property. I see your laryngitis is better."

Despite the heat flooding her face, she wouldn't break eye contact. "Must have been a twenty-four-hour bug."

"Miss Chambers has proven to be a rather . . . resource-ful . . . young woman," Blackthorne said, "given she was able to return your wallet with so little to go on."

"No big deal," Miri said. "I was having trouble sleeping and picked up a James Bond book. When I did fall asleep, something clicked. Sometimes I let my imagination run away with me. Most of it was pure luck. Under other circumstances, I doubt I'd have found Mr. Dalton."

"It's just Dalton, Miss Chambers. I trust you'll remember."

A heavy emphasis on the *Dalton*. The Texas accent tempered the threat in his eyes, but perhaps Mr. Blackthorne hadn't been kidding about Dalton's sensitivity to his given name. She filed it away as another piece of information.

In the bright lights of Mr. Blackthorne's office, she took him in. Absorbed him was more like it. Strong jaw, his lower lip fuller than the upper. The broad nose and unruly eyebrows kept him a notch or two below Greek god status. But he was more than the sum of his features. The man was aware of his looks, but obviously comfortable with them. She'd bet he was *not* the sort who checked his reflection every time he passed a window.

She realized he was waiting for a response. She blinked. "All right, Just Dalton. And I'm Miri."

Mr. Blackthorne cleared his throat. "Miss Chambers is your next assignment, Dalton. If you'll excuse me, I have to prepare for an appointment. The conference room on this floor is available so she can brief you."

Miri watched Dalton's mouth open as if in protest, then close as he and his boss exchanged glares. Although, to be fair, Mr. Blackthorne didn't really *glare*. His face barely changed, but it was obvious Dalton read it perfectly in the instant before his boss slipped on his reading glasses and reached into a wire basket for a file folder.

Tempted to make excuses and leave, Miri knew she would see this one through. When an opportunity fell into your lap—or you happened to find it in someone's pocket—it was fate, and you went where it took you. She extended her hand.

"Thank you, Mr. Blackthorne. It was good to meet you."

Mr. Blackthorne raised his head from the papers and took her hand. "I look forward to speaking with you again, Miss Chambers." He shifted his gaze to Dalton, then back to her. "Good morning."

Dalton held the door for her and they passed through the outer office. Mrs. Scott picked up her computer mouse and studied the monitor, but Miri caught the quickly suppressed grin.

She hurried down the hall as Dalton lengthened his stride and overtook her. He stopped at a door and flipped down a small sign that said, "Occupied." He pulled the door open and gestured her inside. "Make yourself comfortable. I'll be back in a minute."

He disappeared the way they'd come. Miri recalled a water fountain and restrooms along the way, and assumed that's where he'd gone. It was clear enough he had no choice about the assignment—damn, she didn't like being an *assignment.* Would he blow off the job, go through the motions and call it quits? For now, she'd give him the benefit of the doubt, but it was a good-sized doubt. Miri crossed to the large conference table and sank onto a padded leather chair, facing the window. In the distance, she could see the Golden Gate Bridge emerge through the fog.

She held her purse in her lap, clutching the leather strap in a stranglehold. Forcing a deep breath, she clasped her hands on the table. Dalton returned, the scent of commercial soap overlaying the sandalwood. He crossed the room to a wall unit and bent to open a drawer. Aware she was staring at him, Miri snapped her head back to the view out the window, but she wasn't sure it was better than the one behind her.

Dalton tossed a file folder and a yellow lined tablet onto the table and took the seat across from her. From an inside coat pocket, he produced a pen and twisted the cap off. Miri got the impression he was thinking of her neck as he did it.

"All right, Miss Chambers. What is it you want from Blackthorne, Inc.?" He wrote the date, time, and "Mary Chambers" at the top of the page.

"It's Miri, not Mary."

Dalton raised his eyebrows in question.

She shrugged. "Yeah, so I can read upside down. No big deal."

He drew a neat line through Mary. "Miri. Is that short for Miriam?"

"No. It's not short for anything." His gunmetal gray eyes rose from the page, and she felt the uncontrollable urge to explain.

"It's from *Star Trek*. The original series—with Captain Kirk and Mr. Spock."

Recognition flashed across his face. He nodded and wrote *Miri* on the pad. Without knowing why, she liked that he hadn't simply scribbled out the *a* and replaced it with an *i*. Or started a fresh page. He was meticulous, but not extravagant.

"I remember that one," he said. "The three-hundred-year-old kids, right? And the *grups*. Kim Darby."

"Right." She relaxed at his shift to a more conversational tone. After he noted her address and phone numbers, he set the pen down and leaned back in his chair.

"Okay, Miri," he said. "I'll overlook the wallet. How the hell did you find me?"

"I already explained that to Mr. Blackthorne."

"Humor me, please."

She inhaled, getting more sandalwood than soap this time. Thank goodness he'd dismissed the wallet-lifting, which avoided her having to lie, which also avoided the explanation of why she was in Patterson's study, which was fine with her.

"I was really sorry about your wallet. I found your ID, but there was no address or anything, only HLB Imports and Exports. Like I said, I'd been reading some old Ian Fleming, and James Bond's cover was Universal Exports. I thought about how you were sneaking around in the study and how funny it would be if you were really a spy like James Bond."

Dalton said nothing, merely nodded, his eyes narrowing.

Her palms grew wet, apparently sucking all the moisture from her mouth. "Do you think I could have a glass of water?"

He shrugged, pushed back from the table and went to the wall unit. Miri watched as he bent to open a lower cabinet door. The man had a great ass, that was for sure. He returned with two bottles of water, screwed the lid off one and set it in front of her. She gulped half the contents. "Thanks."

He took a quick sip of his water, then placed the bottle next to his tablet. "Go on."

"Okay, so then I got a call from someone where I work—which is really why I'm here. Are you sure you don't want me to get to that? They're kind of connected."

"I'm more interested in knowing how you got from James Bond to me."

Because I'm a daydreaming idiot, that's how.

"First, I called the number on your card. I got a recording saying to make an appointment. But that seemed weird, so I Googled HLB and found an address."

Dalton took another sip of water.

"Anyway, I came by yesterday morning. I was going to drop the wallet into the HLB mail slot, but there wasn't a mail slot. And then I saw the directory that showed Blackthorne, Inc. occupied a lot of office space in the same building."

Dalton rubbed his fingers across his forehead, as if he had a headache.

"Is this making sense?" she asked.

"I'm listening," he said.

"Okay. So, I went home and Googled Blackthorne, Inc. because I was thinking about spy stuff and it was kind of fun trying to see what I could discover.

"I found out Blackthorne did security work and private investigations, which made me wonder—Horace Blackthorne, HLB—you know. Could they be related? And Mr. Blackthorne's middle name is—"

"Langford. I know." Dalton seemed less exasperated. She couldn't be positive, but a smile might be peeking through his gruff demeanor.

"So, I had this fantasy that HLB and Blackthorne were part of some secret agency, which sounded stupid when I thought it through, but I had nothing to lose by coming back this morning—because I really did want to return your wallet.

"The HLB office was still closed, but the big, fancy second-floor office of Blackthorne, Inc. was open. I was trying to figure out what to say when I heard a man talking to the receptionist. I recognized his voice from Saturday night. The Aussie."

"He didn't recognize you?"

"You didn't either, remember, and he didn't get a clear look at me Saturday. Besides, there were five or six other people getting onto the elevator, so I followed him. When he pressed twelve, I got off at ten and waited a few minutes, then took the stairs the rest of the way. There aren't a lot of offices on this floor. Blackthorne's name was on a door, so I went in. I showed Mrs. Scott the wallet and asked if she could get it back to you."

Dalton closed his eyes and grimaced. She'd obviously knocked his reputation down a couple of pegs. She didn't care.

"Go on," he said.

"I waited while Mrs. Scott talked to Mr. Blackthorne. Apparently, he was impressed with my detective skills, so he invited me into his office. We talked, and I mentioned something that concerned me at work. I didn't come here asking for help, but he said he had an available investigator, and I accepted his offer. I had no idea it would be you."

She inhaled, trying to replenish her supply of oxygen. Dalton didn't say anything for a minute, and she braced herself for his wrath.

What she got was laughter, a warm, rolling sound that raised her temperature about five degrees.

Dalton's irritation melted like ice cream on a summer day. Sometimes you were good, and sometimes you were just plain lucky. Miri'd been served a supersized portion of luck. He had a feeling Blackie would be making changes, possibly starting with HLB's name. The fictitious import-export name gave a logical explanation for the international travel they did, but if this little filly broke his cover so easily, something would have to give.

Angry as he'd been, her husky voice while she'd told her tale shot right through him. To the other brain that insisted on distracting him. He swallowed some water while he composed himself, then picked up his pen.

"All right, Miri. Why do you think you need a private investigator?"

She lifted her chin. "*I* didn't. Mr. Blackthorne did, Mr. *Just Dalton.* He's the one who offered your services, remember?"

She was as feisty as she'd been in Patterson's study Saturday night. Which was the real Miri? The thieving waitress or the elegant socialite. A mixture of both, undoubtedly. Studying her—the light brown eyes, her straight nose with a tiny upward tilt at the end, the dip in her chin that wasn't quite a dimple—how had he thought her nondescript? A wide mouth, full lips. And when she smiled, which she hadn't done nearly enough, she could burn off the fog enveloping the Golden Gate. He smiled, trying to coax one from her, and went hard when she returned it. Not good. He cleared his throat.

"I'm sorry. Let me try again. What did you tell Mr. Blackthorne that made him think you needed a private investigator?"

"Three people are missing."

His interest piqued. He sat back and cleared his throat again. "Why don't you explain."

She waited, her expression clearly screaming, *Do you take me seriously yet?*

He dug out a polite smile and leaned forward, getting a hint of her scent. Another dumb move. He shifted back. "I apologize for any misunderstanding. I'll admit I was . . . irritated—"

"Pissed," she said.

He nodded. "Okay, pissed. But I've been assigned your case,

and I'm willing to put Saturday night behind me. I want to assure you, I'm good at my job and I take it seriously." He raised his hands, palms outward. "Truce?"

She appeared to consider it. "Truce."

"Let's start over, from the beginning." He extended his hand. "Good morning, ma'am. I'm Dalton. Would you like some coffee?"

She gave a demure smile, which he knew mocked him, and placed her fingertips in his palm. "I'd love some, Dalton. I'm Miri." She cocked her head and fluttered her eyelashes. "A smidge of cream, if y'all have it. Or milk. Or creamer. Of course, black will be fine. I wouldn't want to be puttin' y'all to any trouble on my account."

The syrupy Southern accent she affected had him choking back a laugh. He thickened his drawl. "Not a lick of trouble, ma'am. You set tight and I'll have it brewin' before you know it."

Dalton stepped over to the coffee maker and started a pot, using the simple mechanics of preparation to center himself. Their lighthearted banter hadn't changed the facts. Miri read him too easily. She knew he was here under protest. No doubt he'd telegraphed his embarrassment at how she'd not only picked his pocket but revealed his shortcomings to his boss. He knew better than to drop his guard, even in civilized San Francisco.

He considered the possibility Miri's case was a setup. That didn't make sense. No matter how irritated Blackie might be, he wouldn't waste the company's time on a nonsense case with a fictitious client. Then again, Blackie'd made it damn clear he didn't think Dalton was ready for serious work. Maybe this was Blackie's way of making him feel useful instead of slapping him with mandatory leave.

Bullshit. Assigning him to what was probably a cut-and-dried investigation was just as demeaning.

He'd research Miri six ways from Sunday before he did anything else. From the way his internal jitters flattened, he knew he'd made the right decision. He hadn't survived without learning to trust his gut.

Feeling more like a professional again, he faced the conference table while the coffee gurgled into the pot. The aroma built a craving for the first sip, pulling his mind away from Miri's enticing scent. He held that thought as he returned to his seat.

"It'll be done in a few minutes. Why don't you start," he said.

Miri nodded, apparently satisfied with their new beginning. "I work at Galloway House." Her eyebrows lifted. "Have you heard of it?"

Dalton frowned. The name was familiar. "Some kind of shelter for runaway kids? Sorry, but most of my assignments are OCONUS, and I'm not in the city much." At her lifted eyebrows, he explained. "Outside the continental US. I normally work on international cases."

Her head tilted a few degrees. "Like with Interpol? Spy stuff?"

He shook his head. "Nothing that glamorous. Sometimes clients run into problems abroad and they're more comfortable with someone from home." The lies of omission came easily as he entered his comfort zone. He shoved aside a fleeting twinge of remorse that he was more at ease with lies than the truth. Those lies kept him alive. He toyed with the pen. "Let's assume I know nothing. Tell me as much as you can."

Miri fussed with her purse strap. "You're partially right about Galloway House, but it's more than a shelter. We cater to teens and moms with kids, but we'll help anyone we can. We give people a fresh start. We provide training, help with job placement, give people confidence to move back into society. Make them productive citizens."

Her eyes sparkled with pride.

"How many residents?"

"It varies—our goal is to move people out, but we provide beds for up to twenty-five. Then there are the daytimers—the ones who live on their own, but take classes or work at the House."

"And your position there?" He wrote Galloway House on his tablet.

"I'm staff—you'd probably call me an administrator. We don't really *have* positions. Except for things requiring specialized skills, like keeping the books, handling publicity, or teaching a particular class, everyone does what they can. I teach some computer classes, but I'll work in the kitchen, or provide a friendly ear. I'll push a mop around if I have to, and I'm not bad with a hammer."

"Sounds like a good place."

"It is. We've helped a lot of people get back on their feet. We have some basic rules—no alcohol, no drugs, and except for a couple of family rooms, the sexes are separated." She gave a little shrug, as if she knew that didn't mean people weren't hooking up for a little action.

He nodded, indicating she should continue.

"Everyone has responsibilities to the House. It makes it seem less like they're accepting charity if they see they're contributing. And if they need more help than we can give—specialized professional counseling, medical care—we refer them to other agencies."

The coffeemaker gave a final sputter. "Coffee's done." Dalton got up, poured two cups and set one in front of Miri along with a metal pitcher from the mini fridge. "I think it's cream."

Addicted to her scent, he hovered beside her while she tipped the pitcher over her cup. The thick white liquid swirled in the hot brew and she nodded. "Thanks." While she stirred and sipped, he walked around the table and sat, letting his general impressions float freely. She definitely cared about her work and the people she worked with. His suspicion Blackie had fabricated the case lessened.

"Tell me what you can about your missing people," he said. "Any reason to think they're connected?"

She nibbled on her lower lip. He stared at the blue lines on his yellow paper, trying not to think about what he'd like to do to those lips.

"I don't think so. But since Mr. Blackthorne offered, it seemed silly not to accept his help—just in case."

Doubts niggled again. Had Blackthorne done more than offer? Had he talked her into accepting help? Made her some sort of deal? He could hear Blackie.

That's a very interesting situation, Miss Chambers. I'm sure there's a very simple explanation. However, as a precaution, I'll be happy to assign an investigator. I have one who's perfect for this kind of a task. He's been under some stress of late, so you'll actually be doing me a favor by letting him work with you. It shouldn't take him more than a day or two.

Well, Blackie wouldn't have come right out and said *stress,* but Dalton had no doubt Miri would have caught on that she was supposed to give him the kid glove treatment. Shit. He tuned Miri back in.

"You should understand, people who come to Galloway House are free to leave at any time. We don't have them sign contracts or make any commitments. Sometimes they'll walk out too soon, thinking they're ready to face life outside after a few days of decent food, hot showers, clean clothes. Especially the teens. Most of those come back in a couple of weeks, once they miss all the extras we offer. Sometimes, they come by for meals—we serve a couple hundred meals a day, no questions asked. Other times, they decide they're happier where they were, or they reconcile with family and go home."

"So what's different about your missing people? What makes you think they didn't decide to leave on their own?"

"It's the way they left. Without saying anything. Or they were in the middle of training and seemed happy—it's more a *feeling* they weren't ready to leave. You pick up when someone's looking at the big picture rather than marking time."

His skeptical streak rose again. A feeling wasn't enough. Then again, he usually trusted his gut. Maybe he should trust Miri's.

"Anything missing when they left?"

She shook her head. "No. As a matter of fact, they took what they arrived with, nothing more, even though we offer things like clothes, toys for little kids, other basic creature comforts."

He picked up his pen, poised to write. "I'll need their names."

She paused, giving him a defiant stare. He stared back.

"Luisa, Cissy and Robbie," she said so rapid-fire they came out as a single word.

Irritation boiled. "Last names?"

Her face slammed shut. "No."

"No?" He put the pen down. "It's kind of hard to find someone if you don't know who you're looking for."

"Our records are strictly confidential. And most of the residents aren't using their full names, or their real names, anyway. We never demand it, and we promise to respect any wishes for anonymity."

"I respect their wishes for anonymity as well. I would never betray a client's confidence. But you have to give me names, or I've got nothing to work with."

She glared at him. "I told you, I can't. I have the same obligations. You said you were good at your job. Are you saying you can't handle it?"

"I'm saying I can't make bricks without straw." He leaned across the table. "I need full names. Pictures. Social Security numbers. Places of employment."

"And I can't provide them."

"Can't, or won't?"

Dalton didn't buy it anymore. She'd proven herself clever, conniving, and a damn good actress. He moved back to his original premise. Blackie put her up to this to keep him occupied. Time to call her bluff. He buried his irritation and brought out a grin, along with as much Texas as he could muster.

"I said I was good, darlin', but I'm no miracle worker. Finding people who don't exist? I reckon not." He crossed his arms and leaned back in his chair.

Miri's mouth hung open. "I'm sorry? You're dropping the case?"

"Sugar, there is no case. I don't know what you and Blackie cooked up, but you can march right back in there and tell him I'm not going to fall for it. I don't need to spend God knows how long chasing a flock of wild geese when there are people who really need Blackthorne's help."

"I'm sorry to have wasted your valuable time." She pushed her coffee cup to the center of the table and stood. Flinging her purse over her shoulder, she marched to the door. Before leaving, she faced him. "I'm sure there's a lost dog or a cat out there you'll be able to find. A case more suited to your talents . . . *Ambrose.*"

CHAPTER 5

Miri sat behind the communal desk in the small back office at Galloway House and reviewed the computer files of the past six months. Although they kept names confidential, outside donations depended upon proof that Galloway House helped people, so they maintained detailed records.

She considered Dalton's questions. So what if he wouldn't help. She knew the ins and outs around here better than he did, and help from a jerk who didn't want to be there would be worse than no help at all.

Armed with a notepad and pen, she browsed case histories. Twenty-seven residents had left in the last six months. Twelve thrived in new jobs. Galloway House's placement service kept in touch with employers, but Miri received more satisfaction when one of the "graduates" called, or dropped a note—or even an e-mail—giving encouragement to other residents, proving the work everyone did here had a genuine payoff. She started to cross those names off her list, then changed her mind. Couldn't hurt to make sure they were still around. She remembered seeing eight more as regulars in the food lines.

"Miss Miri?"

At Will's tremulous voice, Miri glanced up in concern. The eight-year-old had arrived less than two weeks ago, along with his mother, Jillian. For the first three days, he'd stayed in his room or clung to his mother's side, but lately he'd shown budding signs of a cheerful extrovert. A mischief maker, even. Was he here to confess some mishap? She gave him a broad smile.

"Hi, Will. Do you want to talk about something?"

"Someone's crying." He ducked his head and scuffed his tattered sneakers on the floor.

"Who? Is it your mom?"

"Uh-uh." A vigorous headshake sent his blond curls bouncing. "In the kitchen." He bolted from the room.

Miri abandoned her efforts and dashed to the kitchen of the old Victorian mansion. Inside the spacious interior, fully modernized to meet the demands of feeding a hundred or more people a day, Miri inhaled the heady aroma of garlic and onions. Samantha, a frail teenager who'd come to the House a year ago, chopped an onion, tears streaming down her face.

Miri chuckled. "Will said someone was crying in the kitchen. I guess he's never chopped onions."

Samantha wiped her eyes with a towel and gave Miri a friendly smile.

"Wanna help peel potatoes?" Samantha said. "Luisa left, you know, so I'm flying solo until three. Except for Suzie, and she's not quite ready yet."

Miri wandered over to the playpen set up in a corner. She crouched down to peek at ten-month-old Suzie, Samantha's daughter, who stacked colored plastic blocks, then knocked them over and giggled. Although Galloway House boasted a full day-care center and nursery, Miri knew Samantha needed to keep her baby close.

"Hey, kiddo. Not up for potato peeling, are you?"

Suzie giggled again and threw a block out of the mesh pen. Miri retrieved it, then grabbed an apple from a bowl on the counter and took a bite. She fell in beside Samantha. "I know about Luisa. Did she say anything to you?"

Samantha shrugged. "Total surprise. I mean, like she was taking computer classes and all. Wanted a better than minimum wage job." She scraped the chopped vegetables onto a platter and started working on the carrots.

Miri set her apple aside and grabbed a potato. "What are we making?"

"Chicken soup. Tomorrow's lunch for the residents."

Miri wielded a peeler, seeing how long she could make the strip of skin before it broke, remembering the way she and Nancy played that game to take their mind off the chore when they were kids. "She talk about family? Problems? Anything?"

Samantha shrugged. "No different from anyone else who comes here. I think someone was pounding on her, but she wasn't, like, you know, scared he'd come back—you can usually tell. Jumping at every noise, freaking at shadows."

Miri nodded. Samantha would know, having been in a similar situation when she'd shown up at Galloway house, pregnant, with a battered face and broken arm. "I remember. I think her ex is back East, with another woman. He's not likely to come after her."

Samantha gave another shrug. "She seemed happy, but you never know. I mean, people who end up here—well, we're not all that together, are we?"

Miri put down her potato and gave Samantha a big hug. "You're plenty together, Sammi—and you keep cooking like this, we're going to lose you to some fancy restaurant."

Samantha's eyes shone. "You think?"

"I know. Wish I could stay and help, but I've got work to do. I'll round up a volunteer or two for you."

Miri listened to the sizzle as Samantha tipped the onions and garlic into a huge soup pot. She took a deep breath of the aromatic vegetables and savored it on the way to the front room. She hadn't gone five paces before Keisha's gravelly voice bounced down the hall.

"You can't go back there. You take yourself a seat, and I'll have someone come talk to you, but you've gotta wait in this room."

Miri could picture Keisha, her curly black hair with the spiky strands of gray coiling up like springs, her hands on ample hips, herding whoever tried to get past her onto one of the over-stuffed sofas. Obviously whoever waited was an adult because Keisha never used that tone with kids. Probably male, too. Miri lengthened her stride. She'd handle the intake form or direct whoever was waiting to the right person.

She rounded the corner and stepped into the brightly lit room, once a formal parlor.

"Hello, Keisha. Can I help out?"

Keisha's smile revealed a couple of missing teeth. Miri remembered how long it had taken her to smile at all.

"Yes, you can. This man here says he wants shelter, but he says he gotta talk to you personally. I called but you didn't answer, and he didn't want to set down like he's supposed to. I told him he can't go back without you coming to get him first. There's papers to fill out. Those are the rules." Arms crossed over her chest, she jerked her head and glowered in a "so there" gesture, then went back to her seat behind the front counter.

Miri turned to face the visitor. He slouched at the window, his back to her. Tall, broad, wearing a knit watch cap and a wool pea coat over well-worn jeans. Even so, he lacked the posture of someone seeking assistance. She knew exactly what she'd hear when she said, "Hello. I'm Miri Chambers. May I help you?"

At the underlying mockery in Miri's voice, Dalton clenched his fists in his coat pocket. He forced a polite smile, more for the woman Miri had called Keisha than anything else. "I'm kind of down on my luck, and thought I could find help here. One of my buddies told me about this place."

Miri strode behind the counter and stood beside Keisha. "I see." She put her hand on the woman's shoulder. "You did the right thing, Keisha. I'll see what this gentleman wants. We'll be in the back office." She opened a drawer and removed a clipboard. "Meanwhile, can you find someone to fill in for Luisa in the kitchen?"

"Will do." Keisha consulted some papers, slowly running her finger across the pages, like someone new to reading.

When Miri walked away clutching the clipboard to her chest, Dalton followed.

Floorboards creaked beneath his feet. Cooking aromas tickled his nostrils. They permeated the walls, layer upon layer, like coats of paint on an old building. A sense of unease replaced the hunger that gnawed at him on the drive over. Old memories niggled, visions of Rachel, and he pushed them away. He was here on assignment. His past didn't play a part in it.

At the end of a narrow hallway, Miri twisted a faceted glass doorknob and pushed open the door. She crossed to an old wooden desk and sat in a metal desk chair. He stood in the doorway, taking in the space. File cabinets—one wood, two unmatched metal. A set of steel shelves held rows of three-ring binders, assorted books, and a couple of unidentifiable ceramic creations, apparently crafted by young children.

She straightened a stack of papers on her desk. "I'm afraid our digs aren't quite as fancy as what you're used to. We have to mix and match with whatever donations we get."

He stepped inside. "Eclectic, to say the least, but I like it. Shows you're more interested in the product than the packaging."

She gave him a narrow-eyed glare. "Okay, *Just* Dalton. Tell me why you're really here. I don't think you've become homeless in the last few hours. I don't need help from someone who's only going through the motions."

"No, I came to apologize. I was wrong to dismiss you the way I did."

She squinted at him. "Mr. Blackthorne have anything to do with this attitude adjustment?"

He pulled the folding metal chair from beside the desk, flipped it around, and straddled it. "Why I'm here isn't the issue. You've got a problem. So do I. The sooner I solve yours, the sooner I can get back to what I should be doing. Some people are gone and it's worrying you. Tell me why."

Miri glanced around the room. "I think maybe we should discuss this somewhere else."

"You want this confidential?"

She nodded. "I don't know what's going on, but on the off chance someone here has something to do with it, I'd rather not be overheard."

"Have you had lunch? I'm starved."

"I seem to have missed it myself." She hesitated, giving a surreptitious glance toward her purse. "Dutch, okay?"

He recognized pride in her eyes. He'd checked his wallet earlier and she hadn't touched his cash when she'd lifted it. Somehow, he knew paying her own way was important to her. Taking her to Alberto's would be out of the question. "That's fine."

She picked up the phone and explained to someone she'd be gone for about an hour. "Let's go. There's a decent café a couple of blocks away."

He got up and put the chair where he'd found it. "If you're concerned, it might be smarter to get out of the neighborhood." Where he'd be more comfortable.

"I'm not sure—I can't be gone too long."

"We won't be," Dalton said.

She pulled her parka off a hook, and he followed her out a back exit.

"My car's on the next block," he said.

She moved at a rapid clip. Ten yards away, he clicked the remote to unlock the Navigator's doors. Ignoring him, Miri yanked the passenger door open and hoisted herself in.

Before they'd gone three blocks, Dalton noticed his white-knuckle grip on the steering wheel. One at a time, he flexed his hands.

"I'm not the enemy, Miri. I told you I'd help and I don't go back on my word."

"I'm fine," she said, although her narrowed lips belied her remark. "Let's get on with it."

"Good. You think something has happened to your missing people? That they haven't gone on with their lives elsewhere?"

"I do. I'm not perfect, but I've got good instincts. Something's fishy when I'm wrong this many times in a few months."

"So, either your instincts are off—"

"Which they are *not*."

Stopped for a light, he stared at the red signal. Did she believe what she did because she couldn't accept reality? That not all the people who took refuge at places like Galloway House turned their lives around? Did she take personal responsibility? Thoughts of Rachel gnawed at his gut again. The light changed to green and he hit the accelerator harder than necessary. For now, he'd accept Miri's hunches. "Or something's keeping them from coming back."

"Which is what I told Mr. Blackthorne this morning, and you know what happened then."

He sighed. "I'd rather we forget that, okay?"

"Okay." She turned toward her window.

He watched her concern as they drove into the upscale neighborhoods and took an almost perverse delight in her worried expression as he mentioned some of the nicer restaurants in the vicinity. Hell, considering what she'd done, she deserved to sweat. But only a little, he decided. Fifteen minutes later, they sat on a park bench munching hot dogs from a street vendor. After she devoured two hot dogs, he debated telling her about the dab of mustard in the corner of her mouth, but then her tongue found it, which moved him into male discomfort territory.

He fished in his pocket for a butterscotch. "Dessert?"

She smiled and accepted it, barely making contact with his hand. "Thanks."

She unwrapped the candy, and he couldn't take his eyes off the way her lips moved as she sucked on it. He collected their trash and took his time wandering to the nearest trash can. When he returned, he seated himself on the far end of the bench and crossed an ankle over his thigh. "All right. Common denominators. Have you found any?"

She smirked. "There's the obvious. Everyone who comes to Galloway House has one thing in common—they're in some sort of trouble."

"Sometimes it's better to work backward. Take your most recent disappearance, then see if anyone else who's missing has something in common."

Miri chewed her lip. Damn, he wished he had his tablet and pen so he could focus on something else.

"That would be Luisa," she said.

"Which isn't her name, is it?"

"It's the one she gave when she showed up. Whether it's the one her mother gave her is none of my concern."

"I got it. I'm on your side. Tell me what you can about Luisa."

Miri studied her hands. Dalton noted her long, slender fingers and clear-polished nails. How clever those hands had been in his pockets Saturday night. And how warm they'd been while she'd danced with him. He cursed silently. Miri was inching him into terrain he vowed never to visit again. And he'd known her for how long? Not even a day, really. No. He'd follow Blackthorne's orders, find out what happened to her missing people and get back in the field where he belonged.

"She's Hispanic, about five-three, twenty-one years old. She was underweight, malnourished when she arrived, but she bounced back quickly. Literate in Spanish, about third-grade level in English, but she can communicate well in both languages."

"That's a start. What skills did she have? What were her reasons for coming to Galloway House?"

Miri leaned forward, her eyes brighter. Her scent stronger, too. He definitely wanted a notepad—anything—to put in his lap.

"Her skills were of the domestic variety. She worked in the kitchen a lot, helped with laundry, but she was taking a basic computer class. She arrived with no money—her boyfriend packed up and moved out one day—and I know she wanted to get a decent job. She has family in—I don't remember. We don't record that kind of data. I think it's somewhere in South America, but I can't be sure. She talked about bringing them here."

"Any chance she decided to go back to them instead?"

Miri shook her head. "No way. She didn't have the money for that." She slipped her parka sleeve up and checked her watch. "I have to get back. I have a computer class to teach in half an hour."

Dalton stood and reached his hand to help Miri up. As expected, she refused it, which was probably a good thing, considering his state. She walked the edge of the path, her purse slung over her shoulder, holding it with both hands. Totally avoiding any chance of body contact. Another good thing.

In his car, she huddled near the door, although she did rotate her body enough to face him. Navigating through traffic demanded his attention, and he couldn't spare more than an occasional glance her way.

"If you have time," he said, "why don't you make a chart with all the basic characteristics you can think of—like we were talking about for Luisa—and then plug all your other mystery people in and see if anything matches."

"Good idea. I didn't have time to go through enough of the files today. I got as far as eliminating the ones I know are fine."

"What if I come in as a resident? I can poke around a little, ask some discrete questions."

She made a quick snorting sound. "You're too hale and hearty for our typical resident. I'm afraid you'd never blend in."

Dalton stifled a laugh. Blending in was his specialty. But in this case, she made a valid point. Although the few people he'd seen working when he'd arrived at Galloway House appeared hale and hearty enough, he figured they hadn't shown up that way.

"Any kind of job opportunities?" he asked. "Give me access to the way things work, the residents, the staff and all."

"Not right now. We have volunteers for meal service, but they don't get the run of the place. Unless a special problem makes us hire out, we try to be self-sufficient."

"What would you farm out?"

"Things like electrical, major plumbing—things the city insists on inspecting and having done by licensed contractors. But at the moment, everything's working." She paused. "I suppose I can have some kind of a problem with my computer. It'll have to be a good one, though, because I handle all the I.T. stuff for the House. So far, they've never had a problem I couldn't solve."

"What if I showed up after hours?"

"No such animal. Someone's on duty around the clock, and

the office I use isn't private. If I'm not using it, someone else probably is."

"I can usually bluff my way anywhere." Grinning, he darted a glance in her direction.

"Not always with total success, however." Her eyes dared him to keep going.

He dodged the challenge—this time. "Point taken. All right, what would you have me do?"

She stared out the window. "Meet me tonight. Seven o'clock at the South Branch Library."

"Should I come in disguise? Is there a password? Secret handshake?"

She glowered. God, he already loved pushing her buttons. The way her eyes sparked and her lips made a little O.

"Sorry," he said. "That was uncalled for." He pulled out a business card, blank except for his cell phone number. "Here. It'll come straight to me. Any time, day or night."

She shoved the card into her purse without a glance. "Seven. Library."

Chapter 6

After she'd worked with six residents on basic computer skills, Miri retreated to her office where she found three messages from her sister. She grabbed the phone, leaning over the desk to punch the speed dial.

"Hey, Sis. Welcome home. What's up?"

"Are you sure you fixed everything?" Nancy spoke in a low voice, as if she was afraid she'd be overheard.

"As sure as I can be, considering. I checked what I found in Patterson's files. Most of it was Hunter's history. For you, Patterson's got the bio we established years ago. As far as anyone knows, you were Nancy Chambers until you married Hunter. Rayna never existed."

"Do you have the file? Can I see it?"

"No, I left it where I found it. Otherwise he might suspect something."

There was a brief pause before Nancy spoke again. "Of course. I'm not thinking."

Nancy's concern spilled over to Miri. "Why are you so worried? Has something happened?"

Nancy's slow breathing meant she was regrouping. After a lengthy pause, she spoke.

"Hunt had an interview this morning. With Mr. Patterson himself. Hunt called and said there'd been a change in plans, and we'd talk tonight. I was so afraid someone found out I'm a total nobody. Less than a nobody."

"Sweetie, *you're* not a nobody. What you did took more guts and smarts than ten Andrew Pattersons. You're jumping to conclusions. Relax."

"You think? Hunt didn't sound excited."

As far as Miri knew, Hunter never sounded excited. "I don't think. I know. Hunt will come home with good news. Maybe you should chill some champagne and be ready. I'll bet he'll want to celebrate."

"I suppose you could be right. Thanks for listening."

"Always. Love you."

Miri slid the handset back in the base and sank into her chair. Somewhere along the line, their roles had reversed, and Miri had become the strong one, as if all of Nancy's self-confidence dried up when they'd finally begun living normal lives. Nancy loved her husband. For some reason, she lived in fear that it was too good to be true and she'd wake up one day, back on the streets.

Miri hoped she hadn't missed anything at Andrew Patterson's. She thought about the files at home on her laptop—maybe she'd check them, even though she couldn't see how anyone could have traced Nancy's identity back to Rayna Kozwalski. Before the old memories could take over, she reminded herself of the job she had to do.

She tapped away at the computer, making the list of names she'd discuss with Dalton tonight. Before she got very far, movement outside the window revealed people gathering for dinner. With a sigh, she got up and went to the kitchen to make sure they could handle what promised to be a busy evening.

Dalton shook out his tuxedo, going through the pockets before adding it to the pile for the cleaners. In the jacket, he found the brochure he'd slipped inside while he was talking with Grace at Patterson's gala. He smiled at the memory. About to toss the brochure, he remembered Grace's words, and he realized he'd been at the party to do a job and had ignored everything else—including the reason for the whole shebang.

According to Grace, it was something unusual for a patron of the arts. Dalton sat on his couch and perused the slick pages. Emitting a low whistle, he raised his eyebrows. Why would a man whose name was synonymous with theater, music, and fine arts want to get involved with migrant farm workers?

Dalton flipped the page, seeing photos of dirty, too-thin children picking tomatoes, then at the modern trailers, the plans for inexpensive housing in the vicinity of the fields. Of the prototypes already under construction. Very impressive. Medical care, education programs for adults and children alike.

On the back was the inevitable pledge card, plus a list of acceptable in-kind donations. All credit cards accepted. Dalton tossed the brochure onto the table.

His cell vibrated. "Dalton."

Silence. He should have checked the display. He was about to disconnect when he heard a quiet sniffle. "Hello?" he said.

"Dalton?" Miri's voice. High pitched. Trembling. Not the feisty Miri he'd met. Which scared the hell out of him.

"What's wrong?" He was already reaching for his keys.

"Can you . . . I mean, if you're not busy . . . we . . . Elena . . . she's . . ."

"Where are you?" He was behind the wheel.

"The House."

Cursing the traffic, drumming the steering wheel at every red light, Dalton drove across town. He hadn't even waited for Miri to explain. She called; he ran.

He dragged his fingers through his hair. Damn. She'd burrowed into places he didn't let people go. Not since Rachel.

Don't use their names. Don't look at the faces. Never the eyes. You can't do your job if you let it get personal.

Years of dealing with terrorists and hostage rescue taught him that. Yet in a span of days, Miri had created a fissure in his emotional fortress.

He thrust images of previous missions with their gunfire, explosions, and broken bodies from his mind. This was San Francisco, not some third world hellhole.

At Galloway House, Dalton's heart tumbled like a rodeo rider from a Brahma bull when he saw the black-and-white patrol car parked out front. A line of people stretched snake-like from around the corner.

Searching for a parking spot, he finally found a place to leave his SUV three blocks away. He ignored the stares of the sidewalk squatters as he covered the distance to Galloway House at a dead run. At the corner, he slowed to a walk, berating himself for forgetting everything that made him an expert at his job. He channeled the adrenaline, used it to focus. Created a mental checklist. He surveyed the line of people inching into a side entrance of Galloway House. Aromas reminiscent of his school cafeteria wafted out. His brain catalogued the crowd as the shelter's food line and moved on.

He rounded the sidewalk to the main entrance. A bear of a cop stood, arms crossed, in the open doorway. No flashing blue lights on the police car. No ambulance or fire truck. Dalton's breathing approached normal. As he moved to enter the building, the cop broadened his stance.

"Food line's around the corner," the cop told him. His squinty eyes said he didn't believe Dalton needed a meal.

"I'm not here for dinner," Dalton said. "I need to speak to one of the staff."

"Sorry. Nobody's allowed inside. You can wait here or come back later."

Dalton peered over the man's shoulder, but the reception room was deserted.

Miri slipped her cell phone into her pocket when the cop came back into the small parlor off Galloway House's main reception area. Young, probably a rookie sent to do the grunt work. A slender man, not much taller than Miri, in contrast to his older partner who stood at the front entrance like a grizzly guarding its lair. His deep brown eyes matched the color of his skin. Tired eyes, she thought. Much older than his face.

"Okay, ma'am," he said. "Thanks for waiting. Can you tell me if you recognize this woman?" He handed her a photograph.

She glanced at the picture and thrust it back into the pink-brown palm of his outstretched hand. Afraid if she met his eyes, he'd see into her past, Miri focused over his uniformed shoulder, trying to forget the image. Dead eyes, staring into nothingness.

"Elena," she whispered, fighting to get the words past her constricted throat. "I don't know her last name."

He nodded and slipped the photo into his pocket. "That's what two others said, but they have no information about her next-of-kin. They said you might know who to contact to claim the body."

Miri shuddered at the word. Body. A vacant shell, not the living, breathing person who not long ago walked out of Galloway House.

She tugged at her ponytail. Until Dalton got here, she'd try to find out as much as she could and tell the cop as little as possible. Old habits died hard. Following her instincts was another habit she hadn't shaken. Or why would she have called Dalton as soon as the cops arrived with questions about Elena?

"I can't help you, Officer." Glad her voice was steady, she went on. "She left here a couple of months ago."

The cop pulled out his notebook. His demeanor was polite, yet she sensed he didn't want to be here. Probably missing his own dinner. Or irritated that he had to deal with some *homeless* person instead of solving a *real* crime.

"Can I get your name, please?" he asked, his voice a low monotone.

She spelled it for him and watched him write it down. "Where did you find her?" she asked. "How did she die?"

"She was found in an alley about ten miles from here. Appears routine—like she died of malnutrition and exposure."

Routine? Elena was dead. And her death was obviously a low priority for this cop. That might be a good thing. People who needed Galloway House usually preferred a cop-free atmosphere.

"Ten miles away? What brings you here, then?" she asked.

"She had a scrap of paper in her pocket, torn from one of your flyers."

"Galloway House prints thousands of those every year."

"Anything unusual about the way she left?" He'd already shut his notebook, as if the answer wouldn't matter.

Miri shook her head. "No. People leave here all the time." But Elena was on her list of missing people. She felt the blood drain from her face as she imagined all of them dead.

"You all right, ma'am?" The cop's hand steadied Miri's elbow.

She clamped her jaw until the vertigo passed. "Fine." She stepped back, then released the elastic from her hair and shook it out, feeling the tension ease. "Not used to seeing pictures of dead people, I guess."

"Not something you want to get used to," the cop said. His tone was gentler.

"I don't think I can tell you anything else, Officer. Elena wasn't with us very long, and we can't keep tabs on everyone who comes through. She left of her own accord, and she was over eighteen."

Miri folded her arms across her chest. "I don't mean to interfere with your job, but police poking around Galloway House could undo months of work with our residents. One thing we promise is a safe haven, with no questions asked."

He gave her a terse nod and pocketed his notebook. "I understand. This place does a lot of good. If you find out anything else about her, please call the department." He handed her a business card.

She stuck it in her pocket and followed him into the main reception room. He strode to the door, said something to his partner, and the two men left.

Before they closed the door, Dalton burst past them into the room. Concern filled his face as his eyes darted from hers to the cops and back. He took three steps toward her, then came to an abrupt halt, his hands fisted at his sides. "Are you all right?"

If he'd come one step closer, she'd have rushed into his arms. At least one of them was thinking. She inhaled and nodded.

"What happened?" His fists unclenched.

Miri gestured toward the hall and stepped toward her office. Dalton followed. Thankful the room was empty, Miri shut the door and sank into her chair.

"Elena. They found her—dead."

"Who's Elena?" Dalton straddled the same metal chair he'd sat in earlier.

"A former resident. She was one of the names on the list I was going to give you tonight."

"And you're afraid there are more, right?"

Miri toyed with the ponytail elastic she'd pulled over her wrist. "The thought crossed my mind, yes."

"And you think there might be a connection."

She pressed her fingers against her eyelids and studied the swirling patterns. "People who come here are at risk. I've accepted that we can't save everyone, that some will make it and some won't. We hope the ones who aren't making it will come back before it's too late, but that's not realistic. Some of them are going to die too soon."

"Did the cops tell you how she died?"

She lowered her hands and met Dalton's gaze. "They said it was probably malnutrition and exposure. But it's not that cold." She fished the cop's card out of her pocket and tossed it on the desk. "They were more interested in identifying her and getting next of kin to claim the body."

"Unless there were signs of violence, it's understandable," Dalton said, his voice low and even. "People who come here— their lifestyles aren't conducive to longevity."

She almost laughed at the way his drawl made what he said so homey. "You have quite the way with words, Just Dalton. Yeah, they die young, usually because of the way they're living. But we've got to concentrate on what we can do to turn it around for as many as we can."

He lowered his eyes, then gave a noncommittal grunt.

"Don't make it sound so hopeless," she said. "We've helped a lot of people, and we're going to keep on helping them. Speaking of which, with all the ruckus, I'd better see what's happening out on the line. Come on."

"Wouldn't you rather I stayed here and go over the computer files?"

"Not now. I'll have to explain my notes. Besides, someone else will be working in here in about half an hour. What's the matter? You above slinging a little hash?"

She shook her head at his reluctant expression, so like the ones the kids gave when they had to do their homework before they could go out and play. He gave a deep sigh and stood.

Miri led the way. Galloway House's fare was a universe away from what Andrew Patterson served last Saturday, but the people lined up for a hot meal displayed none of the boredom Patterson's guests had while they ate. Nobody here would pick at their food or abandon a half-full plate.

Inside the kitchen, Miri gave a quick nod to the staff and volunteers. She yanked open a drawer and pulled out two navy blue aprons. She handed one to Dalton and slipped the second one over her neck. He stood barely inside the door, motionless.

She shot him an exasperated glare. "It won't do you much good unless you put it on."

Dalton stood off to the side and tied the apron. Miri moved through the space, obviously in her element. She spoke briefly to a young couple opening institutional-sized cans of fruit cocktail. Dalton couldn't hear the words they exchanged above the clatter of empty pans being stacked beside the sink, but the woman frowned and shook her head a lot. The man patted the woman's shoulder. She rolled her eyes and went back to pouring the diced fruit into shallow metal pans.

Dalton stepped forward. "What can I do?"

Eight pairs of eyes met his. He kept his gaze steady, ignoring the unease coiling in his belly, even managing a smile.

"Everyone, this is Dalton," Miri said. "He's going to be helping out tonight. I know you'll show him the ropes."

"What did the cops want?" a beanpole of a man asked. "We're two people short because of them."

Murmurs of agreement from the rest of the group rumbled through the kitchen.

"Oh, relax, Bill," the fruit cocktail woman said. "This Dalton fella looks like he can pull their weight and then some."

An older woman gestured to the counter. "You can start by taking these pans to the dining room. Someone will show you where they go."

Dalton approached a large rectangular pan of something

71

covered in cheese that smelled like his mother's tuna casserole. Some tension left at the immediate return to happier days. He reached for the pan.

"Careful. It's hot," the woman said.

After swapping out full trays of the tuna concoction, green beans, and fruit cocktail for empties, Dalton observed the action in the kitchen. The crew had dwindled to four, and from the way they stopped talking and engrossed themselves in their work when he entered the room, he suspected they were residents. The other four, including the older woman who'd been giving him instructions, were gone. Volunteers, he surmised.

Miri appeared with a fresh stack of sectioned disposable plates. "Can you take these out, please, Dalton?"

"Isn't there something I can do in here instead?" he asked. The mood of the dining room, populated with so many empty stares, stooped shoulders and shuffling feet prickled his innards as if he'd swallowed a porcupine. Although the room was filled with strangers, it was Rachel's eyes haunting him. A hollow-eyed Rachel, not the happy Rachel he wanted to remember.

Miri eyed him curiously, then handed him the plates. She glanced over her shoulder toward two of the workers who filled plates with what he assumed were their own meals. They carried them out, casting wary glances his way.

"They're nervous enough," Miri said in a low voice once they'd left. "You're a stranger and they're not going to feel comfortable with you around. I'll help in here. You can do more good serving. The folks in the line hardly notice the servers and they might say something helpful."

With a glance toward the door, he re-tied his apron, hoping the workers would return. They didn't. "But you're more tuned in to what's normal and what's different."

"You're an investigator," she said, practically shooing him to the door. "I'm sure you're very good at it. Smile, turn on that dazzling charm and scoop food. It's for one more hour, then we shut down."

She was right. The sooner he dealt with this as a field assignment and quit resenting Blackie for sticking him with the job, the sooner he could move on. When Miri pivoted and strode to the sink, Dalton savored her retreat. Trivial or not, the job came with one attractive perk.

"Suck it up," he muttered under his breath and pushed open the door to the dining room.

CHAPTER 7

Miri sat across from Dalton at Gino's Pizza. She raised her eyebrows. "I don't see why you wouldn't eat at the House. There was enough left over. And the tuna casserole's not *that* bad."

A server placed a pitcher of beer between them. Dalton poured two glasses and pushed one across the table. He quaffed half a tumbler and wiped his mouth.

"Got nothing against tuna casserole," he said. "My mama made a fine one. She could stretch her food budget until you could see right through it. I'm sure Galloway House's recipe is tasty, but after breathing it for over an hour, I was ready to leave."

"The added aroma of *eau de unwashed* can do something to the appetite, too, I suppose."

Dalton shook his head. "No, actually, I'm used to that."

"What? Private investigators don't bathe?" Even in the garlic-laden atmosphere, he couldn't hide that sandalwood scent. The one that syncopated her heartbeat.

His eyes widened for an instant, then his expression snapped back to neutral. He slid the shaker of red pepper flakes from hand to hand across the wooden table like a hockey puck. "Stakeouts can get complicated. Not always time for regular personal hygiene."

Working at Galloway House, she'd seen that look before. All too often. The one that said, *Oops. Almost told the truth.* She let it pass. Something about working in the dining room had shaken him. He never made eye contact, and any charm he'd exuded had been forced.

He'd also lost his flirtatious streak, and she hadn't decided how she felt about that yet. Her brain said it was for the best, but something lower down wanted to feel him against her, the way she had on Patterson's dance floor.

Pushing those thoughts aside, memories of Elena invaded, and Miri sobered. "I guess we should talk about the missing people. I made a list like you said, but didn't get very far with a spreadsheet for comparisons before . . . you know."

"Yeah," he said. "You okay?" His tone was hollow.

She stared into his gray eyes. They resembled the ones she saw across intake forms. Empty. No, not empty. Full of despair. "Better than you, apparently, and I knew Elena. What's wrong?"

He rubbed his face. His composure returned when he lowered his hands. "Nothing. Tired."

She leaned back as the server brought their sausage and mushroom pizza. Miri picked up a slice and wrestled with the dripping strands of cheese before taking a bite. "Eat," she said around a chewy mouthful.

He did. Slowly, with frequent refills of his beer glass. Miri ate three slices, Dalton barely finished two. She eyed the three left on the platter.

"All yours. I'm stuffed," she said.

"No, thanks. I'm fine."

Part of her wanted to shake him until whatever was troubling him spilled out. Another part wanted to rock him the way she rocked Sammi's little Suzie.

Nonsense. They'd just met, and his life was his business.

He flipped some bills onto the table. "Be right back," he said.

As she worked her arms into the sleeves of her parka, she watched him cross the restaurant toward the restrooms. Steady enough on his feet. She'd only had half a glass of beer, and the pitcher was empty. Despite the fact that outwardly he appeared sober enough, there were some rules she never broke. She'd switched to root beer when Dalton downed his second glass.

Grabbing her purse, she scooted out of the booth and positioned herself between the restroom and the exit. When Dalton emerged, she smiled and held out her hand, palm up.

His eyebrows arched in question.

"Keys," she said.

"What are you talking about?"

"You're not driving. Or if you are, I'll take a cab."

"I'm not drunk."

"You drank almost an entire pitcher of beer."

"Which in a place like this is barely three beers, and lousy beer at that. Plus, I ate. I said I'm fine. I know my limits." Anger flashed in his eyes, dark and menacing as winter storm clouds.

She kept her tone level, imaginary hands pressed to her ears to block the arguments between Nancy and their mother that reverberated through her head. "The issue is *I* don't know how you handle liquor. I do know I'm not getting in a vehicle with you behind the wheel. Keys or cab. Your choice."

The vein at the side of his neck throbbed. His lips flattened to a thin, white line. In one move, he spun on his heels and jammed his hands in his pockets. He marched to the restaurant door and shoved it open.

Miri followed a wary three steps behind as he stormed toward his car. When he reached the rear bumper, he beeped the remote twice, then yanked the passenger door open and threw himself into the seat. Miri exhaled and crossed behind the car to the driver's side. Dalton stared straight ahead, arms folded over his chest. The keys dangled from a cup holder between the seats.

She worked the key into the ignition. "Seatbelt," she said,

reaching for the lever to slide the seat forward. She fastened her belt, waiting to hear Dalton's click into place before she started the car. "Where to?"

"You want to work, or do you think I'm too drunk to use a computer?" The way he enunciated each word was pure mockery.

"I didn't say you were drunk. I said I didn't want you behind the wheel. It's a rule of mine."

"Fine." He unfolded his arms long enough to turn on the radio. The Eagles were stuck in Hotel California.

Ignoring him, she jammed the car into gear and wheeled into the street. Once she decided where they were going, she settled into the drive. Ten minutes later, Dalton still hadn't uttered a word.

If he was playing a game of wills, he'd grossly underestimated his opponent. Working with troubled souls all day for the past eight years provided plenty of practice in waiting out a recalcitrant teenager. Right now, Dalton wasn't much different. Something troubled him, and she wanted to help, but he had to take the first step.

She shot him glances as they drove beneath streetlights that illuminated the car's interior like a flickering silent movie. The vein in his neck wasn't throbbing anymore. Although he had his eyes fixed dead ahead, she knew he was aware of every peek.

Fifteen minutes later, Miri pulled into the driveway of a small clapboard bungalow. James Taylor's *You've Got a Friend* started playing. She lowered the volume and stared into the night. Memories returned, dulled by the passage of time.

"When I was four, my father drove drunk and killed three people. He died in jail. It didn't keep my mother from drinking, though. By the time I was twelve, she was wasted all the time. When I was fourteen, she walked out one day and never came back."

She switched off the ignition and tossed Dalton the keys. Then she marched up the path to the front door and knocked.

"Fuck. Shit." *Beam me up, Scotty. Please.* Dalton gave it a moment, but when the universe didn't sparkle and the porch stayed right where it was, he sped after Miri. Never mind she'd done the right thing.

He clomped up the wooden steps to Miri's side. "I'm sorry. I was a total jerk."

She didn't move. "I'm not going to argue that one."

Before he could respond, the door opened. A single light bulb—more of a dark bulb, Dalton thought—barely illuminated a small foyer. A rangy African-American woman smiled, her white teeth gleaming. "Miri," she said, her voice barely above a whisper. "I didn't expect you tonight. Come in." She stepped forward and wrapped her arms around Miri.

Still embracing, the two women moved into the foyer. Dalton clenched and unclenched his fists, waiting. What the hell were they doing in a quiet middle-class neighborhood? Not Miri's place, from his preliminary check on her.

"I brought an extra pair of hands, Elsie. Meet Dalton." She motioned for him to join them. "Dalton, this is Elsie."

He nodded, letting his eyes adjust. Instrumental music played softly in the background. Elevator music. Miri shifted and closed the door behind him.

Elsie, nearly six feet tall, all bones and angles with a face like weathered cedar, looked him up and down with curious brown eyes. She wore a faded Raiders jersey over baggy knit pants. Fuzzy pink bedroom slippers covered her feet.

"Welcome, Dalton." She gave him a firm, no-nonsense handshake. "Let's go, then. Miri'll get you started. I'll set things up." Despite a slight scuffing of her slippers, her step as she departed was as no-nonsense as her handshake.

"What the—?" he whispered to Miri. "I thought we were going to—"

"Shh. Change of plans."

He followed Miri into a small laundry room, where she hung her parka on a hook. She handed him a yellow paper gown. "Put it on," she said, slipping into one of her own. "Ties in the back." At the sink, she turned on the water and squirted some soap from a dispenser. "Wash."

He fastened the crinkly paper at his neck and followed orders. Miri was clearly the commanding officer on this op. But he had a bad feeling about this—a *really* bad feeling. Sickrooms and hospitals gave him the willies. Who had they come to see?

When Miri led him down the hall and he heard a baby crying—no, make that babies, plural—he was ready to jump ship.

"Miri—"

"Shh. Keep your voice down. Sudden noises upset them."

As if crying babies didn't upset *him?*

"Go. Sit." She pointed to one of three rocking chairs in a room with five cribs and other bits he recognized as nursery furniture. Elsie fussed over one of the cribs, then brought out a squirming, squalling blanket.

His heart went into triple time forced march rate. Blood rushed in his ears. Before his knees went to full Jell-O mode, he sank into the nearest chair. "What are we doing here?" he said to Miri. "What am *I* doing here?"

"Elsie and her husband Joe are foster parents extraordinaire. They take in the ones nobody else will touch. The mothers were on drugs, or HIV positive, or alcoholics. The babies need human contact. Lots of it."

Elsie appeared in front of him. "Hold out your arms. Come on, don't tell me you've never held a baby."

He shrugged. Words couldn't get past the baseball in his

throat. When he accepted the bundle from Elsie, his hands shook.

Elsie adjusted the infant in the crook of his arms. "Relax. Big guy like you shouldn't be afraid of a tiny baby. Keep his head supported. This is Xavier. He's a little feisty tonight, but he's been fed and has a clean diaper. Figured you might want to start out easy."

Easy? She had no idea. Dalton zeroed his attention on Miri's calm, soothing voice, coaxing her baby to eat.

"If you're okay, I've got some things to do out front," Elsie said.

"We're fine," Miri said. Her furrowed brow meant he'd be toast if he disagreed.

Elsie padded out of the room. Panic-stricken, Dalton looked at Miri. She smiled, which helped relax him. Not a lot, but it helped.

"Hold him close. Rock. Singing is good, too. Or talk to him."

Sing? Talk? He couldn't swallow. Breathing was an effort. He pushed his feet against the floor and set the chair in motion. Xavier didn't seem to notice.

Miri's charge now made slurpy, sucking sounds.

Dalton stared at a mobile dangling above one of the cribs. He focused on the shapes swinging gently back and forth above the crib. Fish. Fish were good.

Think about fish. Snorkeling. Deep sea fishing. Fly fishing. Anything but babies.

Xavier squirmed away, still squawking. Dalton jiggled him. "Shh," he managed.

Would Rachel's baby have been like Xavier? Would she have cared enough to cuddle it? Would it have ended up with strangers?

Dalton tucked the infant more securely into a one-arm hold and used his free hand to tease the blanket away from the baby's head. Xavier's eyes opened. For an instant, those eyes, so big in that tiny face, locked onto his. The baby gave one more wriggle, flailing his skinny arms. When Dalton reached out to tuck the limbs back where they belonged, Xavier's tiny hand fisted around Dalton's finger.

The baseball in Dalton's throat caught fire. Hot tears brimmed behind his eyes, overflowed and trickled down his cheeks. He shifted his head so they didn't land on Xavier's face.

You got it, little fella. Sometimes life sucks.

"Try putting him over your shoulder. You won't break him," Miri said. "Use a firm touch. It makes him feel more secure." From across the room, a not-so-tiny belch resounded. "Atta girl, Zoey."

He followed her suggestion. Holding and rubbing kept both hands occupied. One more distraction.

Miri crooned softly to her charge, who responded with a grunt. "Someone needs a change," Miri said. "Don't you, sweetie?"

Dealing with crap—figurative and literal—that was something Dalton understood. Not that he had any experience in the actual mechanics of diaper changing, but somehow he thought it would be easier to deal with than the crying.

Dalton couldn't fight his growing restlessness. He stood, careful to keep Xavier pressed against him, and paced the small nursery. Four steps one way. Turn. Four steps back. Almost like dancing. He moved his feet in a slow rumba. Xavier stopped squirming. His breathing, right next to Dalton's ear, cycled through ragged and hiccupy to slow and even. The tiny body went limp and boneless, dead weight on his shoulder.

He kept his face tucked into Xavier's blanket. Tears stung his eyes. Dalton couldn't remember the last time he'd cried.

Liar. It was fourteen years ago. It's over. Rachel's gone. So is her baby. Get a grip.

But he found himself on the wrong side of the wall he kept

between himself and his emotions. No matter how he tried to scale it, to get behind it where things made sense, his toes lost their footing, his hands slipped and he tumbled onto his ass. So much for getting a grip.

Miri ambled back to the rocking chair, her hips swaying a maternal cadence. Guys weren't blessed with that gene. He went back to his rumba with Xavier, who made contented sucking sounds.

Miri rubbed her cheek against her baby's face. "Zoey, you're such a sweetie. Someday, someone's going to love you more than anything. You wait. If your first mama can't take care of you, the right one will be here before you know it. You didn't do anything wrong, sweet little Zoey."

The baseball—no, a softball—returned to Dalton's throat. Trapped with an infant he didn't dare disturb, he half-stumbled toward the rocking chair.

Before he got there, the door opened and Elsie tiptoed in. "How are the little darlings?"

Head bowed, Dalton approached her. Her own maternal instincts must have kicked in, because she reached for Xavier. The kid weighed eight pounds if he weighed an ounce, but there was a ton of empty sitting on Dalton's shoulder.

Reaching behind his neck for the tie of his gown, he hauled ass for the door.

CHAPTER 8

"Your man have a problem?" Elsie asked.

Miri gave Zoey one final kiss on her petal-soft cheek and set her in her crib. She stroked the infant's fuzz-covered head. "He's not my man. We're working together. He seemed upset—I thought this would help. Apparently, I was wrong."

"Honey, you go take care of your own things. I'm fine. I got another cuddler coming in, and Joe will be back soon enough."

Careful not to disturb Xavier, Miri squeezed Elsie's arm. "See you."

Crumpling her gown and cramming it into the basket in the laundry room, Miri tried to understand Dalton's reaction. One thing she was sure of—it had nothing to do with being afraid to hold a baby. Parka slung over her arm, she sucked in a breath, counted to five, exhaled and headed for the porch.

From there, she could see Dalton silhouetted behind the wheel of his Navigator. Although the keys still sat in her pocket, she had a feeling he would have hot-wired the car if he'd really wanted out of there. She trotted down the steps and eased the passenger door open. When the interior light flashed on, he swerved his head toward the window.

"You can drop me off at my place," she said, no louder than she'd spoken in the nursery. "We can go over the files tomorrow, if you'd like." She jangled the keys.

"Your call." When he spoke, she smelled butterscotch.

Without touching her, he took the keys and cranked the ignition.

She watched his control return with the engine sounds. "Take me home, then. It's been a long day. Tomorrow's fine."

By the time they reached her neighborhood, Dalton's grip on the steering wheel relaxed. Other than her directions, the only sounds were tires on asphalt. He wheeled into the parking area behind her apartment building and cut the engine.

"I'll walk you up," he said.

"You don't have to."

He tossed the keys in his hand. "About tonight—"

"You don't owe me an explanation." She pulled on the door handle.

"No, I meant—if you want to go over those files, it's not too late." He sat, tossing the keys, staring straight ahead.

Damn, he was unreadable. Did he really want to work? Something had shaken him. Maybe he didn't want to be alone. That was understandable. Not only babies needed human contact.

Stop. You've been cuddling a baby. Your maternal juices are flowing. That's all this is.

Like hell. These juices were anything but maternal.

Something drummed in her ears. Her pounding heart? No, it was coming from the window. She peered across the seat into the indignant face of Mr. Liebowitz from 1C.

He cupped his hands against the glass like a megaphone. "This is a reserved place. You can't park here."

Miri climbed out of the car. "It's okay, Mr. Liebowitz. He's with me. He's dropping me off."

The old man stood his ground. "You want to visit, you find a spot on the street. This lot is reserved for tenants."

"Thanks for the ride. I'll see you tomorrow," Miri said to Dalton. She took her neighbor by the arm. "It's all right, Mr.

Liebowitz. Besides, you know I don't have a car. Technically, the Morgans are in violation for using my spot for their second car."

She steered Mr. Liebowitz to the back entrance and nudged him inside. Dalton hadn't started the car. Miri waved from the doorway and turned toward the stairs.

Normally, a session with Elsie's charges left Miri renewed and uplifted. Tonight, dragging herself up the two flights of stairs to her apartment threatened to consume the last remnants of her energy. Whatever Dalton's problem, it sucked the life from her bones.

Debating the relative benefits of hot chocolate against double chocolate chip ice cream, she unlocked her front door. As soon as she pushed it open, her pulse jumped. Without comprehending how she knew, she sensed someone was inside. She froze. Backing into the hall, she tucked her keys between her fingers and fumbled for her cell phone.

The lamp beside her sofa clicked on. "Miri? Is that you?"

Miri rushed into the room, closing the door behind her. "Nancy, what the hell are you doing here? You almost gave me a heart attack." She sat next to her sister, breathing Nancy's signature scent. That's what she'd noticed.

In the lamplight, Miri noticed Nancy's red-rimmed eyes. She gripped her sister's hands. They were icicles. "Honey, what's wrong? You're not still worried about that background search, are you? I told you, everything's fine."

Nancy sniffled and pried her hands free. "I know." She wiped her hand across her face. "Hunt's on his way out of town. I just spent a week trapped on a cruise ship with his family, plus it's getting close to that time of the month. Doesn't take much to set off the waterworks. I was feeling sorry for myself."

"Okay, let's slow down. What happened with Hunt's job? Didn't he get it?"

"Sort of."

"Nance, work with me here. Start at the beginning." She squeezed Nancy's shoulder.

Nancy shrugged away. "Oh, this is too silly. I shouldn't have come."

"Don't move. I've got the perfect fix." Miri hurried to the kitchen and grabbed a pint of ice cream and two spoons.

"Here we go," she said and sat on the sofa. "Like old times, right?"

Nancy smiled.

Thank goodness.

"Right. But then I wasn't such a basket case." Nancy grabbed the carton and a spoon. "Glad some things never change," she said, scooping out a huge mouthful.

"At least we're eating a better grade of ice cream." Miri snatched the carton and dug in. She crunched on the chocolate chips. "So, tell me everything."

"Andrew Patterson's latest project. He was setting up a whole new division, and Hunt was being considered to run it. I thought it was a great idea because—you know, he'd be helping people."

Miri nodded. "Migrant worker communities. Improving their living conditions."

"Right—So, that meant Hunt would be top dog over all the sites in California."

"Which is a good thing, right?"

"I don't know. Ever since Hunt found out he was up for the position, he's been majorly uptight. He called before, said instead of being top dog and overseeing things from here, he was going to be in charge of one site and have to answer to some higher dog." Nancy skimmed her spoon around the top of the carton, scraping up the softened ice cream. "Which means he'll have to live near the place. He's on his way already—to a one-horse town near the Mexican border."

Miri tried to picture the impeccable Hunter Sanderson mingling with vegetable pickers. No way. But was that Nancy's real worry?

"Are you two having—trouble? Are you afraid he might—you know?—with someone else while he's gone?"

"Hunt? Have an affair? Of course not."

Miri's pulse slowed. "So it's the mingling with the menials you think's got him uptight?"

"I don't know. I sure hope not. It's going to be different for him, though."

"Maybe that's why he's nervous. The change from his normal environment. Or maybe he's trying to be sure he does a bang-up job to impress the socks off Andrew Patterson so he'll give him the top dog spot."

"Maybe." Nancy didn't sound convinced. Was it something else?

"Then there's his family," Nancy continued. "They're aghast their dear son might get his Italian loafers dirty."

"Screw them," Miri said, grabbing for more ice cream.

"Easier said than done."

Miri touched Nancy's cheek. "Tell me the real reason you're here."

Nancy's brown eyes softened. "I keep forgetting you do this kind of stuff—you know, make people tell you their secrets."

"I don't *make* anyone tell me anything. I listen. Encourage them to make informed decisions." She smiled. "And I can usually tell when they're not forking over the whole truth. It's me, Nance. Talk."

"I love Hunt. I'd love him no matter what. I'm not saying rich isn't better than dirt poor, having been both places, but I don't need the big house and fancy clothes to be happy. Hunt told his mother where she can stick her attitude, and I'm proud of him. I know he'll adjust to the conditions of the job after a while. It's just that—oh, this sounds so selfish and lame."

"You didn't come over here to *not* tell me. What's selfish and lame?"

"I'll be stuck—alone—with his mother." Her voice rose half an octave. "She'll expect me to be at her frigging beck and call, like tonight, which is why I came here. It's hard enough to be around her when Hunt's with me. I tell you, the cruise was a living hell. She's five-two, but that woman could look down her nose at the entire NBA lineup. She'll drag me to the country club, to brunches and teas, gallery openings, god-knows what and whine about Hunter working at a job *beneath his station.* And she'll try to guilt me into getting him to quit, all the while letting everyone know *I'm* beneath his station."

"Do you want him to quit?"

"No!" Nancy's response was immediate. "He has a chance to do some good. Real good, tangible good for people whose lives need help. Not simply making the rich get richer."

"So, why not say no when his mother invites you to her soirees?"

"Nobody says no to Mrs. Channing Sanderson. She's already put together a black tie going away party. Saturday night. Please be there. Please? I brought a dress you can borrow."

Miri hugged her sister. "Say it's the red one and I'm there."

Nancy grinned. "It's the red one."

"Nance, you know I'll always be there for you, dress or not. You've got to relax."

Nancy sighed. "I told you it was stupid and lame. I needed someone to talk to. Someone who'd understand." She reached for the ice cream.

"Watch it," Miri said. "Your bracelet." She leaned over and fastened the clasp on the gold link chain that was a fixture on Nancy's wrist. "Got it."

"I keep meaning to have it fixed. I almost lost it at the gym last week." She checked the fastener, then shoved her spoon into the carton. "Where were we?"

"Talking about you and Hunt. Why don't you travel with him? You can probably find plenty to do while he's working." Miri winked. "And it might piss off his mother."

Nancy stopped, spoon midway to her mouth. "Yeah. Why don't I? Dammit, little sister, you grew up with a double-dose of common sense, and I apparently lost all of mine when I tried to fit into the Sanderson mold."

"To get you into that mold, they'd have to break you. And nobody breaks my big sis. Besides, with you by Hunt's side, I'm sure he won't be uptight."

Nancy grinned. "Not for long, anyway."

"Things good in that department?"

"Oh, yeah." Her face reddened.

"What? There's more. Tell me." Miri leaned forward.

"Nothing . . . not exactly, anyway. I . . . we thought . . ." She lowered her eyes. "We decided I should go off the pill." When she raised them, they sparkled.

"Nance, that's fabulous. When?"

"Six months ago," she said.

"And you didn't tell me?"

"I'm trying not to think about it. We're letting Mother Nature decide what happens next, but she doesn't seem in a big hurry. That's probably another factor in my mood swing. Major PMS symptoms, and I was hoping this month might be it." She got up and took the ice cream away.

"Hey, who said I was done? We need to celebrate!"

"I did." Nancy put the carton in the freezer. "You'll make yourself sick."

"Since when are you the boss of me?"

"Always have been."

Nancy came back and sat next to her. Despite the cold ice cream, warmth filled Miri's belly. *Nice to have you back, big sister.*

"Speaking of *that department*," Nancy said. "When are you going to settle down with someone?"

"Not sure I ever will."

"Don't be ridiculous. Of course you will. But be sure you do it for love." She put her hands on Miri's shoulders. "You're a big girl, and I hereby rescind all the threats I laid on you when we were kids. You have my permission to have a fling or two while you're waiting for your settle-down-with-guy."

"Thanks, Sis. You want to bunk on the couch?"

"No thanks. I'm going to go home and start making plans. Love you."

"Love you, too."

Nancy lingered at the door. "Seriously, Miri. Take some time for yourself. Feel free to bring a date Saturday night."

Dalton's image flashed in front of Miri. His lazy grin, his Texas drawl, and the anguish she'd seen and heard from him tonight. She closed the door behind Nancy, then crossed to the window and eased back the curtain. In defiance of Mr. Liebowitz's warning, Dalton's black Navigator remained in the lot.

Seventeen. No, eighteen times. Dalton watched the light from the first floor window grow bright, then dim, as Miri's nosy neighbor pulled the curtain aside, checking to see if he was still here. Well, he was.

Get a life, old man.

Aside from a couple of tenants dropping bags of trash into the Dumpster, there hadn't been any action. Upstairs, the light in Miri's apartment glowed through her draperies. He caught a glimpse of motion and watched the drape slide away, then drop into place. A much more subtle peek than her neighbor's approach, but a peek nonetheless. Popping his third butterscotch, he zeroed in on the window.

After a second or two, that light went out and another went on. Her bedroom, he guessed. He asked himself—again—what he was doing here. He didn't have an answer this time, either.

If she'd changed her mind about working, she'd have called. He should go home.

Home. Home was empty. Empty was not good. Not tonight.

If he had her files, he could work. He damn sure wasn't going to sleep. He'd call, warn her he was coming up for them.

His cell rang as he pulled it from his belt.

"Hey, Dalt."

Ryan Harper. His ex-partner's voice jump-started Dalton's adrenaline.

Dalton rubbed the back of his hand across his eyes. "Hey, pard. Thought you were enjoying some R&R. What pulls you away from that woman of yours?"

"Frankie? She's . . . uh, taking a spa break. Figured I'd check in while she's getting her toenails painted."

"Bullshit. You don't *check in* from Hawaii when you're on R&R with a gorgeous woman. Who called you? Who do I kill?" Dalton waited out a long silence. A shadow floated across Miri's window as she moved through the room.

Dalton growled into the phone. "Come on, Harper. Was it Fozzie?" Blackie would never say anything. But sometimes Fozzie couldn't keep his mouth shut.

"Cool it. I got a standby alert, might have to cut my R&R short. *I* called Fozz, okay? To see if he had any more scuttlebutt about why they'd call me since the boss had been damn insistent I take this time off after the Montana op. Fozz said they were short a man, that you're working a domestic investigation."

"What of it?" Dalton reflexively rubbed his arm where he'd been creased by a bullet on that op.

"Nothing, man. Just touching base. And in case I forgot, Debbie said you owe her a steak dinner. As long as you're in town, you might want to pay up. Take your mind off being stateside."

Dalton thought of Debbie, Blackthorne's miracle-working lab tech. Cute, blonde, ready to rock and roll, and right now, about as appealing as three-day-old fish. His gaze wandered upstairs again.

"Quit playing shrink, Harper. You're no good at subtlety. Blackie's got it into his head I'm off my game. As soon as I wrap up this little job he threw at me, I'll be in the field."

"The boss usually knows what he's doing," Ryan said quietly.

Dalton clenched his fist around the phone. "So fuck me. I got lazy on a dog and pony show assignment. No big deal."

"You know as well as I do, dogs bite and ponies kick."

Bedsprings creaked through the phone. Whispers told him Frankie, Ryan's girlfriend, was back from her pedicure. Upstairs, the light went off in Miri's window. He tried not to think of her getting ready for bed. "Next time you take time off, pard, I'd suggest you pick someplace people won't expect you to come back with a tan. Otherwise, they're going to wonder what you've been up to."

There was a sharp intake of breath from Ryan followed by escalating murmurs from Frankie.

"I, on the other hand, know exactly what you're up to." Dalton lowered his voice, not even trying to be subtle. "She's okay with what you do? Disappearing, half the time without a word?"

Ryan's tone sobered. "Yeah. We had that conversation. Hang on a second." Some muffled sounds, then he was back. "I can talk if you want."

Dalton gripped the steering wheel. "Don't worry about me. You make every minute count, Harper. Every damn minute.

Take care of her. Don't make me come hurt you."

He snapped his phone closed and gave the ignition key a violent twist.

CHAPTER 9

At a whiff of sandalwood wafting into her office, Miri looked up from her computer. She tried to keep shock off her face. Except for his healthy physique, Dalton fit right in with people who needed Galloway House. The weight on his shoulders subtracted half a foot from his height. He was unshaven, with bloodshot, red-rimmed eyes. Blue-black bags under them, big enough to handle a ten-day cruise, said he hadn't slept much, if at all. His hair stood up in all directions, as if he'd been yanking on it. She almost asked him if he was trying to prove he could blend in as a resident.

"Morning," she said. *What the hell is wrong?* "I've got a few more things to do before we can go. Coffee?"

He grunted something that might have been a yes.

"Breakfast's over, but I'm sure we can find something if you're hungry."

His "no thanks" was clearer, but sounded like it was coming from a gravel pit. When he'd called earlier to set up their meeting, she thought it was a bad phone connection.

"Sit. I'll get it. I'm ready for a refill myself." She picked up her half-empty mug.

In the kitchen, a full shift of volunteers prepared for tonight's food line dinner. Since the topic of conversation revolved around whether the Giants would beat the Diamondbacks, Miri guessed they were oblivious to yesterday's visit from the police. Samantha stood away from the volunteers, scooping cookie dough onto baking sheets, humming as she worked. Peanut butter, according to the aroma wafting from the ones cooling on racks.

Miri mumbled a general greeting and filled a thick white mug with coffee from the urn.

"That's stale," Samantha said over her shoulder. "I can make a fresh pot."

"Maybe later. You're spoiling the residents with those cookies, you know."

Sammi grinned. "I enjoy it. Wish I could bake enough for the food line, too."

"Dream on. The budget won't stretch that far in this lifetime, I'm afraid."

Although Miri remembered Dalton drinking his coffee black, she stirred in generous portions of milk and sugar. The man looked as if he had one leg plus a foot in the grave. A little energy boost should help.

She refilled her own mug and forced her curiosity into a little box in her brain, the way she did for all newcomers to Galloway House. When they were ready, they'd talk. Asking questions slowed the process. On a whim, she grabbed a napkin and snatched a couple of still-warm cookies before heading to her office.

Curtailing her curiosity was something she was used to. The full-blown desire to clutch this man's head to her chest and make his pain go away was new. She'd have to find another mental box. A big one, steel-plated, with a heavy-duty padlock.

She made sure she kept her tone upbeat when she entered the room. "Here you go." She set the mug on the corner of the desk, along with the cookies. Dalton sipped the coffee. If he noticed it wasn't his preferred style, he gave no indication. "I'll be finished here in a couple of minutes, and we can go use your fancy computer system. Have a cookie. Samantha's specialty."

Even while he shook his head, his fingers picked up a cookie.

First he nibbled at the edge, then devoured the rest.

"Take them both," she said. "I'll get my purse."

Dalton found his voice on the drive to Blackthorne's office. The coffee and cookies had polished the gravel in his throat, and his smooth Texas drawl was back. Okay, so now she didn't want to offer succor—she wanted to—what? She wanted him. Period.

This was Nancy's fault. Nancy planted a bug in her ear last night, that's all. A *really* big bug. A tarantula-on-steroids-sized bug. Heat pooled between her legs. Her nipples strained at her bra, and she reflexively crossed her arms over her chest, no matter that her parka hid evidence of her response. She glanced his way, but—thank goodness—his attention was on the road.

"Did you find anything your missing people have in common?" he asked.

"Beside the fact they were all women?" she said. "Which isn't much. More than half our residents are women."

"First we collect facts. We'll worry about what they mean later."

After parking in the lot, Dalton led Miri through a side entrance, up a flight of stairs, and down a hallway lined with closed wooden doors. Stopping at one, he gave a quick tap. When there was no response, he opened the door and stepped inside.

"Your office?" Miri asked. There were four desks in the center of the room, pushed together to form one big table. A computer monitor and keyboard sat on each desk.

He shook his head. "I don't have an office here. These are set up for research, and we can use the computers."

Miri started to ask him where his office was but decided it didn't matter. She handed him the jump drive. "Here. I made spreadsheets like you said, but that's as far as I got."

"Let's take a peek." He inserted the drive into a USB port

and pulled the chair back for her.

She reviewed the information she'd put in the spreadsheet. "There wasn't much. Names, dates, if they were dailies or residents, what they did. When they left, how they left. They're all different, though."

"Why don't you copy the files to that computer, and I'll put them on this one." He powered on the one next to her. "We can work in different directions and cover twice as much ground."

Miri dragged the files to the computer desktop and removed the jump drive. Dalton took it from her hand. His fingers drifted slowly down the length of hers, and he must have felt the spark because he yanked away.

She bit her lip and studied her computer monitor. Dalton seemed to be having trouble getting the drive into the USB port. Finally, he clicked his mouse and stared at the screen.

"I've got your spreadsheet up," he said. "Why the asterisks by some of the names?"

"Those left under normal circumstances, but I haven't seen them lately, and after what happened with Elena, I thought I should check them out."

Dalton pulled out a couple of legal tablets from a desk drawer. He passed one across the desk. "In case you want to make notes."

He seemed to be having as much trouble meeting her eyes as she was meeting his.

He tapped a few keys. "Let's find commonalities. Give me the basics. Age, race, special skills. Maybe something will pop."

Good. Something she could think about other than his disarming presence. She added columns to her spreadsheet, filled in a few things she'd been thinking about in the pre-dawn hours.

Those hours when thoughts of Dalton filled her dreams. *Dreams.* That's why she was so uncomfortable. She'd been dreaming about him—okay, so they were erotic dreams of major proportion—and with him here in the flesh, those dreams came back. She sneaked a glance in his direction. Although the real Dalton looked like hell, he beat the dream Dalton hands down. The dream Dalton had no substance. This man sucked the oxygen out of the room.

He leaned forward, depriving her of even more air. His expression was all business. "I want to help. You're going to have to be honest with me, or this is a total waste of time. Are the names on this spreadsheet fake?"

Miri decided to be up front with him. "They're exactly what we have in our files. I'm sure some of them are made up, but what you have is everything in Galloway House's database."

"Good. I don't have my notes from the other day. Which three triggered your concern?"

As she recalled, he hadn't bothered with many notes at the time, but she opted not to go there. Now, he seemed genuinely interested. "Luisa, Cissy, and Robbie. The first three."

"I'll start with them, run them through databases you can't access. Meanwhile, you Google your list and see if you get any hits. You'll be more likely to know if they're the same people."

She clicked open the Internet browser and entered the first name. As expected, "Luisa Fernandez" gave her thousands of hits.

"This could take awhile," she mumbled.

Dalton chuckled, and the sound lightened her heart. "Detective work is nothing like what you see on television. Try narrowing the search. Add San Francisco to your query. Start with the last six months. If we need to go back further, we can do it later."

She sighed and started following links, not really sure what she was looking for.

"Yes!" she said to her screen when her umpteenth search

brought up a newspaper article with a photo she recognized. Becky Crandall, a former resident, beaming as she accepted an award. Miri's eyes brimmed.

"You got a hit?" Dalton swiveled his head in her direction.

Miri nodded as she skimmed the article. "Becky Crandall said she was moving home. Looks like she did, and she won an award for an art contest." Her chest swelled. "I'm so proud of her."

Dalton, sandalwood and all, hovered behind her and read over her shoulder. "Makes it mean something, doesn't it?"

"It's what it's all about." Miri swiveled around. Dalton's face was inches from hers. If she tilted her head up—no, definitely the wrong move. She addressed the monitor. "Guess I'd better keep going."

"I'll cross her off my list."

Had he sighed? Or simply exhaled? She typed the next name into the search engine.

Two hours later, her eyes burned, her neck ached, and she had covered eight names. Only one crossed off the list. "Why don't you have Mr. Spock's computer?" she mumbled. "Ask it a question and it correlates everything and talks to you. No eyestrain."

"I'll see if I can requisition one for you," Dalton said. "Until then, we'll have to be satisfied with these manual versions."

She pressed her eyelids while she waited for a page to load. Dalton was on the phone, his drawl getting deeper.

When she opened her eyes, she blinked in disbelief, but the words on the screen didn't change. Her pulse pounded in her ears.

"Oh, my God."

Dalton whipped his head around at the whispered gasp from Miri. "I'll have to get back to you, darlin'. Thanks," he said into the phone and clunked down the receiver. Miri stared at the computer as if a ghost had materialized on the monitor.

"Find something?"

Her fingers groped for the mouse. He covered her hand with his, squeezing to stop her trembling as he looked over her shoulder at the display. "What's wrong?"

Miri pointed at the screen. "Tania."

Dalton scanned the page, a newspaper article four months old. The body of a vagrant woman, initially discovered under a pile of trash between two Dumpsters, identified after two weeks as Tania Ivanova. With the identification, officials reopened the case. Cause of death not positive, homicide a possibility.

Dalton rolled his chair closer to Miri's. She shoved back and wandered to the window. After bookmarking the page, he stepped behind her and placed his hands on her shoulders. When she relaxed into him, his physical response, appropriate or not, was immediate. He inched his hips away from her. Lowering his head, he spoke softly into her ear.

"I can take it from here. I'll drive you home, or to Galloway House, then come back and keep working."

He waited, feeling her breathing, in and out, in and out. Finally, she shook her head.

"No. I'm all right. It's just that Tania . . . she was so full of life. She didn't always make the right decisions, but she never second-guessed herself. She set a goal and busted her ass to meet it." She exhaled a long breath. "Can I . . . um . . . freshen up?"

When she faced him, her eyes glistened with unshed tears.

"Across the hall on the left," he said.

By the time she came back, he'd followed the threads and pieced together enough information for a case outline.

"Okay," she said, sliding into the chair beside him. "What did you find out? What can I do to help?"

He faced her, saw the determination in the set of her jaw, the steady way her gaze met his.

"Did Tania leave without notice? I didn't see any address information on your spreadsheet."

Miri shook her head. God, he wished she wouldn't do that—it dispersed her scent as if she sprayed the room with a Miri aerosol.

"She said she had a place to live, a friend from school she'd re-connected with. Somewhere south of here, but I don't remember. The article said they found Tania outside of Santa Barbara, but that doesn't ring a bell. She seemed so excited. Sammi—Samantha—one of our residents, made a special chocolate cake for her."

Miri's face fell. "Good Lord, that's pathetic. I can't remember where she was going, but I remember a damn chocolate cake."

Resisting the temptation to caress her, he laid his hand over hers, pleased when she didn't pull away. "Hey, don't get upset. You had no way of knowing anything like this would happen."

From the pain in her eyes, she'd remember more than chocolate cake from now on.

He gave her hand a gentle squeeze, then rolled his chair back to his own computer, searching for the right way to pose the questions he had to ask. "We need to approach this from all angles. It's important to keep things impersonal."

"Impersonal? Two people I knew are dead. That's personal."

"It's a matter of being able to do the job. Emotional responses keep you from seeing things clearly."

"So, people you know die and you plod right on as if nothing happened?"

He felt the blood leave his face and he clenched his jaw until he was afraid he'd crack a tooth. His ears buzzed. *No. Life stops. But you find a way to keep going. You build your wall and don't let anyone get through.*

He croaked out a response. "If you want to do the job, sometimes that's the only way."

She narrowed her eyes. "That may work for you, but I can't pretend I didn't care about these people."

"We're not in the same line of work. And I'm not saying you shouldn't care. But I'm going to ask you to be objective. If that's too hard, I understand and can take you back."

"No. I'll stay."

Normal background sounds replaced the buzzing in his ears. He wiped his hands on his jeans and picked up the pen. He tapped it on the legal pad until he was sure his hands were no longer shaking.

"From what I've found, the cops didn't work too hard on Tania's case. Once they identified her, they followed a few leads, but there wasn't enough evidence of homicide."

Miri toyed with the computer mouse. "I can't help but feel responsible. I should have prepared her to avoid whatever killed her."

"Why would you assume her death was related to something you did or didn't do for her? You're not responsible for everyone who comes through Galloway House."

"You're right. Intellectually, I know it. But emotionally, it's another story." She wheeled her chair back from her desk and faced him. "Tell me something. The article said they'd found a vagrant. What makes the cops assume that?"

Dalton shrugged. "Logical assumption, most likely. The neighborhood was one frequented by the homeless. No ID, shabby clothes. No one reported her missing."

"So, tell me. If the body they found under the garbage had been wearing expensive clothes, fancy hairdo, manicured nails, whatever—would the cops have dismissed the case as easily?"

"Probably not," he admitted. "They've got only so much manpower, only so much money for investigations." His stomach churned with the memories. "It's a sad fact of life, but they prioritize. If they didn't think she'd been murdered, what would they investigate? Another unfortunate death, one of who knows how many every year."

"And if she had been murdered?"

He focused on Miri's eyes, golden where Rachel's had been vivid blue. *Stay in the present.* "I can't tell you. I hope they'd do whatever they could to find whoever did it."

"You think it was easier to assume it wasn't a homicide, so they could close the case?"

He exhaled, only then aware he'd stopped breathing. "Miri, I'm not fighting you here. I don't even disagree. But it's reality, and sometimes it sucks. It's like triage in a hospital. If you spend too much time on a hopeless case, then other people you might save will die. And I'm sure the cops don't sleep much better than the doctors when they're stuck having to choose."

"You're trying to tell me I should accept Tania's death—and Elena's—because of who they were. That nobody cared about them."

Unable to sit, he strode to the window and stared at the parking lot. "I didn't say that. But the reality is, the odds of people like Tania and Elena dying the way they did are higher than for your typical middle-class citizen. And their cases aren't going to get a lot of attention."

He tried to bury the images of Rachel, swallowing past a burning tightness in his throat. Miri's scent grew stronger, her light tread approached. He blinked, pinched the bridge of his nose, scrubbed his face with his palm. He ached to reach out to her, to take comfort from her, the way she'd comforted baby Zoey. He jammed his hands into his pockets and leaned against the window.

She meandered through the room, then sat down on the edge of the nearest desk.

"What you said before," she said, running her fingers across the pens in a mug on the desk. "About priorities. Maybe there's a good side." She picked up one of the pens and wiggled it between two fingers. "Nobody can help Tania anymore. Or Elena. If the police start a big investigation, they'll talk to everyone who comes to Galloway House." The pen wiggled faster. "We're nothing if we can't offer a safe haven. So, maybe if the police aren't investigating, we'll be helping more people. If they're too scared to come because they're afraid of cops, we can't do anything for them."

"I can make a few calls. See if I can get the cops to compare notes on Elena and Tania."

She shook her head. "That'll bring them in. Isn't there a way you can do it without them?" One corner of her mouth lifted. "You being a super-sleuth and all."

Her upturned mouth was enough to release some of his tension. His phone jangled, and gave her a quick grin as he reached for it.

CHAPTER 10

Miri tried to finish another search while Dalton grunted unintelligible sounds into the phone, nodding, shaking his head, writing notes. This time, the writing wasn't neat and tidy, and she gave up trying to decipher his scrawl.

"Thanks, sugar. I owe you," he said in an over-the-top drawl. He averted his face and murmured something into the phone.

The twist in her belly was *not* jealousy. How could you be jealous when you'd just met someone, and he irritated the hell out of you half the time? She rested her chin in her hands to hide the flush she felt rising to her cheeks.

Dalton apparently didn't notice, thank goodness, because he attacked the keyboard, his gaze flitting between it and the monitor.

The door flew open. A young woman—mid-twenties, maybe—breezed into the room behind a toothpaste ad smile.

"Hey, Cowboy, what about that steak dinner you owe me?"

Dalton leaped to his feet and hurried toward her on an intercept course. "Debbie. What are you doing here?"

Miri ducked behind her monitor. Debbie seemed oblivious to anything other than Dalton. She wore a white lab jacket that hit her mid-thigh. Whether she wore anything underneath was up for grabs.

"I've got three analyses running that don't need my babysitting, and someone said they saw you up here. When did you get back? And if it was more than a day ago, I'm going to be very hurt that you didn't call."

Peering around her computer screen, Miri took in the short, spiky blonde hair, the deep blue eyes that had to be contact lens-enhanced, and the clunky boots that somehow exuded the elegance of strappy stilettos. She thought about her own standard jeans and ratty sneakers.

Debbie launched herself at Dalton's neck.

Okay, so this time the belly-twist *was* jealousy. She cursed herself for feeling it.

Dalton pecked Debbie's cheek and peeled her away. "I've been busy."

"I heard you got grounded, but I didn't believe it. Are you really stuck on some dumb domestic?"

Miri adjusted her polo shirt and rose from behind the monitor. "Hello. I'm Miri Chambers, Dalton's dumb domestic." She extended her hand. At least Debbie had the decency to blush as she gave Miri a firm handshake.

Dalton's face was a few shades redder than normal, too. "Miri, this is Debbie, one of Blackthorne's finest lab techs. Deb, Miri."

Debbie gave her an embarrassed grimace. "I'm *so* sorry. My manners have atrophied. Too much time alone in the basement trying to give these guys what they need. I'm Deb. Can we start again?"

Miri had to laugh. "Sure. Getting off on the wrong foot seems to be a Blackthorne tradition."

Debbie lifted her eyebrows at Dalton. He shrugged. "My personal life got in the way of our first meeting."

This time Debbie laughed. One of those disgustingly charming, musical laughs. "I didn't know you *had* a personal life."

Miri smiled at Debbie. "Mr. Blackthorne offered Dalton's services to investigate some missing people. We've been doing some research this afternoon, but I'm sure we'll be finished in time for him to take you to dinner."

"That's okay," Debbie said. "I like it better when he owes me one." She ran her fingers down Dalton's chest. "Right, Cowboy?"

"Um . . . right."

"I'll let you two get back to work. Nice to meet you, Miri."

"Nice to meet you, too." Miri waited until Debbie had one hand on the doorknob. "Oh, Debbie? Do you have the time?" She kept what she hoped was an innocent expression on her face as Debbie checked her bare wrist. Miri dangled the timepiece from her fingers.

Debbie's mouth dropped open. Her eyes went saucer-wide. Then she laughed, a warm, reverberating tone this time. "Touché." She strapped the band around her wrist. "Watch it, Cowboy. She's good."

The door clicked shut.

"Um . . ." Dalton said. "That was Debbie."

Miri nodded.

"She works in the lab."

"I gathered that."

"She's a damn good tech."

"I'm sure she is."

"We're friends." Dalton rubbed his jaw. "It's not like we have anything serious—oh, shit. This is awkward."

"It shouldn't be. You've got a life. Mr. Blackthorne dumped me into it, but I don't expect you to give up your friends. Or explain your relationships."

"I don't have a *relationship* with Debbie."

"Fine. Why don't we forget the whole thing and get back to work?"

She rounded the desk and sank into the chair.

"In a minute." Dalton stepped across the room. He leaned down until his scent threatened to strip the composure she'd tried so hard to maintain during the Debbie encounter. He rested his palms on the desk.

She swallowed. With more effort than she was willing to admit, she met his eyes. Heat smoldered behind the storm clouds. Heat that hadn't been there when he'd looked at Debbie. "Wh . . . at?"

"You lifted her watch."

She fussed with the mouse. "I gave it back."

"Did you take anything else?" He tucked a finger under her chin until their gazes met again.

"No. Of course not. It was . . . like a reflex, I guess."

He slapped the desk. She jumped.

"*That's* a reflex. Picking pockets is *not* a reflex."

She fisted her hands at her waist. "Well, it is for me."

"You want to explain?" He traced her jaw line with a forefinger.

A quivering shudder ran down her neck. She shook her head. "It's something I do when I get . . . nervous, I guess." Or jealous, apparently.

He bent down, a hand on each arm of Miri's chair. "Where'd you learn it?" His lips moved closer. His breath warmed her cheek.

"New Orleans." At least that's what she tried to say. As soon as she got to the "Or" his lips were on hers. Warm, pliant lips. Tender, gentle lips. Did she moan? He increased the pressure a hair. Yep. She definitely moaned. She met his increase and raised him another fraction.

His tongue ventured over her lower lip, more in question than demand. She parted her lips in subtle invitation. Her tongue found his. Teased, drew back. His followed. Danced, darted. Entwined.

Dalton closed his eyes, savoring the kiss. Miri's lips were so soft. She tasted so sweet. And this was so wrong.

Damn! He had no business kissing her. She was a Blackthorne client, for God's sake, and vulnerable. He didn't take advantage of women, vulnerable or not. He tried to pull away, but his lips clung to hers as if trapped by some all-powerful magnet. He clenched the chair's armrests because if he touched her, he might not be able to stop.

He nibbled her lip. She ran her tongue along his teeth. She made a sound somewhere between a whimper and a moan. He groaned. This was barely a kiss, yet he was rock hard. His jeans shrank half a size. Bells rang.

When Miri pulled away and bent over for her purse, he didn't know whether to curse or give thanks. Wiping sweat from his upper lip, he did both.

As she opened her cell, she flipped her bangs, revealing tiny beads of perspiration on her forehead.

Miri answered her phone with a smile and a breathless, "Hey, Sis."

With his back to her, he adjusted his jeans, worked at getting his breathing under control. Stupid, stupid, stupid.

"Be right back," he mumbled, heading for the door. In the hall, he bent over a water fountain, thinking a cold shower would be more effective than a cold drink. Things were not settling fast enough. He took the stairs to the third floor and poked his head into the anteroom of the communications center. The fax machine held a stack of pages in the output tray.

He waited, but the clerk wasn't around. He found the faxes addressed to him and settled into one of the chairs against the wall. Leafing past the two reports his contacts had provided about Tania and Elena, he stopped at the cover sheet headed *Chambers, Miri.*

He stared at the black-and-white print until the words blurred. When he'd requested the information, Miri was a pain-in-the-ass client. A woman who'd picked his pocket and embarrassed him in front of his boss.

Then, not five minutes ago, he'd been stuck in a lip-lock he didn't want to end, while a crack radiated like a spiderweb across the wall of his emotional fortress. To read the pages he held would put Miri right back into pain-in-the-ass client territory. Never mind that it was the smart, professional thing to do. Professional was the last thing on his mind.

Things snapped back into perspective. He *was* a professional, dammit. He pulled the cover sheet aside and started reading. He finished the first page. Everything there was consistent with what she'd told him about her life and job. He dug through the papers for the next page. Nothing but the reports on the two dead women. He went back to the fax machine, searching for the pages he must have missed. Nothing. He read the cover sheet from Miri's report more carefully.

Two pages including cover. That was it? Miri's existence faded into nothingness eight years ago.

Most five-year-olds left longer paper trails. He'd have to do the search himself.

He braced himself for Miri's reaction. If it was going to hit the fan, he might as well get it over with. He crammed the pages into an envelope from the counter. Mentally plastering the cracks in his wall, he marched down the hall.

Rounding the corner, he slowed his pace to a leisurely stroll. At the door, he counted to ten before opening it.

Miri glanced up from the monitor. If she was thinking of their kiss, she hid it well. That was fine with him. It should never have happened. So, why couldn't he forget it?

"Any good hits?" he asked.

She pushed her chair back and stretched her arms over her head. He couldn't help noticing how the movement lifted her breasts, which led to visions of what it would be like to cup them in his hands, which led to those places he had declared off limits. Before she lowered her arms, she reached behind her neck and fanned her hair. He casually positioned the envelope in front of him, ignoring its contents. Time for that later, when he was thinking clearly.

"I've Googled until I'm cross-eyed, and I'm starting to think this whole thing is simply a bunch of unfortunate coincidences. I found two more people, and they're fine."

"Are you saying you want to give it up?" In which case she wouldn't be a client. He wasn't sure how he felt about that.

"I don't know. It happened so fast. Mr. Blackthorne offered to help, and it made sense, but you keep saying there's no connection, and maybe you're right."

"You're in charge," he said. "If you don't think there's a problem, say the word."

"I wish I knew. But you were probably right from the beginning. It's a wild goose chase, but I don't think there are any geese. My instincts aren't perfect, and the law of averages says that eventually I'll have a bunch of wrong hunches, one after another. Like tossing a coin and getting ten heads in a row. It can happen." She reached for her purse. "I've been gone most of the day, and the House is short-staffed. If you don't mind driving me back, I'll be out of your hair and you can get back to what you really want to be doing."

No, he wasn't going there. He gripped the envelope a little tighter.

She tilted her head, her eyes questioning. "If it's a problem, I can take the bus."

Right. He was supposed to talk. As long as he didn't mention what he really wanted to be doing, he should be fine. "No. I'll give you a lift." At least he hadn't stuttered. He hoped he wasn't blushing. "Are you sure, though? You really want to drop this?"

She sighed. "Yes. No. Hell, I don't know. You're right. The

cops are right. People leave and don't really owe us an explanation. I suppose I was hurt that they didn't stick around, but it's time I face reality. Now that I've had time to think about it, I'm surprised Mr. Blackthorne even suggested you investigate."

Dalton wouldn't bring up the obvious answer. That this was nothing more than busy-work, an assignment meant to keep him occupied but out of trouble. "It's your decision, but why don't you think about it for a while? Go home, regroup, get things in perspective."

"Maybe you're right." She reached for her purse. "Let's go."

Why did he want her to stick with the case? As they walked to his car, he tried to convince himself it was because the investigation warranted more time and effort. That there might be a few more days sitting side-by-side with Miri couldn't possibly have anything to do with it.

They approached his car, but he didn't press the remote until his hand was on the passenger door. Irritation flickered across her face, but she stepped back and allowed him to open it. What the hell. He moved away, let her haul herself into the seat, enjoying one last view of her delightful rump.

He still held the envelope with the faxes and tossed it on the backseat before climbing in.

Despite the questions swirling through Dalton's head, he couldn't find the right approach. He almost laughed out loud. He had the reputation of being able to sweet-talk anyone out of anything, but Miri tied his tongue in knots. She sat, cupping her elbows, staring out the side window. With a sigh, he punched the radio button.

When Dalton pulled into one of the parking slots behind Galloway House, Miri leaned across the console. With a feather-light brush of her lips on his cheek, she grasped his hand between hers. "Thanks for everything, Just Dalton." She hopped out of the car.

He watched her trot to the back door and slip a key in the lock. After she'd gone inside he discovered a scrap of paper she'd slipped into his hand. He unfolded it and stared at a phone number he didn't recognize.

CHAPTER 11

Miri had lost track of how many times she'd punched all but the last digit of Dalton's number into the phone over the last three days. Did she really want to know if more people she knew were dead? And if he found them, what good would it do? They were adults—most of them, anyway. They'd made their choices, and there were still so many more people she could help. Or was she looking for an excuse to see him again?

She slid the receiver back onto the base, convincing herself that toe-curling kisses aside, he was a man with too much baggage. She had enough of that with the people she dealt with all day.

What she needed was something different. Something light, fun, frivolous.

Who was she kidding? She had four new residents, a leaky water heater and Will had smuggled in a puppy. A very un-housebroken puppy. Who had time for frivolous?

The phone rang, and she jumped. Taking a calming breath, she picked up. "Galloway House. How may I help you?"

"Hey, kid. I figured you might need a reminder about the party."

Nancy. Her going-away party. Why had she promised to show up? Stupid question. Because she couldn't say no.

"Right. Tomorrow night. Eight o'clock. At the witch's castle. I'll try."

"Miri, you promised. Hunter's back for the weekend, and

then we're both going to Santa-something-or-other. Mrs. Sanderson's doing the full-blown martyr bit—her poor, brave son, setting off into the wilderness to bring indoor plumbing to the destitute. Sheesh—I've talked to Hunt. It's not like that at all, but to listen to *her,* you'd think these people were all drug-crazed lunatics living in tents. I need an escape hatch."

And you need to get out.

Although Nancy didn't speak the words, Miri heard them as if they were broadcast over the PA system at Candlestick Park. "I'll be there."

"With a date."

Dalton's image flickered. But he hadn't called since they'd parted company. "I can't promise that much."

"I could set you up. I think Buddy Higgenbotham's on the prowl."

Talk about the antithesis of frivolous. "God, no. I'll find someone." Who was she kidding? Nobody she knew had a tux—except Dalton. Why wouldn't the man stay out of her head?

The receiver slipped off the ends of Miri's fingers. She adjusted it on the base, staring at it for several heartbeats before she picked it up and punched in Dalton's number—all the digits this time. Much as she dreaded what could only be termed groveling, the alternative—an evening with buck-toothed Buddy Higgenbotham and his oversized adenoids—was a definite no.

After seven rings, as she was about to hang up, Dalton answered, breathing heavily. Thoughts of what she interrupted flooded her brain with pictures she didn't want to see. Before she could slam down the receiver, he spoke again.

"Miri?"

Great. Caller ID.

"I'm so sorry. I didn't think—I mean, I'm interrupting—I'll let you go."

"Miri, wait. Is something wrong?"

A rhythmic thumping came through the line. Her face heated. "No, nothing's wrong. I thought—never mind. I shouldn't have called."

Still breathing heavily, he called to someone. "I'll catch up. Go on without me."

"Umm . . . Are you sure you want to be talking to me right now?"

"What? I'm eight miles into a ten-mile run, but I can talk."

"You're running? Like in exercise running?" She leaned back in her chair.

"Yeah. PT. Physical Training. What did you . . . you mean you thought I was . . . ?"

"Something like . . . that."

"Well, it's nothing like . . . that, I can guarantee. What do you need?"

"A favor. Kind of a big one."

"More people missing?"

"No. I need an escort for tomorrow night."

Dead air. The silence brought the heat back to her face. "I shouldn't be bothering you. It's nothing. You've probably got a date already. It's last minute. And a Saturday." Buddy Higgenbotham wasn't *that* bad. She could tolerate him for an hour or two, adenoids and all.

"It's no bother. What time?"

"Just like that? What if I told you it's black tie?"

"I'd say I'll drop by the cleaner's on my way home and pick up my tux. What time?"

He sounded so matter-of-fact. Like she was still an *assignment*. Maybe that was a good thing. "The party starts at eight."

"Seven-thirty all right?"

"Fine."

"Miri!" Keisha swung into the doorway, grabbing the jamb to stop herself. "You have to come see. She's dead, I think."

Miri swore Keisha's dark skin paled. "Gotta go," she said into the mouthpiece even as she slammed the phone down. "What's going on?" Miri asked Keisha.

"I saw her." The woman was breathing more heavily than Dalton—as if she'd run a marathon, not just down the hall.

"Who?" Miri gripped Keisha's shoulders. "Slow down. Talk to me, Keisha."

"Luisa. Explosion. On the TV."

Miri put her arm around Keisha and guided her to the recreation center. A handful of residents gathered around the television, transfixed. "Okay, Keisha. Tell me what you saw. Who you saw."

"Luisa. There were cops. Lots of cops. A bunch of women, and Luisa be there. And—" Keisha burst into tears. "I think she be dead."

Hearing Keisha's speech patterns revert to ones she'd been taking pains to unlearn, Miri settled her onto a sofa. "Relax, hon. It'll be all right."

Miri stared at the breaking news broadcast, which displayed a smoldering house and a lot of cops and paramedics. "What's going on?" she asked the group. Everyone spoke at once, but Miri sorted through the cacophony, processing what she needed.

"Meth lab exploded."

"About an hour ago."

"That place on Holden."

"Near the park."

Miri's heart leaped to her throat. The park. Where she'd told Sammi to take Will and his puppy. And Suzie.

"Where's Sammi and Will?" Miri asked. No one answered. "I said, has anyone seen Sammi or Will?"

The group exchanged glances and gave a collective head shake.

Miri ran.

Her sneakers pounded the concrete. She dodged and snaked her way through alley shortcuts. She smelled smoke mixed with chemicals. Ahead, tall green trees marked her goal and she pressed harder.

"Sammi! Will!" She started calling as soon as she hit the edge of the park, wondering which way to turn. Why had she ever thought the park was too small? They'd be at the playground, right? She veered left, down the dirt path. "Sammi! It's Miri. Answer me if you're here!"

She slowed to listen, straining to hear anything over her labored gasps.

Dalton's breathing filled his car, drowning out the road sounds. Once again, Miri called and he'd dropped everything to rush to her aide.

Three days at the Blackthorne training compound, immersed in PT until every muscle screamed, hadn't kept her out of his head. She was with him on every step through the obstacle course, whispering to him on the firing range, a shadow hanging out of reach on the forced marches. She was the hostage they rescued in countless simulations.

A brazen waitress, picking his pocket—and he hadn't asked her what she was doing in Patterson's study.

A silent socialite, melting into his arms as they danced.

Proud, strong, intelligent, compassionate, and one hundred percent female. Damn her.

Miri had said someone was dead and then hung up. He'd run the last two miles all out, catching and passing the rest of the team, stopping long enough to ditch his pack and rifle before barreling out of the compound.

No doubt, the team thought he was crazy. They were probably right. Miri *made* him crazy. He took a deep breath, then another. Crazy got people killed. Routines, training, practicing until everything was automatic—that kept you alive.

He was in a total dead cell zone, otherwise he could call the compound and they could monitor the public safety bands. All he'd been able to find out before he lost contact with the civilized world was that a meth lab exploded, not far from Galloway House.

Even knowing he was at least ten minutes from any kind of signal, he punched buttons on the radio, trying to get more information. Maybe Jupiter was aligned with Mars or something, and he'd pick up a station. Yeah, right after Santa Claus dropped out of the sky with his reindeer.

The onramp to I-80 never looked more inviting. He merged into traffic, hit the radio and reached for his cell phone, reminding himself Miri'd been talking to him when the explosion happened.

A call to Blackthorne's offices got him some bare-bones information. Names of the dead or injured were not being released. The fire was contained; the cops were investigating. The fact that the radio broadcasts weren't saying much allayed a fraction of his anxiety. Of course, a meth lab blowing up in that part of town probably wouldn't get more than a cursory mention.

How much did someone have to be worth to make the news? How much to interrupt regularly scheduled programming? Were there crawlers with updates at the bottom of television screens? Crap. He had no business assigning value to people's lives.

To Dalton, all that mattered was that Galloway House was *near* the explosion, not *at* the explosion site. So why was he in a panic? Miri wouldn't get involved. Would she?

Pictures of her, racing to the rescue, evading cops and firefighters, running into a chemical-filled house, wouldn't stop playing in his head.

No. Miri would be fine.

He repeated that to himself over the next thirty-six miles, more emphatically when all he got was voice mail on both Miri's cell and Galloway House's main line. Sitting in stop-and-go traffic on the Bay Bridge, he found the detachment he needed to think things through. His mind played with the pieces, testing how they fit. A meth lab. Something tickled the edge of his brain. Taking advantage of yet another stop in traffic, he reached into the backseat and retrieved the envelope he'd dropped there when he'd driven Miri home.

He found the reports on Elena and Tania. He eyed the sheets, searching for anything drug related. A horn sounded behind him.

Relax, asshole. Moving ahead six inches isn't going to get you there any faster.

He lifted his foot from the brake and his car closed the gap. "Methamphetamines" popped off the page in both reports. Could there be a connection to Miri's missing people?

Too much of a stretch. They'd found those two in entirely different places, Tania as far away as Santa Barbara. Should he mention it to Miri?

Although she claimed to have a handle on the reality of Galloway's population, Dalton didn't buy it. Deep down, she imposed her optimistic goals on each of them. Drugs weren't part of the Galloway picture; therefore, she didn't want to admit her residents might be users.

That, he understood. Too well. He didn't know Rachel had a problem until it was too late.

Fuck. That was fourteen years ago. This was now.

The nearer he got to Galloway House, the harder his heart thumped. He hadn't changed out of his filthy sweat-soaked pants and shirt, but the sweat running down his back was the ugly, cold sweat of fear.

He tried Miri's cell phone again.

Nothing. Another honk. Another gap closed.

Across the bridge at last, Dalton repressed his impatience. For years, his existence depended on waiting for the right moment. On following plans. Using his brain. The one above his neck.

Traffic crawled, but at least it moved. The sun hung low in the sky, and despite his sunglasses, he squinted against the glare. With his goal so near, the last few miles seemed to stretch out as long as the rest of the trip. Commuter clogged streets, pedestrians—why not a damn marching band? That would really slow him down. Finally he arrived, parked, and managed to restrain his pace at something under a run to the front door of Galloway House.

Inside, a different face sat behind the counter. Female, middle-aged, was all he bothered to notice. He scanned the room, but no sign of Miri. Before he opened his mouth, the woman reached under the desk, pulled out a clipboard and gave him a sympathetic smile.

"Welcome to Galloway House. I'm sure we can help you. What kind of assistance do you need?"

As he stepped toward the counter, he saw her lean back an inch and her nostrils flare. Her smile widened as if to cover her reaction. He rubbed his fingers across his jaw. He hadn't shaved since Tuesday morning. They'd been running simulations all night, and then a little live-fire drill followed by a ten-mile run in full gear. He glanced at his filthy cargo pants and mud-encrusted T-shirt. Hell, he could smell himself.

He suppressed a chuckle. Looks like there was one person who thought he'd blend right in with the Galloway House crowd.

"I'm looking for Miri Chambers."

Her lips formed a polite, professional smile. "Miss Chambers isn't here, but I can help you." She poised a pen over the clipboard. "Your name?"

"Dalton—but I don't want the kind of help you're offering. I need to find Miss Chambers." Dammit to hell, he'd had over an hour to consider all the possibilities and come up with a credible way out of this scenario, which he should have predicted. Which he *would* have predicted if his brain had been functioning at half his normal standard. He tried for his guaranteed to open any door smile, and the effort was beyond him. Well, there was always Plan B. Beg. "Please, ma'am? It's important."

The polite smile shifted to genuine concern. "No. She left a while ago—after the explosion—and she hasn't come back yet."

"Maybe someone else would know. I wouldn't bother you, but like I said, it's important that I find her."

"I'll call someone," she said. "Maybe you'd like a hot meal while you're waiting? The dining room will be serving at five." She picked up a phone.

Voices drifted from down the hall. He pivoted and followed the source, ignoring the woman's pleas that he wait. He found a room occupied by half a dozen women while a sitcom played on the television. Several seemed engrossed in the program, but one peered up from her needlepoint.

"I'm looking for Miri Chambers," he said. "Have you seen her?"

"Ran out like a bat out of hell," one woman said.

"Right after the explosion," another added.

God, would she have run *toward* the disaster? Why?

"She was asking about Sammi, remember?"

"Yeah, Sammi and Will. They come back?"

There was a silent exchange of glances, a few shrugs, and the needlepoint lady said, "Sammi was going to the park. Took her daughter and Jillian's kid. And the pup."

"Where?" Dalton asked.

"Clifton and Holden," one of the others said. " 'Bout three

blocks that way." She waved an arm in a sweeping gesture that covered at least three compass points.

"Thanks."

Dalton jogged back to the door, colliding with a baby stroller coming in. He caught himself before he landed on the floor and stared into the large, startled eyes of a toddler. "Hi, there," he said.

Her chin quivered.

Great. He was scaring babies. He found a grin. "You're okay, aren't you, kiddo?"

A female form reached into the stroller and snatched the child into her arms. "It's okay, Suzie. The man did an oops."

"I'm sorry, ma'am. I wasn't watching where I was going."

"No problem." She barely met his eyes, trying to hold onto the child and maneuver the stroller past him.

"Sammi," the woman at the counter said. "This man's looking for Miri. Says it's important. Have you seen her?"

Sammi nodded. "At the park. Reggie ran away."

Dalton helped her get the stroller inside. "Which way is the park?"

Sammi tilted her head to the left.

Dalton ran.

CHAPTER 12

Miri reached for Will's shoulder. "Get out of the bushes. You need to come home. Now."

"We can't go. Reggie's in there, Miri! We have to get him out." The dog's leash hung from Will's hand. The desperation on his face made the decision a no-brainer.

She glanced into the distance. The wind blew the smoke—and more importantly, the chemicals—in the opposite direction. Still, she kept her breathing shallow.

Miri nudged Will behind her. "Okay, let's see what we can do. But stay back. He's scared enough. You be ready with the leash."

"I'm sorry. I didn't mean to let him go, but he wanted to run and play."

She tousled his hair. "I know, sport."

"We can't leave him here. He needs me."

Not as much as you need him.

Miri crawled under the bush, fixing on the whimpering sounds from its depth. Of course the puppy would bolt for something with thorns.

"I see him. His collar's stuck."

"It's okay, Reggie," Will called. "We're saving you."

Will's voice startled the already frightened pup and he jerked deeper into the greenery. Miri reached into the shadows, ignoring the scratches. Her fingers touched leather. She inched forward on her belly, straining to grasp the collar. "Got you," she whispered. She tugged. The soft fur beneath her fingertips wriggled free. A blur of brown-and-white sped past.

"Grab him, Will!" She scrambled out, brushing the leaves and dirt from her hands. Turning, she saw Will's blur join Reggie's. They were both running *toward* the explosion site. She raced after them. "Will, no! Stop!"

She caught up, grabbed his arm. "Stop. You can't go there, Will. It's too dangerous."

Tears welled in his brown eyes. "It's all my fault. I shouldn't have let him off the leash. Is he going to die?"

Miri crouched to meet Will's eyes. "I'm sure he'll come home when he gets hungry."

"Does he know the way?"

"Dogs are smart about things like that. Hey, I have an idea. How about we go home, get some hamburger meat and come back? He likes hamburger, doesn't he?" She gave him a conspiratorial smile.

Will flushed at the exposure of his forays into the kitchen for dog treats. He scuffed at a pebble. "I guess so."

"I know so. Let's go."

Will darted ahead, calling after Reggie. When he crashed into a tall figure dressed in black, Miri's pulse jumped. Rather than sidestep, the man leaned into Will. Although she'd never felt uncomfortable in the neighborhood, knowing there was a meth lab so near elevated her level of wariness. She straightened her shoulders and strode toward the man.

"Will," she called, her voice louder than usual. "Let's go."

White teeth appeared behind a wide grin on the grimy stranger's face. "Are you two lookin' for this?"

He held out a squirming brown and white puppy.

"Reggie!" Will shrieked, reaching for the dog.

"Dalton?" Miri ran forward. "What are you doing here?"

"I was in the neighborhood. Thought I'd take a stroll through the park."

"First things first," Miri said. She collared the puppy and snapped on his leash. Once she secured Reggie, she looped the leash around Will's wrist, with a quiet admonition to hold tight. He gave a solemn nod and crouched to the ground, burying his face in the dog's fur. Watching the two scruffy creatures delighting in the reunion, she grinned. A bathtub at Galloway House would be challenged tonight.

She turned her attention to Dalton, who hadn't said anything since his initial greeting. In comparison, he'd been ready for a spread in GQ the last time she'd seen him. His hair was matted, he hadn't shaved in days, and judging from his bloodshot eyes, hadn't slept, either. There was definitely not a whiff of sandalwood anywhere in his vicinity.

Will trotted ahead with Reggie at his side, any danger apparently forgotten. Dalton dovetailed his fingers in hers and drew her closer as they walked. She felt his chest bellow in and out, as if he'd been running. He'd said he was running when he'd called, but surely he'd driven here. Was he trembling? Or winded? She stepped away enough to study him.

She absorbed the way his T-shirt hugged his broad chest before it dipped into the waist of his cargo pants. The strong biceps beneath the short sleeves. She caught a glimpse of a healing gash at the base of the sleeve. He must have noticed her scrutiny.

He tugged the sleeve down, covering the scar. "A little too much *eau de unwashed?*"

"No. I'm deciding if I like you better in a tux, or like this." His mouth curved up. Heat flooded her face. "Did I really say that out loud?"

"Afraid so." He cocked an eyebrow. "So, which is it?"

"Haven't decided. Were you on a stakeout or something?"

Dalton shook his head. "Training. Routine stuff."

"I didn't know private investigators had to keep in shape like that."

He drew her back against him. "You never know when we'll be called on to look good in a tux."

She accepted his arm around her shoulders. After crawling in the dirt and bushes, she couldn't get much dirtier.

Before they reached Galloway House's entrance, Dalton stopped her. "Are you okay with your decision about checking into your missing people?"

Miri raised her hand. "Will, go inside and take care of Reggie. Your mom should be back from work. Let her know you're home."

"Okay." Will picked up Reggie and breezed through the door.

Miri thought about Dalton's question. "You found something?"

"I don't know. But maybe we should talk. How well did you know Elena and Tania?"

"Apparently not as well as I thought. What do you have?"

He glanced around. "Not here. Your office?"

"Do you need the computer or privacy?"

"More the latter."

"Then my office isn't the best place."

He gave her a wry grin. "I think this is where I say, 'your place or mine?' but you might misconstrue my intentions."

"And what exactly are your intentions?"

"Honorable, Miss Chambers, I assure you."

The exhaustion in his eyes gave her a sudden urge to rock him. She was about to decline his suggestion when she envisioned the picture of Elena the cop had shown her. If there was the slightest chance of a connection, she owed it to Elena, and maybe to others, to follow through.

She rubbed her neck. "I've got a laptop at my place."

"I've got a hot shower at mine. And my neighbors don't pay attention to comings and goings."

"Maybe that's what worries me."

He rested his hands on her shoulders and rotated her to face him. Behind the exhaustion, something else showed in his eyes. Pain? Anguish?

"I'll never do anything to worry you." His voice was a husky whisper. "You can count on that."

Her mind whipped through an automatic spreadsheet of options, none of them better than another. His place? Hers?

"I have a shower, too," she said. "And I need to get into some clean clothes."

He grazed a finger across the back of her hand. "You need some first aid."

She'd forgotten the sting of a criss-crossing of scratches over her hands and arms. "It's nothing."

"They should be cleaned." He cradled the back of her head. "Let me take care of you. Just this once."

Maybe that's what she wanted. An hour or two not being responsible for everyone.

"Let me make sure everything's all right and get my bag," she said. "We have a supply of clothes here. They might not be the greatest fit for you, but they're clean."

"I take it that means my place is out."

"Unless you live around here, mine seems more sensible." She had faith he'd leave when she asked. At her place, she at least maintained the illusion of control.

The twinkle in his eyes said he understood. "I've got spare clothes in my car."

"For disguises when you're tailing someone?"

His grin was genuine this time. "Maybe. Or maybe because I never know when I'm going to need clean clothes on the job."

"I'll bet you were a Boy Scout, too."

"Guilty as charged. All the way to Eagle."

"All right, Boy Scout. Wait here. I won't be long."

He saluted.

She inched open the door, determined to ignore the incessant demands that would surround her when she stepped inside. It was Friday, she had the weekend off, and even Mrs. Sanderson's party sounded good. She hesitated, then pushed the door closed.

"What's wrong?" Dalton asked.

"For the time being, nothing. And I intend to keep it that way. Come with me." She trotted down the steps and jogged to the rear entrance, Dalton half a pace behind. "Wait here." She slithered through the door, grabbed her bag, then darted outside again.

Dalton stepped away from the wall, where he'd been leaning. "What was that all about?"

"Nothing." She pulled out her cell and called the House.

Keisha answered. "Miri? You all right?"

"I'm fine. And I'm officially off duty until Monday." She snapped the phone closed and looked at Dalton. "Well? Where's your car?"

Dalton leaned his hands against the tile in Miri's shower as the steamy water sluiced over him, whirlpooling acres of muck down the drain. The bathroom was small, clean, and totally Miri. No fancy labels, merely no-frills utilitarian products that would get the job done. An oversize T-shirt hung from a hook on the door. No doubt what she slept in. She'd emerged from the bathroom in sweats covering her from wrist to ankle, barefoot, her damp hair fastened in a ponytail. That he hadn't embraced her right then was a testament more to his exhaustion than his self-control.

He closed his eyes. Three days of an adrenaline-enhanced

existence meant he was going to crash soon—big time. Thoughts of the neatly-made double bed in the adjoining bedroom—no, he wasn't going there. Get real. Sleep was first and foremost on his mind. Dead-to-the-world, round-the-clock, dreamless sleep.

As if that would happen. Miri insisted they wait until they were clean before they spoke of his findings, which was fine with him. He never felt dirty roughing it with the team, but in Miri's presence, he was all too aware of the way he looked—and smelled.

He flipped the cap of the shampoo bottle sitting on the windowsill in the shower and squirted a liberal dollop into the palm of his hand. As he lathered it through his hair, a familiar spring breeze scent filled the shower. Whoa. One part of him wasn't *completely* exhausted.

Ignoring his response and thankful he'd used most of the hot water, he hurried through the rest of his shower. A new disposable razor rested on the edge of the sink. He fetched a canister of some pink shave gel from the shower and dealt with his overgrown stubble.

Being clean lightened his spirits, and he slipped into the jeans and Longhorns sweatshirt from his duffel. For good measure, he brushed his teeth.

He opened the bathroom door to release some of the steam, and a delicious aroma, second only to spring breeze–scented shampoo, enticed him to the kitchen.

Miri was setting plates on a small table in an alcove of the kitchen.

"Smells fantastic. You didn't need to go to any trouble."

"Nuking leftovers is hardly trouble."

"What can I do?"

She eyed him from head to toe and back again, her gaze resting on his face. "Sit before you collapse, I think."

He pulled out one of the ice cream parlor–style chairs with

its blue-and-white checked seat. "The shower worked wonders."

"A hot meal should be even better." She retreated to the kitchen and returned with two plates. "You're in luck. I was on a cooking spree last week. Most nights I grab something at the House, but I had an uncontrollable urge to try something different."

Dalton inhaled the aroma in front of him. "I think I might be in heaven here, darlin'."

"It's nothing fancy. Pork tenderloin with a spice rub. Maybe you should taste it before you decide."

"No question." He forked up a piece of pork and chewed, savoring the spicy flavors against the tender, mild meat. "Definitely heaven." He scooped some mashed potatoes. "You mind if we hold off on business for a few minutes? I've been living on field rations for days. If you can call it living."

"Can I ask a question?"

Her voice was hesitant. He put his knife and fork on the plate. "Anything."

"What do you really do?"

He picked up the fork and shoveled another bite, formulating an answer as he chewed. "I do investigative work for Blackthorne, Inc. You know that."

"You're the one who said detective work was mostly staring at computers. I couldn't help but notice the gash on your arm. How did you get it?"

Had she recognized it as a healing bullet wound? "It's nothing. Sometimes the people we investigate don't like it when we find them." He took a sip of water. "Most of what I do is confidential. I meant it when I said I respect a client's privacy. I have to ask you to trust me on that."

"All right."

Something about the way her eyes squinted when she spoke told him she wasn't totally convinced, but she dropped it, and they finished the meal in a wary silence.

When her plate was empty, Miri rose. "Why don't you go into the living room? I'll take care of the dishes and you can tell me what else you found. I assume it was about Tania and Elena."

"I'll help."

"It's no bother—it'll take me two minutes. Go. Relax. The kitchen chairs aren't very comfortable, especially for someone your size. I hardly use them except for a cup of coffee."

The soporific results of the hot shower and meal gave Miri's overstuffed couch an almost overwhelming attraction. Instead of relinquishing himself to its lure, he wandered the small living room. Stopping at the small entertainment system, he browsed her CD collection.

"Anything you want to hear?" she called from the kitchen. "Feel free."

"You like jazz."

"Good work, super-sleuth. Whatever gave you that idea?"

He gave a quiet chuckle. "My outstanding powers of observation."

The water stopped running and she padded to his side. She reached around him and tilted a case from the shelf. "I thought I told you to sit." She gave his shoulder a gentle shove toward the couch.

Familiar music filled the room. Memories of his grandmother's house. It took several seconds to register. "Glenn Miller?"

She nodded. "*In the Mood.* I didn't know what you liked, so I went with a compilation of classic jazz."

"I think our signals got crossed," he said.

"What do you mean?"

He reached for her arms, gently pulling back the sleeves of her sweats. The scrapes and scratches gleamed under what he assumed was an antibiotic ointment. "I was supposed to be taking care of you, remember?"

"Seemed like you needed it more."

So much for his reputation of having the best poker face on the team. "Let's get started." He motioned her to the couch. She scooted into a corner, one leg tucked under her.

He retrieved the envelope he'd dropped on the end table when they'd arrived and situated himself at the opposite end of the couch. "What did you know about Tania and Elena?"

"Elena was about twenty-three. We helped her find a job doing alterations for a dry cleaner, but she dreamed of being a dress designer." Miri pulled the elastic out of her hair, slid it over her wrist and ran her fingers through the damp locks. He felt her raise a barrier of detachment, something he knew too well, but she couldn't eradicate the compassion. "I guess impatient describes her. We tried to make her understand there weren't any shortcuts to success. She quit after a few weeks. I wondered if someone was trying to take advantage of her—"

"Sexually?" he interrupted.

Miri nodded. "She wouldn't talk about it. Then she was gone. Nobody heard from her until the cops showed up with her picture."

"Tania?"

"Runaway. Bad family situation. Her father used her as a punching bag. She took it, figuring if he was beating her, he was leaving her mother alone."

"But she left."

Miri snapped at the elastic on her wrist. "Her father died."

"You know how?"

"She never said and we don't ask. If you're asking if I think she had something to do with it, the answer is no. But I can't tell you why. Instinct."

"Did either of them do drugs?"

"No way."

"How can you be sure?" The words exploded, harsh and demanding, surprising even him.

She jerked upright. "We've got strict anti-drug policies."

Thoughts of Rachel swamped him. He struggled for detachment, reaching into the depths of his control to keep his voice neutral, his features bland. "Users can get around them."

Her eyes clouded. "What are you trying to say?"

He focused at a point on the wall behind her. "They found evidence of methamphetamines in both women."

"No. No way. Absolutely no way."

"That's not what the medical reports showed."

"You got their medical reports? I thought we agreed no cops."

"At the time, we were looking for similarities. And I didn't go to the cops. I have some connections. This was off the official records." He handed the faxed sheets with the summary of the autopsy findings to Miri.

She scanned the pages, then slammed them onto the coffee table. "Impossible. This is a mistake. They both hated drugs. Neither used before coming to us. Elena lived as a resident for months. There's not that much privacy—someone would have seen the signs. *I* would have noticed."

Conviction and indignation flowed in her voice. His dinner congealed in his belly. "Can you be sure?" His voice came from far away, ringing in his ears.

Miri's hand rested on his thigh, barely touching, but it scorched like a branding iron. She didn't speak. When he met her gaze, her eyes sucked him in, dragging him down until he was drowning in their amber depths.

"Rachel. My wife. Died of an overdose."

"What happened?"

The words hung in his throat before he could speak. "We were the perfect small-town couple. The whole cliché thing. Buddies in grade school, awkward friends in junior high, while we tried to get a handle on the boy-girl thing." He swallowed, remembering. "You know—roping calves one day, and then there's a school dance, and you don't know what to make of her all dressed up."

Miri nodded, the dip of her head almost imperceptible. She waited, leaving a void demanding to be filled. Like a bronco bursting into the rodeo ring, his words tumbled out.

"I couldn't see a future in town—Dad was selling off more and more of the ranch and getting ready to retire. I joined the Navy. Serve my country, get college paid for. Rachel stayed with her parents while I did my training."

He drew a ragged breath. "Once I was out of Basic, she couldn't wait to get out from under her parents' roof. I was based in San Diego. We moved. I shipped out. I thought . . . I thought she was happy there, making friends. I didn't know. She never said . . . her letters and e-mails . . . upbeat. Shore leave—" he clawed his fingers through his hair— "was good.

"I had no idea—no clue—" Damn. His throat felt like sandpaper. His chest ached. His eyes burned. "She was lonely. She hooked up with some people. Not the quiet life she was used to. Partied, they gave her drugs. To take the edge off, but they consumed her until that's all she lived for." He hung his head, stared at the floor.

Miri gave his thigh a gentle squeeze. "It's hard to help when you're not around."

"Dammit, if I'd have known, I'd have gone AWOL to get her help. There was nothing anonymous like Galloway House around. Maybe if there was, and she'd found it, or—shit, I don't know. I had to piece it together when I got back. I didn't know until after—I had to tell her parents—" He choked on the words. "She was . . . pregnant . . . when she died."

He hadn't noticed when Miri got up, but she pressed a glass in his hand. When he lifted it toward his mouth, the alcohol fumes stung his eyes. He swallowed a mouthful, the fire burning all the way to his belly. Then he set the glass down.

She settled onto the couch beside him, not making contact, but close enough for her body heat to radiate through his jeans.

After a moment, she asked, "When did she die?"

"Fourteen years ago this month. Next week."

"Can you forgive me?" A tear trickled down her cheek.

"Forgive *you*? What?" What could she possibly have done?

"I thought—I thought you had this *thing* about the kind of people I deal with. That you couldn't handle being around them. That you were—I don't know—above them. But you were remembering." More tears followed the first. "Oh, God, Dalton. I dragged you to Elsie's and made you deal with babies—that must have hurt so bad. I am *so* sorry. So damn sorry."

He fought for control, clenching his jaw, his fists, every muscle in his body. "I can't believe I told you this. Nobody outside my family knows. Not even the people I work with. And they're closer than family sometimes."

She handed him his drink.

He pushed it away. "I'm driving, remember."

"When's the last time you slept?"

His shoulders twitched upward. "Been awhile."

"The couch pulls out. It's made up."

He took her wrist, held it like a lifeline. "You know what?" he whispered. "I don't even know if the baby was mine."

CHAPTER 13

Miri stepped to the bathroom sink and splashed cold water on her face before bringing a pillow and extra blanket to Dalton. He hadn't moved since she'd pried away from his grip and left him on the couch. His hands hung limply between his knees. His eyes stared, glazed, into the distance. At least his ragged breathing had steadied.

She crossed to the CD player and turned it off. When she approached the couch, Dalton gave no signs he noticed.

Could he be asleep?

Her heart tugged. She fluffed the pillow in the corner of the couch and unfolded the blanket, wondering if he'd simply tip over if she nudged his shoulder. Before she could turn off the lamp, his hoarse whisper filled the silence.

"No."

"Okay." Her fingers dropped from the switch. "You need sleep. Lie down." She indicated the pillow.

"Don't . . . don't go."

The effort it took him to ask was palpable. She sank onto the couch and set the pillow on her lap, both an invitation and a barrier. Patting it, she whispered again, "Lie down."

His head hit the pillow with a shuddering sigh that seemed to resonate from the depths of his soul. Leaning over him, she tugged gently on the blanket and arranged it over his shoulders.

"Sleep." She stroked his hair. "I'm here."

Curled on his side, Dalton found her hand. She held it, feeling it relax as he finally surrendered to his body's demand.

Propping her feet on the coffee table, she scrunched into the couch cushions and rested her head against the back. She wrestled with the idea that Tania and Elena had been mixed up with drugs but couldn't wrap her brain around it. She closed her eyes. Dalton's slow, rhythmic breathing lulled her. The last thing she remembered before drifting off was the way his warm fingers remained curled around hers, even in sleep.

Sometime later she awoke, her neck stiff, her feet freezing and her calves sore where they rested on the edge of the coffee table. One thing was certain. Remaining here for the rest of the night was out. Dalton waking up with his head in her lap was not something she was ready to deal with. She needed time to regroup. She unclasped his hand and laid it on the couch near his face. Carefully, she extricated herself from under him, supporting his head on the pillow as she eased it back down. His breathing never altered.

She tiptoed to her bedroom. Two A.M. With luck, she might get a few hours of real sleep before Dalton awoke. While she lay there, she mulled over the right approach for the morning—to offer sympathy, companionship, or merely pretend he'd fallen asleep without saying anything to her. Hell, for all she knew, he'd been so exhausted he *wouldn't* remember a thing.

She sighed. Nothing was ever that easy. Besides, *she'd* remember.

The next time she opened her eyes, sunlight filled the room. She squinted at the clock. When was the last time she'd slept until ten? Dangling her legs over the side of the bed, she waited for the cobwebs to clear before venturing out. To her surprise, Dalton was exactly as she'd left him, except the hand that had held hers now hung to the floor.

She trotted downstairs to pick up her newspaper from the lobby. When she got back, Dalton hadn't stirred.

She set a pot of coffee to brew, then took a shower. Feeling more alive, she sat in the kitchen and read the paper while she sipped her coffee. She found news of yesterday's explosion in the middle of the local section. She refilled her mug before finishing the article. Eight people dead, no names released, pending identification and notification of next of kin. Detached, clinical language, with undertones of *good riddance, one less drug house and eight fewer people to run through the legal system.* Keisha swore she'd seen Luisa on television, but nothing in the article confirmed hers was one of the bodies. She squinted at the blurry photo in the article, trying to identify anyone she knew. Fire engines, cop cars, medics loading a stretcher into an ambulance, and a Dumpster, which reminded her of Luisa. Tears threatened.

Movement from the living room caught her attention. Almost eleven. Schooling her features into a friendly but neutral expression, she prepared for the inevitable morning-after awkwardness even though there hadn't been a traditional night before. Should she take the proactive route? She poured another mug of coffee but had second thoughts about initiating the conversation.

Dalton sat on the couch scratching his head.

Don't be silly. Bring him the coffee.

She hesitated at the counter, her back to him, speaking to the coffeepot. "Good morning. Did you sleep well?"

"What time is it?" His voice was thick, but not hesitant. Maybe he *had* forgotten. As if. Someone like Dalton didn't forget coming unglued. Especially in front of a woman. "Ten-fifty-four," she said. "Coffee's ready."

"Ten-fifty-four in the *morning?*" He bolted to his feet. "Shit."

"Is that bad? Did you miss an appointment or something?"

"Fourteen hours. I slept *fourteen hours?*"

"More or less. You were tired."

"Six hours. That's a long night. I don't sleep fourteen hours." He stomped to the window and pulled back the curtain, as if something outside would disprove her words.

"Okay. I confess. I set all the clocks ahead, and it's really four in the morning. Of course, getting the sun up that high in the sky took a little more doing, but yeah, you only slept six hours."

Shaking his head, he did a circuit of the living room, mumbling, "Fourteen hours." He cut his eyes in her direction, looking bewildered. "Excuse me." He disappeared in the direction of the bathroom.

When he emerged, he'd put on his shoes, dampened and finger-combed his hair, but the incredulity hadn't left his face. His duffel hung over one shoulder. She held out the coffee mug. His gaze moved from the mug to her face, to his watch and back to the mug.

"Thanks." He sipped and paced the room, dropping his duffel by the door. After half a dozen circuits, he poured the remains of his coffee into the sink and rinsed the mug, seeming not to notice she leaned against the counter barely six inches from him. "I should get going."

He moved to the table at the entry where he'd dropped his cell phone yesterday evening. He checked the display then clipped the phone to his belt.

She stayed where she was. "Are we still on for tonight?"

Confusion crossed his face. "Tonight?"

"A going away party for my sister. Black tie, remember?"

"Oh, yeah. Right. Tux. Seven-thirty." He gave a quick smile. "Seems like you called a year ago. I'm in."

"Seriously, I'll understand if you want to cancel."

"Don't be silly." His eyes caught the paper on the counter. "The explosion. Anything in the news?"

"Nothing much." She related what she'd read.

"Want me to poke around?"

All right, then. Last night hadn't happened. It worked for

her. "Luisa Fernandez. A former resident. Keisha said she saw her on television during the news coverage."

"Luisa Fernandez her real name?"

She glowered. "We went through that yesterday."

"You're right. Sorry. Description?"

"Hispanic. Twenty-two. Five-eight, thin. Dark hair, long when she left. She wore a St. Christopher around her neck on a silver chain. Never took it off."

"Thanks. That helps." He gathered his things. "See you at seven-thirty."

"Right."

Until he remembered how he'd revealed his deep, dark secrets. How long before he called to cancel?

Dalton sat on a marble bench on the Sandersons' patio, staring at the lights reflecting off the lagoon-themed swimming pool. Being stuck in a tux for the second time in a week wouldn't be so bad if Miri would stop pretending he didn't exist. Hell, at least at Patterson's gala, he'd had a job to do, and Fozzie had been there for distraction. Fozzie and the rest of the team had gone wheels up in the pre-dawn hours—hours when he'd been dead asleep on Miri's couch.

He glanced over his shoulder again. Miri had attached herself to her sister as soon as they'd stepped through the door, and nearly an hour later, the two women circulated through the room like a pair of conjoined twins.

He'd laid himself wide open last night, every bit of raw, naked pain exposed to someone he barely knew. Was she embarrassed? Afraid she'd embarrass him if she mentioned it?

Like a coward, he'd picked her up for the party, pretending last night never happened. When she'd opened the door wearing a flame-colored cocktail dress that did more than merely hint at cleavage and clung to her curves, he shot to attention like a teenager.

Aside from uttering a few navigational directions, she spent the drive staring out the window. A glacial chill rested between them. He vowed to confront the awkwardness on the ride home because, damn, she stirred things inside him he thought had died with Rachel.

He returned to contemplating the flower-shaped candles floating on the pool in their lily pad holders. He watched a pink one drift by for the third time when the approaching click of heels on the flagstone raised hopes that Miri had decided to join him.

No, not Miri. The scent was all wrong. He pasted a polite smile on his face and turned, half-blinded by the glaring lights mounted under the eaves.

"Dalton? I thought I recognized you. Don't tell me you're still searching for that special someone?"

He rose, his smile widening into a genuine one. "Grace. It's nice to see you again." He gestured her to the bench. "Would you like to join me?"

"Thank you." She extended her legs, crossing them at the ankles. Very shapely ankles. She sighed. "Ah, much better. What an old broad like me is doing in these shoes is a question for the ages. What is it that makes women victims of some man's idea of attractive footwear? I'd take them off, but that would scandalize the Sandersons. I can see the gossip column headline. 'Mrs. Grace Ellsworth Bares Bunions.' "

Patting her silver hair, she moved her head from left to right, then took a small compact out of her evening bag and touched up her lipstick. Dalton's radar hummed as he recognized the subtle moves of someone making sure they weren't being watched. In that instant, he regretted not having added Grace's name to the list when he'd run background checks.

She smiled at him, her voice soft, her lips barely moving. "Did you investigate Andrew Patterson's project?"

Her cheerful countenance didn't match her words.

He followed her lead, giving a quiet laugh as if she'd told a clever joke. "Afraid not. I saw the brochure. It looked very . . . philanthropic."

She fluttered her hands in front of her lips. "My Edgar used to say, 'A leopard doesn't change his spots,' if you know what I mean. Andrew Patterson has devoted his life to making money. Why start giving it away?"

"I thought he donated a lot to charity, funded museum and theater trips and the like for school kids."

"Barely scratched the surface of his income from the museums and performing arts center. Believe me, he hasn't given away a dime that didn't net him a dollar somewhere else."

High-heeled footfalls approached. She grasped his forearm. "It was so nice seeing you again. I'd better be getting back inside. Mr. Patterson is coming to send the young Sandersons off with his best wishes."

Dalton stood and helped Grace to her feet. As she adjusted the lapel of his tux, he leaned forward and planted a soft kiss on her cheek. Although she'd been smooth, he knew he'd find a card in his breast pocket.

"I'm sure our paths will cross again," he said.

She gave a friendly wave as two couples walked out onto the patio. "It's a lovely night, isn't it?"

They nodded, lifting their drinks in a silent salute and Dalton mumbled a greeting of his own. His curiosity piqued, he followed Grace at a casual distance. Inside, the Sandersons' spacious living room was a scaled down version of the previous Saturday, except for the bright colors on the women. He scanned the room, seeking Miri's scarlet.

The crowd became mere background. She turned in his

143

direction and a smile lit her face. He tried, not successfully, to keep a goofy grin from spreading over his. Never removing his gaze from his target, he excused himself through the obstacle course of people. As he closed the distance between them, he realized her gaze was trained somewhere over his shoulder. To his left, the sea of guests shifted, effectively stonewalling him as they closed the few gaps between himself and Miri.

Easing his way around a portly couple who seemed to inhabit five times the space their combined bulk required, Dalton found a tall, blond Ken doll standing with Miri. A Ken doll with Miri's arms around him, and the grins on both their faces said they were much more than casual cocktail party acquaintances. The kiss they exchanged wasn't one of those society air kisses, either. Quick, not passionate, but definitely a *we're good friends* kiss.

His heartbeat drummed in his ears. He shoved his fists into his pockets and pivoted toward the center of the room, crashing into Mr. and Mrs. Portly.

"Excuse me," he muttered.

Apparently oblivious to his intrusion, they continued their animated discussion, rocking back and forth as he attempted to get by. After some fancy footwork, Dalton timed his moves with theirs and avoided a collision.

The conversational din dropped to a low murmur. A hand grasped his sleeve. "This could be interesting."

Dalton lowered his eyes toward the quiet voice at his side. Grace smiled at him and linked her arm with his. "Over here," she said and steered him to a gap between two large wooden bookcases.

Despite the lack of a band, it was as if a drumroll filled the room. All conversation ceased, and caterers scurried to provide flutes of champagne to the guests. Andrew Patterson, his teeth flashing brilliant white against his tan, strode to the staircase in the center of the room. He glided upward until he perched high enough to be visible to all without over-exaggerating his importance.

"And let the show begin," Grace said. She lifted two crystal flutes from a waiter and handed one to Dalton.

Patterson swept his hair from his forehead, emphasizing the white streak against the jet black. "Friends. First, I apologize for being late. Second, I thank the Sandersons for putting this evening together on short notice. And last, I promise that I did not come with any intentions of fundraising." He paused for the undercurrent of laughter that rippled through the room.

"Like hell," Grace said.

Dalton studied her, but her expression was one of rapt attention. He decided it would be wise to mimic it.

"Most of you have known Hunter Sanderson for years—some of you for his entire life," Patterson continued. "Although I had the pleasure of meeting him recently, I knew immediately he would be the perfect choice to oversee my new project. I'm confident that within a very short time the living conditions of those souls who help put food on our tables will be vastly improved." His eyes scanned the crowd, and he dipped his head as a king might command attendance. Dalton watched as Miri's Ken doll emerged from the crowd, which parted like the Red Sea at a wave of Moses' staff.

When the Ken doll joined Patterson—one step below him, Dalton noted—Patterson raised his glass. "A toast to Hunter Sanderson, and the beginning of the newest Patterson enterprise."

On the stairs, the two men tapped their glasses and sipped champagne. So, Ken was Miri's brother-in-law. Good thing he hadn't grabbed him by the collar and punched his lights out. Shit. He shoved those feelings aside and watched the action on the staircase. Ken—no, Hunter—turned his back on the crowd and said something to Patterson. There was some minor head shaking from both men. Patterson's color deepened, his smile faded for an instant, and when it returned it was forced. Patterson clapped Hunter's shoulder and escorted him down the staircase. Handing off his champagne glass to a passing waiter, he worked the room, managing to shake hands with guests while never releasing Hunter from his grip.

"What happened up there?" Dalton asked.

"You saw it, too, then." Grace tilted her head to meet his gaze. "Hunter said something, and Patterson was *not* pleased." She smiled, and the corners of her eyes creased. "I think I'll go offer my congratulations to the guest of honor."

Dalton resumed his quest for Miri, sifting through the feelings she aroused in him. Aroused being the operative word. Not good. He tried switching gears. What could have triggered that fleeting standoff between Patterson and Hunter? Hunter spoke and Patterson hadn't liked it. Beyond that, he had nothing.

Maybe Grace would ferret something out. He gazed in her direction, but she'd disappeared like morning mist on a warm day.

Who the hell was she?

A flash of scarlet caught his eye. With a stride indicating she wasn't used to high heels, Miri approached, moving through the crowd as if the room were empty. Her gaze met his, then moved to the champagne flute in his hand. Her lips—full, lush, and as scarlet as her dress—narrowed.

"You okay to drive? Because if we need a cab—"

He handed her the glass, stretched his arms to the side and touched his fingers to his nose. "Totally, Officer." Did he detect the start of a smile? He grinned, trying to coax it all the way out. "Seriously, I had one glass of champagne an hour ago. As you can see, the one you're holding has barely been touched. And I've been eating. Shall I walk a line for you, too?"

Even the hint of her smile disappeared. Shit. He'd gone too far. "Sorry," he said. "Did you want to leave?"

"If you don't mind." She marched, a little unsteadily, toward the door. He waited half a beat so he could trail behind her. Those high heels made for some delightful hip action.

She brushed off his assistance climbing into the SUV. He tugged off his bow tie and dropped it in a cup holder before starting the engine. Miri stared out the side window. Ten minutes later, she hadn't looked at him or said a word.

"Miri. About last night."

She faced him. At last. "Did you find anything about Luisa?"

Okay, she wasn't going to bring up his meltdown. He could wait. "I called in a favor or two. I should know by Monday, if it hasn't already hit the news."

"You must have a lot of people who owe you favors." Her words hung in the air like so many icicles.

Where was a red light when he needed one? Traffic demanded his attention so he couldn't watch her. "What are you talking about?"

"Don't play games with me, *Just* Dalton. Drive. I'll give you everything when we get to my place."

Which couldn't be soon enough for him. He checked his mirrors and stomped on the accelerator.

Chapter 14

Miri shoved her anger aside, which to her frustration, was far too easy. When she'd found Dalton's envelope under the coffee table this afternoon, she'd been ready to do him grievous bodily harm, or at least cancel the entire evening—but that wouldn't have been fair to Nancy. She garnered a small helping of satisfaction from the way he clenched his jaw and his knuckles whitened on the wheel.

She shouldn't have drunk so much champagne. Turning her head, she watched the streetlights fly by so she wouldn't have to deal with how damn luscious he looked in that tux. And his scent. If only she didn't have to breathe. The man must pump pheromones along with his cologne. Being furious with him didn't seem to make him any less enticing. Besides, he'd been a good sport when she'd abandoned him for Nancy. She cracked the window, hoping the cool air and exhaust fumes would reverse his effect on her.

Enough. She let her mind drift to the way she and Nancy had kept Mrs. Sanderson at bay all night. The biddy was polite enough not to make disparaging remarks when someone else was present, and Miri made sure Nancy was never alone. And when Mr. Patterson arrived, Mrs. Sanderson had no choice but to rave about how wonderful it was that her son, his wife, and even his wife's *sister* were doing such *good works for the poor downtrodden masses.* Miri's lips twitched in an involuntary smile.

The car stopped. This time, Dalton parked on the street in

front of her building. Guess he'd had enough of Mr. Liebowitz. They'd left the party at eleven, so it wasn't yet midnight. Why did Cinderella come to mind?

The car door opened beside her. Dalton's hand hovered. What the hell. As Prince Charmings went, he was way up there. She took his hand. Warm, dry and strong, it sent a tingling jolt from her fingers to her toes.

When she stepped out of his car, he smiled. She raised her eyes to meet his gaze, but it was too low for eye contact. As if they knew he was watching, her nipples stiffened. If a glance could do that to her, could it be happening to him? Well, she wouldn't stoop to his level. *She* had more class than that. She kept her eyes lifted.

After she unlocked the entry door, she crossed the small foyer and paused at the foot of the stairs. Champagne and three-inch heels. Not the best combination. She should have eaten more canapés. She grabbed the railing.

"After you," she said. She swept her arm upward.

He tilted his head in question.

She shrugged. "You had your turn, now it's mine. I'm going to enjoy the view."

He arched his eyebrows but took the lead. She followed. Being mad at him didn't matter. She did love his manly assets.

As soon as she opened her apartment door, the sight of the envelope on the entry table undid most of her mellow. She marched inside, threw her purse onto the couch, and snatched it from the table.

"You forgot this."

"Right." His tone was matter-of-fact. "Thanks."

The fury she felt when she'd found it flooded through her again. She almost smacked him with it. "That's it? Thanks? I think I deserve more than that, *Just* Dalton."

He closed the door and she noticed her too-shrill voice,

sensed her rapid breathing. One part of her brain said too much champagne left her a few synapses short of reasonable, but the part that made the words gush from her mouth didn't seem to understand.

It wasn't until he tugged at the envelope that she realized she clutched it in a death grip. She let go, only to stumble backward. Dalton grasped her forearm. She shrugged away.

"Don't touch me." Her voice echoed in her ears. She didn't sound convincing.

He stepped closer, cradling her face in his hands. His eyes bored into hers. A smile played across his lips. Yummy, tempting lips.

"How much champagne did you drink?"

She frowned. "Not that much." Then again, the wait staff kept her glass full and she hadn't kept track. "I'm not drunk."

"Of course you're not. How about some coffee?" He was already walking toward the kitchen. "It might be smart to eat something, too."

She flopped onto the couch and kicked off her shoes. "I'm trying to be mad at you, you know."

"I figured that out. I'm the super-sleuth, remember?"

Cabinets opened, water ran, the refrigerator opened and closed. Dalton returned with a large glass of water.

"Drink." He held it in front of her. "You'll be glad in the morning."

"I did *not* have that much champagne." She scooted away from him, got off the couch and stood erect. She stretched her arms out to the sides and aped his mock sobriety test. Then she walked to the window and back. Without the heels, her step was almost perfectly steady. Okay, she had a light buzz—a glow, maybe, but she wasn't *drunk*. Not even tipsy. "I should have eaten more, and I was tired. Am tired. I wasn't the one who slept for fourteen hours."

"Drink." He shoved the glass into her hand. "You'll wake up without a headache. Even a little champagne can be nasty the next morning. Eight ounces of prevention."

Glowering, she lifted the water to her lips. "You're lucky I don't throw this at you. How dare you investigate *me*. I was the client. Or the *assignment*." She gulped the water and shoved the glass back in his hands. "And I'm not drunk." The throbbing at her temples had nothing to do with champagne.

She found the envelope and yanked out the page with her background check. "What business did you have—what right did you have—to invade my privacy like this?"

He took the paper and glanced at it. The lightbulb flashed. He rubbed the bridge of his nose.

She waited. Nothing. "Well? Aren't you going to say something?"

Lowering the page to the coffee table, he flattened his yummy, tempting lips before speaking. "I'm working on it. But I have a feeling no matter what I say, I'll make things worse. If I explain, will you even listen?"

"Are you saying I'm close-minded?"

"See? We're already fighting and I haven't started."

She regrouped. No matter what, he deserved his turn. Let him rationalize away. Crap. She *was* being close-minded. She wouldn't last ten minutes on the job if she judged the people who came to Galloway House this fast.

"Go ahead." She folded her arms across her chest. "I'll listen."

He worked off his jacket and draped it over the back of her easy chair. "I'll get the coffee."

She followed him into the kitchen. "If you don't think it'll be too crowded, do you mind if Ben and Jerry join us?"

"Always welcome in my book."

She opened the freezer. "I'm calling the Chocolate Chip

Cookie Dough. You can have Vanilla or Chocolate Peanut Butter Swirl."

"Vanilla's fine."

He poured two cups of coffee as she scooped ice cream into bowls and carried them to the dining room where she could keep her distance. This wasn't sharing a pint of ice cream on the couch with her sister. This was giving a fair shake to a man who'd professed to want to help her but ran a background check. She'd read the page and knew her past wasn't there. But she couldn't control the anxiety snaking through her as she wondered if he had more information squirreled away somewhere.

Dalton sat across from her. He spooned a good chunk of his ice cream into his coffee and stirred, gazing into the cup as if the words he searched for would appear.

She ate her ice cream and waited.

"Background checks are routine," he finally said. "Blackthorne gets a lot of clients who aren't totally . . . forthcoming . . . about themselves."

"You assume I lied to you?"

He sipped his drink, then stirred the rest of his ice cream into the cup.

She put down her spoon with a clunk. "You *did* assume I was lying."

He leaned forward, his elbows on the table. "Are you thinking this through? Do you believe everyone who comes to Galloway House is telling you the truth?"

"Of course not." Her response burst out, apparently of its own accord. With the tip of her spoon, she drew designs in the melting remains at the bottom of her bowl. "But we don't check up on them. We respect their privacy." She'd lost most of her anger. All that remained was the fear he knew more than what was on that page.

She brought the bowls to the kitchen and rinsed them. Dalton materialized behind her, close enough so his body heat radiated through her, in sharp contrast to the cool water running over her fingertips. He reached around her and shut off the water. She braced her hands on the edge of the sink, afraid to turn around. His hands rested on her shoulders and suddenly, the decision was made for her, and she faced him, meeting his eyes. Warm eyes. Caring eyes. Eyes that defused any last vestiges of anger.

He tucked a strand of her hair behind her ear. "Should we talk before or after I kiss you?"

"Yes," Miri whispered.

He wove his fingers through her hair, letting the silken threads cascade over his hands. She lifted her head, her brown eyes accentuated by thick, dark lashes. When she half-closed her eyes, gold shimmered on her eyelids. He touched his mouth to hers.

Her lips parted. He nibbled on her lower lip, tasting coffee and chocolate. Lord, he could devour her. He moved his hands downward, tracing her back with gentle caresses. He tried to pull away, to slow down, to be tender and gentle. But her mouth opened wider and her tongue found his. Restraint vanished.

He tilted his head, angling his mouth over hers. Tenderness gave way to plundering. He needed more. His tongue probed deeper. The ice-cream chill of her mouth rapidly blazed into fiery heat.

She whimpered. He moaned.

He cupped her buttocks through the fabric of her dress. Her breasts pressed against his chest. His heart thudded against his ribcage. Blood roared in his ears.

Her hands, damp from rinsing dishes, clutched at his neck. He lifted her to the countertop where her lips would be level with his.

153

She stroked his hair. Every strand sent an electrical shock through him. He couldn't remember a kiss that consumed his entire being like this. Hell, he couldn't remember his name.

Dalton. That was it. It echoed in the distance. Muffled. Sounded like Miri's voice. He leaned closer, murmuring her name in return. Something pushed at his chest. His hips pulsed against her, his tongue danced in rhythm.

"Ambrose!"

The word shot through him, severing the connection. Panting, he jerked away.

"Too fast," Miri said.

Her dilated pupils darkened her eyes to pools of chocolate. Her chest rose and fell, matching his own labored breathing. Her cheeks were flushed. She ran her tongue across kiss-swollen lips.

Speaking was a challenge. Instead, he lowered her from the counter. Taking her hand in his, he led her to the living room and sat on the couch. She hesitated, then squeezed his hand and sat across from him in the oversized easy chair. Wise move. He had a steel I-beam between his legs that begged for attention.

Get a grip. She's right. It's too fast.

He exhaled a shuddering breath. What he needed was a long, sub-zero shower. Shifting uncomfortably, he watched as Miri smoothed her dress over her legs and folded her hands in her lap like a schoolgirl waiting for the teacher to call on her. Except she wouldn't look at him.

Right. Talk. Get back to business.

He cleared his throat. "Okay. That took care of the kissing. I guess it's time for the talking."

She nodded, studying her fingers.

"You want to decide where we start?"

She shook her head.

He smiled. "I've got to admit, my brain's not exactly running on all cylinders right now, darlin'. But I think we're either going to talk about your missing people—because I don't believe for a minute that you're satisfied it was all a coincidence—or we're going to talk about who the hell you are and how come a standard background search only goes back eight years."

Her eyes lifted at last. They widened, then retreated to fix on her fingers, which fussed with the fabric of her dress. Her chest rose and fell once. She shook her head, flipping her hair and tucking it behind her ears. She squirmed in the chair.

He waited.

She licked her lips. "My sister and I were practically street kids. I told you my dad went to prison and my mom left. Even before she did, Nancy and I were on our own."

Her voice was low but steady. "Nancy did whatever it took to put food on the table and clothes on our backs. Almost anything. Mom turned tricks, but Nancy swore she'd never do that." She gave him an earnest stare. "I believe her—I know she wouldn't let men near me. But we begged, shoplifted, ran street scams."

"Where did you live?"

Her fingers danced on the arm of the chair. "Down South until I was sixteen. New Orleans area, mostly."

He glanced over his shoulder at her CD collection. "Where you learned to appreciate jazz?"

She nodded, smoothing her hair behind her ear again. "Nance and I hustled for street musicians. She had a decent voice and a good body—I made sure the audience paid for the music."

"By picking pockets."

"Like I said, we did what it took to survive." Pride and defiance radiated from her eyes.

"Social Services didn't help?"

"We stayed under the radar. We moved so often, they never found us, assuming they bothered."

His chest ached. Although she'd obviously accepted her past, he could understand her wanting to forget it. And hide it. Which she'd done well, or the Blackthorne research department would have found her. Or she was lying. "I don't hear the Southern accent."

"Good. We both worked very hard to lose it."

He distanced himself. Made her a generic interview subject. "How did you disappear?"

"We came to San Francisco when I was sixteen. Nancy was eighteen. We were lucky. We found Galloway House, and they gave us the help we needed. We'd changed our names. Like I said, they don't require ID."

"Who were you before?"

"I've always been Miri."

"Miri who?"

She narrowed her eyes. Shook her head. "Nope. That's all you get."

"Why? What would it hurt to tell me your real last name? I'm not going to use it against you." He rested his ankle on his knee, glad things had settled enough to get comfortable again. "Or did you do something worse than pick a few pockets? Even if you did, I'm sure it's too late for any prosecution."

Except for homicide. No. Whatever she was, whatever she'd done, she wouldn't have taken a life. He'd bet his own on that.

"Not for me. For Nancy. She's afraid of what the Sandersons would do if they found out she was something they'd scrape off the bottom of their shoes."

"Her husband?"

"I don't think he'd mind—he truly loves her. But she's not sure it would be worth the risk, and I've promised to respect that. Saying for better or for worse, and then having to live with the for worse part are two different games."

"And what's the worst that could happen?"

She twirled a lock of hair. "Nancy's afraid his parents would disinherit him. Disown him. Or get Patterson to fire him. Who knows?" She lowered her eyes once more. "That's why I was in Patterson's study that night. To make sure his background check hadn't uncovered anything. That the PI he hired didn't find anything except the identities we created."

"And he didn't, I'm guessing."

Her eyes twinkled. "It's not that hard, really. Find a one-horse town where the hall of records burned down, and there's your place of birth. Nobody can verify your birth certificate. And fake IDs are easy enough to get on the street."

Her hands settled at last. There was an underlying serenity, as if she'd emerged from the confines of a cocoon, ready to spread her wings and soar through a world, seeing it from an entirely new perspective.

His groin stirred again. He glanced at his watch. "It's after midnight. I should be going." He stepped behind the chair and retrieved his jacket.

Miri got to her feet. "Dalton?" She stretched out a hand.

He let his fingers slide down hers. His pulse quickened. Emotions he'd kept tamped down wormed their way toward the surface. He was afraid she'd ask him to stay. If she did, he wouldn't be able to say no, and he knew it wasn't the right time. "What?"

She met his eyes head on. "About tonight. I was confused. I wanted to be mad at you—because if I wasn't mad at you, I was afraid I'd—you know—what started in the kitchen. But it's too soon. Nancy said maybe I should have a fling. But I'm not sure I could have a fling and walk away. Not from you."

Her cheeks glowed bright pink, and he found that all the more endearing—and arousing. His sort of women were definitely the fling sort. Like Debbie. Mutual tension relievers. Itch scratchers. Tonight he found them all totally unappealing.

"Shh. I know what you mean. I'm flattered." He kissed her palm. "And that's why I have to leave. But I want to see you again." He held his breath, waiting for her answer.

"You said you'd have more information about Luisa on Monday."

That wasn't what he had in mind. But it would have to do.

CHAPTER 15

Miri scrubbed the makeup off her face, wishing she could scrub away her body's reaction to Dalton as easily. And not only the physical reaction. She'd known him a week, and in one night she had revealed things about her past that nobody but Nancy knew.

Maybe it was because he'd bared himself to her. For the first time, she found someone she trusted.

Too antsy to stand still, she wandered into the bedroom and pulled back her bed covers while she brushed her teeth. The phone rang. Who would call after midnight? Nancy? Her mind whirled, her pulse kicked into overdrive as she grabbed the handset, rushed into the bathroom, and spit a mouthful of foamy toothpaste into the sink.

"Miri? Thank goodness you're home. I didn't know who else to call."

She tried to connect the voice to a person, but the voice hovered one notch below hysterical. A female voice, and to her relief, not Nancy. "Slow down. Who is this?"

"Sammi. Miri, you have to tell me what to do."

"All right, Sammi. It's all right. What happened? Where are you?"

"I'm at the front desk. But you need to go to the police station. They took Jillian."

Will's mom. "When? Why?"

"I don't know. She called from the police station."

"Where's Will?" Miri tucked the handset under her chin and went back to the bedroom.

"He's here. Asleep. He doesn't know."

"Okay, Sammi." Miri opened drawers, grabbed underwear and a sweatshirt. "Look in the top right drawer under the counter. There's an emergency call list. Find the number for legal services."

"I already called. I got a recording. She's gone for the weekend. That's why I called you."

Miri snatched a pair of jeans from her closet. "You did good, Sammi. I'll take care of things. You hang tight. Be there in case Will wakes up, okay?"

She clicked off the phone and tossed it on the bed. Where was her cell phone? She shrugged into the sweatshirt and did a circuit of her apartment.

Calm down. You're worse than Sammi.

Her everyday tote hung on a hook by the entry. Right where it belonged. She yanked it down and fished inside for her cell, punching the speed dial she'd programmed with Dalton's number.

She waited for the call to go through, and a thought slammed into her like a bolt of lightning. Every time she'd needed help, she'd called Dalton. She tried to tell herself it was because she didn't trust cops. Or that it was logical to call him. He couldn't be more than a few minutes away, and no busses ran at this hour, and a cab would be expensive and—and he'd kissed her like there was nobody on the planet except the two of them. She tingled at the memory. The phone clicked.

"Miri? Hey, darlin'."

The mere sound of his drawl erased some of her panic. "Um . . . one of the House's residents is at the police station. I don't know what happened, and the lawyer we use is away. I thought—"

"On my way."

To rescue the fair maiden.

The chill air on her legs sent her to the bedroom for her jeans. Why did he scramble her brain? She was *not* a maiden in need of rescue. Thrusting legs into the denim, she tried to come up with a reason Jillian would be at the police station. Like so many people who arrived at Galloway House, Jillian was a victim who had finally been pushed too far. Miri recalled Jillian the day she'd arrived in reception. Strawberry blonde, petite. Nice clothes, well groomed. Not coming from poverty. Unable to keep the trembling from her voice, yet she'd maintained an upbeat façade. Being brave for her kid, who cowered behind her.

Miri zipped and buttoned her jeans, jammed her feet into socks and sneakers and snagged her purse. She checked for her wallet, ATM card and checkbook as she went to the shoebox in her closet for her emergency cash.

Minutes later, a quiet knock on the door made her jump. "That was quick," she said when she opened it.

"I was in the neighborhood." He gave her a sheepish grin. "Walking. Cooling off."

"Can you drop me at the police station?"

"Let's go." His hand on her back as they hurried to his car provided a security blanket. By the time they were on the road, she'd centered herself again.

"You do this often?" Dalton asked. "Bail people out of jail in the middle of the night?"

"Me? No. We've got paralegals we can call, and there's even a full-fledged lawyer who donates some time. This is a first for me."

"What happened?"

"I don't know. Sammi—she's the one who called me—said Jillian called from the police station." Her insides twisted at the thought of Jillian in jail. And Will. The one thing they had going for them was each other.

"Tell me about her. Why do you think the cops would want her?" Dalton's tone was calm, back in investigator mode.

"I can't imagine. She showed up a couple of weeks ago, scared to death. Her husband was one of those control freaks. Made her stay home, keep the house immaculate. Gave her a pittance of an allowance." Miri couldn't keep the fury from her voice. "An allowance. Like this was the fifties. And he made her account for every penny. She didn't say, but I think he abused her physically, too. She had a bunch of bruises when she arrived—said she was clumsy."

"Why did she put up with it? Or protect him?"

"Why does anyone put up with abuse? They think it's normal. Or they're at fault. Or they have nowhere to turn." Her nails dug into her palms from clenching her fists.

Although Dalton watched the road, some extra sense said he was studying her. "Did anyone hurt you?" he asked, his voice barely audible.

"Never. Neglected, ignored, but physical abuse? No, Mom never did that. She loved us, but she didn't know how to keep her own life together."

"What do you think made Jillian leave?"

"I think her husband started working on Will. They wouldn't talk about it, but I'll bet Will figured out things weren't right. My guess is he tried to defend her, and Daddy didn't like it. Will didn't leave Jillian's side for days after they arrived."

They drove the rest of the way in silence. She watched Dalton, his jaw set, his hands gripping the wheel. His eyes seemed attentive to the road, but his brain, she'd bet, was somewhere else.

At the precinct, Dalton parked the car in the half-empty lot. She opened the door and hopped out. "Thanks for the ride."

He slid out of the car. "I'm with you. I might be able to cut some red tape."

She shoved the door shut. "I'm all right. Jillian's my responsibility."

As she circled the car on her way to the entrance, Dalton grabbed her by the shoulders and spun her to face him. Under the sodium glow of the parking lot lamps, his gray eyes appeared almost gold.

"Jillian is *not* your responsibility. She's a grown woman who has to learn to live with the consequences of her actions."

"She's part of Galloway House. That makes her mine."

He curled a finger under her chin and tilted her face up. "You can't be a mother to everyone, Miri. If she did something wrong, we'll get her the help she needs."

"If she's not my responsibility, she's sure not yours."

"Let's get her out. We'll deal with the details later." He took her hand and led her toward the entrance.

We. He'd said "we." Something warm wrapped around her heart.

Dalton held the door for Miri and entered the police station behind her. A maintenance man mopped the tile floor of the empty lobby. A pine scent filled the room, not quite strong enough to disguise underlying layers of sweat, urine, and vomit. "Wait here. Let me ask." He stepped to the glass-enclosed counter and spoke through a metal grate to the man seated at the desk.

"We're looking for Jillian—" he shot Miri a questioning glance.

She joined him and leaned her face close to the grate. "Durbin. I don't see why she would be here. She's—"

Dalton squeezed her hand to cut her off. It was ice cold. "Jillian Durbin. Can you let us know why she's here?"

The man fiddled with the computer mouse. Dalton read the identification badge on the man's shirt. A civilian, not a sworn officer. Dalton smiled. "Hello, Craig. All we need is a little information. Has she been charged?" He hoped Craig wasn't a wannabe cop who'd raise every official hoop for them to jump through.

Craig motioned them to wait and picked up a phone. "Let me do the talking," Dalton whispered to Miri.

She arched her eyebrows. "Jillian doesn't know you. She'll be freaked enough without some guy in a tux coming to talk to her."

"I meant I'll talk to the cops."

She nodded and he saw the exhaustion behind her anxiety. "The best thing you can do is be calm. Try to relax."

"Relax. Right. I'll go sit over there," she said, tipping her head toward the chairs against the wall.

God, he wanted to hug her. Take her home, put her to bed. Let a lawyer handle this. She deserved at least one twenty-four-hour period of being just Miri.

What was he thinking? She *was* being Miri. Clenching his fists, he turned back to the counter. Craig set the phone down and leaned closer to the grate.

"Have a seat, sir. They'll be out shortly."

Miri raised her gaze as he crossed the room. Apprehension filled her eyes. Her spring breeze scent cut through the police station smells. He sat, clasping her fidgeting hands to quiet them. As if the energy demanded an outlet, her foot tapped a rapid tattoo on the floor.

"I think it's going to be okay," he said. "The clerk said they'd be out soon. If they'd charged her, they wouldn't let her out here to talk to us."

The relief on her face made him long to bottle the *it's all right* feeling flooding him, loosening everything inside. Something to pull out and inhale on those missions when there was nothing to do except wait for it all to hit the fan.

The heavy wooden door beside the reception counter opened. Miri leaped to her feet and rushed across the lobby toward the slight strawberry-blonde woman dwarfed between a linebacker of a uniformed cop and a husky man in a rumpled blue suit, tie loosened, top shirt button undone. Salt-and-pepper hair, overdue for a trim. Most likely a detective, if the badge hanging from his coat pocket was any indication. One who'd been on duty too long.

The uniform crossed the lobby with barely a glance in their direction. A man in a tux and a woman in jeans didn't rate a lifted eyebrow. "Night, Hank," he said over his shoulder, pushing the door open.

Rumpled Suit stepped forward. "Detective Henry Braddock," he said. "Let's sit down." He crossed to the chairs in the corner, farthest away from the door.

When Braddock sank into a chair and rubbed his eyes, Dalton recognized the weight he carried. Long days, longer nights and wondering if it was worth it. That the man was on the job said it was. Braddock's gaze said he recognized some of the same in Dalton.

Miri sat next to Jillian and wrapped an arm around the frightened woman's shoulder.

"Is Will all right?" Jillian asked. "Can we go home?"

"He's asleep," Miri said. "What happened?"

Detective Braddock broke in. "Ms. Durbin made a rather serious error in judgment, but in return for her cooperation, we're not going to charge her." He gave Jillian a stern look. "This time. You'll remember what we talked about?"

Jillian sniffed, wiped her eyes and nodded. "Yes. I'm sorry."

"It seems Ms. Durbin thought she could pick up some cash working for meth dealers. They've got a clever enough scheme, and if their lab hadn't blown up, we might still be looking."

"Jillian couldn't have anything to do with drugs," Miri said. Annoyance dripped from her voice.

Embarrassment flooded Jillian's face. "I needed the money," Jillian said, her voice trembling. "They told me it was legal. They swore. But those people are dead."

Braddock looked at Miri. "Thanks to Ms. Durbin's information, we're a few steps closer to the ringleader. She assures me what she and the others did has nothing to do with Galloway House."

Miri bristled. "Galloway House deplores the use of drugs, Detective Braddock. And our residents understand we have a zero-tolerance policy."

"So Ms. Durbin said." Braddock furrowed his brow as if he wondered how anyone could be naïve enough to think drugs weren't commonplace in the environment of a shelter.

To his surprise, Dalton found himself sharing Miri's irritation at Braddock's assumption. "How about you explain a little more, Detective?"

"With the restrictions on buying the basics for methamphetamines, the dealers have to find new ways to get the quantities they need." He looked at them like a patient schoolteacher explaining the obvious to a group of elementary school students. "A group of local dealers offers money to the homeless and indigent—loads up a van, gives them cash and drives them all over town to grocery stores, convenience stores and drugstores. They go inside, buy the allergy meds and move on."

"But you need ID," Miri said.

"If the folks don't have it, the dealers are more than happy to provide some." Braddock ran his fingers over the stubble on his jaw. "And since there's no centralized computer system, and most of the smaller shops don't record the information anyway, there's no way to tell that someone like Ms. Durbin here hasn't popped in right after buying the quota from the store across the street."

"They gave us ten dollars a store," Jillian said. "I can't make that much at my job. Not fast enough."

She seemed on the verge of breaking down. Dalton faced Braddock. "Are we free to go? Is there any paperwork?"

Braddock gave a weary sigh and a wry chuckle. "Isn't there always? But no, not for you." He turned to Miri. "You'll let us know if you hear any more of this, won't you? Galloway House does good work. It'd be a shame to have to shut it down."

Miri stood up, hands fisted on her hips, eyes blazing. "As I said, we have a no-tolerance policy. And I'll make sure the word gets out."

Braddock handed her a card. "Call if you hear anything."

Dalton itched to offer help, do something to get one more drug pusher off the street, but he knew Braddock wouldn't let a civilian get involved in his investigation. Braddock must have read something in his expression because he handed him a card as well.

Tomorrow, he'd see what he could do about getting more information. Tonight, two exhausted women needed to get home.

"Let's go," he said.

"Wait." Miri faced Braddock. "The meth house explosion. Is that your case?"

Braddock sighed and dragged a hand through his hair. "Among others, yes."

"Can you tell me—one of the victims? Was there a Luisa Fernandez?"

After a pause, Braddock answered, his tone flat. "We're not ready to release names to the public, ma'am."

He didn't have to. Dalton read it in Braddock's eyes. So had Miri.

"Detective, please. It's important," she said. "The news said eight people died. Have you identified the rest of them?"

"Not yet, ma'am."

"Can you tell me if any of them were women?"

"Yes, ma'am, that much I can."

"Miri, we should get Jillian home."

She shook her head. "I need to know. What if—?"

She didn't finish the sentence, but he filled in the blanks easily enough. *If they were her missing residents.* She'd gone pale. Too pale. Dalton wrapped his arm around her. "There's nothing we can do for them now. Tomorrow. I promise."

"Please," Jillian said. "I need to get back. Check on Will."

"You're right," Miri said. "Things will be clearer in the morning." The two women trudged toward the door. He moved to follow, but Braddock caught his elbow.

"We'll talk," the detective said.

CHAPTER 16

Miri helped Jillian climb into the backseat of Dalton's car and settled in beside her. The sadness in Braddock's eyes lingered in her thoughts. Luisa was dead. Were the other victims people she knew? But Dalton was right. There was nothing anyone could do for them. Jillian, however, was very much alive.

"Talk to me, Jillian. Something important made you go along with that man. Let us help."

"I've really screwed up this time. Vic's going to get custody of Will."

"Vic? Your husband?"

Her head bobbed. "He wants me back. I'm sure he's already hired detectives to find me. I need to take Will somewhere safe. Far away."

"Jillian, you have to tell us everything." *Us.* When had she started thinking of Dalton as part of an *us*? Probably about the same time he started talking about *we*. Miri caught Dalton's eye in the rearview mirror. He gave the tiniest of nods, encouraging her to go on. She clasped Jillian's overactive hands in hers.

Jillian half-closed her eyes. "Vic wasn't always that way. When we were first married, he was kind and gentle. He changed when his father died. In little ways at first. Drinking, losing his temper. After, he'd be so sorry. But I couldn't do anything well enough to please him. He started punishing me when I didn't meet his standards."

Miri's stomach clenched at the all-too-familiar tale.

"When I got pregnant, he seemed to get better. But one day something set him off—he got so mad, he shoved me too hard. I lost my balance—I was about six months along and getting used to dealing with the basketball belly. I crashed into a kitchen chair and fell. He panicked—it really shook him. For the rest of my pregnancy he was perfect. And when Will came, he was the proudest dad in town."

Jillian's eyes, brimming with tears, met Miri's. She squeezed Jillian's hands, offering reassurance without interrupting. Nothing to staunch the flow of words now that Jillian was willing to release them.

"Will wasn't an easy baby." Jillian's voice sounded distant. Detached. "First colic, then teething, lots of colds, and when he was six, he needed an operation. A leaky heart valve."

Not Daddy's perfect son. Miri concentrated on Jillian, trying to keep the contempt for Vic off her face. "He seems fine."

Jillian gave a half-hearted smile. "Yes, he's perfectly normal. But while he recuperated, he developed a love of books and showed some artistic talent. Vic thought that was too namby-pamby and put Will down every chance he got."

They turned down the street to Galloway House. Jillian's attention shifted to the window. Her feet jiggled up and down on the floor, as if that would speed the ride. Her hands were already on the seatbelt.

Dalton barely parked the car before Jillian released the door. Bolting outside, she flew to the House's entrance, jerked on the handle of the locked door. Her finger reached for the night bell, but Miri stopped her with a gentle touch to her forearm.

"Let me," she said and pulled out her key. "No need to disturb anyone."

As soon as the door swung open, Jillian darted upstairs. Miri let her go. Sammi sat on one of the couches in the lobby, half-dozing, Suzie asleep in her arms. She started to rise, but Miri motioned her to stay. "Give her a minute to see that Will's all right."

"What happened?" Sammi whispered. "What did she do?"

Miri sensed Dalton behind her. Sammi's eyes widened, moving from Dalton back to Miri.

"Sammi, this is Dalton. He's been very helpful."

Dalton didn't move, resting a hand on Miri's shoulder. "We met yesterday, I believe," he said. "I had a near-collision with your stroller."

Miri heard the thickened drawl. Without looking, she knew he was giving Sammi his lazy grin. She fought the urge to lean against him, to slide her arm around his waist and steal some of his strength. To let him take over. But that wasn't an option. Galloway House, its residents, and its problems were hers.

Confusion, then recognition flashed over Sammi's face. And then a glimmer of interest. Female interest. Yeah, Miri thought. Even tired and rumpled, Dalton in a tux was a commanding masculine presence.

"I should put Suzie down," Sammi said. "I'll be happy to do desk duty until Keisha comes on."

"What happened to Angie?" Miri asked, noticing the empty reception desk.

"I told her I'd cover for her." Sammi stroked Suzie's hair. "That I'd wake her if anyone showed." A flash of panic crossed her face. "That was okay, wasn't it?"

Miri shoved back the rising tide of weariness. "Don't worry about it. You did fine." She glanced at the clock. After two, and Keisha would be in at six. "I'll put on some coffee and take care of it. Get some sleep. Suzie needs an awake mom in the morning."

"Thanks." Sammi moved toward the hall.

"Sammi?" Dalton stepped forward. "One question before you go." Somehow, he managed to sound apologetic and commanding at the same time. And damn charming.

Sammi swung around, an eager-to-please smile on her face.

"Do you know anything about people being paid to buy medicine for other people? Cold and allergy pills, not prescriptions."

Sammi wrinkled her nose at Miri. "Is that what Jillian did?"

Miri nodded. "Do you know anything about it, Sammi? It's important."

She gave her head a shake. Suzie whimpered softly. Sammi shushed her. "No, no. Nothing."

Dalton flashed another easy grin. "If you hear anything, though, you'll let Miri know right away, won't you? It doesn't have to be a Galloway House resident."

Sammi gave a solemn nod. "Sure. I don't get out of the kitchen a lot, but I'll keep my ears open."

"Thanks," Dalton said. "You go on and get that pretty baby to bed."

Sammi almost floated up the stairs.

Miri folded her arms across her chest. The adrenaline rush passed, leaving a bone-deep chill in its wake. Sandpaper filled her eye sockets. "I've got things covered," she said to Dalton. "You can go home, get some sleep. Thanks for everything."

"I had fourteen hours last night, remember. You're the one who needs to crash."

"What we need and what we have to do aren't always the same," she said. "I'm going to put on a pot of coffee."

"Sounds good."

His gray eyes grabbed her. She hesitated but only for a heartbeat. "I guess if you want a cup for the road, you can hang around for a bit." A bit. Not long enough for her to surrender to the urge to let him take charge.

He shoved his hands in his pockets. "We need to talk to Jillian. Now. Before she has a chance to make up something.

There's a lot she hasn't told us yet."

There was that *us* again. Some of the chill left her, replaced by a heavy ache in her breasts. She headed toward the kitchen, chiding herself for letting Dalton inch inside her. There was one person in her life she'd been able to rely on. Nancy. Everyone else took what they needed, then disappeared.

She forced a businesslike tone. "I'll get her. Right after I start the coffee."

He followed her down the hall. She stopped, half-turning.

"No. You wait here in case she comes downstairs before I get back." Or was it because she didn't trust herself alone with him?

His footsteps retreated, and she was torn between relief that he'd acquiesced and disappointment that he hadn't.

In the kitchen, she concentrated on measuring precise amounts of water and coffee into the coffeemaker, trying to find order in everything swirling through her mind with the familiar task. With a shaky exhale, she flipped the brew switch. Afraid if she sat down she'd fall asleep, she paced the room, wondering what she could do for Jillian and Will. A restraining order, maybe. It dawned on her that she'd never asked where Jillian came from. For all she knew, Vic lived out of state.

The aroma of brewing coffee cleared some of the cotton batting from her brain. First thing Monday, she'd get Jillian an appointment with the attorney. First thing tomorrow morning, she'd call a House meeting and see if anyone knew anything about the meth scheme.

She rubbed the knot forming in her belly. Had she missed any signals? Residents with extra spending money? Unusual purchases—little luxuries? Furtive whispers, conversations stopping when staff was around?

No. She hadn't seen anything. Was she so blinded by her optimism that she could turn everyone around?

The coffeepot gave its final sputters. She pulled two mugs from the cabinet. In one, she nuked some milk, then added hot coffee to it, stirring in a generous spoonful of sugar. The other she left black.

Carrying the coffee down the hall, she detected low voices from the reception room. Good. Jillian had come downstairs. She rounded the corner and stopped in the doorway. Dalton and Jillian faced each other on the sofa. He was giving her that lazy smile, and the sparkle in her eyes wasn't from tears. He might have handed her the moon draped in a necklace of stars.

He'd met Jillian half an hour ago, and now they sat there like they'd come back from a date, not the police station.

The man oozed charm. It poured off him like syrup over a stack of pancakes, as much a part of him as his gunmetal gray eyes and the curl in his hair.

Why did she think she was different from any other woman he came in contact with?

Motion and a shadow from the doorway grabbed Dalton's attention. Miri carried two mugs across the room.

"Don't let me interrupt." With a clunk, she set one on the end table beside him. "You want some coffee, Jillian?"

"No, I need to get some sleep."

Miri went behind the reception desk, dragged the chair out and flopped down. She made a show of squaring piles of paper, leafing through the contents of a file folder and positioning the phone near the edge of the desk.

He glanced at Jillian, who didn't seem to notice anything unusual in Miri's behavior. For all he knew, Miri was a compulsive neatnik. He flashed a smile. "Jillian was telling me how Will's been training Reggie."

"They're good for each other," Miri said.

Dalton wrapped his hands around the mug, letting the

warmth dispel some of the chill from the night air seeping through the poorly fitted windows. "We were waiting for you to get back before we started discussing what happened."

"I'm back. Let's discuss."

He ignored Miri's attitude. Something had ticked her off, but he needed to deal with Jillian and Will. If Vic really wanted to find them, a good investigator could track them to Galloway House. He took a sip of coffee.

"Jillian, what did you tell the police? Did you tell them about Vic?"

"No." Jillian shook her head vehemently. "I answered all their questions about the man who paid me to buy the cold pills. I gave them descriptions of the others in the van. But we all used the names on the fake IDs. I don't know their real names."

Miri leaned forward across the desk. "Jillian, did you recognize anyone? Regulars from the food line? Anyone from classes?"

Another head shake, not so vehement. "I haven't been here that long. I'm working at the motel most of the day, and nights I'm with Will." She looked from Dalton to Miri. "Honest. You can call my boss. I haven't missed a shift."

"I believe you," Miri said. The glare she threw Dalton dared him to disagree.

"We both do," he said, biting back the urge to ask her what the hell was going on. He kept his tone even. "Jillian, the police are investigating the meth dealers, and that's their domain. What I'm concerned about is why you think your husband will find you, and what he'll do if he does."

"Nobody embarrasses Victor. For word to get out that his wife left him because he whacked on her and his kid would destroy his standing in the community." She made a sound between a laugh and a snort. "And nothing is more important to Victor than his standing in the community."

"What community?" Dalton asked. "Would your paths cross here?"

"With Vic, you can never tell. He knows people everywhere."

"Where did you come from?" Miri asked.

"Let's leave it at a few states away and one hell of a long bus ride."

"Why do you think he'll find you?" Miri asked.

"He will. He always gets what he wants. It's a matter of time. That's why we need to keep moving. But I used up everything I managed to save, plus what I borrowed from a friend."

Her words set the hair on the back of his neck on end. Years of experience kept an easy smile on his face. "Your husband know this friend?" He took another sip of coffee.

"I doubt it. We met at a cooking class, but that was over a year ago, and I don't see how Vic would connect us."

"He let you take classes?" Dalton asked. That didn't sound like a total control freak. Not the sort who kept hourly tabs on his possession.

"He was okay with 'womanly classes'—" she crooked her index fingers to put air quotes around the words "—like cooking or flower arranging. As long as the house was clean and dinner was on the table." She gave a wry grin. "He did like his home-cooked meals.

"And I never went out of my way to make friends. The people I met in the classes—we'd be together for a few weeks or a month, then go our separate ways."

"What about mutual friends?" he asked. "Yours and Vic's. Did the two of you socialize a lot?" Much harder for someone to be discreet about his inquiries if a large pool of friends and acquaintances might get suspicious.

"Lots of socializing, although I don't know that I'd consider those people true friends. Victor liked having his doting wife at his side. We invited people over, went to their homes. Went to events. Anything to schmooze his way up the ladders he wanted to climb."

Her voice dropped, her eyes grew vacant, as if she relived some of those events. The ones where she hadn't been doting enough and he'd let her know afterward. From Miri's expression, it was clear to her as well. She left her hiding place behind the desk and perched on the edge of the coffee table.

"Vic thought I should schmooze the wives," Jillian said. "The rich ones, of course. Be a lady who lunched. I played cards with them once a week, and that was about all I could stand."

She yawned and Dalton stepped up the pace of his questions. "Sorry. I know you want to get to bed. You said none of your social circle knew Vic beat you? One person in your cooking class?"

Jillian nodded. "If someone knew, I'm sure they would have said something to me." She tugged on her fingers. "He was careful not to hit me anywhere it would show."

Despite the knots tightening in his belly, Dalton kept his voice calm. "Okay, that's good."

"Good? Why?" Miri asked. "That means nobody's going to tell the authorities Vic's wife ran away because he beat her. He gets away with it?" Indignation colored her tone. "What *is* he telling people. How's he explaining his wife not at his side? And taking Will?"

"I'm sure he's got me visiting a sick relative or something. He's probably invented a grandmother or sister I don't have. Nobody'd bother to check."

Dalton picked up the dropped thread. "I meant it's good because if nobody suspects, Vic won't feel so pressured to get Jillian back to show everyone she's fine. He can take his time because everyone will believe his story."

He leaned forward, like a friend, not enough to threaten. "Jillian, I need you to trust me. If your husband is serious about getting you back, and if he hired an investigator, I need to know what kind of a trail they might pick up. Especially your financial situation."

"Not much in that department. I'd sneak extra cash when I used my debit card. An aunt sent money for Christmas and birthday gifts, and I squirreled that away, too. One of my cooking school friends loaned me some cash."

"Credit cards?" he asked. "ATM?"

She shook her head. "I've watched enough television to know better."

He felt more optimistic that she was a few steps ahead of Vic. But she was using her maiden name, which wouldn't be too much of a stretch for any halfway decent PI, and he was sure Vic wouldn't have hired anyone but the best. And he worried that if Vic found the cooking school friend, he'd find a way to make her talk.

He finished his cold coffee and set the mug on the table. Miri's eyes snagged his and he knew, no matter how irrational, he'd made his decision. He took Jillian's hands in his. "Jillian. I work for a company that has a lot of experience with people who don't want to be found. If you want me to, I might be able to help you disappear."

Her eyes widened. "Really?"

He nodded. She shifted her gaze to Miri, who shrugged.

Speaking more to Miri than Jillian, he went on. "I know Galloway House has an excellent reputation. And I know they do a lot of good. But eventually, Vic is going to think about places like this."

"I know," Jillian said. "That's why I need to keep moving."

"Which is no life for you and Will," he said.

She eyed him warily. "How much will this cost me?"

"Don't worry about it. Why don't you go upstairs, get some sleep. Have a nice, normal Sunday tomorrow, and I'll have some answers for you by Monday."

Hope replaced the despair in her eyes. Even more than gratitude, that look gave meaning to his job. But the look also meant he'd have to do some fast talking and a lot of string-pulling with Blackie.

On the other hand, Miri's eyes held more questions than either hope or gratitude. With a spark of irritation as well. He avoided meeting them until Jillian left the room.

He inhaled a long breath, exhaled slowly. Tried for a smile. He patted the couch cushion beside him. "You want to get some sleep? Let me return the favor from the other night?"

"Go home, Dalton," she said, moving behind the desk. She didn't sit, though. She placed both hands on the desktop and leaned forward. "I appreciate what you're doing for Jillian and Will. But I need to sort things through. Alone."

"Miri—you're doing good work. Don't ever forget it."

She shook her head. Sadness filled her eyes. "Good night, Dalton."

He took one pace toward the desk. She stiffened, which stopped him as quickly and painfully as the time he'd run into the sliding glass door to his grandmother's patio when he was six.

He told her what he'd told himself so many times. "It's not your fault. None of this is. You do what you can."

And then you lie awake wondering if it will be enough.

Chapter 17

Dalton shoved thoughts of Miri inside one of the compartments he kept in his brain, where he put things to be dealt with later. If only she'd stay there, instead of sneaking out and hovering in front of his eyes. Closing them didn't help—her image was etched inside his eyelids.

He poured a generous shot of scotch and settled into his leather recliner, his one piece of what he considered grown-up furniture. Maybe concentrating on Rafael would displace the visions of Miri. But thinking of the drug lord brought him to Jillian's plight, which segued right back to Miri.

He sipped the whiskey as he listened to the night sounds filtering through the open kitchen window. Leaves rustling in the trees. A dog barking. In the distance, the drone of traffic lulled him into that ethereal place between being asleep and awake.

He woke a little past dawn to a stiff neck and a cottony mouth. After a shower and breakfast of leftover Chinese takeout, he felt moderately revitalized. He bundled his tux to take to the cleaners tomorrow, then drove to Blackthorne's offices.

Walking down Blackthorne's deserted halls at seven o'clock on a Sunday morning filled him with a sense of gloom. He shook it off. He let himself into one of the computer rooms and worked on a cup of vending-machine coffee while he searched computer files for Blackthorne's list of hideaway homes. When a name jumped out at him, he choked on his coffee and ran, coughing, out to his car. Rummaging through the pocket of his tux jacket, he found the card Grace slipped into it at the Sandersons' party.

The card showed a neatly penned telephone number. Nothing more. He compared it to the one on the computer. The same. His pulse raced, but as he reached for the phone, his mama's words echoed in his head.

A civilized person doesn't call before ten on a Sunday morning unless someone's died.

He glanced at his watch. Seven-forty. Giving in to Mama's deeply ingrained rule, he refrained from calling. He'd use the time to dig into Grace's background.

Satisfied with his internal compromise, he clicked through the information in Blackthorne's files. Whistling softly as he read, his innate respect for Grace grew tenfold. She and her husband spent decades in the Intelligence community, beginning in World War II. When her husband had died, she volunteered her services to Blackthorne, Inc., opening her home and offering cover stories for people on the run or those who might need to lie low for a while.

He paced the room. Had she ever taken in one of the people he'd rescued on an op? Would she be willing to help Jillian and Will start a new life? Excitement, the kind that preceded a new mission, thrummed through his veins. He peeked at his watch again.

Eight forty-five. Close enough. He picked up the phone.

Miri stood on Grace Ellsworth's spacious front porch and shook her hand. "Thank you so much." She embraced Jillian, then crouched to hug Will and scratch Reggie's head. "You be good, guys."

Will swiped his hand across his mouth, smearing a trail of sugar cookie crumbs. "You'll come visit, won't you, Miri?" His voice trembled as he clung to Jillian, much the way he had when she'd first met him.

"I'll sure try, kiddo. And your mom has my number. You can call me anytime."

Grace stepped forward and placed a hand on Will's shoulder. "Will, there's a park with a huge playground not far from here. After you get settled, maybe you can show me what Reggie can do."

Will's eyes brightened. After one final tousle of Will's hair, Miri trotted down the porch steps to where Dalton waited in his car, cell phone to his ear. Miri's spirits lifted.

She climbed in and buckled her seatbelt. He mumbled something into the phone and set it down.

"Ready," she said.

He nodded and backed out of the driveway. She leaned out the window and gave one last wave to the trio on the porch.

On the ride home, she struggled to stay awake. Last night—more like early this morning—she'd collapsed on the couch as soon as she walked in the door. She'd managed about three hours of sleep before Dalton called to tell her he found refuge for Jillian and Will, but they needed to get going right away.

"What happened to 'have a normal Sunday'? Do you really think someone's going to storm Galloway House and yank her away in front of everyone?"

"Not really. But since I found a place for them, I'd rather not take any chances. If whoever's involved knows she was at the police station, they're liable to want her conveniently out of the way," he'd said.

Sleep-deprived, she'd obeyed without question, not bothering to change clothes. She'd awakened Jillian, telling her to pack everything while making sure Will wasn't frightened by the sudden urgency of their departure.

Now, with them safely ensconced in the warm, caring

atmosphere of Grace Ellsworth's home, where Jillian would serve as a live-in cook and housekeeper while establishing a new identity, her breathing returned to a normal pattern for the first time all day. Until she started wondering how that sweet woman could finagle a new identity for Jillian. New identities definitely fell into those shadowy areas of the legal system.

It was one thing to let him help her, but she'd put the lives of two other people—one a mere child—in Dalton's hands when she'd hung up the phone and told Jillian to pack. She decided she didn't want to go there. Not yet, anyway. Accepting Dalton's plan meant she trusted him.

She looked across the car at him. No white knuckles on the wheel. A half-smile on his lips. In control of himself and the situation.

"I don't think I thanked you for what you've done," she said. "Like I said last night, Jillian's not your problem."

He stared straight ahead. "I wanted to help."

"How did you put this all together so fast?" she asked. "Have you known Grace Ellsworth a long time?"

His shoulders inched up a fraction, then dropped. "Not really. As a matter of fact, I met her the same night I met you. At Patterson's gala."

"What?" A flash of panic zipped over her. "How can you be sure she's going to consider Jillian and Will's safety? How can you trust her if you just met her?"

"Sometimes, you know. I'd say you and I trust each other, wouldn't you?"

He smiled. Damn, she couldn't keep her indignation boiling when he did that. Especially when he had a point.

"Yeah, but—"

"Grace has been on Blackthorne's list of safe houses for years. I met her at Patterson's, and again at the Sandersons'. She seemed perfect for the situation."

Miri tried to remember Grace but couldn't place her. "I don't suppose you ran a background check on her?"

He smiled again. "As a matter of fact, I did. She has quite a colorful history."

"Colorful? What's that supposed to mean?" The word conjured thoughts of some art thief or smuggler or something equally underhanded. "She's not an ex-gangster or anything, is she?"

He chuckled. "Nope. A genuine spy." He glanced at her with narrowed eyes. "And I trust you'll not repeat it."

Mollified, she mumbled an apology. Not only was she dealing with dead people and drugs, she'd gotten involved with a super-sleuth and super-spy. Her head swam. She chalked it up to lack of sleep and vowed to sit down and get her thoughts straightened out once she could string two of them together. Right now, her entire repertoire of thought processes was confined to the hunk of delectable masculinity sitting two feet from her.

And no matter how much she tried to convince herself that he was simply a plain, everyday, run-of-the-mill person who happened to have the XY chromosome configuration, no different from the countless other males she dealt with daily, it wasn't working. Her heart pounded, her palms and her mouth did that wet-dry thing again. And she wasn't going to think about all the other things going on where the car's vibrations rumbled through the seat to her bottom.

For half a moment, she considered giving in. Having that fling. Then she remembered how charming he'd been when they'd sat in Grace's living room. Like he'd been with Jillian. With Sammi, and for that matter, with Mr. Blackthorne's secretary.

Funny, but it didn't bother her. So what if he was naturally charming? A fling with someone charming had to be better than one with a bore.

Stop it. You're tired. And grateful. And too damn horny for words.

She squirmed in the seat and wrapped her arms across her chest so he couldn't see her headlights shining like beacons. Something they seemed to do every time she thought of him.

He glanced her way. Smiled. And squirmed in his seat, too.

"Um . . ." She summoned enough spit to lick her lips. "We should probably discuss . . . what's going to happen . . . with Jillian."

"We will." His voice was husky. "Eventually."

She stifled a groan of longing, closed her eyes, and drifted.

She hardly noticed when he got off the interstate well before her exit. Or pulled up in front of a redbrick apartment building in a quiet residential neighborhood. Or opened her door. Unfastened her seatbelt. Half-lifted her out of the car.

"Where are we?" she felt obligated to ask, although she had a good idea.

He didn't answer, merely took her hand and led her up the boxwood-edged stairs into the building. When they reached the door, he said, "My place."

"Dalton, I—"

"Shh." He pressed a finger to her lips. "Galloway House is under control, right? It's officially your day off?"

She nodded. "But—"

Dalton escorted her to an elevator, pushed three and encircled her with his arms. He dipped his forehead to hers. "No talking. No thinking. Let me do this for you. Please?"

"Do what? You've done enough."

"What I meant to do the other night."

Desire coursed through her like a spring stream overflowing its banks. But a tiny portion of her brain dammed the surging tide. *Be sensible. Don't let your hormones make this kind of decision.* "I . . . I don't know."

He stroked a tendril of hair away from her face. "I do. Trust me?"

To help her with her problems? Yes. To penetrate her emotional defenses? She wasn't sure.

The elevator dinged, the doors slid open, and Miri allowed Dalton to guide her down the carpeted hallway. Unlike her building, the hallways exuded air freshener, not homey cooking smells. Then again, maybe Mrs. Liebowitz's stuffed cabbage or Sophie Lavia's garlic-in-everything didn't smell like home to people who lived in Dalton's building.

Thinking of food made her mouth water. Much better than Sahara dry. God, she was tired. And, to listen to her stomach, hungry, although the thought of eating seemed too much effort.

Dalton unlocked a paneled wooden door and pushed it open. She tensed. If Dalton noticed, he didn't react. Inside, he steered her across a sparsely furnished living room to a black leather recliner, settled her down, and raised the footrest.

"Don't go away. I'll be right back." He brushed her temple with his lips, then disappeared.

As if she could move. The chair molded to her body. It smelled like leather and Dalton. Trying to escape the thoughts playing bumper car in her head, she studied his apartment.

Standard apartment issue off-white walls. Neutral carpet—something between beige and grey. Empty walls. The boxy couch, striped in a brown and tan fabric, worn at the edges, looked like it would be more at home in a fraternity house. Maybe it had been.

A dark green footlocker strewn with newspapers served as a coffee table. From the sounds of a refrigerator door opening and glasses clinking, she guessed Dalton was in the kitchen. Not exactly what she'd expected. Dalton approached with a glass of orange juice. He set it on the table beside the recliner.

"A little energy boost," he said. "Back in a bit."

Definitely not what she'd expected. "Thanks," she called after him, as much for the juice as for delaying the decision she'd have to make. She picked up the glass and took a swallow. Tangy and sweet, it went down easily, and she drained the contents without stopping.

More clunking noises. When Dalton returned, he gave her the grin that grew sexier every time she saw it. He held out his hand. "Come with me."

Warily, she grasped his hand and levered herself out of the chair. She followed him around a corner and into—a breakfast nook, where two plates of scrambled eggs and toast sat on a square wooden table.

He pulled out a ladder-back chair. "Sit. Eat."

Most definitely not what she'd expected. "What's this? Are you feeding me?"

He lowered himself into the opposite chair. "Well, I'm not going quite that far. I figure you can manage a fork without my help."

"But—I thought—I mean—you brought me to your place—and—you *cooked for me?*"

He picked up his fork. "Don't let 'em get cold."

She took a tentative bite. Creamy. Perfectly seasoned. "These are *good.*"

"Don't look so surprised. Scrambled eggs isn't exactly what I'd call cooking, but it's one of the few things I do fairly well."

Suddenly ravenous, she devoured the eggs and toast.

"More juice?" he asked.

"Maybe a little."

He went to the living room and retrieved her empty glass. "I could make some more eggs if you want," he said from behind the refrigerator door.

"No, thanks. These were perfect."

He handed her the juice. "Feeling better?"

Well, she wasn't hungry anymore. And she was a lot more relaxed. Was this where he expected her to pay for her breakfast? Her insides twittered.

Draining the orange juice, she couldn't help but notice the way his eyes went dark and smoky. He took the empty glass from her hand, his fingers trailing over hers with an electric touch.

"Come," he said. He caressed her cheek.

She shivered.

Heart pounding, she took his hand and followed him through the kitchen, down a narrow hallway to his bedroom. Nothing but the king-sized bed registered. She reminded herself to breathe as he pulled back a navy blue comforter and a pale blue sheet.

"Sit. Relax."

"*Come. Eat. Sit.* I'm not Reggie," she muttered, obeying nevertheless.

He smiled and knelt to unlace her sneakers. His touch was gentle as he slid them, then her socks, from her feet. He toed off his shoes and draped his socks over them. He patted the center of the bed. "You're tired. Lie down. On your stomach. If you're more comfortable, you can leave your clothes on, but if you want to undress, I'll leave for a minute."

Clothing-optional sex?

Her mouth dropped open.

He laughed.

Her face flamed. "I'm not sure what you want from me." She was no virgin, but this was the strangest foreplay she'd ever experienced.

"Darlin', let me take care of you. Like I wanted to the other night. Lie down."

She eased onto her belly, muscles tensed.

His hands kneaded her neck. Slowly, they moved down to her

shoulders, finding the tension, working until the knots disappeared. He leaned forward until his lips were by her ear. His
breath fanned her cheek. "When we make love, darlin', you're
going to want it. But you need to sleep. I promise, nothing's going to happen here except a massage. Which would be easier
without your sweatshirt on. May I?"

She mumbled a yes. He reached for the hem of her sweatshirt, and she helped him slide it over her head. Trust. She did
trust him. She unfastened her jeans and lowered them. He
touched the clasp of her bra. Waited for permission. Her fingers
met his and together, they worked the hooks free. He slipped
the straps down her arms. She lifted her torso enough for him
to pull it away.

Naked except for her panties, she felt the sheet settle over
her. He shifted it aside enough to access each part of her, then
replaced it as he moved on. Any remaining self-consciousness
evaporated. Warm, strong fingers demanded relaxation from
weary muscles. By the time he got to her calves, she floated on
a cloud into oblivion.

CHAPTER 18

Dalton paused, listening to Miri's steady breathing. He crossed the room and closed the drapes so the afternoon sun wouldn't disturb her when it hit this side of the building in a few hours. He shook his head as he closed the bedroom door. The two of them definitely gave new meaning to "sleeping together."

And what the hell was going on with that, anyway? Less than an hour ago, he had nothing on his mind beyond wild, frantic sex. A little friendly persuasion and she'd have been willing. He'd be rid of this annoying hard-on, and she'd be asleep in his arms instead of alone. That was normal. This was—absolutely crazy.

He brewed a fresh pot of coffee and fired up his laptop. He checked in with ops control at the compound. The team was in one of those countries that ended in 'stan, on schedule to rescue six hostages while Uncle Sam dragged on with negotiations. Hell, by the time the official negotiations were wrapped up, the hostages would be home with their families and Blackthorne's boys would be on their next mission.

Anything on Rafael? he typed into the Blackthorne message system. Jinx was on duty and usually kept an ear to the ground.

Nope. He's in the wind. Rumors he's switching to arms dealing. Or smuggling diamonds. For all we know, he's trafficking humans. Or retired to the beach.

Thanks. Anything else going on? With an ear tuned for sounds from the bedroom, he waited for Jinx's message to appear on his screen.

Drug crackdown on the Mexican border. Dealers looking for new ways to transport the product. DEA and Border Patrol territory.

Right, Dalton thought. No client. Blackthorne wouldn't get involved. Nothing ever stopped the flow, only rerouted it.

Thanks. Keep me in the loop. He signed off, regretting he wasn't on a field op.

But he *was* on an op, albeit an unusual one. Might as well figure out how to tell Blackie he'd stepped over the lines of a domestic investigation. Like into the next county.

Well, sir, you ordered me to work with Ms. Chambers, and this is where it led.

Yes, sir, I know we don't normally provide refuge for local citizens.

Yes, sir, Mrs. Ellsworth will expect compensation for her trouble.

Yes, sir, I fucked up. Big-time.

He figured his personal budget could probably cover a month or two before anything hit the fan, but he knew better than to keep something like this from Blackie. Why the hell was he even considering shelling out the money?

Try the truth. For the first time in almost fifteen years, I met someone who takes away the empty feelings inside. And I'd give my left nut to keep her safe and happy.

The thought was a sucker punch to his belly. And another response lower down.

He pushed away from the table and crept to the bedroom door. Leaning his ear against the cool, hard wood he listened to Miri sleep. Slowly, carefully, he eased the door open. The curtains didn't block all the light, and he watched her, on her belly as he'd left her, with her hair fanned across the pillow. Under the thin sheet, her form lay like a sculpture waiting to be unveiled.

The ache in his groin intensified, and he adjusted his trousers in a futile attempt to accommodate his growing erection.

She stirred. Pushed her hair from her face. Her eye opened.

"Go back to sleep," he whispered. "I didn't mean to wake you."

She angled onto her side and shook her head, sending her hair fluttering. "I flunked naptime in kindergarten."

He took a hesitant step into the room. She smiled, lazy and seductive. The blood left above his neck roared in his ears like the aftermath of a firefight. When he got to the edge of the bed, she peeked out from under a veil of silken hair and raised the sheet. Not enough to reveal her body, but definitely enough to be an invitation.

"One of us has too many clothes on," she said.

He remembered the first time he'd heard her speak. When she'd sounded like she'd spent a night making passionate love. That was nothing compared to her husky, not-quite-awake tone now. What would she sound like in an hour?

His shirt was off before he finished the thought. He took more care with his pants as he worked them down. All the while, his gaze never left Miri's face. Not quite awake, yet definitely aware. Her tongue as it swiped across her mouth. Her lips, parted slightly, revealed a glint of white teeth. Her half-lidded eyes, drawing him in. Barely able to breathe, he slipped into bed beside her.

Warmth from the sheets enveloped him. Miri's scent heightened his arousal, something he didn't think possible. Propped on an elbow, he brushed her hair away from her face. With a fingertip, he explored from the arch of her brow to the contour of her ear, afraid if he used more than a single finger, the sensation would overwhelm him. He traced the curve of her neck, continued along her shoulder, her torso, his touch follow-ing the dip at her waist to the elastic of her panties. Her choice of underwear suited her perfectly. Practical cotton, but low-cut bikinis. Sensible, with the tiniest hint of vixen.

"Are you sure about this, darlin'? Because if you're not, I have to leave right now."

She answered by pressing her lips against his, her tongue probing, seeking, dancing. Tormenting.

He groaned with relief and plundered her mouth, rolling over her, straddling her, moving his kisses to her neck, her collarbone and back to her lips. Her fingers threaded through his hair, each strand shooting jolts of electricity straight to his throbbing cock. He fondled one of her round, soft breasts. She wriggled under him, making tiny whimpering sounds.

He thumbed her nipple, pebbled into a taut peak. "You like that?"

Her moan said yes. With effort, he abandoned her mouth and laved her other nipple. She clutched his head, pressing it tighter against her breast. He twirled the tiny erect bud with his tongue, scraped it with his teeth. Concentrating on bringing her pleasure, he tried to ignore what she was doing to him. Slow down. Breathe. He shifted so he was beside her again. One hand sought her panties. Slipped inside, caressed her curl-covered mound.

"Off," she whispered, lifting her hips, tugging at the elastic. With the last barrier lost beneath the sheets, he dipped a finger inside her wet heat.

Her hips moved, and he matched her rhythm, seeking the nub of her pleasure. Already perched at the edge of control, he craved—needed—to be inside her. But not until she was with him on that precipice. His mouth returned to her breast, suckling, nipping. She writhed. Moaned. Or was that him?

A warm hand fondled his balls. Encircled his erection. Stroked. When her fingers toyed with the moisture building at the head, he pulled back.

"Wait," he gasped.

He reached for the edge of the bed. His nightstand never seemed so far away. Straining fingertips made contact with the drawer pull. Found a condom. Tore it open. Not quite ready to give up the flesh-on-flesh contact, he set it on the pillow beside him.

Her hands found their target again until he thought he'd die.

"Darlin', slow down. Let me." His fingers and tongue thrust in rhythm, mimicking the motions of lovemaking. Her hips gyrated faster, her head thrashed back and forth, and her moans grew louder.

He groped for the condom and sheathed himself. Kneeling over her, he stroked damp hair from her face and placed a kiss on the tip of her nose. She lifted her knees, opened herself to him.

He slipped inside her and gasped. So wet. So tight. So perfect. He stayed there, motionless, gazing into her eyes. Her lips curled upward.

"Kiss me," she said.

Supporting himself on his forearms, he leaned forward to do as she asked. When he did, she thrust her hips upward, drawing him farther inside. Her arms wrapped around his back, pulling him closer. At the same time, her muscles gripped him from inside.

"I . . . am . . . going . . . to . . . die," he said.

"Not yet, please." She gave him a bewitching smile and gently seesawed her hips. Barely moving, holding him against her, keeping him from moving.

He savored the sensation as pleasure built. He moved his lips to her nipples once more. She squirmed. Gasped. Her hips pistoned, and they fell into the instinctive motion, tempo increasing to a frenzy until his control was a razor-sharp wire and he was hanging on by his fingernails.

Miri bucked under him. As his point-of-no-return approached

like a herd of stampeding cattle, her fingertips dug into his butt and she screamed. His world exploded, and he was sure he screamed, too.

The pounding in Miri's chest slowed to a bearable rate. The rainbow-hued shards that had become her universe rearranged themselves into Dalton's bedroom. Breathing came under control. Dalton's weight pressed her into the mattress, but instead of pushing him away, she wrapped her arms even more tightly around him, wishing she could slide inside his skin.

Sated, dozing, she was dimly aware of a shift in positions as total relaxation sent her under. Later, floating to the surface, she felt Dalton curled behind her, his arm draped over her, his hand tucked between her breasts. She gripped his hand and snuggled tighter into his warmth.

He nuzzled her neck. "I think you finally passed naptime."

Sunlight sliced beneath the curtains. She checked the red numerals glowing from the nightstand clock. Two-seventeen. "I guess so. Miss Ballenger would be so proud. Of course, I'm not sure she would have approved of your methods. She was more the storytelling type."

"I'll be happy to tell you a story," he said. "It's about a man and a woman. And the man's got this . . . problem." He took her hand and placed it on his erection.

"Yeah," she said. "The woman noticed. She thought she was lying against a big stick, and it was poking her in the back. She asked the man to help her get rid of it."

Dalton murmured in her ear. "The man said he'd be glad to help. First he put a magic spell on the stick." He slid away and she knew he was getting another condom. She smiled at how quickly he returned, sheathed and ready.

He wrapped his arms around her again. "Then he showed the woman a secret place to hide the stick." He lifted her thigh enough to slide his cock against her entrance.

"Which moved the problem from one place to another." She took him and guided him inside. "But the woman liked where he put the stick. She tried to hide it deeper in the secret place."

She rocked her hips. One hand tormented her nipple and the other moved between her legs, rubbing circles around her center. Pleasure shot through her.

"And the woman . . . wanted to . . . keep the stick there . . . forever." Her brain detached, and there was the sensation of Dalton filling her, of ecstasy coursing from breast to groin. "Oh, God. Don't stop. Don't. Ever. Stop."

Flesh slid along flesh. The fairy tale became guttural sounds, moans and gasps, and then she convulsed around him.

"More," he said, not relenting. "Go over again. For me. With me." His fingers cast another magic spell.

"So, you gonna tell me about him?"

At the sound of Keisha's voice, Miri abandoned her class outline and the page she'd been staring at for the last twenty minutes. "Who?"

"Whoever put that smile on your face, sister. And that swing in your walk. I ain't seen you like this since—hell, I ain't *never* seen you like this." Keisha came into the office and set a coffee mug and a plate of oatmeal cookies in front of Miri. She hiked her ample hip onto the edge of the desk. "Spill."

"That obvious?" Stupid question. She'd been able to think of nothing but Dalton's lovemaking all day.

"Child, you might as well hire a band and have a parade."

Miri rotated the coffee mug. "He's someone who was helping me out."

"I'll say he done—did—a good job, then."

Heat rose to Miri's cheeks and she picked up the mug, using it as a shield. "I didn't mean it like that—he helped me with

Jillian and Will."

"I kinda noticed they was—were—gone."

Miri peered over the rim of her mug. "And as far as you're concerned, they were never here."

Keisha nodded. The residents were highly protective of one another's secrets, and Keisha mother-henned them all.

"They okay?" Keisha asked.

"They're in a good place."

Keisha gave her a narrow-eyed stare. "I know you're not the sort to give *that* kind of a thank you—even for doing something big. He gotta be special, right?"

"Okay, he's hot, and kind, and it sort of—happened." Like three times. Might have been four, but she'd insisted he drop her off at her place right after midnight. The heat in her face sizzled through her entire body. She snatched a cookie from the plate and took a huge bite. She waved Keisha toward the door. "I have work to do," she mumbled around the mouthful of crumbs.

Keisha gave her an exaggerated wink. "You go, girl." She straightened. "Oh, and there's a Detective Braddock in the lobby."

Miri leaped from her chair, barely catching the mug before tipping its contents onto the keyboard. "What? Why didn't you tell me?"

"I just did. Ain't gonna hurt him to cool his heels for five minutes. If I came in here and told you about him first, I'd never have found out about your man, now, would I?" She pivoted and sashayed down the hall.

Miri gulped a mouthful of coffee, trying to wash down the cookie, scalding her tongue in the process. Cursing under her breath, she rushed down the hall, slowing her pace when she approached the reception room. Detective Braddock stood by the counter, legs slightly apart, hands behind his back. His pose allowed a glimpse of the gun at his belt. He looked as worn as he had Saturday night.

He nodded brusquely as she entered. "Ms. Chambers."

"Detective. Sorry to keep you waiting. What can I do for you? Do you have information about Luisa?"

He shook his head, although she got the impression he wasn't willing to share what he knew.

"No, I came to discuss another matter." Shoving his hands in his pockets, he cast his eyes toward Keisha.

"I understand. Would you like to talk in my office? Can I offer you some coffee?"

He scratched his head. "Thank you, ma'am. That would be nice. Black is fine."

"I'll be right back."

He wanted to discuss another matter. She quelled the automatic apprehension and distrust while she went to the kitchen. If he wasn't here about Luisa, had he found out about her past?

Stop. You're worse than Nancy. You've got nothing to hide.

Somehow, despite all the time gone by, she couldn't shake the way she felt around the police. Afraid they'd catch her picking pockets. Afraid they'd come take her mother away the way they had her father. Although she knew they served the community and cared about its citizens, logic couldn't surmount the ingrained responses years of dodging cops had instilled.

She poked her head into reception and, with a nod, invited the detective to her office. Gesturing him to the chair, she closed the door behind him and sat behind her desk.

"Have a cookie," she said, sliding the plate in his direction. She set his coffee beside it. "Sammi, one of our residents, bakes them." Small talk. Delaying the inevitable. Cops didn't come bearing good news.

"Thanks." He took a sip of coffee, then set the mug down,

leaving the cookies untouched.

Keeping her expression as neutral as she could, she waited. Let him ask a question before she'd volunteer anything.

He cleared his throat. "A Victor Vaughn is behind some discreet private investigation inquiries as to the location of his wife, Julie Ann. I happened to notice the sheet come through internal channels. The description matches your Jillian Durbin."

Fear prickled her skin. Still, she waited.

"You wouldn't know if she's the same woman, would you?" He picked up a cookie. Rotated it in his long, thick fingers. His eyes demanded an answer.

"She came here a few weeks ago. Gave her name as Jillian Durbin. We don't ask a lot of questions, detective. It kind of defeats our purpose."

"Would you have any idea—that is, of course, if we assume these two women are one and the same—why she would have left her husband? I did a little checking, and Victor Vaughn is a well-respected man in his community. Plenty of money. Lots of connections. Makes me wonder why someone would leave all that comfort to live at Galloway House—no offense intended."

"None taken."

"Of course, if she is the same woman, and she came to Galloway House from a comfortable standard of living, one might suspect that maybe she wasn't as . . . cherished as Mr. Vaughn's investigator indicated."

Miri's mind swirled through her options. Was Braddock on Vic's side? Would Vic have offered a reward for Jillian's return? Vic was wealthy. Cops didn't make much money. Could she lie to this cop? His eyes seemed to be twin lie detectors.

He chewed the cookie. Sipped his coffee. "I talked to Mr. Dalton. We had a very interesting conversation."

He set the mug on the table and stood. "I wanted to let you know that I called Mr. Vaughn—figured I'd cut out the middleman and give him my official report."

Sweat trickled down Miri's neck. She stayed seated, afraid her knees would cave in if she tried to rise. Dalton couldn't have betrayed Jillian. Or her. Could he? How well did she really know him? "And?"

He gave a noncommittal shrug. "I told him we haven't seen anybody matching his wife's description. I suggested he might try New Mexico. Albuquerque attracts runaways. Cost of living isn't too steep, weather's reasonable."

She couldn't keep relief from her face. "Thank you, Detective."

"Never could tolerate abusers. Make sure Ms. Durbin stays away from New Mexico, though."

"Definitely."

He shifted in his chair and pursed his lips a few times. "Your friend also said you were worried about some missing people."

Miri's pulse kicked up. "Did you identify more meth lab victims?"

"No, ma'am. That's another reason I'm here. He said you'd feel better knowing if they were women you knew."

Knowing they were dead? She'd rather convince herself they were success stories, like Becky Crandall. But the wondering haunted her. "What can I do?"

He reached into a breast pocket and extracted an envelope. "Do you recognize any of these?" He pushed a small stack of pictures across the desk.

A cold sweat filmed her hands as she reached for them, trying to put thoughts of Elena out of her mind. Relief tricked through her when the first picture belonged to a total stranger. She shook her head. "No, not her." She let the photo drop to the desk.

"Go on, please."

"Oh God, that's Cissy." She leafed through the others quickly, but not without recognizing two other former Galloway House residents. Barely able to speak, she identified them for Detective Braddock.

"Thank you, Miss Chambers. That helps a lot." He slipped the photos back into the envelope.

"How? Why? What happened?"

"We're still investigating," he said. "The lab was situated in the basement. Poor ventilation and the fumes probably would have killed these women even if the place hadn't exploded."

"Why would they do it? Leave here, where it's safe and clean, and—" Her voice cracked.

"Money, most likely. Like with your friend Jillian."

"You think they're connected?"

He shrugged. "We have to consider all the possibilities. Jillian gave us a lead and we're following it."

"What lead? Maybe I can help."

Detective Braddock hesitated before he replied. "She got the impression that there was another recruitment level. That if she proved herself buying the meds, there might be something more lucrative in it."

"Such as?" Miri leaned forward.

The detective shrugged his beefy shoulders. "We think it was working in the meth lab. Quite likely, once they showed up, they weren't allowed to leave."

"Jillian wouldn't do that. And she would have said something."

"It's funny what people will or won't say when they've got a lot to lose. But no, I believed Jillian when she said she didn't know anything about the meth lab. However, if you, or anyone you come in contact with, has information, I'd appreciate a call."

"Definitely."

"Keep up the good work," he said. He picked up another

cookie and walked out the door.

Miri went back to her class outline. Her notes made less sense than before. She doodled spirals in the margins. Braddock had done her—and Jillian—a big favor. For that, she owed him. But the sense of failure wouldn't leave her alone.

She picked up her cell and punched in Dalton's number.

CHAPTER 19

Dalton maintained an at-ease position while Horace Blackthorne adjusted his reading glasses and leafed through his report on Jillian and Will—the one he'd spent half the night and most of the morning writing. No way he was getting out of this office with his ass unscathed. That Blackie squeezed him in this afternoon made it clear enough. So did the pity on Madeline Scott's face when he'd arrived for his appointment.

Blackie glared at him. "You did this so I'd send you back into the field, right? After our last discussion about who decides what assignments are suitable for the company, you continue to take matters into your own hands?" He smacked the pages with the back of his hand and dropped them onto his desk.

"No, sir." He'd run every possible scenario through his head while he waited for Blackie to see him, and the only one that worked was a good offense. With a deep breath, he plunged in. "You made the initial assignment. I followed through and made a decision. I was afraid for a client's safety, and time was of the essence."

"Bullshit. This Jillian and her son aren't clients. I assigned you to investigate Miss Chambers' concern for missing people."

"With all due respect, sir, you threw that assignment at me to get me out of the field. It was a *pro bono* job and you assumed if you put me on mandatory leave, I'd take matters into my own hands. I followed through as instructed. After investigating the situation, Miri—Ms. Chambers—agreed that missing people were not unusual given the circumstances of residents of a halfway house. However, during said investigation, your aforementioned non-clients came to my attention as needing safe refuge from an oppressive situation. Something, as you know, that Blackthorne's covert operations teams are well trained to handle. I was merely carrying out my training. Sir."

Blackie waved his hand at him like he was shooing a cat. "Cut the crap and sit down. *Aforementioned? Oppressive situation?* What the hell's gotten into you? You eat a dictionary for breakfast?"

Without breaking eye contact, Dalton sat in the client chair. "I stand by my decision. If you want, you can deduct Mrs. Ellsworth's subsidies from my paycheck."

Blackie huffed. "I spoke with Grace. She's taken a shine to your—" he waggled his glasses "—*rescued hostages* and is willing to foot the bill herself. God knows, she has enough money." He gave an unexpected chortle. "You charmed the daylights out of her. Nobody's immune, are they?"

Heat rose to Dalton's face even as relief inundated him. "I wouldn't know, sir."

"Next time, come to me first. I know you're used to split-second decisions when you're on an OCONUS op, but domestics are different. There are actually legalities involved. Minor details like our licenses, for starters."

"Yes, sir."

"One more thing." Blackie snapped his reading glasses into their case. "Grace seems to think Andrew Patterson's migrant project might be edging into some gray areas. Given her history, she's likely to assume there's something shady about a summer day in Death Valley, but I told her I could spare someone to do a little discreet checking. She seemed to think you might be suitable."

His first thought was of Miri's sister—okay, his second

thought after Miri. After a third thought, he leaned forward. "Why me? I'm a field operative, not a trained investigator. You've got at least a dozen people on staff who can squeeze data out of a computer much better than I can. Why not put Zeke on it?"

"You're questioning my judgment again?"

"No, of course not." *Right, Dalt. Dig the hole a little deeper.* "I'm curious, that's all."

"I think you're suitable for the job. I don't recall restricting you to computer searches, although I agree they are a necessary starting point. If you uncover something that requires more than your skills can handle, I trust you'll report it, and I'll assign someone with the necessary specialization." He tilted his head. "I need a subtle, preliminary investigation."

"I think I understand. So, what's shady about Andrew Patterson?"

"If Grace knew that, she'd have told me, wouldn't she? Patterson's image is squeaky-clean. And he's a client, one who pays well. But if he's operating outside the legal system, I don't want his money."

So, the dog-and-pony show with Fozzie had netted the contract Blackthorne wanted. "I understand. Under the radar."

"Think Carlsbad Caverns."

"You have anything beyond Grace Ellsworth's suspicions?"

"Not a thing. That's your job."

"On it." He stood to leave.

"One minute." Blackie's features softened. "You've got a big heart, son. Your grandma would have been proud."

Dalton swallowed at the uncharacteristic sentiment. "Thank you."

"Go on—but remember you're in the states, and our laws hold. We don't need cowboys."

"I'll remember."

As Dalton left Blackie's office, the shredder whined behind him.

Maddie took her eyes from her computer when he walked by her desk. He rubbed his butt and grinned. "He's in good form today."

She tilted her head and pouted in mock sympathy. Returning to her monitor, she applied fingers to keys and clattered away. He had one hand on the doorknob when he heard her mutter under her breath.

"Reamed you a new one, did he?"

He swerved, not hiding his surprise. "Maddie, my dear. Such language."

She reddened. "It's my daughter. She's been visiting. I'm afraid her more colorful vocabulary is rubbing off."

He crossed back to her desk and kissed her forehead. "Change is good. You have a great day."

"You seem in bright spirits, considering."

He smacked his butt. "Fast healer." He left her to her work and took the elevator to the second floor. Investigating Andrew Patterson would take longer if he had to do the searches himself, but the fewer people involved, the fewer chances something might get back to Patterson.

He opened the door to the same workroom he and Miri shared earlier that week. The memory tightened his groin. He couldn't decide if she was more of a distraction when she was with him or when she wasn't.

With him, he decided. He made a silent promise to forget Miri and spend the rest of the day earning his keep.

"All right, buster. Let's see what you've got," he mumbled to the computer.

Internet articles about Patterson's migrant project were all hype and fluff. The same as he'd seen on the brochure. Disappointed, but not surprised, he backed up and started again.

After an hour spent reading about the Andrew Patterson Modern Art Gallery, the Andrew Patterson Symphonic Hall, and the Andrew Patterson Theater, he knew he'd never survive as a desk jockey. He rubbed his neck while the computer brought another batch of hits. It would take an army of researchers weeks to ferret out everything about Andrew Patterson. Well, he didn't have an army, and Blackie wanted results sooner than that.

He wandered to the window, staring across the parking lot to rest his eyes. What would Patterson be hiding? What triggered Grace's suspicions? In his experience, there were two basic lines of investigation. Follow the money or find the woman. When he thought back to what Grace said at Patterson's fund-raising gala and at the Sandersons' party, he dismissed the woman angle—temporarily. Money had raised her hackles.

Damn, *anything* was better than tracking financials. He braced himself for hours staring at screens full of numbers, then trying to find correlations with more screens full of more numbers. He rubbed his temples as if the inevitable headache had already materialized. Maybe a cup of coffee would help. At the very least, it would put off the drudgery for a few minutes.

Two hours later, his eyes burned and the headache pounded in full force. Blackthorne's databases churned out yet another screen full of Patterson investments and investors. Why couldn't the monitor flash, "Shady Migrant Worker Files" and be done with it?

He glanced at his watch. Almost six?

Time flies when you're having fun.

He grabbed his notes and strolled to the break room in search of some aspirin. He popped three, washed them down with a paper cup of tepid tap water, thinking about a cold beer.

In the parking lot, he leaned against the front of his SUV. The cool evening air helped erase both the swirling visions of computer readouts and the throbbing in his head. Maybe Miri would like a cold beer, too. He unclipped his cell phone, momentarily puzzled by the dark display. Right. He'd switched it off while he was waiting for his appointment with Blackie. He pressed the "on" button and got the chime telling him he'd missed calls. He unlocked the car and slid into the seat while he listened to his messages.

Miri's voice brought an immediate smile to his face. Another part of him responded as quickly. He punched the call back button and an unfamiliar voice answered.

Miri paced the sidewalk in front of the bus stop. One hand clutched the cell phone in her jacket pocket, the other, balled in a fist, thudded against her thigh. A million perfectly good reasons why she hadn't heard from Dalton raced through her head. But the one that rose to the top of the list no matter how many times she tried to bury it said, *he's no different from anyone else. Takes what he wants and leaves. Threw her a bone by sending Braddock over.*

Memories of the past few days said otherwise. He cared. He'd gone to bat for Jillian and Will. And that massage—he could have had her right there, but he'd waited until she made the first move. And when she did—she tingled at the memory. He'd been a compassionate partner in bed, giving her two orgasms for each one of his.

A black car whooshed into the bus lane at the curb. A Navigator. The window lowered. Dalton's voice floated out.

"Want a lift?"

She flew into the car. "Why didn't you return my calls? What have you been doing?" She regretted the anger in her tone and wiped her hands across her mouth. "Oh, God, I didn't mean to sound like that."

A bus swung in behind him. "Looks like I caught you in

time." He pulled away from the curb. "I turned off my phone because I was in with the boss. He frowns on interruptions. Then he put me to work, and I needed to score some points, so I didn't turn it on until a little while ago."

"Score some points? Did I get you in trouble? Because of Jillian?"

"Nah, it's cool."

His grin undid her. She clicked the seatbelt and spent time testing it, adjusting it just so, avoiding his gaze. "I shouldn't have bothered you at work. I know you're busy."

"Don't worry about it. When I returned your call, someone said you were off duty. Then I listened to your next three messages and was afraid if I called back, you'd hang up on me."

She buried her face in her hands. "I've got an impatient streak, don't I?"

"That last message sounded a little more than impatient." His tone was only half-joking.

"Sorry. Detective Braddock came by, and I wanted to talk. I'm over it." More or less. He hadn't been available when she needed him, and she got through it on her own. The way she always did.

"He called me, too. I told him about Jillian's husband."

"Yeah, thanks. But he showed me pictures. Of the people in the explosion."

"And?"

"I knew three of them."

A momentary silence filled the car. "Aw, darlin', I'm sorry I wasn't there for you."

Was he? His hand pressed her thigh. Tension evaporated. "It wouldn't make a difference. They're dead. Nothing will change that. It's up to the police to investigate. All I can do is try harder to make sure nobody else from the House ends up like that."

"You hungry?" he asked, clearly trying to move her thoughts

in another direction. "Just dinner. No strings. I know a great sushi place."

That was something Galloway House didn't offer. The gnawing in her stomach made the answer obvious.

Later, at her apartment, he took the key from her hand and slid it into the lock. "May I come in? I'd like to ask you a few questions."

There was nothing suggestive in his gray eyes. "Sure." She went inside and hung her coat on the hook by the door. "Work related?"

"Yes."

"Coffee? Tea?"

"If you're having some."

Pleasantries. Small talk. She'd accepted his invitation for a sushi dinner, hoping a quiet evening would erase the pictures filling her mind. He'd filled her with fascinating stories about his first experience with sushi—in Japan, no less. By unspoken agreement, they didn't talk about the meth lab, but then, nothing in their conversation touched on what they'd done last night, either. Kind of an out of sequence first date.

"Have you talked to your sister?" He sat on the couch. In the middle. Was she supposed to sit next to him, or did he want the entire sofa for himself? She chose the easy chair.

Stop overthinking everything. Relax. Answer the questions. Make conversation.

"She called this afternoon. She's happy. She's thinking about teaching."

"She likes the new lifestyle?"

"It's only been a day, but I don't think Nancy cares. She's going to feel productive—be productive—and that's important."

"How's the project coming? Patterson's."

Is that what he wanted? To grill her about what Hunter and

Nancy were doing? She gave a noncommittal shrug. "Moving right along, I guess. Nance said they're building solid structures, and she likes the cottage she and Hunt are living in, and the construction noise and dust won't last forever."

He studied his fingernails. "At the party, it looked like Hunter and Patterson were arguing, that's all."

"Oh, that. Yeah, Nance told me Patterson had been trying to talk Hunt out of letting her go with him. I guess he's not used to people telling him no." A current of unease rippled through her belly, and she didn't think it was the octopus sushi roll. "Why are we talking about Nancy and Hunter? If you want my help, you have to be open about it. What are you working on?"

"Maybe tea would be good idea."

Miri stood. "So would trust and honesty." She'd revealed Nancy's secret to him. If he was going to use it to hurt her, he'd have done it already. Or was someone else looking? "Are you investigating my sister?"

He rose from the couch. "I'll help you with the tea."

She scowled. "Because if you are, you can forget the tea, and anything else you have in mind."

"No, no. I'm not investigating your sister. Or her husband."

Confused, she went to the kitchen and filled the kettle while she ran through the options. "Patterson? You're investigating Andrew Patterson? Mr. More Money than God Patterson?"

"I didn't say that." He stepped behind her and put his hands on her shoulders. "It would be nice if you didn't announce it to the entire building."

She spun around, trapped between the sink and his overwhelming maleness. She laid her hands against his chest and felt the thumping of his heart. He stepped back, staring over her shoulder at the darkened window. She could almost hear the gears whirring as he wrestled with a critical decision. And she knew she was a part of what he was deciding, that his answer could drive a permanent wedge between them.

His features relaxed. One corner of his mouth lifted. He traced her jaw line. "Will you work with me?"

Although her brain told her it would be better if they parted company, leaving her with untarnished memories of one fantastic night, some non-logical part of her did an internal fist-pump that he accepted her as more than a sexual partner.

Somehow, no matter how she'd tried to keep her emotional distance, he'd managed to chip away at the wall she kept around her heart.

She returned his gesture, scraping her fingernail against the scratchy stubble of his jaw. "What can I do?"

They sat at her tiny table sipping tea while he told her about Grace's suspicions.

"Well," she said. "In my opinion, Patterson seems a bit full of himself, but Nancy thought working for him would be a big step for Hunter. What did Grace pick up on?"

He shook his head. "Nothing. A feeling, she said. That the migrant housing project was totally out of character."

"It does seem strange. I mean, there are enough ways to do good works and stay in his area of expertise. Head Start programs, music, art classes. The things the school board never has the money for. A man like Patterson would know you can't cut them from the curriculum and raise well-rounded kids. Why would he throw his money into migrant programs?"

"You're probably right. It doesn't make a lot of sense."

"Hey! Maybe he's paying back an old, personal debt."

"Like?" His eyes brightened. "You have an idea?"

"Don't look so surprised." She stuck out her tongue. "What if he's got some connection to migrants himself? Like, his parents or grandparents came out of poverty and made good." She grinned. "It can happen, you know. Not everyone with money is born into it."

He appeared impressed. She glowed inside. Partners. Sharing information. Brainstorming. It felt right. Energy bubbled to the surface.

"Good idea," he said. "Tomorrow, I'll go back further. I've been scrutinizing the Patterson of today, not where he came from. Mostly following the money."

"What do you have so far?"

"Not a lot. I'm going over what financial records I can tease out of Blackthorne's databases." He gave her a puppy-dog look. "I could use another pair of eyes."

"I might have a set I'm not using much." Except for staring at him, which she was trying her damnedest not to do. "But are you allowed to show it to me?"

"Most of it's public record. Besides, my boss told me I could ask for help. I'm asking."

There was an evasive quality to his tone, but that was his business. Right now, if there was something going on that might hurt Nancy, she didn't care if she was treading into areas of gray. "I'm in."

"Great." He went to the living room and fished something out of his jacket pocket. "You can transfer what I have to your laptop." He returned and handed her a flash drive.

The glide of his fingers across hers reminded her of the magic they'd created yesterday. How his touch, his mere presence, filled her with an indefinable sense of being complete.

She inserted the drive into the USB port and powered up the laptop. When her desktop icons appeared on her screen, the files she'd appropriated from Patterson's study caught her eye.

"I wonder if there might be something in these files," she said, clicking one open.

"What?" He leaned over her shoulder. She would *never* get tired of the scent he brought with him.

"Some files I took when I was in Patterson's study that night.

213

One looks like plans for a remodeling job."

"May I?" He rested his hand over hers on the mouse.

She sucked in a breath. He didn't react, merely moved her hand and the mouse until the cursor pointed to the file. Apparently the connection didn't send the sparks through him the way they did her.

"Be my guest." She went to pull her hand out, but his grip tightened. His thumb stroked the back of her hand. Okay, so maybe it did.

He nuzzled her neck. "I love the smell of your hair."

"I love the smell of you, period. Your aftershave, and . . . you."

He laughed, deep, from his belly.

"What's so funny?" she said.

"Nothing—I was thinking about what I normally smell like on the job."

Before she could consider what he meant, a word jumped off the screen.

She jerked upright, forced the cursor back and clicked the mouse. "What the—"

Dalton moved back in time to avoid a collision between Miri's head and his chin. "What did you find?" He leaned around her, trying to get closer to the screen. All he could see were schematics.

Her hand relaxed under his. "My mistake. It's nothing."

"A strong reaction for a nothing." He lifted her hair off her neck and let it float down over his hands. "I'm starting to get a reaction, too. But it's not a nothing."

She shook her head. "I saw the word Hobart. For a second, I thought it said Holden, the street where the meth lab blew up. But it's a construction company. There are no dates on this. For all I know, this was done years ago or might be planned for years in the future."

He nudged her aside, then sat in the chair. "Don't go," he said and pulled her to his lap. "I want to poke around a little."

"Yeah, I get the idea." She wriggled against him. "You're awfully good at that."

"I had every intention of working when I came up here."

"Then let's work. I've got a full day tomorrow, and Tuesday's my volunteer night. At Elsie's."

Her eyebrows lifted in the obvious question. *Would he join her?* Rocking babies. His breath caught.

"Hey, no sweat," she said. "I don't expect you to come along." She swiveled, straddling him, and ran her fingers through his hair. "I understand."

"I should be over it," he said. "But I don't think I could do that again. Not now, anyway."

"I'm glad you said that." Her eyes were golden, warm and caring.

He stroked her chin. "Why? I thought you wanted me to come along."

"I do. But I know the time has to be right." She covered his hands with hers. Brought them to her lips. "And I'm glad you were honest. You could have said you were busy, had other plans, made some excuse."

Emotion flooded him until it seemed too much for his body to contain. "I don't think I can lie to you, Miri." He kissed her, and it was familiar and new at the same time, yet still Miri.

Time stopped for the duration of the kiss. When she broke the connection, he felt a different kind of emptiness. Not the dull ache he'd lived with for so long. This was specific. An ache that said, "Miri's gone." He clutched her head to his chest.

"I want you," he said. The sound was more growl than words.

"You mean the extra pair of eyes?"

"Darlin', I don't want your eyes. But you can bring 'em along."

CHAPTER 20

Memories of their night fueled Dalton through the next two days. Miri had her job, her commitments, and he had his. Determined to find something to support Grace's suspicions or prove them unfounded, he confronted the computers, not caring if he went blind doing it.

So far, Miri's idea hadn't panned out. Patterson's personal history was above reproach. His past, plastered over the Internet, filled countless magazine features and newspaper articles. Dalton wouldn't be surprised to find someone making a documentary on the man's support of the arts. Solid, upper-middle class parents. Solid, upper-middle class neighborhood. Scholarship to Harvard where he'd excelled in both the arts and business. Made his first fortune at twenty-four. His second, three years later. Moved his parents to a solid, upper-upper class neighborhood.

Dalton sighed. Back to following the money.

He'd traced Patterson's financial records to their original source—Patterson Enterprises, Inc. But there were layers upon layers of subsidiaries, holding companies, tax dodges he held no hope of understanding.

This was ridiculous. Blackie must have been crazy to think he could find anything in a maze of financial records. He was a field operative, not a computer geek.

Wait. He gave himself a mental slap upside the head. Blackie hadn't said stick to computers. No, he'd said keep the investigation off the radar.

He saved the last downloads to his flash drive and shut off the computer. Time to play his hole cards. Sometimes the best way in was right through the front door. He picked up the phone.

"Grace? I could use a little help."

At three that afternoon, dressed in his second-best suit, Dalton sat in Andrew Patterson's outer office. Dark wood paneling lined the walls. Plush carpet the color of port wine covered the floor. Instead of the expected potted plants, marble pedestals held works of art, from pre-Colombian to modern glass. Behind a substantial desk, a conservatively dressed young woman flashed him the occasional smile, revealing perfect white teeth. Madeline Scott, only twenty years younger.

"Are you sure I can't get you something, Mr. Drummond? Coffee? Tea? Bottled water? We have some excellent pastries. Or some fresh fruit?"

"That's most generous ma'am, but I'm fine."

She seemed disappointed. "I'm sure Mr. Patterson won't be much longer." Another smile peeked out. "He's on an international conference call."

"Not a problem." He drizzled more Texas into his speech. "I'm grateful he's willing to see me on such short notice. I really appreciate you squeezing me in."

"Oh, I had nothing to do with that."

He widened his smile. "I don't believe that for a minute. People like Mr. Patterson rely on others to keep them on schedule. If he's seeing me today, it's because you found an opening, and as I said, I'm much obliged."

Her cheeks reddened. "Mr. Patterson is always happy to discuss his projects."

"How is his quest to improve the living conditions of the

migrant workers coming along? I was at his gala and was most impressed."

In the midst of a canned, although animated, recitation of the hype he'd been reading for the past three days, her gaze shifted to her phone. "Excuse me, Mr. Drummond, but Mr. Patterson is off the line. I'll let him know you're here before he gets busy again."

He stood and straightened the bolo fastener on his string tie, reviewing the cover story he and Grace established. Competent, but not flashy. Nothing to have Patterson chafing at the bit to go along with his proposed scheme. Nothing to encourage Patterson to dig too deep. "I do thank you, Miss—?"

"Grantham. Belinda."

"Well, I thank you again, Belinda Grantham."

She pushed her chair back and glided across the carpet to open the door for him. Dalton held back long enough for her to announce him, then stepped into Andrew Patterson's private space, his cowboy boot heels sinking into the plush like it was river silt. As in his reception area, Patterson's office displayed the tools of his trade, with art rather than books on his shelves. More dark wood paneling and a cherry wood desk the size of an aircraft carrier deck dominated the room. Patterson sent a welcoming smile across the vast space before walking around to shake his hand.

"Come in, Mr. Drummond. Can I get you some coffee? I'm about ready for an afternoon caffeine hit myself."

"It's not necessary, Mr. Patterson. No need to go to any trouble."

"Nonsense. It's no trouble at all. Part of my routine. It's a Kona blend I'm sure you'll enjoy."

Of course it was no trouble. All Patterson needed to do was push a button, speak a few words, and Belinda would appear. "In that case, I'll be happy to join you."

Instead of pushing an intercom, Patterson leaned out the door with his command. Crossing through the office, he paused to accept the business card Dalton extended. One of several he'd created earlier this afternoon.

"Lone Star Growers Consortium," Patterson read. He set the card on his desk and descended into his oversized leather chair. "Please. Sit."

Dalton sat in a junior version of Patterson's throne. "I've been hearing good things about your project."

Patterson nodded. "I can't say I've heard of your company, Mr. Drummond." His eyebrows twitched. "But then, most of my endeavors have revolved in different circles, so to speak. My current project is a voyage into uncharted waters."

"I noticed."

"Indeed?"

"I do my homework, Mr. Patterson. And in reality, I work for a Texas consulting firm. The Consortium is my current client, and I'm here on their behalf." He paused, ready to drag out another business card, hoping he wouldn't have to.

"Go on." Patterson leaned back, his pale blue eyes attentive.

Dalton met his gaze. "The Consortium is a collection of Texan produce growers trying to improve business. I've been researching California growers for the past month. Your name has come up on more than one occasion. As a matter of fact, I was at your fundraiser not long ago." Dalton kept a pleasant smile on his face although his pulse kicked up to a rapid trot. "One of my clients was kind enough to give me his invitation when he couldn't attend."

He and Grace agreed that it was possible Patterson would remember him from the gala, and they decided to be aboveboard about it. Better to say it first rather than deal with that uncomfortable, "Don't I know you from somewhere?" repartee.

He went right on, not giving Patterson time to ask which client, although he and Grace covered that as well. "I was most impressed with your endeavor. And, I admit, more than a little surprised."

"And what surprised you?"

"You're a patron of the arts. What information I've been able to find doesn't remotely approach the realms of manual labor."

"I felt it was time to get closer to the earth, so to speak. The arts are lofty pleasures, but without basic human survival needs, it's difficult to appreciate them." Patterson displayed a plastic smile. "I'm a businessman. I hoped that by bringing my talents to another facet of life, I might do good for a broader cross-section of our society."

Dalton nodded in feigned approval. "I understand. And from what I've seen, you're doing very well."

Before Patterson could respond, there was a light tap on the door. It opened, and Belinda breezed in, carrying a large silver coffee service and two delicate white china cups trimmed in silver.

"Here you are, sir," she said, setting the tray on the credenza behind the desk. Dalton couldn't help but notice a more rugged coffee mug sitting beside a sculpture of a breeching humpback whale. The ornate service was for his benefit.

The tray held a platter of assorted cookies as well as the coffee. Belinda poured, doling out a smile in his direction. "Cream? Sugar?"

"Black is fine."

She nodded, handing him a cup and saucer. She placed a second in front of Patterson, who took two cookies and set them on his saucer, his eyes paying more attention to Belinda's rump than his snack.

"Will there be anything else, Mr. Patterson?" she asked.

He shook his head in dismissal, and she sauntered toward the door.

Dalton wondered if all the wiggle was for Patterson's benefit. "Very efficient. Easy on the eyes, too."

Patterson chewed on a cookie. "I don't mind admitting I like attractive things. A good admin is worth her weight in gold. A good *and* attractive admin? Priceless." He winked.

Dalton relaxed at the obvious change in Patterson's attitude. A couple of good old boys who happened to be businessmen.

Patterson picked up the second cookie, holding it in the air between them. "What is it you want from me, Mr. Drummond?"

Dalton replaced his cup in the saucer with a quiet clink. "Well, Mr. Patterson. Lone Star has reached a plateau. They've recently acquired substantial acreage, but the supply of workers can't justify expanded planting. No point in letting crops rot. Like everything else nowadays, we need a gimmick. Something special to attract a bigger and better workforce."

"I would hardly call raising the level of basic creature comforts a gimmick." Patterson waved the cookie again, then broke it in two and popped half in his mouth.

"You're right," Dalton said. "Poor choice of words. But the bottom line is, your projections are for an increased, more stable employee base. The Consortium needs that as well.

"I'd be mighty obliged if you'd share some of your expertise. Maybe let me visit your construction site, see your project in action? Maybe even see how you wrangle your rich investors?" He held his hands out, palms up. "I can assure you, Lone Star has no interest in competing with you. We want to maximize our own share of the market. With the current labor laws, it seems harder and harder to get workers."

Patterson pursed his lips. "Texas, you say? I suspect the tighter borders might cut down on your workforce."

"Not *my* workforce. I'm a simple consultant looking for methods, not people. The members of the Consortium follow the law, I'm sure."

Patterson nodded at the obvious lie. Dalton returned the nod. How many Texas pickers carried green cards, much less valid US citizenship? The man had to know that held true for California's labor pool as well. Was Grace concerned that Patterson might be edging into the wrong side of Immigration? That by being involved with the migrants, he'd be associated with gray areas of the law?

Patterson sat up straighter, in total PR mode. Tempted to turn around to see if a television crew had materialized, Dalton struggled to keep a straight face as Patterson went into his spiel.

"I see the workers as human beings first. People who are putting food on our tables. They deserve a more comfortable life than what many camps offer. If I can be of help, we, the consumers, have everything to gain. A healthy workforce, both physically and mentally, is more productive. And increased productivity benefits everyone."

"Spoken like a true businessman." When Patterson's eyebrows came together, Dalton hastened to go on. "And that's why I'm here, sir. Everything I've heard about you points to the fact that you are one top-notch businessman. If you'd be willing to share some of that expertise, then our Texas growers will also have better conditions and increased productivity."

"Perhaps. I have thought of my project as a prototype for others like it, although not quite this soon. Our first community is only the beginning." Patterson poured another cup of coffee, tilting his head toward Dalton's cup and lifting his brows.

"Thanks," Dalton said. He stood and moved nearer the desk, sliding his cup closer to Patterson. His hand stroked the smooth wood. "Very impressive. Antique?"

Patterson shook his head. "No. Just old. It was the first piece of office furniture I bought. It made me feel successful. Gave me the confidence I needed." He chuckled. "And kept me motivated to burn the midnight oil to pay it off."

"I will say, it's obvious you've put in the hours." Dalton took his cup to the credenza and tipped in a little cream. He rubbed his belly. "Never liked adulterating a good cup of joe, but doc says if I refuse to cut out the coffee, the cream makes it easier on the stomach lining." He picked up the bronze whale. "Right fine piece of work. I remember the first time I saw one of these creatures in the Texas gulf. Blew me away." He checked the bottom. "Sandie Casper. Gotta remember that name."

He made a pretense of strolling around and admiring more of Patterson's office accoutrements before returning to his chair. "I'm sorry. You're a busy man, and here I am, acting like I'm at one of your museums."

"Not a problem. I'm glad you enjoy my little collection."

"It's time to cut to the chase." He perched on the edge of his chair. "If you had financial support, would you consider expanding your migrant project into Texas?"

Patterson's lips pursed in and out. "Perhaps."

Dalton straightened his spine and delivered the lines like an often-repeated sales pitch. "I have the authority to open a discussion of a cooperative effort between Patterson Enterprises and the Consortium. Anything from a consultation to a partnership."

Patterson stroked his chin like an imaginary beard. "I'll have to think about that. May I call you?"

"Of course. I'll leave my number with your assistant." He stood. "I'm in California for a few more days. It would be very helpful if I could see your operation before I leave."

"I think we can arrange something. I'll have to check with my foreman."

"I'll look forward to your call."

Patterson stood and shook Dalton's hand once more. "You've given me some interesting ideas, Mr. Drummond. Thank you for stopping by."

On his way out, Dalton paused, waiting for Belinda to finish a phone call.

"I think you need to be more careful, Wendy," she said. "Talk to you next week." Frowning, she shook her head and replaced the receiver.

He stepped into her line of vision. Her cheeks reddened.

"My sister," she said, apparently flustered at being caught on a personal call. "New boyfriend."

"Younger sister?" he asked.

She nodded. "Guess I'm overprotective."

"Never hurts to have someone watching out for you." He smiled. "I'll leave you my card. I'd be obliged if you make sure the number gets into Mr. Patterson's address book. I'll be expecting his call."

"Right away, Mr. Drummond." He wandered toward the door, ostensibly admiring one of the paintings while he watched her add his number to her computer. Patterson probably hadn't placed a call himself in twenty years.

"Y'all have a good day."

"One minute," she said. She handed him a card. "This is my direct line. It'll save you going through the main switchboard." Her cheeks flushed a dusty rose color.

"I'm very much obliged for that, Belinda." He tipped the brim of an invisible hat and let himself out the door.

In the elevator, he programmed the number she'd given him into his cell and set it for a distinctive ringtone. Then he called Grace.

"I've planted some seeds in his mind," he said. *And a couple of bugs in his office, too.*

CHAPTER 21

Butterflies the size of fruit bats flapped inside Miri's stomach. She opened her medicine chest, surveyed her bathroom counter, making sure she hadn't forgotten something. Her doorbell rang, sending the bats into a swirling frenzy. Telling herself she was overreacting, she flipped off the light and strode to the door.

She hadn't seen Dalton since Sunday. Five whole days. They'd barely talked, agreeing they'd get more done if they cut out the phone calls that stretched a morning coffee break into the lunch hour.

"I've got grant applications to write," she'd told him, "not to mention two new residents who need constant hand-holding."

"I should be working, too," he said.

"We can live until Friday without seeing each other, can't we?" Her brain insisted it was the right thing to do, but there were body parts lower down that ached every time she thought of him. Which she'd done all too often.

He'd called last night with an offer she couldn't refuse. Get real. He could have offered to take her skydiving and she wouldn't have refused, even though she couldn't jump off a three-foot wall without leaving her stomach behind.

Now, seeing him, even distorted through her peephole, tumbled her heart, bringing a mix of pain and pleasure. A new feeling, not unpleasant.

She opened the door. "Hi," she managed, but it came out all squeaky. His reply was a croak. She stood there, inhaling his scent. The temperature rose at least ten degrees. His crooked grin made her knees wobble.

"Ready?" he asked.

Embarrassed she'd squeak again, she nodded and picked up her carryall. He tugged on the strap. "Let me get that," he said.

She nodded again.

His grin widened. "Helps if you let go."

She stared at her fingers, wrapped around the black fabric. With heat suffusing her face, she released the strap and slung her purse over her shoulder. "Ready."

"No trouble getting off work early?" he asked.

"No. I don't think I've used any vacation days in three years, and there are enough volunteers to cover for me this afternoon. And I've told staff I'm taking Monday off, too."

"Good." He glanced at his watch. "We can beat most of the Friday traffic if we hit the road."

"Let's go, then." She sidled past him and waited in the hallway until he was out the door so she could lock up. He kept his distance and seemed unusually stiff. Uncomfortable. "Is something wrong?"

His eyes slid over her, lingering on her lips. "I was thinking, that's all."

"About what? Are you worried that Patterson figured out you're an imposter?"

"No, I was thinking that if I get any closer to you, we'll never leave. And I was awfully close to kissing off the whole trip in favor of your bedroom."

"Highly unprofessional." Taunting him, she edged closer. Ran her fingers down his chest.

"Woman, I can barely walk as it is."

"You going to be able to drive? You know, will you fit behind the wheel?"

He glowered—but only with his mouth. His eyes twinkled.

"Downstairs. Now."

She skipped down the two flights ahead of him so he couldn't see what must be a totally goofy expression on her face.

Twenty awkward minutes later, they were on the 580.

"I'm definitely going to have to get bigger jeans," he mumbled.

"What?"

He cocked a grin. "You heard me."

She'd given up crossing her arms in his presence. He knew damn well what he did to her. "This might be a very long drive."

"I thought we'd stop for dinner, then find a motel and spend the night. No point in pushing it. I'm not expected until tomorrow. This way we can enjoy ourselves and be at her place by ten tomorrow morning." He waggled his eyebrows. "Or maybe eleven."

Eager as she was to see Nancy, her thoughts of a night in a motel with Dalton outshone everything else. "Sounds perfect."

"All right. Tell me how your meetings went."

Good. Back to reality. "Ended up being more of a combination speech, memorial and lecture. I caught the dinner crowd Monday and again Thursday. I hope they listened. Detective Braddock wanted to be there, but I convinced him he'd scare too many people away. I promised him I'd relay any information and promised everyone anonymity if they know anything or if anyone approaches them."

"Any takers?"

She sighed. "Not yet. But I'm hoping the explosion scared them enough not to get mixed up in anything like that. I think it hit home with the residents."

"Let's try to forget that for the next few days, okay?"

"Yeah. The cops have the resources." Deal with the living, she'd convinced herself. And enjoy some self-indulgence. As if he'd read her thoughts, Dalton sent a lopsided grin her way.

"So, what have you heard from Nancy?" he asked. "You didn't tell her you were coming, right?"

She shook her head. "You told me not to. I haven't talked to her except for one call after she got there. She's probably running herself ragged trying to do everything at once. Set up the house, get a job—heck, maybe she's got one already. Or created one. I can see her organizing a schoolroom in the garage or starting a daycare center."

"Two of a kind."

"I owe her everything. She's the one person who was always there for me. So, yeah, I guess some of her rubbed off."

Strains of *My Favorite Things* drifted from the radio. She closed her eyes, swallowed by the melodious soprano saxophone.

She sensed Dalton's gaze. "John Coltrane. I get goose bumps listening to him."

He upped the volume and didn't say anything until the song ended. The station broke for a commercial and she turned the radio off, angling in her seat to face him.

"So, we've got hours of driving, and the scenery sucks. You hardly said anything on the phone last night. Spill, super-sleuth. How did you get Patterson to agree to a trip behind-the-scenes at his project? You went in as a rich investor, right? Mega-donor? 'Let me peek and I'll give you a kazillion dollars'?"

"Nope. Too hard to keep a cover intact—he'd know all the players, have all the contacts. It's better to stay on the outskirts, come from somewhere new. If he can't find me, he'll assume he doesn't know where to look. It won't send up the same kind of red flags."

"Are you worried about red flags?"

His gaze drifted into space, then returned to earth. "Always. But I covered myself."

She waited. He seemed willing to talk, but not beyond the immediate realm of her questions. "Am I treading into forbidden territory?"

His lips twitched. "No, not really. You're in this with me. I'm not used to explaining my methods, that's all."

"Well, if I'm in it with you, shouldn't I know your cover?"

Tension lines appeared in his brow. "It'll be blown as soon as we get to your sister's." He faced her, wordlessly telling her he knew she'd have mentioned him to Nancy. Had undoubtedly pointed him out at the party.

"I can talk to her. She'll keep the secret."

He shook his head. "No point in making her lie to her husband over something that will probably blow over in a few days."

"But I'm confused. Why did you invite me along?"

His eyes twinkled. "Aside from the obvious reason?"

She was *not* going to last sitting in this ever-shrinking vehicle for five or six more hours. "Yeah, aside from that one."

"I'm working on it." He reached for the radio.

She intercepted his hand, trying to ignore the inevitable spark. "Please. Talk to me. Maybe I'll come up with an idea or two."

After adjusting the mirrors and rubbing his neck, he asked, "How well do you know Hunter?"

"Fairly well, considering. We don't socialize all that much— don't exactly run in the same circles. He's—rich. Ultra-polite. Proper. Almost stodgy sometimes. But he loves Nancy, and Nancy loves him."

Dalton didn't say anything.

"You think there's something fishy going on and he's in on it?" She ran it through her brain, couldn't fit Hunter Sanderson into that scenario. "He's been married to Nancy for over three years. She knew him for at least two years before that. If he was doing anything illegal, she'd know. And I'd know. We can't keep secrets."

He tilted his head. "I thought you said she could."

"*From* each other, I mean. *For* each other . . ." She remembered all the things she and Nancy had done. "That's different."

"You don't think she'd do the same for her husband? Even if it meant keeping something from you?"

She chewed her lip as she considered that one. This wasn't like the old days, when their very survival depended on them being close. The nights they'd shared a bed, or a mattress in an alley, huddled together for warmth. How they'd grown to know each other's thoughts. As close as twins, despite the years separating their ages. She thought back to the night Nancy surprised her in her apartment. To the party at the Sandersons'. To the excited phone call when she'd arrived at her new place. She didn't see Nancy that often anymore. Could her sister hide things from her? Face to face, Miri didn't think so. But keep them out of her voice over the phone? She hated to admit it was a possibility.

"I'd know," she said to Dalton. "If she lied, or tried to hide something, I'd know."

His gray eyes left the road and bored into hers, as if he could see the inkling of doubt.

"Easier not to lie to begin with," he said. "Don't have to think so hard."

How well she knew. "Then tell me what version of the truth we're going to be using."

"Like I said, I'm working on it."

Bits of conversation alternated with stretches of companionable silence. Dalton stole a peek at Miri, eyes closed, in the reclined passenger seat. They'd stopped for dinner before the L.A. snarl and crawled through the city outskirts without any unusual delays. He planned to spend the night at a quiet motel somewhere in the Beaumont or Banning area, which would give them time for some pleasant recreational activity and enough sack time to arrive with clear heads tomorrow morning. He sucked on a butterscotch and worked on the thermos of coffee he'd filled at the restaurant as I-5 stretched out in front of them.

While Miri dozed, he ran choices through his mind. Normally, he worked with a team of trained field agents anticipating moves, getting in, attaining their objective, and getting out as a single unit. Miri asked the right question. Why *had* he invited her along? On an op, everyone had a job, an area of expertise. If it would take six people to get the job done, they sent six people. Not five. Never seven.

Was he trying to earn points by giving her a chance to see her sister? Bullshit. Nancy had been gone one week. No, Miri did have something to offer. If Nancy or Hunter tried to hide something, Miri would know. Would she protect them? Could he read Miri after knowing her such a short time?

On an op, he often had a split second to decide who he could trust, who he could believe. His instincts served him well. But another part of him weighed in where Miri was concerned. He shifted his eyes in her direction. She slept, twitching at the corner of her mouth from time to time. Was she was dreaming about tonight? He smiled, anticipating the night ahead. He let her sleep. Later, she'd be awake. He took another slug of coffee.

The sky darkened, although dark was a relative term. City lights invaded, swallowing most of the stars. On his first sea voyage, out in the middle of nowhere, the thick blanket of stars filled him with awe. Here, it was nothing but headlights as the miles slid under his tires.

Dalton tugged on his seatbelt, where it was getting far too acquainted with his bladder. Twenty miles to the next exit. He pressed harder on the accelerator. Miri stirred.

"You okay over there?" he asked.

"Fine. You got your plan yet?"

"Rough draft. We show up. You have your sisterly reunion with Nancy. I'm going to trust you to get an overall feel for whether she thinks there's something fishy going on."

"Like?"

"You're her sister. You said you can read her. Ask some basic, friendly questions. Is she happy? Is he happy? Is she picking up unusual vibes?"

"Vibes? You want me to get out a crystal ball, or should we hold a séance?"

He laughed. "You know what I mean. Does he disappear and not tell her where he's going? Mysterious phone calls? How's their financial situation?"

She rolled her eyes. "And this is why you're a super-sleuth?"

No, he was a field agent, stuck pretending to be a super-sleuth. He adjusted the seatbelt again. "You created the title, not me."

"Okay, well what sleuthing have you done so far? You never told me what happened in Patterson's office."

"Not much. I met him, suggested the company I worked for might be interested in sharing information—or paying for it. Planted a few bugs in his office and left."

"Bugs? Like spy stuff? That's illegal." Her eyes twinkled. "What did you find out? Aren't you afraid he'll find them?" She paused. "If he does, won't he know you planted them? And then he'll call Hunter and warn him."

Her excitement was intoxicating. "Slow down. First, he won't find them. I took 'em out."

"But why? You only put them there a few days ago, right?"

"Super-sleuth handbook, chapter five, section eight. If it's gone, they can't find it. Besides, I got what I needed." Not much, but enough to know his cover hadn't been blown, and Patterson was mildly interested in including Texas in his scheme.

"I wish I could have been with you."

"No you don't. It's endless hours of waiting and listening. The range on those bugs isn't far. Means you have to camp out somewhere close enough to pick up the transmissions but not be conspicuous. Boring." And no place to piss. He yanked on the seatbelt again. Think about something else. Six more miles, according to his odometer.

"So, how did you get the bugs out?" she asked.

"Trade secret."

"Dalton! Tell me. Did you crawl in through the ductwork? Or do they self destruct?"

God, he could eat her up. "I like that last idea. Maybe Research and Development will create it. No, I put on a pair of coveralls, carried a clipboard and walked in when Patterson and his secretary were at lunch."

She frowned. "Don't they do that on TV?"

"Super-sleuths get their best ideas watching television. Or maybe it's the other way around."

The exit ramp came up at last, and he beelined for the first gas station.

"Pit stop," he said, wheeling into a slot near the restrooms, half out the door almost before he put the car in park. After he finished getting rid of what seemed to be the entire San Francisco bay, he splashed cold water on his face. Enough coffee. Another hour or so, and they could call it a night. The tired face in the mirror grinned at him.

Someone pounded on the door. He opened it, surprised to see Miri. Her face was the color of pre-dawn fog.

"We have to go. Now. To Nancy's." She spun on her heel and ran to the car.

He raced after her, trapping her against the car door. "Slow down. What happened?"

"I don't know. But something's wrong. Hunt called. We have

234

to go." She yanked on the door.

"Okay, okay. Take it easy. Rushing into things without think-ing isn't the answer. First, let me gas up the car and you can explain. Tell me everything he said."

He swung over to the pumps. While the gas flowed, he cupped Miri's face. Some color returned to her cheeks. He tilted her chin and brushed his lips against her forehead. She grasped his hands. Hers trembled.

He worked free and gripped her shoulders. "Deep breath. You're shaking."

"Sorry."

"It's all right. Start at the beginning. I'm on your side, remember that."

She inhaled, exhaled, then met his eyes. "Hunt called. He didn't say much, asked if I'd talked to Nancy lately. If we planned to get together. When I said I hadn't, he said never mind. Then he hung up."

"And this is unusual?"

"Dalton, he was scared. I've *never* heard him like that. His voice shook. He stammered. That's *not* Hunter. Something's wrong, and we have to get there. Something's happened to Nancy. I can feel it. She's not home, and Hunt was looking for her."

The fear in her face convinced him, but he knew he'd have done it anyway. Miri asked, he dropped everything and ran. "We're out of here as soon as the tank is full."

"Can't we fly?"

He shook his head. "By the time we get to an airport and ar-range a flight, we could be there. Plus, it might be handy to have our own wheels." And his guns, which would require major airline hoop-jumping.

"Okay. So, drive."

He replaced the fuel hose, ripped his receipt from the pump

and got into the car. Miri was already buckled in. He twisted the key in the ignition. "Um . . . did you use the facilities? It's going to be a couple of hours at least."

She nodded. "Before he called. Let's go. Please."

"You know, we'll probably get there, and Nancy and Hunter will be laughing about their crossed communications."

"I hope so. But it's like there's this huge hole in my gut that's telling me she's in trouble."

"So why wouldn't Hunter tell you?"

"I don't know. He might be embarrassed to admit he doesn't know where she is. In his circles, that would be airing one's dirty laundry in public. He's—proper."

"Okay." He searched for the right words. "I have to ask this. Don't get upset, please. Is there a possibility Nancy might be somewhere and not want him to know about it?"

Even in the dim light, he swore Miri's eyes flashed with indignation.

"Like she was having an affair?"

"That's one possibility."

"She's been there a week. I can't believe she'd have met someone and cheated on Hunt that fast."

"And him? He's been there longer. Do you think *he* might have met someone and Nancy found out?"

Her answer wasn't quite as fast coming back, but her "no" exuded confidence.

He took a few breaths. "Does he treat her well?"

She hesitated. "You think she's running away—because—like Jillian? No way. No, no, no way."

He figured each "no" jumped about ten decibels. "I had to ask. Consider it one less thing to worry about."

"You might spend a lot of time checking on unfaithful spouses for your job, but it's not that way for everyone. Nancy and Hunt have a great marriage. She was so excited about playing a part in his work, and if there were problems, he'd never have let her come along."

He paused, trying to ignore the blow to his pride. She thought he spent his time peeking into motel room windows. Better to let her think that than tell her what he really did. She'd accepted him as a private investigator. What would she do if she knew the truth? To hell with reality. Time for that after they solved their current dilemma.

"Makes perfect sense." He changed lanes, overtaking a semi. The road was clear, and he increased his speed. "Next question. When he called, did you tell him we were a couple of hours away?"

"No. He hung up before I said much of anything. Should I call him?" She held the phone in her hand, punching buttons and staring at the screen.

He pondered her question. Although Miri's instincts were probably spot-on, there was that remote possibility that Hunter Sanderson's call had been a ruse—an alibi to show him as the caring husband, while he unburdened himself of a wife he no longer wanted. In a remote town, away from everyone she knew, an accident would be accepted much more easily than in the upper crust circles of San Francisco. Unfortunately, in his work, he saw the worst case scenario all too often. Ugly as it might be, considering those one-in-a-million chances saved lives more than once.

"I think we should wait awhile."

CHAPTER 22

Miri held the phone, Hunter's number displayed on the screen. Her finger hovered over the send button. She stared at it while her mind untangled, then transferred her gaze to Dalton. The pain behind his eyes spoke volumes. She let the phone slip into her lap. "All right."

Outside, she watched each marker count down the miles, silently urging Dalton to go faster, faster. Her foot pressed the floorboard, pushing an imaginary accelerator pedal.

"We'll get there. Better if you relax." Dalton's voice, quiet and soothing, floated across the car.

"My sister could be in terrible trouble, and you want me to relax?"

"The hard part is knowing when there's nothing you can do. And accepting it. Worrying makes you reckless. Reckless people make mistakes. Mistakes can get you killed."

She tore her gaze from the window and studied his face. There was something new there. He seemed totally—focused. Intent and relaxed at the same time. He drove, checked the mirrors, changed lanes when needed, almost as if he was part of the car. Yet his tone chilled her enough to make her shiver. Was there a death beyond his wife's weighing on his conscience? Had it been his mistake?

She recalled the tension he'd carried after an evening rocking babies. Yet now, when there was the possibility they were riding toward danger, a mantle of calm surrounded him. Was he simply humoring her? Didn't he believe her? Hunter had freaked. Hunter never freaked.

"Something *is* wrong, you know," she said.

He gave no indication he was catering to the whims of a silly female. "It's definitely a possibility." He inched his chin toward the radio. "Music? Might help the time pass. There are some CDs in the console."

She lifted the cover and pulled one at random. The car's interior was too dim to read the title, and she didn't really care what it was. She popped the case open and slipped the disc into the player.

Country music thumped from the speakers. A female singer complained about falling to pieces. Dalton's fingers tapped the steering wheel in rhythm. Rather than try to find something she liked, she let the CD play. Dalton smiled in her direction. "Patsy Cline. The best."

So much for changing the CD. Besides, at this point, she didn't think even John Coltrane could distract her. She tried to listen, but her mind wouldn't hold on to the melody or process the lyrics. Outside, only the changing numbers on the mile markers proved they'd made headway.

"Hand me my jacket, darlin'."

"Huh?" The interior of the car was comfortably warm, but she reached over the seat and snagged his parka. "You cold?"

"Nope. Check the right outside pocket."

She held the jacket up, orienting herself to left and right, and lowered a finger into the opening. Plastic met her touch. She reached deeper into the pocket and felt hard lumps.

"Help yourself," he said.

She pulled out a small bag of candy. As she wrestled it open, a whiff of butterscotch floated up.

"Mind unwrapping one for me?" he said. His hand hovered, palm up, between them.

The simple task of twisting the yellow cellophane from the candy seemed beyond her, but she convinced her fumbling fingers to behave. When she dropped the disc in his palm, he gripped her hand. His squeeze said he'd make everything all right. She tried to believe it.

Not loosening his grip, he raised her hand to his lips and sucked the candy into his mouth. His tongue caressed her palm while his thumb rubbed circles on the back. He released her with a kiss.

His voice rumbled from his chest. "I'd share this one with you, but that might get us killed."

Butterscotch and sandalwood surrounded her senses. "Thanks. I'll have my own. This time." She tipped out a candy and dropped the bag into the console. Guilt assaulted her. Thinking of sharing a butterscotch kiss wiped out thoughts of Nancy. Dalton encompassed her entire being. Whatever he was thinking—and she bet a motel room and a bed topped the list—had no business in his head when her sister might be dead. Oh, God, that couldn't happen. Nancy couldn't be dead. She refused to consider that possibility.

Headlights from a stream of oncoming semis illuminated Dalton's face. Filled with compassion, not lust. Realization hit her like a trumpet fanfare. He'd been distracting her, not out of a testosterone surge, but to keep her mind off Nancy. Helping her pass the time while there was nothing to do but watch the mile markers flash by.

"Water's in the cooler in the back," he said. "There are some wipes in the glove box."

Her fingers traced the sticky palm of her opposite hand. "Do you anticipate everything?"

He chuckled. "Would be great if I could. Figured if my hand's sticky, yours is, too."

"Oh. Yeah." She reached for the glove box and found the

packets of wet wipes. "You want one?"

"You can do the honors."

She tore open the packet and unfolded the towelette, swiping the cold, lemon-scented wipe over her hand before using it to clean Dalton's.

She sucked her butterscotch, swearing she wouldn't look at another mile marker until she finished. "Can you tell me about any of your cases? Anything interesting, or exciting?"

Another shrug.

"Can't talk about them, or won't?" she asked.

"Little of both. The more interesting ones fall into the *can't* category. The others are boring."

If another semi hadn't illuminated the car's interior, she might have believed him. She crunched on the candy and peered out the window.

Ten miles closer.

Dalton left Miri to her musings. He lifted his cell from the console well and punched the speed dial number for the covert ops control center.

"Hey, Cowboy! How's it hangin'?"

"Fine, Zeke. Is the team back?"

Miri's head jerked away from the window. He pressed the phone tighter against his ear and concentrated on Zeke's words.

"Airborne. ETA at twenty-three hundred. Smooth sailing all the way."

Knowing nothing was ever smooth sailing, Dalton shared the relief he knew any team felt once they'd completed a mission. "Tell 'em to have a brew for me."

"Why not come out and join us? You're not banned from the compound, right?"

"Actually, I'm working on another project. I need a favor."

Eyes wide, Miri leaned forward and he gave her a reassuring smile.

"Can you monitor the Riverside County sites?" he asked.

"Can I? You mock me, sir. Of course, but what am I looking for? Riverside County's huge."

If anyone could slip in and out of computer databases undetected, it was Zeke. "Anything unusual to do with migrant workers. Missing persons." He hesitated, avoiding Miri's eyes. "Nancy or Hunter Sanderson. A new housing project funded by Andrew Patterson. Crap, anything at all unusual. Start around Santa Angelino and work out—probably toward Mexico."

"With or without local help?"

"I need you to run solo for now, pard."

"You're not going rogue on us, are you? I know you're hot for Rafael, but don't blow your career."

"This has nothing to do with Rafael." But he sure as hell wished it did. With Rafael, he knew where he stood. In that world, everyone was a bad guy. "I got the job from upstairs, but it's under the radar."

"Gotcha. I'll be in touch."

"I'll owe you."

"Damn right." Zeke disconnected.

"What was that about?" Miri asked. "What team? Where are they back from? Who's Rafael? Does he have something to do with Nancy?"

"You ask a lot of questions, don't you?" He'd known before he made the call that Miri's involvement in the case might prove troublesome. The trick would be making sure he isolated this case from the rest of his Blackthorne duties when he talked to her. His training, where maintaining a cover was second nature, seemed to evaporate in her presence.

She offered him another butterscotch. "Why not? There's nothing else to do. Besides, we're on the same side here, right?"

"Rafael's a leftover from another case," he said, accepting the candy but setting it into a cup holder. "Nothing to do with Nancy."

"So what about the rest? You were asking about migrant workers along with Nancy. And Hunt."

He nodded. "I called Blackthorne's offices and asked someone to do a little investigating."

"But we're not calling the local cops. I figured that much out. Why? Won't they have more resources than we do?"

He smiled at the "we." Then again, she *was* part of this, regardless of how much or little help she'd be. "Until I know more, I'd rather not show my cards."

She nibbled her lip. "I get it. You think the worst of everyone first."

Ouch. But close to the truth. Too close. "Not everyone." He reached over and stroked her thigh.

She pulled her leg away. "You did a background search on me."

"Darlin', I did that after you became a professional obligation because that's the way it is in this job."

"Wouldn't you rather see the glass as half-full, not half-empty all the time? It's got to be a depressing lifestyle."

"I prefer to think of it as an ounce of prevention. Not knowing something important and getting ambushed—that's depressing." He cut his eyes in her direction, but she seemed willing to let the matter drop. "Next exit's ours. Should be there in under half an hour."

Miri slid one hand up and down the seatbelt strap, making a scraping sound. She leaned the other against the window as she peered into the darkness. The scraping stopped and both hands made a visor against the pane.

"Are you sure we're going in the right direction?" she asked after they'd pulled off the highway and onto the 86 spur.

"There's nothing out there."

"You said she lived out in the boonies. The GPS coordinates are right." He tapped the small dash-mounted unit.

"You're sure it's not broken?"

"Relax, darlin'. It's working fine, and we're almost there. I want you to be calm. There's a chance this is all a misunderstanding and Nancy will be home."

"I wish I could believe you. But . . ."

"Miri, we're going on your gut instinct here. He didn't ask you to help. He might not be all that glad to see you. Or want you to know if Nancy really is missing."

"I keep telling you, I can feel it."

"Okay. We'll take the half-empty glass. She's not there. If your brother-in-law is as upset as you say, we'll want to keep him calm, not fan the flames. Can you do that?"

"I'll try."

"Darlin', you need to practice what you'll say. He's expecting me—as the man Patterson sent—tomorrow. Arriving tonight is bad enough, but you're going to be a total surprise. Start with that. You tell him you were coming down to see Nancy."

"But—"

"Practice. Make it sound natural. Something like, 'Hunt. I was on my way down to surprise Nancy when you called. You hung up before I could tell you. You sounded worried. Is everything all right?'"

She nodded. "How do I explain you? I mean, I can't pop in with a date."

"At this point, my investigation is secondary. Tell him the truth. That someone hired me to check into Patterson's project. He might be pissed, but you can vouch for me and make him understand that if Nancy's missing, I'm no longer on that job. That I want to help. The important part is he's gotta trust me."

Houses appeared in the distance, and soon they were in a

dark and quiet area of small, widely scattered residences. He followed his GPS directions through the last few turns and navigated to the driveway of a bungalow, verifying the address on the mailbox. Miri fidgeted in her seat.

"This is it," she said. Her seat belt clicked and retracted with a clunk.

He stopped, backed a few yards into the driveway and killed the engine, reaching for Miri's arm before she could leave. "Wait a second."

"Why?"

He leaned over and kissed her gently on the lips. "What are you going to say?"

Her gaze rolled heavenward. "Hi, Hunt. Is Nancy back yet? I was on my way to surprise her when you called."

"Not bad, darlin', but try not to say it all in one breath, and take longer than two seconds. Remember, you're concerned, not panicked."

"Easy for you to say." She opened the door. "Is this where you say 'Break a leg?' "

"Go. Walk, don't run. I'll be right behind you. Wait on the porch." He let her start down the drive, then dug through his pack for his Glock.

CHAPTER 23

"Hi, Hunt. I was in the neighborhood," Miri muttered under her breath as she strode toward the door. "Yeah, right. I always drop in on people at ten-thirty at night."

She fought to stay calm as she walked up the dirt path. Faint moonlight and a pair of yellow porch lamps gave her enough illumination to keep from twisting an ankle in the ruts and potholes.

The porch steps creaked. Despite the urge to pound on the door, she followed Dalton's instructions and waited. The stucco could use a fresh coat of paint. Was it white, or a faded yellow? Why did she care? Delaying the inevitable. Dalton's touch on her shoulder came without warning. Her breath hitched.

"There's a light on in back. Seems to be the kitchen. Silver Escalade in the carport."

She hadn't noticed. That's why he was the super-sleuth. His matter-of-fact tone calmed her. Slightly. She lifted her hand and tapped on the door. No response.

Dalton said, "I don't think he heard you." He stepped forward and rapped with enough force to be heard two doors down.

A light came on at the window. The door opened. Miri stifled a gasp.

Hunt's normally impeccable appearance rivaled Dalton's the day he'd shown up at the park to rescue Reggie. Blond hair stood up in unruly spikes. He dug his fingers through it. On his jaw, gold stubble stood out in stark contrast to his pasty complexion. He'd aged ten years since the night of the Sanderson's party.

"Miri?" His voice was a hoarse croak. He held a tumbler half full of golden liquid, and Miri smelled whisky on his breath. He blinked several times. "God, Miri. Why are you here?"

"Hunter." *Calm. Relaxed. Concern, not panic.* She exhaled, then drew in a quick breath. "You didn't give me a chance to talk when you called. Dalton and I were already on the road. What's wrong?" No way could Hunt expect her to pretend things were copasetic.

His eyes, normally a brilliant green, were dull and bloodshot. He shifted his gaze to Dalton, then back to her, as if he couldn't trust what he saw. He gulped from his glass and tugged at his hair.

"Mr. Sanderson?" Dalton spoke in a calm, reassuring tone. How did he do it? Of course, Nancy wasn't *his* sister. "We need to talk. May we come in?"

Hunt stood as if anchored to the worn carpet. Miri stepped forward and took his hand. She pried the glass from his fingers and slid her arm around his waist. "Let's sit down, Hunt."

"Guess you should come in," he said. Miri walked alongside him as he trudged to a small beige sofa in the living room.

She could do this. This was what she did, for God's sake. Took care of distraught people, listened, ferreted out what they were really saying, separated it from what they were trying to hide. She helped Hunt lower himself onto the couch and sat beside him, holding his hand. Her peripheral vision caught Dalton sliding an armchair closer.

She focused on Hunt. "Nancy isn't here, is she?" When he didn't respond, she went on. "How long has she been missing, Hunt? It's me. Miri. Talk to me. I'm on your side."

He looked at his hands, then around the room. "I need a drink."

"Later, Hunt. First, we talk."

He blew out a ragged breath. Miri forced herself not to flinch as the alcohol fumes stung her eyes.

"She's happy." There was defiance in his tone. "She doesn't mind living here." He swept his arm around the small room with its shabby furniture. Lowering his head into his hands, he kneaded his temples. "I think she feels comfortable. Maybe more than at our San Francisco house."

Miri nodded. She and Nancy lived in a house not much different from this during the few happy years of their childhood, when they were a family.

"Start at the beginning, Hunt." She mouthed the word, *coffee* in Dalton's direction. He hesitated. She jerked her head toward the kitchen.

"Who's he?" Hunt said, apparently registering Dalton's presence for the first time.

"That's Dalton. He's a private investigator, and he's good. He'll know what to do." She hoped.

Hunt blinked several times. His gaze moved from Dalton to Miri. "Private investigator? How? I didn't . . . what's he doing?"

She ignored his real question. "He's going to make some coffee."

"Don't want any." He massaged his stomach. "Had plenty."

"Well, we've been on the road a long time. I'm sure Dalton would like a cup."

Hunt moved to get up. "I should help. I'm being rude."

Miri gripped his hands and drew him back. "It's fine, Hunt. Tell me what happened."

"I didn't want her to come, you know. We argued about it. I told her she should wait until everything was established. Andrew Patterson thought that would be a better move, too. But she insisted."

Miri smiled sympathetically. "I know how she can be when

she makes up her mind to do something."

He scrubbed his face with his hands. His long, slender fingers trembled. "From the minute we got here, she was going like gangbusters." His shoulders straightened, and the man Miri recognized as her brother-in-law reappeared. Someone who maintained his dignity and control. "Patterson's plans include an extensive community center, and she took it upon herself to make it special."

"That sounds like Nancy." Miri smelled the aroma of brewing coffee.

Dalton returned with a package of Fig Newtons and set it on the table. "Coffee's going. I thought you might feel better if you ate something."

Barely glancing at the package, Hunt reached for the cookies and extracted one. With it halfway to his mouth, he froze, as if his arm had turned to stone. Staring at the cookie, he dropped it onto the floor. Miri bent to retrieve it. Nancy's favorite, she remembered as she set the fig-filled square on the table and pushed the package away.

"Wednesday," Hunt whispered. "I haven't seen her since Wednesday. She went shopping on Tuesday—" he gestured toward the Newtons. "Wednesday morning, I had a trip to Indian Wells." He seemed calmer. "You know, there are more millionaires per capita there than anywhere in the U.S. I figured we could get some funding. I tried to talk Nancy into coming with me, but she wanted to work on the center. Plus, I think she said one of the local kids was sick and she wanted to take him to the doctor."

"Were things all right between you when you left?" Dalton asked.

Hunt answered, watching her. It was as if he'd heard Dalton's questions but hadn't connected them to the man's presence in the room. "Sure—I mean we have our own opinions about things, and we disagree from time to time, but who doesn't? I wanted her with me. To be honest, it's easier to schmooze at social events if you're a couple. She huffed a little—said I was trying to keep her away from the people who needed help, that I thought they were beneath us—the way my mother did."

"Go on," Dalton said.

"So, I went alone. And yes, I let her know I wasn't happy about it." Hunter stared at the ceiling. "Squeezing money from rich people can be a royal pain." One corner of his mouth twitched in something between a grin and a sneer. "That's why they're rich. They hang onto their money." He gave a quiet snort. "I should know. I was brought up in that environment.

"Anyway, in order to meet everyone, you have to start with the two-martini lunch, then afternoon cocktails, pre-dinner drinks, after dinner drinks, and on into the wee hours. I can pace myself, but when you're trying to cover as much ground as possible in a day, it gets to be a bit much. I called to tell Nancy I was getting a hotel room, and I'd be home Thursday morning. She didn't answer, but I wasn't worried." A grimace crossed his face. "I was three steps beyond buzzed and didn't think twice about it. Figured she was in the shower, working on something for the center, making friends—anything. It wasn't unusual." He choked back a sob. "I should have followed up."

Miri reached for him. "You couldn't know. Don't blame yourself. We'll find out what happened."

"Right." Hunt looked from Miri to Dalton again, confusion in his eyes, apparently clicking on the third person in the room. "You're an investigator?" He rubbed his neck. "How did you know—what made you think—why are you here? I didn't tell anyone." He gave Miri an apologetic glance.

Dalton leaned forward and rested his arms on his thighs, his hands clasped between them. "Mr. Sanderson, I'm going to be straight with you. We weren't coming about Nancy. It's almost a coincidence we're here." He paused, as if waiting for Hunt to question him. When Hunt didn't respond, Dalton continued.

"There are people who think this undertaking is a bit off the wall for Andrew Patterson and wonder if there's more to it than meets the eye. I was working with Miri on a Galloway House issue, and our paths dovetailed. When I was sent here to check things out, I invited Miri along to pay a surprise visit to her sister."

Hunt stared into the distance, as if he was trying to assemble a thousand-piece mental jigsaw puzzle. "Check what out?"

Miri waited for Dalton to explain.

"Patterson's project," Dalton said. "I was sent to make sure it really was a prototype community for migrant workers."

Hunt nodded in slow motion. "Right. I got a call. Someone is coming. Tomorrow." He tugged his hair. "His name is Mr. Drummond."

Dalton unclasped his hands and sat up, keeping on a level with Hunt. "There is no Mr. Drummond, Mr. Sanderson, and I'm here tonight. I posed as Drummond when I met with Patterson. It's a long story, and I apologize for the charade."

After another pause, Hunter rubbed his neck again, then worked his shoulders. His posture straightened and some light returned to his eyes. "You're not investigating me, are you? It's Patterson?"

"I said I'd be straight with you, and I meant it. I'm investigating the project. If there's anything unusual going on, I'll follow it back wherever it leads. If it's to you, I'll have to report it."

Miri watched Hunt, waiting for him to bristle at the hint of impropriety. Instead, he nodded like a wise old man on a mountaintop. He stroked his stubbly chin as if it were a full grown beard. "I see." He rose from the couch, back straight, shoulders square. "I'll get the coffee."

★ ★ ★ ★ ★

Dalton followed Sanderson and Miri into the pristine kitchen. Aside from brewing coffee, the man probably hadn't fixed himself a meal since he realized Nancy was gone. While Sanderson brought cups out of a cabinet next to the sink, Dalton opened the refrigerator.

"We've been on the road awhile," he said. "Would it be all right if I raided your refrigerator?" Without waiting for an answer, he pulled out a carton of eggs, butter, and milk.

Miri gave him a nod of understanding and found a bowl and frying pan. "Let me help Dalton. Hunt, why don't you sit down?" She lowered two slices of bread into the toaster. By the time Dalton cooked the eggs, she'd finished toasting more bread and located plates. From a drawer, she found silverware and set three places at the table.

Dalton put a plate piled with scrambled eggs and toast in front of Sanderson. If he noticed that his portion was triple the size of Dalton's or Miri's, he didn't say anything. Once he swallowed the first bite, he devoured the rest in silence.

"Dalton's a wizard with scrambled eggs, isn't he?" Miri said when Sanderson finished the last morsel on his plate. "I'll bet you feel better."

To his surprise, Sanderson cleared the table and filled the sink with soapy water.

"Nancy hates coming home to dirty dishes," he said. "I hired a housekeeper when I first got here, but her kids were sick, so Nancy gave her the week off."

Miri moved to get up, but Dalton stayed her with a hand to her shoulder. He joined Sanderson at the sink, picking up a towel and drying.

"I have to ask this straight out, Mr. Sanderson. Please don't take offense," Dalton said. "You and Nancy—"

Sanderson responded immediately, as if he anticipated the

question. "No. I said it before. We weren't having marital problems. Coming here was something she wanted." He wiped the side of his nose with the back of a soapy hand. "She was like a kid again."

Dalton tilted his head at Miri, silently asking if she detected anything off in his tone, his words. She shook her head.

"Good," he said. "That narrows our search since we can assume she's not running or hiding. Where have you checked? Have you called anyone? The local cops?"

Sanderson snorted and spun around, scattering droplets of water. "Sure. The police chief himself came out, off duty, in his fancy clothes and new Lexus. Like I'd called him away from something *important*. 'You know, Mr. Sanderson, this was a big change for your wife. Dragging her down here away from all her people. She's a grown woman, Mr. Sanderson. You can file a report if you insist, Mr. Sanderson, but if it'll make you rest easier, I suppose I could put a lookout order on her car.' The whole time he's eyeing me as if I'm either a wife-beater or a cuckold. The man probably couldn't find his ass with both hands and a GPS."

Miri's chin dropped and her eyes widened. Maybe she didn't know Hunter Sanderson as well as she thought.

"I drove around, looked for her car. Checked the new community center. I called the hospitals, too," Sanderson said, a trace of relief in his voice. "She hasn't been admitted anywhere around here."

"Could she have been with friends?" he asked. "You said there were some sick kids. Maybe she ended up taking them to the hospital."

"She'd have called," Miri said emphatically.

Sanderson nodded. "Cell reception around here can be erratic, but if she was anywhere with a land line, she'd have used it if her cell wasn't working. Besides, she hasn't had a lot of time to make friends. She talked to some of the workers, trying to get a feel for what they wanted, but we haven't been here long enough for her to start much socializing." He rubbed the back of his neck. "This isn't the luncheon crowd."

"So where could she be? What do we do?" Miri looked back and forth between Dalton and Sanderson. "If someone took her, wouldn't they call? Send a ransom note? She could be lying in a ditch somewhere."

Dalton flinched at Miri's outburst. Sanderson blanched.

"I should have done more. I . . . God." He sank to a chair and buried his face in his hands. Dalton gave him the privacy he needed, shaking his head at Miri. She understood his silent admonition and mouthed, "Sorry."

Sanderson spoke, his voice muffled through his fingers. "I thought . . . maybe, maybe the chief . . . that there was a grain of truth . . . maybe . . . maybe she was with someone. I hadn't called her until very late. She could have been angry, gone off to teach me a lesson. I don't know why. She's not the vindictive sort. And—" he looked up, red-faced "—and the way I was brought up, we don't air our little domestic squabbles in public. I convinced myself she'd be back this morning. Then by lunch. When she missed dinner, I started to panic, and that's when I called Miri." He turned toward her, pleading and apologetic. "I thought she might have confided in you—told you what she was doing."

Dalton took a breath that started at his toes, then slowly blew it out. "Okay, Mr. Sanderson." He rested his hand on the man's shoulder. "Hunter. Let's figure out what we're going to do."

Sanderson dried his hands, folded the towel, and slipped it through the handle on the oven door. "Let me use the john, and I'll be right back."

"She's in trouble, isn't she?" Miri whispered after Sanderson left the kitchen. "She and Hunt might disagree about stuff, but they don't *fight*. She wouldn't run away even if they did."

Of course not. After a childhood of abandonment, neither sister would leave someone they loved. He almost wished it was a domestic issue. It might make it harder to find Nancy because she wouldn't want to be found, but she'd be safe. The pain in Miri's eyes jabbed him in the gut. He enveloped her in a tight embrace, inhaling the scent from her hair.

"You have to be strong, darlin'. We're going to deal with this." He released her and guided her to the living room. "But I'm gonna need some more information."

"Like what?"

He heard Sanderson's approach. "Later," he whispered.

Sanderson sat on the edge of the armchair. Dalton took a seat across from him on the couch, with Miri claiming the other end. Dalton recognized the blank expression on Sanderson's face. It usually meant someone admitted defeat. When it was one of the bad guys, it was a welcome sight. Now it sent an almost palpable feeling of despair through the room.

"First thing," Dalton said, "is to forget anything about pride. No making up stories, no hemming and hawing. She's missing, you want to find her, and you'll take help where you can get it. No matter what kind of looks people give you. No matter what they might be thinking."

"I understand," Sanderson said.

"Okay. Let's start with your police chief. What's his name?"

"McClusky."

"First name?" He'd have Zeke run a background check.

"Al. Not sure if it's Albert or Alfred. Hell, could be Algernon for all I know. He's always saying, 'Call me Al.' "

"All right. I'll see what I can find out."

"The cops aren't doing anything, are they?" Miri said.

"I doubt it," Sanderson said. Bitterness filled his tone.

"Unfortunately," Dalton said, "there's no legal reason the

cops are obliged to follow up on a missing adult in good physical and mental health. There's no law saying a person has to tell anyone when she picks up and leaves, whether it's for a trip to the grocery store or for good. So even if he's a jerk, McClusky hasn't violated the letter of the law."

Miri leaned forward, her jaw muscle clenching. "What works to our advantage at Galloway House doesn't help on this side," she said. "Most abused women are glad the cops don't come rushing as soon as they leave."

Dalton directed his attention to Sanderson. "I work for a company with a lot of resources," he said. "I can use some of them."

"Of course," Sanderson said. "Do whatever it takes. I should have done more already."

"I have to be honest," Dalton said. "It's not going to be cheap."

Sanderson didn't blink. "Whatever it takes."

Dalton's phone trilled. He pulled it from his belt, glanced at the display, then lifted the phone to his ear. "Zeke. Whatcha got?" He frowned at the garbled response. "You're breaking up, man. Where are you?"

"It's this end," Sanderson said. "Try the front yard by the sycamore tree."

He nodded. "Be with you in a second, Zeke." He opened the front door and stepped onto the drive, almost colliding with a small figure racing toward the house.

"Whoa, little lady. Take it easy."

She sidestepped, as if he was a minor obstacle in her path, and bounded up the stairs. "Miss Nancy," she called, her voice ragged over her heavy breathing. "*Donde esta* Miss Nancy?"

"Hang tight, Zeke." He opened the front door. "Miri?"

CHAPTER 24

At the sound of her name, Miri jumped from the couch. A girl, not more than twelve, she estimated, raced into the room, sweeping it with a frantic gaze.

"Carmen. What are you doing here? It's the middle of the night." Hunter was on his feet, gripping the girl's shoulders, trying to calm her.

"Roberto." She gasped for air.

"Her younger brother," Hunt explained. "What about Roberto?"

"He is very sick." Carmen struggled to get the words and catch her breath at the same time. "Mama. Sent me. Get. Miss Nancy."

Miri dashed to the kitchen and returned with a glass of water for the child. Carmen drained the glass, then shook her head. "Mama says Roberto needs the clinic. He coughs so much and has a big fever. Mama can't wake him. She asks if Miss Nancy can drive."

Miri's instincts waged a battle. Taking the child to a doctor would draw her away from Nancy. "Is there anyone else who could take him?"

"No. Mama has tried. No one can help."

"How far is it to the hospital?" Miri asked.

"The emergency clinic is about fifteen miles away," Hunt said. "There's a small hospital attached, but the nearest major facility is at least an hour from here."

Hunt buried his face in his hands. When he looked up, his entire demeanor changed. He was calm, in charge. "Carmen, wait here." Back straight, he strode into the kitchen.

Miri crouched to meet Carmen at eye level. "Hi, Carmen. I'm Miri. I'm Nancy's sister."

The girl gave her a nervous smile, her gaze following Hunt.

Miri took Carmen's hand and led her to the couch. "Sit for a minute. He'll be right back."

The girl nodded, wide-eyed, but seemed grateful for the shift in responsibility.

"When did you see Nancy, Carmen?"

"Two days, I think. Maybe three?" She lowered her eyes. "I am sorry, I do not remember."

Miri sat beside the child and held her hands. "Did she tell you anything about what she was doing? Anything she was working on? Anyplace she might be going?"

Carmen gave her head a rapid shake. "I know she goes to the old center. She asked everyone what we want." Her eyes lit up. "She said we will have a new center. With many books, like the library. And computers."

"Do you like school?" Stupid question. What kid did?

"Yes," Carmen said. "Mama says if I finish school, I can have a better life than picking. Only Papa goes to the fields, and he is north. There is more work."

Hunt returned and flashed a smile. "Carmen, I called Doctor Gerardo Montero. He's a good friend of mine. He's going to go to your house and examine Roberto and decide if he needs to go to the hospital."

Carmen stood, her hands clasped at her waist. "Thank you, *Señor* Sanderson. I must go home, to help Mama." She walked toward the door.

"Wait," Hunt said. "You can't walk back, not alone. I'll drive you." He slid his eyes toward the kitchen, as if willing the phone to ring. "I've got my cell, Miri, if someone calls."

"I'll go. You wait here. You said half the time there's no decent cell reception. I won't be long." She squeezed him in a quick embrace.

Carmen darted out the door and Miri followed. She passed Dalton as he paced, cell to his ear, under the sycamore tree. Dalton said something into the phone, then lowered it. "What happened?"

"Her brother's sick. Hunt called a doctor friend. I'm running Carmen home." She shooed Carmen toward the Escalade. "Get in the car." Turning back to Dalton, she said, "I've got my cell. Did you find out anything?"

"Zeke's working on it." He traced her jaw, and a warm glow ran through her at the understanding transmitted in his touch.

"I won't be long."

"Go," he said. "There's nothing you can do here."

Wandering the front yard, Dalton focused on Zeke's words, not Miri.

"No reports of the Sanderson woman's car," Zeke was saying. "Nothing in the local cop shops or county sheriff's office."

"Damn it, Zeke, don't tell me what you didn't find. There's got to be something."

"Sorry, man. Nothing on the missing woman. But I did find some murmurs about your Patterson guy."

Dalton stopped mid-step. "What?"

"Seems the contractors he's hiring have less than a blue ribbon reputation. Although technically, he's not hiring them, but he owns the company that is. Hobart Construction."

"So he's cutting corners on code? What's that supposed to mean?"

"Chill. I poked around his financial holdings. Found some interesting stuff."

"Cut to the chase, Zeke. I'm working on no sleep here."

"Some of the companies have legitimate reasons for purchasing large quantities of chemicals used in the production of methamphetamines."

Dalton leaned against the sycamore tree. "You're shittin' me. Patterson is into drugs?"

"That's the easy answer."

"Holy crap."

"You do have a way with words."

"Anything on Chief McClusky?"

"Still digging. His surface finances check out, commensurate with his salary."

"Below the surface?"

"Working on it. But I'd bet the next round of beer that he's got a nice secondary income source. I'll get back to you."

"Thanks, Zeke. Keep digging." He pressed the end call button and dashed for the house. He flung the door open. "Sanderson. What do you know about drugs? Meth in particular."

Sanderson bolted upright on the couch, rubbing his eyes. He grunted something. "Guess I dozed off." He jumped to his feet, apparently remembering. "Did you find Nancy?"

"Drugs, Sanderson. What do you know about them?"

"I'm not on drugs. And I don't deal. What are you talking about?"

"Scuttlebutt has it that Patterson's been investing in companies that could have ties to meth production."

"Meth?" Sanderson said. "Of course, there's a lot of poverty here, and I'm not going to pretend drug use isn't going on, but meth usually comes across the border already made. Why would Patterson be manufacturing it?"

"I didn't say he was. It's one more thing to look at. The border's been beefed up. Harder to get the drugs across. Back in San Francisco, they're paying indigents to go from store to store, buying allergy meds. You see anything like that here?"

Sanderson shook his head. "I can't see that working. Most of the people go to the free clinics. There are only two or three places in town where they could buy meds, and they wouldn't be driving to another town. Most of them don't have cars. In season, they're bussed to the fields and brought home at the end of the day." He drew his hands across his face. "These are poor people, but from what I can see, most of them are trying to make an honest wage. If they were doing anything else, why bother picking? And what could this have to do with Nancy?"

"Beats me." He stifled a yawn. "I worked all day, and we've been driving since this afternoon. I'm going to crash for half an hour. Zeke'll call if he finds anything. Why don't you try to get some sleep?"

"I couldn't." He walked around the desk, straightened books on a shelf, moved the desk lamp so it was perfectly centered.

Dalton recognized the symptoms of helplessness. "You're no good to anyone if you're exhausted. Grab a shower. Go lie down. I'll take the couch."

Sanderson hesitated.

"Trust me. This is what I do, Sanderson. Go. I'll wake you if I hear anything."

"I guess a shower would be good." He gave a weak laugh. "I'm probably rank."

Experience told him Sanderson willingly relinquished control. Let someone else be in charge. Which also meant someone else could take the blame if things hit the fan. Sanderson trudged out of the room. Dalton clenched his jaw. Nothing would hit the fan. Not on his watch.

He headed for the couch and a combat nap. As he lay down, he remembered his fourteen hour journey through oblivion at Miri's. Not this time. Setting his internal clock for thirty minutes, he closed his eyes and sank into immediate sleep.

Headlights jerked him awake. A glance at his watch told him he'd been out twelve minutes. It would have to do. He got to his feet and crossed to the window. Sanderson's Escalade drove into the carport. Exhaustion and stress couldn't keep the smile from his lips as he went to greet Miri.

The kitchen door flew open and she stomped inside. "Any news on Nancy?"

"Not yet," he said, holding her by the shoulders. "Is there any chance—any remote chance at all—that Nancy would be involved with drugs?"

Miri stiffened and pulled away, eyes flashing. "Nancy use drugs? Absolutely not."

"Whoa, darlin'. Calm down. That's not what I meant. Would she be trying to work *against* drugs if she found people using them?"

She sank onto one of the kitchen chairs. He stepped behind her and massaged her neck.

"God, that feels good," she said, dropping her head. He moved his fingers outward, kneading the taut muscles. She whimpered. "This isn't what we were supposed to be doing tonight, is it?"

No, damn it, it wasn't. He bent and kissed her neck. "Life happens, darlin'."

She spun around in the chair. "It sure does. Nancy and drugs? After all the anti-drug lectures she gave me as a kid? Yeah, she'd take it upon herself to do something. In a heartbeat. You think that's why she's missing?" Concern clouded her features.

"It's all we have to go on. If someone wanted her because she's rich, they'd have been in touch."

"So, what do we do?" She craned her neck toward the doorway. "Hunt's got to have ideas."

"Wait a minute." He pulled a chair around and straddled it.

"There's another angle we haven't considered."

"What angle?"

He lowered his voice. "What if this is connected to Nancy's past? Could she have any secrets that might be valuable to someone?"

"I don't see how. We were anything but valuable."

"Hunt doesn't know about your pasts?"

"Not unless Nancy said something in the last week. I know she felt guilty about not confiding in Hunt, but she always thought if his family knew, the consequences would be worse than the guilt."

"I need you to tell me." He braced himself for her indignant refusal.

"You won't tell Hunt?"

Taken aback by her response, he rewound his planned counterargument. "No. That would be your call."

"No, it's Nancy's call." She glanced toward the doorway again, then stood. "Let's go outside."

He followed her to the sycamore tree, more determined than ever to find her sister. That she'd confide such a well-guarded secret reinforced how frightened she must be. She sat on the ground, leaning against the tree. He lowered himself to her side, curling her into him. The half-full moon cast silver shadows as a breeze ruffled leaves under the clear night sky.

"Her name was Rayna. Another *Star Trek* name." She picked up a twig and toyed with the dirt beneath the tree. "Rayna was the robot woman from 'Requiem for Methuselah,' if you remember your Trek. Kirk fell in love with her."

"I remember. The Roman soldier who couldn't die. Keep going."

"We were born in a little town about fifty miles from New Orleans. Belle Vista. I already told you what our childhood was like. After Dad went to prison, Mom moved us to New Orleans and things went from lousy to miserable. Nance and I survived. When we moved to California, Nancy changed her name from Rayna Kozwalski to Nancy Crater."

He tried to make the connection, but couldn't. "Another *Star Trek* episode?"

She nodded against his chest. " 'Man Trap.' The first episode ever aired. Nancy was this creature who could change her appearance and be what people expected."

"Right. The salt monster." He smiled as he recalled the creature's grotesque appearance and compared it with Nancy's sleek good looks.

"Yeah. Nancy liked the chameleon idea. I wanted to keep Miri, but I took Chambers as a last name. Nancy thought it would be better not to be sisters on paper."

"You're losing me. Are you hiding your relationship to Nancy?"

"Not exactly. Anybody asks, we say we had different fathers."

"Okay. One last thing." He snuggled her closer, enjoying her softness. "Aside from wanting to get a fresh start, was Nancy hiding something—anything else—as Rayna?"

Miri ran her fingers over his knee. "I can't think of anything special. Our whole lives were about hiding in those days. We were poor, we broke some laws, but nothing on a grand scale. We wanted to eat, not get rich."

"Could revenge be a motive?"

"Revenge? I can't imagine anyone being pissed enough to track us down over the loss of a few bucks or a watch. Not after all these years."

"All right." He stood, helping her up. "I'm going to see what Zeke can do with this information."

She stiffened, then slumped. "I suppose you have to."

"He'll be discreet, and nobody's going to find out what he knows except me."

She blinked those golden-brown eyes, and in the moonlight, fear shimmered from their depths.

"It'll be fine, darlin'." He embraced her, tipping her face up and lowering his. His lips brushed her forehead. She wrapped her arms around him, her heart pounding. Her soft breasts pressed against his chest. The pre-op rush and the warm female curves in his embrace undid him. With a subdued groan, he cradled her face, pressing his mouth to hers. He slid the tip of his tongue across her lower lip. Her lips parted, accepting him. She returned his gentleness with an urgent need. He allowed the kiss to deepen, matching her urgency with his. Too soon, he pulled away, running the tip of his finger across her mouth where his lips had been.

"Go get your brother-in-law."

CHAPTER 25

Miri didn't bother knocking on Hunt's bedroom door before opening it. She found him sprawled on his belly on top of the bedcovers, a towel beside his naked body, the lamp on. She stopped. Turned away. Cleared her throat. For an instant, she regretted waking him, thinking this was probably the first time he'd rested since he discovered Nancy was missing. But only for an instant. He might hold the key to finding her.

"Hunt. Wake up." She hovered in the doorway.

"Huh?" He jerked awake, blinking against the lamplight. "You found her?" He raised himself to his elbows.

"No. Dalton thinks there's a drug connection."

"Nancy doesn't do drugs." He fumbled for the towel. She averted her eyes while he wrapped it around his hips.

"I know. That's not it. Dalton's checking with his people. Get dressed and come out to the living room." She backed toward the door.

"Wear something black," Dalton called from the other room.

"What?" Hunt said. He scrubbed his hands over his face.

"Black," Dalton repeated. "Harder to see in the dark."

"Got it," Hunt said, not questioning Dalton's request.

At Dalton's touch, she spun around. "Do you *always* have to sneak up on people?" Behind her, the door closed.

"You have anything black with you?" he asked, ignoring her retort.

She thought through what she'd stuck in her bag and shook

her head. "No. Jeans and some tops. I think there's a dark green one."

"Black is better. Can you borrow something?" He pushed past her, tapping on the door before thrusting it open.

Hunt wore black denims and was slipping a long-sleeved black jersey over his head. She stepped into the room. "Hunt, I'm going to raid Nancy's wardrobe, okay?"

He pointed her to a small walk-in closet. She pulled a pair of black jeans off a hanger. In the dresser, she found an assortment of shirts in basic black. She selected a long-sleeved silk turtleneck and a heavier polo. She held them both up for Dalton's approval.

"Layer them," he said, then disappeared.

She gathered everything into the bathroom and got ready. For what? Her sister was missing, there was something going on with drugs, and she was going out at two in the morning because a man she'd known barely two weeks said so. She splashed her face with cold water and scrubbed it dry with one of Nancy's ultra-plush face towels.

Exhilaration erased any tiredness from her body. She should be afraid. Shaking, not tingling. Why?

The face in the mirror smiled. *Because Dalton won't let anything happen to you.*

A ridiculous assumption, but logic did nothing to wipe away the grin. Their kiss under the tree cemented her confidence that Dalton would make things right.

Dressed, she gave her reflection a quick salute and went to find the men.

Dalton stood in the living room wearing dark camouflage-patterned cargo pants and a matching shirt. He gave her a succinct once-over. "You have any black shoe-polish?" he asked Hunt.

Visions of smearing black goo over her face almost made her

laugh. "Are we playing soldier?" She put her fingers to her cheeks.

Dalton pointed at her sneakers. "For your shoes."

He'd changed from sneakers to black boots, she noticed.

"I'll get it," Hunt said. "Anything else?"

"You need something to cover your hair. Watch cap would be fine."

She noticed Hunt's blond hair, suddenly aware that it glistened in the low illumination of the living room lamp. She sobered. This wasn't a game.

Hunt left, then came back with a roll-on bottle of black shoe polish. She set to painting it over her scuffed but clearly white sneakers. No biggie. Almost time for a new pair anyway.

"No cap here—we didn't bring much stuff," Hunt said.

"Hooded sweatshirt?" Dalton asked.

Hunt shook his head. "It's white."

"I've got a cap with my gear," Dalton said, then faced her. "Put your hair up."

Nerves fluttering, she dashed back into the bathroom and rifled through the drawers. She found clips to secure her hair in a twist atop her head. Her fingers trembled, and a clip bounced from her hands to the floor behind the wastebasket.

"Damn." She toed the plastic container out of the way, tipping it over in the process. "Double damn." Reality set in, undermining some of the confidence of Dalton's kiss. A sudden need to use the facilities hit. She hurried to replace the contents of the wastebasket, gathering the usual assorted cotton balls, swabs, and lipstick-smeared tissues, before her hand rested on an empty box. She picked it up, automatically checking the label. She froze. A pregnancy test. She let the box fall back into the basket as an ice ball formed in her stomach.

When she finished, Hunt was waiting in the bedroom. He gave her a weak grin as he stepped toward the bathroom.

"Nerves," he said.

She took his elbow. "Hunt, there's a pregnancy test kit in the trash. Was . . . is she . . . are you—?"

His face went parchment pale. "We think so." He shook out of her grasp and hurried into the bathroom, kicking the door closed behind him.

Moments later, they assembled in Dalton's Navigator. Hunter protested, saying his car was less likely to arouse suspicion since he often drove through the area. Dalton vetoed it, pointing out that was exactly why they shouldn't take it.

"Until we know who has her and why, you're going to have to be invisible," he said. "Assuming someone does have her. Let's not show our hand yet. Miri, take the back. Sanderson, you ride shotgun and navigate."

Dalton assumed control. His drawl barely evident, he spoke as though he was a general commanding his troops. Which she and Hunt were, she figured. Hunt seemed more than willing to accept Dalton's leadership. She climbed into her seat and buckled up next to a large green duffel bag. "Ready. Let's go."

"Before we leave," Hunt said, "I want to know everything you know."

A muscle in Dalton's jaw clenched.

"Damn it," Hunt continued. "She's my wife. She might be carrying my child."

Dalton smacked the steering wheel. His head snapped toward Hunt. "You're both happy about it?"

"Of course we are." Hunt's voice bristled with resentment. "What kind of a question is that?"

Dalton lowered his head to the wheel. Putting aside her anxiety to get going and find Nancy, Miri reached around the seat and patted Hunt's shoulder. "He has to ask. He has to consider all the possibilities."

"Sorry, man." Dalton said. "Miri's right. If she didn't want a kid, that could mean she went off somewhere to—you know. Over and done before you got back, and you'd never be the wiser."

When Hunt spoke, it was a whisper. "No. She—we—wanted this. Want this."

"Hey, that's a good thing. Like Miri said, I have to consider everything. Sometimes it's the ugly side, but it's nothing personal. We're going to find her. Zeke's been checking. He said her credit cards haven't been used, and no hits on any ATMs."

"How is that good?" Miri asked. "All you've got is what she isn't doing, or where she isn't."

"Eliminating possibilities," Dalton said. "Increases the odds she's around here somewhere, not quite so many places to look."

"Speaking of looking," Hunt said. "Where are we going dressed like cat burglars?"

"We'll start with where she'd most likely be and work out from there. You said she was busy planning the new community center. Anywhere else she went regularly?"

"Maybe the old center," Hunt said. "Beyond that, I wouldn't know. She hasn't been here long enough to do anything *regularly.* And I checked both those places."

"Let's check again," Dalton said, starting the engine. "Which is closer?"

"The old center," Hunt said. "It's about two miles from the trailer park. Some of the older kids hang there."

When they got to the main road, Dalton killed the lights. Miri's heart thumped as her stress level kicked up another few notches. As if he sensed her unease, Dalton reached over the seat. She took his hand, strength flowing into her like an IV infusion. When he let go, a butterscotch candy lay in her palm.

Dalton centered himself, slowed his breathing, let his eyes adjust to the dim light. As his SUV bounced along the poorly paved road, Blackie's words bounced in his head. *Don't need any cowboys.* Was that what he was doing? Playing cowboy because Blackie grounded him?

No, he was being careful. Nancy was missing in an environment where the worst-case scenario kept popping to the surface. Poverty, drugs, maybe a police chief on the take. What else?

"What's the immigration situation here?" he asked. "A lot of coyotes?"

"Coyotes?" Miri asked from behind him.

"People smugglers," Sanderson said. "They sneak groups of people across the border, taking all their money, promising them a better life in the states. The death rate is astronomical, but the coyotes don't really care. They get the money up front."

"That's terrible," she said.

"The people are desperate," Dalton said. "They figure they've got nothing to lose. Unfortunately, too often they're wrong, and what they lose are their lives. Crossing the desert is tough even for an experienced survivalist."

"And a lot of these poor souls try it in the heat of summer." Sanderson swiveled to involve Miri in the discussion. "Since they started requiring passports at points of entry, more people who might have entered on a fake ID are resorting to paying coyotes."

"What about the people who work the fields around here?" Miri asked.

"Most of them have been working the same fields for years. I don't know how they got into the country initially, and that's not what I'm here for. I'm simply supervising the construction for Patterson's project and trying to raise a little public support."

Dalton heard the unspoken, "Don't ask, don't tell."

"There aren't many people left, though," Sanderson continued. "A lot found jobs at the aquaculture plants near Mecca."

Miri leaned forward. "Carmen said her father's up north."

"That's another place they've gone," Sanderson said. "It's a vicious cycle—the growers can't get pickers because the living conditions are horrifically sub-standard, so the pickers go somewhere else, and the crops rot. They lose money, so they can't afford to improve living conditions. They don't plant as much and don't need as many pickers. Patterson hopes by providing better living conditions, he can break the cycle. More planting, more crops, more pickers."

Sounded a lot like Patterson propaganda. On the surface, it made sense, but would it actually come to fruition? Dalton winced at his pun.

"There," Hunt said. "On the left."

Dalton stopped about twenty yards away, under a small stand of trees where the SUV wouldn't be visible from the road. "This was the community center?" The small concrete-block building screamed abandoned, from the dark, broken windows to the sagging roof. "Center of what?" There was nothing around.

"The old trailer park," Sanderson said. "The former owner hauled all the trailers away about five years ago. Sold 'em for scrap is my guess. This was the only permanent structure. Technically, it's condemned, but the older kids—hell, probably some of the younger ones—still come by," Sanderson said. "They hang around the old playground out back."

Dealing drugs, Dalton thought. "Why would Nancy come here?"

"I know she came by at least once to see for herself what the conditions were like, to meet the kids, get their input for the new place," Sanderson said. His voice caught. "Damn it, she was busy. I was busy. She was excited, I could tell, but we never sat down for the 'what did you do today, dear?' stuff. We usually saved that for Sunday mornings. If . . . if we'd made more time."

"Hey, shouldn't we go in?" Miri said, clearly trying to pull

Sanderson's thoughts away from any guilt.

Sanderson cleared his throat. "Yeah. But I've got to warn you. The inside's disgusting."

"What's the layout?" Dalton asked Sanderson.

"You walk into one main room. Two bathrooms in the back on the left, but I wouldn't recommend going near them, and a small kitchen on the right. I haven't been here since I first arrived. Nothing but junk inside."

"Miri," Dalton said. "There should be a couple of flashlights in the duffel." He turned to Sanderson. "And there's one in the glove box."

Sanderson leaned forward. "Got it."

"Wait," Dalton said as both flicked on their lights. "Let me make sure we're alone first." He hadn't seen any signs that anyone was using the building, but if they were, they'd have heard the car. He reached over the seat to Miri. "Hand me the penlight, darlin'."

She put it in his hand like a scrub nurse handing a doctor a scalpel. "Wouldn't the big one be better?"

"Not until I do some basic recon. I won't be long." He spoke to Sanderson, lowering his voice. "I'll flash the light two times if it's okay to join me. Three times, and you haul ass. Keys are in the ignition." The man nodded his understanding.

Miri spoke up. "Pretend I'm not here, why don't you? Don't want to scare the little lady?" Sarcasm coated her tone, but he heard fear underneath.

"Merely a precaution," Dalton said. He killed the dome light and let himself out, leaving the door ajar. Sanderson crawled over the console into the driver's seat.

Once he was away from the car, Dalton took the Glock from the pocket of his cargo pants and tucked it into his belt. Using the faint moonlight for guidance, he stole along the edge of the road toward the building. Someone had locked the front door.

He stifled a laugh. A credit card would open it with no trouble. He worked his way around the structure, alert to any motion, but sensed nothing. The pong of ammonia assailed his nostrils as he passed under the two small bathroom windows. He continued his way around the perimeter.

In the backyard, he froze at the sight of what appeared to be a monster camouflaged by shadows. A high-pitched screeching sound cut through the normal night noises. He drew his Glock and crept toward the apparition.

Chiding himself when the monster morphed into a playground slide and the sound came from a rusty swing set in motion by the breeze, he did an about face. Time to go inside.

Boards covered all but the two bathroom windows, which were too small for him to squeeze through. He tried the back door, not surprised it was unlocked.

A cursory sweep of the space revealed nothing but debris and detritus. Holding his breath, he checked the two bathrooms. Empty, but obviously used long after the plumbing stopped working. Nobody in the kitchen. He toed the cabinet doors open. Four eyes glowed from under the sink. Two cats darted past. He unlocked the front door and flashed his light twice in the direction of his SUV. Almost instantaneously, two shapes emerged, jogging side by side.

"Did you find anything?" Sanderson whispered.

"Aside from a playground set masquerading as a Tyrannosaurus, not much. Why don't you see if anything belongs to Nancy."

Sanderson took the big Maglite from Miri. He moved from one pile of junk to the next, kicking aside fast-food bags, cups, mold-encrusted tin cans, an old sneaker, and other assorted discards. Miri coughed. Small wonder. The stench was enough to make your eyes water. Miri stayed with Sanderson, and Dalton went to give the kitchen a closer look.

A broken camp stove suggested squatters might have used

the room. He poked through a pile of rags. Some lengths of rubber tubing. No doubt people used the place to shoot up. Aware he'd grown careless, he stopped using his fingers and moved things with his feet. No need to get stabbed with a used needle. Shit, he should warn Miri and Sanderson.

"Watch out for needles," he called. "This is a hype hangout."

When he got no reply, he went back to find them. Sanderson knelt on the floor, staring at his clenched fist. Miri crouched beside him, her hand on his shoulder.

He rushed to them. "You find something?"

Sanderson opened his palm. Miri shone the light. Something sparkled in his hand.

"Nancy's bracelet," Sanderson said, holding up a length of gold links. His voice was a hoarse whisper. "I kept telling her to get the clasp fixed." He pressed his fingers to his temples.

Dalton's head throbbed. Damn. Where were his brains? "Outside. Both of you. Back to the car. Now!"

CHAPTER 26

The urgency in Dalton's tone sent Miri running. Footfalls drummed behind her. At the Navigator, her heart pounded more from fear than exertion. She spun around to see Dalton half-supporting a stumbling Hunt.

Another wave of adrenaline crashed over her. "What's wrong? Hunt, are you hurt?"

"I'm okay." He pulled away, coughing, and craned his neck toward the structure. "Nancy."

"She's not inside, man," Dalton said. He grabbed Hunt's shoulders. "That's what matters."

"But . . . what if she left something else?" Hunt shrugged away from Dalton's grasp. "There could be more evidence. Maybe . . . maybe she tried to leave some kind of clue."

Dalton leaned against the car's fender. Miri's first rational thought was Dalton discovered a bomb, but if so, they'd be halfway home by now, not standing under the trees.

Okay, too much thinking, none of which was giving her answers. "Why did you rush us out here?"

Dalton's shadowed hands ran across his face, as if he was pulling down a shade. She'd bet his expression would be unreadable in bright sunlight.

"Crap," he muttered, pushing past her to get something from his duffel. He used the penlight long enough for her to see it was a large bandana. "This place is a health hazard."

"Yeah," she said. "It stank."

He shook out the bandana and folded it into a triangle. "I should have caught it sooner, but I thought it was the plumbing. Someone's been cooking meth in there, and my guess is it was used fairly recently."

Miri's breath caught. "Meth?" Something tickled and teased at a long-buried memory that refused to surface.

"No question in my mind," Dalton said. "And my next guess is there are enough residual chemicals to be dangerous. How long has it been empty, Sanderson?"

"Can't say for sure. I know it's been shut down for months. That's one of the reasons the community center is top priority for Nancy. Patterson agreed, I think, because construction was almost done when I arrived."

"You'd think he'd have wanted to get the homes done first," she said. "What's the point of a community center if there's no community to use it?"

"He wanted to show the locals his commitment, and keep the growers optimistic. Trying to keep the town alive." Hunt yanked his cap off and threw it to the ground. "But enough of this—we're wasting time."

Dalton bent to retrieve Hunt's cap. "One minute. Sanderson, you and I will go back in, look and leave. Fast. You see something that might be a clue, it comes outside. Grab first, check later." He rested his hand on Miri's shoulder. "You stay here, darlin'."

She almost protested, but the thought of going back in there even if it *wasn't* a health hazard turned her stomach. And the elusive memory set her nerves on edge. "Yes, sir," she said, adding enough sarcasm to disguise her relief.

"You're on lookout," he told her. "If anyone approaches, drive to the community center and pick us up. No lights."

"Why not move the car closer?" Miri asked.

"Can't see enough from there because of the curve in the

road. From here, you can watch both the road and the building and be out of anyone's line of sight."

Made sense, but she felt like a sitting duck alone out here. "You're the boss," she muttered.

Dalton handed Hunt the bandana. "Cover your nose and mouth." Dalton hitched his shirt up to cover the lower half of his own face. "Keep as much of your skin covered as possible. Even residual chemicals can cause nasty burns. Miri, there are latex gloves in the duffel. Outside pocket. Cardboard box."

She found the box and held the flashlight while the men donned the gloves. "Hurry back," she said.

Dalton tugged the shirt from his face and kissed her forehead. "Warp speed."

"Transporter would be better." Her skin tingled where his stubble rubbed. She savored the sensation as they jogged away, trying to ignore the sense of abandonment. She climbed into the driver's seat. Inhaling deeply to calm herself, she noticed there wasn't a hint of sandalwood in the car anymore. Only sweat and chemicals.

She sniffed again. Cooking meth, Dalton said. She knew that smell. But from where?

Relax. Don't try so hard. It'll come to you. Do your job.

She twisted in the seat, leaned out the window, trying to scan in all directions, wondering if she'd notice anyone if they didn't arrive by car. Her fingers found the keys hanging from the ignition. She pretended to turn them, rehearsing in case they needed her. Her feet barely reached the pedals, so she adjusted the seat.

Another look at the path. Nothing. Her gaze continued to the house. A flashlight's glow shone from a window, then disappeared. She sent mental messages.

Hurry. We have to find Nancy. Get away from those chemicals.

A ripple of fear snaked down her spine with the memory of a mother and three kids who'd shown up at Galloway House.

They'd run from a home where her husband cooked meth. They'd been hospitalized for several days before moving away to live with the woman's aunt somewhere in the desert. And something about one of the kids' severe liver damage. Or was it kidneys?

How long had Nancy been inside? Maybe someone stole Nancy's bracelet and dropped it, and Nancy had never been here at all.

But, dear God, what if she had been, and what if she *was* pregnant? What about the baby? She'd barely run the possibilities through her mind when she heard foliage rustling. She held her breath, straining to pinpoint and identify the sound. Her hand rested on the keys, her fingers twitching them to a soft jingle. She clamped them in her damp palm.

A small furry blur raced in front of the car. A larger furry blur followed. Cats? Foxes? Definitely animals. Telling herself it was normal night stuff, she took slow, even breaths, waiting for the adrenaline jolt to ease. That smell again. And this time, the memory came back. She closed her eyes.

She was six? Seven? She and Nancy. Dragged somewhere with Mom. A house? Apartment? It smelled like that. She was cold, tired. Her jacket wasn't warm enough. Underneath, she wore nothing but her pajamas. And there was a man with Mom. He smelled like that, too.

"You girls be good," Mom said. She'd shoved the two of them into a tiny bedroom. They huddled together on a single bed. No sheets. Just a scratchy blanket. Miri's skin itched with the memory. Noises from the other room, but Nancy sang, telling Miri to join in. "When the Saints Go Marching In."

When the noises stopped, Miri slept. She woke up when the man came in and pulled at her pajama bottoms. Nancy kicked him. Hard. In the place she'd told Miri to kick if someone tried to touch her wrong.

The man fell. He curled up on the floor like a dog. Nancy screamed for Mom, but she didn't come. Nancy dragged Miri outside, and they ran and ran until they couldn't run anymore, and then they hid in the alley until morning, and then they went home, and Mom was asleep on the couch.

Movement brought Miri back. Gasping, shaking, filmed in sweat, she wiped tears from her cheeks. Had they found Nancy? Please, let her be all right. She had to be all right.

Dalton and Hunt appeared on the path. No Nancy. Her heart sank. Both men walked upright, their strides sure and even, neither leaning on the other. She flung the door open, grabbed a flashlight, and rushed toward them.

"Did you find anything?" She played the light over their faces. Hunter squinted and covered his eyes with his arm. She lowered the beam to the ground. "Sorry."

"Nothing," Dalton said. "Let's go check out the other site."

She climbed into the backseat. Hunter wiped his face with the bandana. Before she fastened her seatbelt, the car sprung to life. Dalton hung a rapid three-point turn, spinning dirt and gravel. Thrown sideways, Miri grabbed the *oh shit* handle for balance. They drove without lights until they hit the road. She stared out the window. It seemed strange to see even the short distance illuminated by the headlights after being in darkness.

Dalton seemed calmer. At least his driving was. A muffled chinking sound came from the front seat. She peered around to see Hunt shifting Nancy's bracelet from one hand to the other. The brief glimpse of his face in the flashlight beam had ripped her heart. Afraid anything she said about Nancy's exposure to meth chemicals would destroy his control, she leaned forward and rested her hand on his arm. He pressed his hand atop hers and left it there. As they drove, she listened to the quiet clicks as he tossed the bracelet in his other hand.

Dalton pulled his eyes off the road to check his cell display. Crap, he'd gotten better reception in the middle of the jungle. "Here," he said, handing the phone to Sanderson. "Tell me when I can make a damn call."

"Should be fine around the next curve in the road."

"Who are you calling?" Miri asked from the backseat.

"Nobody, apparently." Where were the communications specialists, the folks who made sure everything worked? Not to mention the controller who would have a handle on all the pieces. Running an op as a civilian sucked.

"Got it," Sanderson said.

"Punch five," he said, swerving to avoid a pothole.

Sanderson obeyed and handed it back. Dalton held the phone to his ear, relieved when Zeke's voice sputtered through. "About time, Cowboy."

"Tell me you've got something, and make it good."

"Nothing on your woman. Yet. I've run all the hospitals within a hundred miles. No hits. Nothing on her car, either."

"So, what *do* you have?" He glanced at Sanderson, the man's face both eager and apprehensive. Another pothole caught him off guard and the car bounced. He wished for a headset so he could deal with driving. He considered the speaker setting on his cell but thought better of it. Sanderson deserved to know, but he might not understand the way Zeke parceled out information. To civilians, he'd come across as flip and uncaring. He tried flashing a brief smile at Sanderson but didn't think it reassured him.

Silence. Dalton checked the cell, which displayed one lousy bar. "Zeke?"

"What's going on?" Sanderson asked. "Have they found something?" His voice shook. Zeke's voice came back. Dalton raised a finger, signaling Sanderson to wait.

"I'm here, Cowboy. I got the results of some cross-reference searches. Seems a Wendy Grantham was arrested yesterday for smuggling at the border in Calexico."

"What does that have to do with—?" Wait. Grantham. The name rang a bell. Patterson's secretary. But she was Belinda. An alias? Before he could put the pieces together, Zeke continued.

"I got a hit because it matched someone in Patterson's office."

"Right. But—"

"Sisters," Zeke continued. "Border folks are very interested. She has a string of gift shops in San Diego, LA, and Santa Barbara. Sells cheap Mexican crafts. Apparently they found large quantities of allergy medications in her last batch of pots and baskets."

Too similar to what was going on in the Bay area. His eye twitched. "You think it could be connected to what I'm doing?"

"Too early to tell," Zeke said. "Hunter Sanderson works for Patterson. Belinda Grantham works for him, too. No stone unturned, but there are a lot of pebbles in the stream here."

He stared at Sanderson. No, he'd bet his next field assignment the man wasn't a drug smuggler. And if he was wrong, after he found Nancy, he'd kill him. But first, they needed to find Nancy.

"I could use some backup here."

"Figured," Zeke said. "I talked to the old man about it."

Dalton nearly dropped the phone. Zeke called Blackie in the middle of the night? He braced himself. He couldn't get much higher on Blackie's shit list. "What did he say?"

"He's mobilizing a team."

"What?"

"I told him what you told me. And that you had a client. Plus, I gave him some of the stuff I'd been digging out."

"And somebody was going to tell me this *when?*"

"Cool your jets. If you'd checked your missed calls, you'd have noticed we've been trying to reach you for the last . . . thirty-eight minutes."

Sanderson tapped on the window. "Right turn up there."

Sanderson's words registered. "Right. Right turn. Hang tight, Zeke. Give me a minute."

He set the phone in the console and made the turn, aware Miri was leaning as far forward as her seatbelt allowed. He inhaled, trying to erase some of the chemical stench with her fresh scent.

"What's going on?" Miri demanded. "Someone found something, didn't they?"

They entered a construction area near the sloping base of a range of rocky foothills. Land was bulldozed and graded; dirt roads wove through the complex, but there was only one building at the far end of the development, nestled near the hills. Trees and boulders stood scattered throughout. As if it wasn't cost-effective to move them. Not because the developer wanted to leave things in their natural state. If they could maneuver their equipment around them, they stayed.

He drove toward it, then slid the car next to a large Dumpster about thirty meters from the structure and shoved the gearshift into Park. "Maybe."

"God. God. Is she—?" Sanderson's voice was barely audible.

"Hey, don't go there." He unfastened his seatbelt and angled around so he could see both Sanderson and Miri. "Do you know a Wendy Grantham? Belinda's sister."

Sanderson gave him a blank stare.

"Belinda is Patterson's secretary," Dalton said.

A glimmer of recognition dawned. "We've met. Belinda, I mean. Briefly. In Patterson's office. She brought coffee. Never heard of Wendy. What does this have to do with Nancy?"

Damn, this was *not* what he did. He dealt with terrorists. Rescued hostages. Interrupted drug deals. Arms deals. He did *not* find missing wives and deal with terrified relatives. Someone else took care of that part of an op. He almost wished Nancy was inside the building, tied up, blindfolded, and surrounded by tangos. That, he could handle. Go in, clear the room, get her the hell out of there. Turn her over to the people who cared about her and disappear into the wind.

Miri's hand on his shoulder brought him back. He swallowed. "Sanderson. I don't know much. We're working on it. I can't give you anything else, but reinforcements are on the way."

"Reinforcements?" Miri asked. "Who? What for?"

"That's what I'm trying to find out." Blackie wouldn't have mobilized a team to find Nancy. Yeah, he'd put a number of operatives on it, especially with a wealthy and prominent client, but not covert ops teams. He'd use his investigators. His *real* investigators.

"What's your twenty, Cowboy?" Zeke's voice came through, calm and detached. In total controller mode.

Dalton grabbed the cell. "Halfway between Bumfuck and Buttcrack," he muttered. "Hang on." He squinted at the GPS and relayed the coordinates.

"Got it. Let me do some checking. Back at you in fifteen."

Zeke's words brought Dalton into his own comfort zone, and for the first time in too long, he felt in control. Never mind he had two civilians with him. Never mind he had no clue what he was doing. Never mind he had nothing but a couple of handguns. The snarl in his gut loosened.

"Roger, Zeke. Line's open." Without disconnecting, he put the cell in his shirt pocket. He put buying a handsfree earpiece on his list of things to do when this was done. On the job, they used company gear, and for his private life—well, he really hadn't gotten around to having much of one and never bothered with frills. Hell, his phone was so old, it didn't even take pictures.

He swiveled in the seat. Miri's eyes pierced through him, demanding answers. Sanderson twisted and untwisted the bandana, afraid to voice the questions in his eyes. Afraid of the answers.

Dalton kept his tone light. "Blackthorne is sending some of his men. Probably has something to do with drugs. I should get you back to the house. When Zeke calls, I'll know more." He did a lot better charming strangers. These two could hear the lies of omission.

"No way."

"Absolutely not." Both voices chimed in unison. He'd expected no less.

"Nancy could be inside," Sanderson said. "I'm not going anywhere until we've looked."

Dalton checked his watch. Thirteen-and-a-half minutes until Zeke's update. Plenty of time to make sure Nancy wasn't in the building. He nodded.

"Before we go in," he said, "I need to know what to expect."

They got out of the car and assembled beside the hood. Dalton scraped the dirt into a smooth surface. He aimed his Maglite at the spot. "Show me the floor plan."

Sanderson pulled his keys from his pocket and dropped to his haunches. Using a key as a pencil, he etched a square in the dirt, then divided it into three sections. "I'm no architect." He tapped the middle. "This is the general purpose room." He cleared his throat and continued as if he were giving a real estate tour. Dalton let him continue at his own pace.

Sanderson went on. "Meetings, maybe movies, dances, parties. Furniture's due in next week." He divided the right-hand section into three parts. "Two sets of multi-unit restrooms over there, complete with showers, plus some storage closets." He traced a line to the far end of the room. "Kitchen's back there."

"What's on the other side?" Dalton asked.

Sanderson pointed to the middle of the line. "Door here. Opens into a hallway leading to four smaller rooms, plus two more single bathrooms. Nancy's been working to turn them into kid-friendly spaces." His voice choked on the words.

Miri put a hand on Sanderson's shoulder, but her eyes were on Dalton. "Can we go?"

"The important thing is to be prepared," he said. "I know this seems to be taking too much time, but walking in blind isn't worth the risk."

"He's right," Sanderson said. "What's your plan?"

"Nothing fancy. I go in first. You wait outside until I say it's okay." His eyes were on Miri's face as he spoke, but she seemed to accept the need for structure. "All right, team. Let's move."

Like a colt eager to run, Sanderson led the way to the door. "Light?"

Miri shone her flashlight and Sanderson selected a key. His hands trembled and it took two tries to slide it into the lock. He twisted the knob, then stepped aside. "Go for it."

Standing to the side, Dalton eased the door open. Waited. Listened. Nothing but silence. And the smell of paint, although traces of ammonia lingered in his nostrils. He swept his flashlight around the space. Freshly laid industrial carpet covered the expanse of a large room. Dusty boot prints marred its pristine surface, the only traces of another presence. Sanderson's hand nudged his back.

"Wait here. And get down below window level." Dalton stepped inside. Despite the barren surroundings, his neck prickled. He wrapped his hand around the grip of the Glock in his pocket.

You're getting paranoid.

Maybe so, but he withdrew the weapon. How many times

had he gone into buildings to yank out hostages? More than he cared to count. Telling himself that was the reason he was on edge, that it was nothing more than the usual unknown-building-in-the-dark syndrome, he moved quietly toward the bathrooms. There was no way he'd surprise anyone. Their arrival hadn't exactly been stealth. If anyone was there, they'd be waiting for him, not the other way around. He opened the first door, then entered the men's room, systematically checking the stalls.

Yep. Nothing. The ladies room and supply closet were empty, as was the kitchen. He crossed the room to the door on the other side.

Sanderson's description was dead on. He stood in a hallway with six doors. One by one, he verified each room was clear. Yet the prickling at the nape of his neck didn't subside. He stepped into the last room, as empty as the others. He inhaled something more than paint and drywall. Something earthy.

CHAPTER 27

Miri sat on the ground under the window, hugging her knees to her chest. Hunt paced a short distance away, tossing Nancy's bracelet from one hand to the other. She motioned him over. "Save your energy."

"Can't sit," he said. "What's taking him so long?"

"He seems to know what he's doing."

"Well, if he's not out in two minutes, I'm going in. He doesn't know Nancy. I do, and if there's any evidence she's been here, I'll see it."

Miri stood and gathered Hunt into an embrace. His entire body quivered, as if an electrical current ran through it. "We'll find her."

Looking over his shoulder, she noticed the white logo on the Dumpster. Hobart Construction. She pictured the plans she'd seen on Patterson's computer file. Coincidence? "You didn't say anything about a basement. Is there one?"

"What?" He wormed out of her arms.

"I saw some plans for basement renovations done by Hobart Construction in Patterson's files. Maybe it was for this building."

"I don't know. I never saw the plans, and the place was in the finishing stages when I got here." He shoved the bracelet in his pocket. Although she couldn't see his expression in the dark, she sensed a change in his body language. When he spoke, confidence filled his tone. "If there is a basement, she might be there. We have to tell Dalton." He dashed past her and opened the door. "Dalton!"

Miri reached for him, but Hunt was already inside. What the hell. Sitting on her butt wasn't getting anything done. Besides, it was cold out here. She flipped on her light and followed him in.

"Dalton, where the hell are you?" Hunt said. He waited about three seconds, then strode to the right. The kitchen and locker rooms, Miri recalled. She darted after him, grabbing his elbow.

"Wait. If he's not answering, something must be wrong. Don't go barging in like that."

He shook her off. "I've waited around doing nothing long enough. If anything bad was going to happen, we'd have heard it. No gunshots, no explosions. It's the middle of the night and there's nobody here. Enough is enough." He marched toward the back of the room. "Nancy! Nance, it's me. Hunt."

Miri stood, rooted, as she tried to decide whether to follow Hunt or search for Dalton. He couldn't be missing, too, could he?

She had no means to protect Hunt, and if there were problems, no reason for both of them to get caught. Decision made, she crossed the room to the open doorway at the left.

"Dalton?" she called softly, not sure if she should whisper or shout. Hunt had already made enough noise. She raised her voice. "Dalton?"

"Hang on a second." His voice, muffled, came from somewhere down the hall. "Last room on the right."

Following the flashlight's narrow beam, she rushed toward the voice, stopping two paces into the room. It was empty. "Dalton? Damn it, where are you?" She swept her light across the space. Industrial carpet on the floor, a window to her left. Hinged louvered doors open across from her. Seconds later, Dalton emerged, wiping his hands on his pants.

Miri jumped back. "Shit. You scared me to death. Why were you hiding in the closet?"

He motioned her to him, hooking a thumb over his shoulder. "I wasn't hiding. There's something in the back wall."

She pointed her light along the space. "Looks like a wall to me."

"Here." He held her hand, guiding her beam to the corner, about six feet up the wall. "See that?"

She ignored the way his touch made her wish this wasn't happening. That they were tucked away in a motel room, wrapped in each other's arms. That Nancy and Hunt were home, talking about babies.

Too bad. Those were wishes. This was reality. She stepped into the recess of the closet and followed the beam to an oval indentation. She touched it, feeling cool metal instead of the sheetrock it was painted to match. "What is it?"

Dalton stepped around her and put his fingers into the slot. Slowly, the wall slid to the right. "A pocket door." He bent forward and waved his light into the opening.

"In a closet?" she asked. "Where does it go?"

"Down."

She peeked over his shoulder, seeing a ladder-steep staircase leading to a tiny room about six feet square. Too small for the basement plans she'd seen. "You think it's for storage?"

"If so, it's in a strange location. Where's Hunter? He might know more."

Hunt. She'd forgotten about him. "He's on the other side."

"He's here." Miri pivoted as Hunt stepped into the room. "Someone going to fill me in, please?" His eyes darted back and forth. His voice held an irritated edge, as if he clung to a razor-thin blade of control.

She stepped back into the room. "There's a hidden door in the closet. And some kind of storage room below."

"Is Nancy there?" Hunt asked.

"It's an empty storeroom," Dalton said.

"Are we still playing cat burglar?" Hunt asked. "You think anyone who could possibly matter doesn't know we're here?"

"Not anymore," Dalton said. "Anyone wanted us, they'd have made their move."

"Good." Hunt slapped his hand against the wall switch and illuminated the room. "I flipped the breakers." He tore his cap from his head and dropped it on the floor. In two strides, he shoved Dalton aside. "I hope you don't mind, but I'm going down."

Miri moved toward him, but Dalton took her by the arm. "Let him go. He needs to see for himself."

Hunt peered down, then reversed and descended.

Dalton moved toward the hall.

"Wait," Miri called. "Do you think Nancy's—" She checked to make sure Hunt hadn't reappeared. "You know, is she—?"

"Ah, darlin', come here." Dalton crossed back to her and wrapped her in his arms. "Don't think that. Positive attitude."

She melted into him, rested her head on his chest, putting her worries aside for a moment. An altogether too brief moment.

He took her hand and kissed her palm. "You okay?"

She nodded.

Before Dalton released her, Hunt's voice echoed from below. "Get down here. Bring your lights."

As one, they bolted. Dalton zipped down the steep staircase as if it were a fireman's pole. Miri followed, a little less gracefully. Dalton's hands at her waist told her she was near the bottom, and he swung her to the ground.

No lights down here, she noted, switching hers on. Dalton's washed out her feeble beam, so she flicked it off.

"Over here," Hunt said. Metal shelving units stood against

two of the walls. He stood next to one, shining his flashlight over it. "There's something behind this."

"Hang on." Dalton tried to reach Zeke on his cell. Crap. No reception down here. He shoved Sanderson aside, not all that gently. "Let me."

"Damn it, man, if my wife is in there—she could be hurt."

"And if she is, she'll need a husband to take care of her. In case it's a trap, I go first. Show me what you found."

"Here," Sanderson said. "I heard something. And maybe I'm crazy, but I swear I smelled Nancy's perfume."

Dalton ran his hand along the metal frame. He pressed his ear to the wall. "What did you hear?" he whispered to Sanderson.

"A humming sound. Like some kind of machinery."

He strained, but heard nothing. As far as perfume—well, Sanderson was desperate for any sign of his wife. All Dalton could smell was his own body, which exuded meth lab chemicals.

"Look," Miri said in a stage whisper. "Over here."

He crossed to the other side of the shelving unit where her light illuminated the metal supports.

"It's hinged," she said, pointing to two hinges almost hidden behind the posts.

Although the shelving unit was fixed to the wall, a barely visible gap ran to the ceiling in line with the post, all but obscured by the shelving framework. "I'll be damned. Sanderson, give me a hand."

Together, they pulled on the shelf unit, but nothing happened. Dalton sensed Sanderson's growing frustration.

"Wait," Miri said. Instead of pulling, she pressed, and the unit popped forward several inches, bringing the wall with it. "We have a cabinet with a lock like this at Galloway."

"Way to go, Miri," Dalton said, giving her a thumbs up. Her grin gave him a quick jolt of energy.

Sanderson grasped the edge of the door and pulled. It slid smoothly open, revealing a short, narrow concrete block hallway with a concrete slab floor and a wooden door at the other end. Someone had gone to great pains to create this hideaway. Unlike the other doors, this one had no discernable opening mechanism.

Motioning Sanderson and Miri to hang back, he crossed the narrow space and leaned his ear against the wood. It sounded . . . hollow. "This is getting old," he grumbled.

"Can we get in?" Miri asked.

From behind the door, someone sneezed. Quiet, muffled, but a definite sneeze. Then two more.

Sanderson's flashlight dropped to the ground with a resonating clunk. It spun around, sending a miniature searchlight around the room. Dalton glared at him.

"That's Nancy," Sanderson said. "She always sneezes three times. Like that." He pushed Dalton aside.

"Quiet." He clapped a hand over Sanderson's mouth. "Give me a second to think." He almost dismissed the man's insistence his wife was behind the door, writing it off as wishful thinking. It could've been a dog or cat.

But he knew it wasn't. He knew he could recognize any of his team by their breathing, the way they walked, and yes, even the way they sneezed—although on an op, they'd know better.

Sanderson squirmed free. "Nancy! Are you all right?"

Footfalls and scraping sounds filtered through the door.

So much for thinking. He leaned down and pulled up his pant leg, removing his backup weapon, a snub-nosed thirty-eight revolver, from his ankle holster. "You know how to use one of these?" he asked Sanderson.

Miri's eyes widened.

Sanderson retrieved his light, then took the gun from Dalton's hand. He flipped open the cylinder, spun it and clicked it shut. "Yes, as a matter of fact, I do."

"You do?" Miri said. Dalton could tell she was learning more about her brother-in-law tonight than in the years she'd known him.

"Shooting team at Harvard, although I prefer a rifle," Sanderson said.

"Well, let's hope we don't need to use your skill." He wondered if Sanderson would shoot a human being. A lot different from targets. In the dimly lit corridor, he saw Sanderson's eyes. The man would defend himself and do what it took to save his wife. Dalton prayed it wouldn't come to that. "Miri. Go back upstairs to the other room, please, darlin'. Sanderson—in the corner, if you don't mind."

Dalton pulled his Glock out.

Sanderson backed up, looking at him. "What are we doing?"

Adrenaline surged. Standing in a narrow hallway with no cover, he was an easy target. He held the flashlight up at what he assumed would be eye level for someone opening the door. No light bled through, so he assumed it was dark inside. Even a split second while someone reacted to a bright light in his eyes would give him the advantage he needed. Then again, the light sure as hell made him as easy to hit as the side of a barn.

Hoo yah. He flashed a grin at Sanderson. "What anyone does when they want to go a callin'." He rapped three times. "We knock."

Nothing. He counted to ten, then knocked again. This time, the door eased away from him, opening an inch, then two. Dirty fingers appeared, curled around the edge. Small fingers. A child? He lowered the beam of his light about a foot and got a glimpse of deep brown eyes before they squinted shut. The youngster darted back into the darkness.

Dalton gripped the door and gently pushed it forward, angling himself behind it until it was open all the way. He stepped around, Glock in one hand, Maglite in the other.

Holy crap. A spacious room, maybe twenty feet long and sixteen wide. Like the building above, it was newly built, although definitely used. A barracks was the first thing that came to mind. Metal bunk beds—five protruding from each wall like so many teeth. Twenty beds. He noted the rumpled bedding, piles of clothing and revised the vision from ship-shape barracks to college dorm. A six-foot tall concrete wall at the back partitioned the space. Who lived here? The child was gone.

"It's okay," he called to the empty room. "Nobody's going to hurt you. Come out, please."

From behind him, Sanderson burst through the doorway. "Nancy! It's Hunt. Where are you?"

Sanderson had heard right. A soft mechanical humming filled the room. Generator, was Dalton's automatic assessment. Lights came on. Seconds later, a door opened at the far end of the room, beyond the last bed on the right. A ragtag assortment of Hispanic humanity emerged, stepping uncertainly into the space.

"Please," said one, a leathery-skinned man who could have been thirty or eighty. "You will not send us back. Please." He eyed Dalton's Glock. "We are doing as you ask."

Dalton lowered his weapon but kept it in his hand. Before he could say anything, Sanderson rushed to the center of the room, turning from one face to another.

"My wife," he said. "Nancy. Where is my wife? *¿Donde está mi esposa?*" He shoved the revolver into his pocket and brought out a wallet. Holding it open, he pointed, handed it to the man. "*Mi esposa.* Nancy."

The young girl who'd let them in looked at the wallet, took it from the old man, then approached Sanderson. *"Señora Nancy?"*

"Yes," Sanderson said, hope filling his voice. He tapped the billfold. *"Si.* Nancy."

"Señora Nancy es enferma," the child said. She pointed behind her.

"Is there anyone else with the *Señora?"* Dalton asked.

"She is alone," the old man said. "We are all here."

Maybe. Dalton held his Glock at the ready. He indicated Sanderson should do the same with the revolver.

Sanderson shook his head.

"Do it," Dalton said.

Miri appeared at his side. Damn, she was supposed to be in the other room. Why didn't she listen to him? He grabbed her arm before she walked into his line of fire.

She glared at him. "She's a little kid, for God's sake. These people don't want to hurt us."

"I sure as hell hope you're right," Dalton said. "But I've seen good men—and women—die at the hands of eight-year-olds. Tell me I was wrong later. When we're safe. As a matter of fact, maybe you'd be better off upstairs."

Miri's hands fisted at her hips. "She's my sister. You can't dismiss me."

"Damn it," Sanderson said. "Nancy's in there. Sick, according to the child. You two can stand here and argue, but I'm going in. Now."

Dalton reminded himself that Sanderson and Miri weren't part of Blackthorne, that they weren't used to taking orders and obeying them without question. He plucked his phone from his shirt pocket. He laid it in his palm like a peace offering. "Miri, if you don't mind, would you please go outside and contact Zeke. Find out what's going on?" He tried to keep the sarcasm from his voice, unsuccessfully, to judge from the eye-roll he got from Miri. But she snatched the phone and retreated. "Tell him purple," he called after her. She glowered over her shoulder.

Dalton spoke to the group assembled in front of him. "Please. *Por favor.* Stay here." He motioned to the old man, their apparent spokesperson. "I don't want anyone to get hurt. Do you understand me?"

The man nodded. "*Si.* Yes. I speak some English."

"What's behind that wall?" Dalton pointed to the partition.

"*Baño.* Bathroom. Showers."

"One second," Dalton said to Sanderson. He strode across the room and checked behind the wall. An empty bathroom, standard gymnasium locker-room issue. What the old man said was the truth. A fraction—a very tiny fraction—of his concern eased.

"Please tell everyone to wait here," he said to the old man. He smiled at the child. "Let's go. *Señora Nancy, por favor.*"

The girl eyed his gun warily but slid her hand into Sanderson's.

"It's about damn time," Sanderson muttered.

Dalton marched to the doorway, Sanderson and the girl at his heels. He stood sideways at the closed door and, Glock at his side, reached for the knob.

CHAPTER 28

Purple, Dalton had said. Good grief, was she in the middle of some cloak-and-dagger scenario, complete with secret passwords? Miri climbed the ladder into the closet, hurried through the house and stepped onto the porch. Hunter must have turned on every light in the place, down to bright carriage lamps flanking the door. She checked the phone's display for a signal, then held it to her ear. "Um . . . Zeke? Are you there? Dalton sent me."

A brief interlude of silence, then a deep male voice with a faint trace of a Minnesota cadence asked who she was.

"Miri Chambers. He's—you—are looking for my sister, Nancy Sanderson."

"Don't suppose he's around to confirm that, is he?"

"Not exactly," she said. "We found a secret underground room, and he's checking it out. He gave me his phone and said to ask you what's going on."

"That all he said?"

Feeling like an idiot, she added, "He said to say . . . um . . . purple."

"Good to hear. Is the cowboy all right?" Zeke asked.

Okay, so she really *was* in the middle of secret-password land. Or dreaming, but she didn't think that was the case. "He's fine. But there's no cell reception where he is, and he's kind of busy."

"Explain, please." She detected an undercurrent of worry in his tone.

Shaking off exhaustion, she gathered her thoughts. "We found a bunch of people—probably illegals—hiding in a basement. One of them said Nancy was with them, but Dalton sent me out here. He and Hunter—that's my brother-in-law, Nancy's husband—have guns and they're checking it out."

"Ten-four. If your sister's with Dalton, ma'am, she's in good hands."

"Got her." The voice was coming through the phone, but sounded far away. "ETA in less than two."

An Australian accent. And a familiar voice. A helicopter whirred. She stepped away and searched the skies.

"Ma'am, please get inside." Dumbfounded, she stared at the phone, then into the surrounding darkness and back up to the sky. Aside from a half moon and some stars, she saw nothing.

"Are you talking to me?" she asked Zeke, or whoever was on the other end of the line. "If I go inside, I lose the signal."

"Yes, ma'am. Miri. It's Zeke again. All right. Try to stay as close to the building as you can to keep the connection."

Amid more crackling, Aussie's voice came over the phone. "Can you hear me, Miri?"

"Yes. Where are you? *Who* are you?"

"Right. We were never introduced at Patterson's, were we? I'm Fozzie, and I'm about five hundred feet above you. I work with Dalton. A couple of our mates will be joining you shortly."

As he finished speaking, two shadows emerged from behind some trees, taking human form as they jogged in her direction. She backed toward the house, leaning against the wall for support. "Umm . . . I see two people, but how do I know they're your men?"

Another crackle, then a green light appeared, tracing a circle above the head of one of the figures.

"I had them give you a signal," Fozzie said. "What did you see?"

She took a few steps forward, improving the reception. "A green light."

"Those are my men. Ryan Harper and Hotshot McCade. Point them to Dalton, if you will."

She nodded, then realized he couldn't see the gesture, although she thought he should be able to hear all the new information rolling around in her head like rattling maracas. "Yes, sir."

The two men arrived, clad in the same dark camouflage as Dalton. The resemblance ended there. They wore packs on their backs, headphones with microphones at their cheeks and weapons. Big weapons. Lots of weapons. She told herself these were the good guys, that she should be glad to see them, but the words weren't getting past the panic filling her.

"Miri Chambers?" one man said.

She nodded.

"I'm Ryan," he said, white teeth making a fleeting appearance. "Where's Dalt?"

She started to lead the way.

"No, ma'am," Ryan said. "Tell me. You stay here with Hotshot."

The other man touched the edge of his watch cap with two fingers. Creases crinkled at the edge of his blue eyes. "I'll escort you to the helo. You'll be safe there."

Helo? She thought of their arrival. Okay, helo was a helicopter. Good. She wasn't too scared to put two and two together. Somehow, she found the ability to speak. "My sister is down there. Along with her husband and maybe a dozen terrified immigrants. If you think I'm going to crawl into a hole—or a helo—you can—well, forget it."

The men exchanged eye-rolling glances and shrugged.

"Confirmation on the vehicle," Ryan said. "Crashed about half a klick away. We have the package."

Package? Had he called her a *package?* She was about to retort, but Ryan's eyes got a faraway stare and he put his fingers to the headset before turning his back. He said something she couldn't understand, and she realized he wasn't talking to her. He stopped, then he and Hotshot did that glance-exchange thing again. Hotshot unzipped Ryan's pack and pulled out another headset. "Here," he said. "This is for Dalton, but you can borrow it."

He helped her adjust it, explained what she'd be hearing, and what to press when she wanted to talk. Fozzie's voice in her ear made her jump. "Miss Chambers, I'm in a helicopter about a hundred meters from your position. I can hear everything going on, and my job is to make sure everyone's safe."

Safe from what? Some helpless migrants?

She pressed the button the way Hotshot showed her. "Umm . . . okay. But I'm not leaving my sister."

"I understand. Please stay close to my mates, and do whatever they say. I don't think you'll have any trouble."

"We're on our way," another voice said. Hotshot waved her inside. She pointed down the hall. Hotshot led, and Ryan motioned her forward. She was following two men dressed for a combat zone.

I'm dreaming. It's late. I must have fallen asleep watching a war movie.

She rubbed her eyes, hurrying after Hotshot. "Last door," she said, not sure if she was talking to the men with her or an entire audience of total strangers on the other end of her headset. "On the right."

The men moved, silent as ghosts, down the hall and into the room. She pointed to the closet, with its open door. Hotshot disappeared and caught her the same way Dalton had when she descended.

"Where?" came through her headset.

Fozzie's voice crackled through. "Heat sources about ten yards ahead, at two o'clock."

Reflexively, she checked her watch. It was almost four, not two. She rubbed her eyes. Slowly, the words registered. Direction, not time.

Hotshot was examining the shelving unit, which had closed behind her when she'd left Dalton. With a barely contained smirk, she strode forward and gave it a shove, enjoying the quick lift of Ryan's eyebrow and the thumbs-up from Hotshot when it opened.

Three feet away from the second door, Ryan halted their progress with an upraised hand. "Does it open the same way?" he whispered.

"I'm not sure. I wasn't in here. But I think Dalton knocked."

"How novel," Hotshot said. He motioned them to stay where they were, stepped forward and raised his knuckles.

The child followed Dalton into the adjacent room, which, unlike the brightly lit one they'd come from, was dark. Their kitchen and dining room, he guessed from shadowy shapes of tables and kitchen appliances. A moan came from the floor, and he flipped on his flashlight. Nancy slouched against the wall, eyes closed, wrapped in a blanket.

Sanderson shoved past him and crouched at her side. "Nance—it's me." He pushed the blanket from her head. "God, you're burning up. What happened?" He gripped her hand.

Her eyes opened. "Hunt?"

"Sweetheart, yes. I'm here. You're going to be fine, baby." He cast imploring eyes to Dalton, seeking confirmation.

Dalton shut the door, then knelt beside them. Sweat glistened on Nancy's upper lip, damp tendrils of hair clung to her face. He brushed them away, revealing a purple bruise on her forehead. Her mouth was swollen and an assortment of abrasions marred her cheek and jaw.

He gave her his best smile. "Hello, Mrs. Sanderson. Nancy. I'm Dalton, a friend of Miri's and your husband's. We're going to get you out of here and to the hospital, okay?" Her eyes, glazed with fever, seemed focused on Sanderson. Gently, he took her chin in his hand, careful not to move her head. "Nancy, listen to me a minute. Where are you hurt?"

"Hurts."

"Tell us where, baby." Alarm filled Sanderson's voice. "Who did this to you?"

"My head." She raised her hand to the lump on her forehead. "Don't remember."

"Give me your penlight," Dalton said to Sanderson. The man slapped the cylinder into his hand. Dalton flipped it on and shone it in Nancy's eyes. Her pupils contracted.

"You know what you're doing?" Sanderson asked.

"Basic emergency first aid. Her pupils look good, but I want to check for other injuries." He unfolded the blanket. She was wearing torn, dirty sweatpants and a stained sweatshirt zipped to the neck, its hood pillowed behind her head. Expensive sneakers, but not what he expected after seeing her at the Sanderson's going away party.

"Take her shoes off," he told Sanderson. "Carefully. Don't move her more than necessary." For what that was worth. Hell, she'd probably been moved plenty getting her here.

While Sanderson worked on Nancy's shoes, Dalton ran his hands down her arms, watching for any indication he was hurting her. She didn't flinch. Gently, he pressed her belly. The muscles contracted under his touch, but she didn't cry out.

"Shoes are off," Sanderson said.

"Nancy, can you move your toes?" There was no response, and he fought a surge of panic. "Nancy, look at me." She didn't take her gaze from her husband.

"Nance, wiggle your toes, baby. Come on," Sanderson said.

Both feet rotated in circles. Dalton let go of the breath he'd been holding. "Good."

Sanderson grabbed the flashlight. "God, is that blood?"

Dalton noted the red-brown stains on her sweatshirt. "I'm not sure." He touched one. Dry and hard. Pieces flaked off in his hand. "I think it's mud."

"The clothes," Sanderson said. "They're not hers, except the shoes."

Dalton reached for the zipper, lowered it and found bare skin where he expected a shirt. Sanderson's hand covered his.

"I think I'd rather do that myself," he said.

Dalton backed off. "Okay. Check her for any cuts, blood, anything. Keep talking to her. While you do, I'm going to try to find out what happened."

Dalton sought the child, who cowered on the floor in the corner. He left Sanderson with Nancy and knelt at the child's side.

"Sugar, tell me what happened. Nobody's going to hurt you." She blinked her big, brown eyes but said nothing. He swore under his breath and repeated his question in Spanish.

Her expression said she'd understood, but she remained silent. "Here you go, Sugar. Want a candy?" He offered a piece from his butterscotch stash. She grabbed it and gave him a shy smile. "It's okay to talk to us." He shoved his Glock into his waistband, raising his hands, palms outward. "I'm Dalton. A friend. *Amigo.* What's your name? *¿Su nombre?*"

"Juanita," she whispered. She pointed to the door. *"Mi abuelo habla inglés."*

And her grandfather probably knew what was going on. "Let's talk to him, okay, Juanita?" He stood and extended his hand. Without taking it, she popped to her feet and opened the door.

When the light streamed in, Dalton inspected his surroundings. The room was more than a kitchen and dining hall. He shone his light over the assemblage of equipment. Fuck. Another God damn meth lab. Remembering the waiting child, he swallowed the curse behind his lips. Her white teeth flashed the first smile he'd seen. He found one to return.

The child darted through the doorway.

"Oh, God, Nancy. Baby," Sanderson said, his voice shaking. "Come back. Wake up."

"What?" Dalton rushed to them.

"She passed out. She said something about an accident. In her car. God, do you think there are internal injuries? She's got bruises on her torso." He paled. "If she was . . . she could have lost . . ." He splayed his hand over her belly.

"Hey, none of that." He squeezed Sanderson's shoulder. "We're going to get her out of here and to a hospital. I'm sure the docs will fix her right up."

Sanderson's lips narrowed. He wasn't buying any of it.

" 'Scuse me, *Señor.*" Dalton jerked around at the voice.

The old man shuffled in, glancing over his shoulder. "Someone comes."

Dalton gave Sanderson one more squeeze. "Stay here. I'll be right back."

He followed the man into the dorm. At first, he thought everyone had disappeared, until muffled stirrings drifted from the bath area. He motioned the old man to join the others hiding there and approached the entrance to the room. Although he heard nothing, hair bristled at the base of his neck. He gripped the Glock.

He had one hand on the deadbolt when four quick raps sent his heart to his throat. He froze. Seconds later, two more knocks, not as rapid, vibrated through his hand.

He twisted the thumbscrew and yanked the door open.

Two heavily armed men stood there. "Don't shoot, Cowboy,"

the taller one said.

"Damn you both to hell." Dalton slapped Hotshot on the arm, then grabbed Harper in a bear hug. "It sure is good to see you."

Miri peeked around the wall of masculinity and gave him a finger wave. "Zeke sent them." She pulled off a headset and dangled it from her hand. "I'm not in Kansas anymore, am I?"

He wanted to kiss her. Hell, he'd kiss all three of them. "We've got a medical situation." He slipped the headset on. "Who's controlling?"

"That would be me, mate," squawked from the radio. "Can't leave you alone for a minute, can I?"

"Fozzie, you son of a bitch—get us the hell out of here."

"Where's Nancy?" Miri stepped into the room, searching the empty space. "Where's *everybody?*"

"Nancy's next door." He pointed to the rear. "Miri, go with Hotshot."

Miri raced across the room, Hotshot at her heels. Once she was out of sight, he confronted Harper. "What the hell is going on that Blackie would send an ops team?"

"Smuggling. Both the medicinal and human variety," Harper said. "Border patrol requested assistance. Not to mention a Mr. Sanderson willing to pay big bucks for the return of his missing wife. So here we are."

"Sounds like Blackie bent some of his own rules, but what the hell." Dalton adjusted the lip mic. "Hey, Fozzie. I've got an injured woman. Can you airlift her to the nearest hospital—belay that—the *best* hospital? Probably San Diego?"

The silence following his question sent a cold, metallic taste to his mouth. "Fozzie? What haven't you told me?" He glared at Harper.

"Sorry, mate," Fozzie said. "No can do. There's another shipment on its way, about two klicks out."

"Shipment of what? Damn it, if I'm part of this team I need to be brought up to speed. And if I'm not, then I'm taking the woman to the hospital myself."

Harper reached forward and grabbed his arm. "The short version seems to be that the coyotes are doing more than bringing people across the border. They're working with the drug smugglers. They promise the people jobs, only the jobs turn out to be cooking meth. And we've got another group on its way."

"Group of what? Smugglers or illegal aliens?"

"Aliens? You make them sound like monsters from outer space." Miri's voice rang through the room. "They're people, you know. Trying to improve their lives."

Behind her, Sanderson and Hotshot carried Nancy to the nearest cot and laid her down. Sanderson sat beside her, holding her hand. Miri knelt on the other side, smoothing Nancy's hair. Hotshot shrugged out of his pack and set it on the floor.

"How are we going to get her up that staircase?" Sanderson asked. "Won't it be risky to move her that way?"

Hotshot rested his hand on Sanderson's shoulder. "Glenn McCade. I'm a medic," he said. "They call me Hotshot. May I take a closer look?"

Sanderson relinquished his spot, but not his hold on Nancy's hand. "She said there was a car accident."

Hotshot pulled a field kit from his pack and set to examining Nancy. Dalton noted Sanderson didn't have any problem with Hotshot opening Nancy's sweatshirt.

His headset crackled. "Topside, mates. Trouble coming."

CHAPTER 29

In unison, the men's faces went stone cold. Tentacles of dread slithered over Miri. Ryan tapped the headset at his ear and said something she didn't catch. Dalton's gaze, filled with uncertainty, met hers, and ice settled in her gut. He extended his arm, but it seemed to say, "Keep away," not, "Come with me."

She rose from the floor beside Nancy. His arm dropped. He shook his head.

Replies cascaded through her brain. *Stay. Let them take care of it. Nancy needs you. I need you.*

"Go," echoed in her ears, as if someone else spoke the words.

Without another glance, Dalton whirled on his heels and followed Ryan out the door, leaving a hole in her heart, although she wasn't sure why. She didn't *love* him or anything like that.

"Keep everyone quiet," Hotshot said. "We'll be back as soon as we can." He got up and loped across the room after his teammates.

It hadn't been three seconds, and they were gone. An eerie silence descended over the room.

"How could they leave?" Hunt said. "Nancy needs a doctor. A real doctor. Why have these people been holding her prisoner here?"

Miri blinked back hot tears. "Hotshot said he was a medic. He wouldn't have left if he didn't think she'd be all right for a while." She didn't sound convincing, even to herself. Who were those men? And why did Dalton fit in so easily? One thing was certain. The man was no private investigator.

She shoved thoughts of him into the recesses of her mind, something to deal with later when Nancy was all right and she'd had some sleep.

"Hunt?" Nancy's voice, weak and shaky, snapped Miri's attention to Nancy. Relief surged when she saw her sister's eyes open.

"I'm here, baby. Look what I found." Hunt slipped the bracelet around Nancy's wrist.

She smiled, then winced. "My bracelet. Where?"

"At the old center."

"Roberto." She coughed. "Asleep inside. Tried to get him outside. Must have fallen off."

"How long were you in there, Nancy?" Miri asked.

"Few minutes. Drugs. Had to get Roberto out."

"That's my baby." Hunt caressed Nancy's forehead.

"Ow," she said.

"Hey, Sis." Miri's smile came more easily as worries of long-term exposure to meth chemicals dissipated. "That's some goose egg. How are you feeling?"

"Been better."

Movement caught Miri's eye. She turned as an old man came out of the bathroom area, stopping at the foot of the bed. A young girl followed, shyly peeking from behind. The man glanced around, as if searching for Dalton and his men.

Hunter stormed toward the man and grabbed him by the collar. "Why didn't someone get in touch with me?" The fury in his voice gave Miri goosebumps.

"Please, *Señor.*" The man bowed his head. "We did not know. She had no bag. No cards. No one has phones."

"When?" Hunt said to the man. "When did this happen?"

"*Miércoles.* Wednesday night, very late."

"That was days ago! Someone should have found me. Told me."

"Hunt. No. It's not their fault," Nancy said. She struggled to sit up, but Miri pressed her down. "The coyote took everything. He threatened to kill them. And their families at home. Please. They've tried to take care of me."

Hunter's gaze alternated between Nancy and the old man. Breathing heavily, he stared at the man who stood wide-eyed and motionless. Finally, Hunter sighed and released his grip. "I'm sorry. Thank you for looking after her."

"Dalton said they'd be back," Miri said. "And that we should be quiet." She stroked Nancy's hand but fixed her gaze on the man. "I'm Miri. Do you know what happened to my sister?"

"I am Paco," the man said. "Your sister, she help when the coyote try to . . ." He drew the child closer to him. The child buried her face in the man's chest.

"He didn't . . ." Miri said.

"No." Paco gave his head a violent shake. "But if *Señora* Nancy had not arrived . . . She is brave woman."

"What were you trying to do, Nancy?" Hunt asked. "You could have been killed." The words didn't match his tone or the tenderness in his eyes.

"It wasn't in the plan." Nancy sighed. "These people need help. Paco is trying, but it's a vicious cycle." She coughed and grimaced.

"Don't talk," Miri said.

Nancy shook her head. "They come for freedom. The coyotes keep them locked up here, cooking meth. Until they get too sick to work. Then they let them go and bring in another group." She closed her eyes.

"She's always helping, isn't she?" Miri said.

"Yes, but it's usually at the fund raising level," Hunt said. "Donating clothes to Dress for Success."

"I'm here, you know," Nancy said, her eyes closed. "You don't have to talk about me as if—" A paroxysm of coughing cut her off. Miri and Hunt exchanged alarmed glances.

"Don't talk, baby," Hunt said. "Save your strength." To Paco, he said, "Can you tell me more about how Nancy got hurt? How long has she been here?"

"*Si. Por favor,* but first, can we not be hiding? It is not comfortable in the back."

"Of course," Hunt said.

The man whispered something to the girl, and she scooted behind the wall. Seconds later, a line of people snaked in, heading for beds, eyes downcast. Miri counted twelve. Two men, four women and six children who seemed between six and preteen. The women encouraged younger ones to lie down, but most perched on the edges of the mattresses, staring at the floor. Their fear was tangible.

Nancy's eyes snapped open. "Hunt . . . I don't feel so good," she whispered.

"Sick? Pain? What?" he said. He gripped her hand in both of his.

"Something . . . feels . . . wrong. Inside."

Miri clenched the bed frame, its cool metal growing warm under her grip. "We need to get her to the hospital. I'll go see what's going on. We've got an hour or two before it gets light. It'll be safer if I go now." She kissed Nancy's forehead, alarmed at the heat beneath her lips. Hunt's protest was halfhearted.

"*Señorita?*"

Miri peered into Paco's face, concern adding even more wrinkles to his leathery skin.

"Is another way out," he said.

"Not upstairs, through the house?" An easier way to get Nancy out?

311

He shook his head. "I will show you."

With one last squeeze of Nancy's hand, Miri followed Paco through the room where they'd found Nancy. His feet dragged across the floor, but his back was straight, his head erect. He approached a cheap kitchen hutch housing a microwave. Clutching the corners, he rolled it out on its casters. Miri hurried to help. No longer surprised by anything in this house, she noted the pocket door behind the hutch and slid it open. Cool air smelling of earth drifted in on a night breeze. Her small flashlight did little to illuminate the space beyond the room. Paco moved around her and bent over. When he straightened, he held an electric lantern.

Miri squinted into the darkness, trying to see what lay beyond the range of the light. "A cave? Some kind of a tunnel?"

"*Sí*. Tunnel. There are many of them through here. First, for people to cross the border. Now the drug cartels have made many more." He stepped forward, holding the lantern aloft. Miri followed.

Most of her concentration was on her footing, avoiding stones and uneven spots on the path. Instinctively, she crouched, although the ceiling was several feet above her head. The walls seemed to grow closer, the ceiling lower. The silence wrapped itself around her and her mouth felt as dry as the dirt that surrounded them.

"How long have you been here, Paco?" she said, to ease her growing tension more than needing an answer.

"In U.S., four years. I work the fields, saving money to bring my family from Mexico. I make a foolish mistake, agree to work for the evil men to get money faster."

"Evil men?"

His pace quickened. "They tell me to help meet others who have crossed the border. I do, but they make us cook the meth and will tell the police and Immigration if we do not. Finally, I have enough to send for my granddaughter and her uncle. Juanita, she arrives three days ago. But Matteo—" his voice thickened.

Sadness clawed at Miri's heart. "Oh, Paco, I'm so sorry."

"Is a rough journey." His shoulders slumped. "Many do not survive."

"How did you meet Nancy?" she asked, changing the subject.

"I meet the new arrivals and bring them the last distance. Miss Nancy found us, although I do not know how. It does not matter. She drives up. She sees the coyote who is touching Juanita. The car hits the tree. She runs from the car, she yells, pulls Juanita away. The coyote hits her. She fights back. 'Run,' she tells us." He averted his gaze. "There are women and children. We take them to safety."

It'd been a long time since Nancy needed street skills, but Miri almost smiled knowing how her sister would defend herself. "You had to think of the children."

"*Sí*. And our families back home. We cannot go against a coyote."

He sounded so forlorn, Miri's heart went out to him. "I understand. You can't blame yourself."

Paco stretched his arm out. "Here." He raised the lantern in a sweeping motion.

Miri looked where he indicated but saw nothing but rocks and brush. Paco pulled branches aside, then slid between a gap in two boulders. "Out here."

Miri followed him to the tunnel's end. Or its beginning, thinking of the people running from a life imprisoned by poverty, then imprisoned again instead of enjoying a life of freedom and opportunity.

The legality of what these people were doing flitted across her mind, and she swatted it away like a pesky fly. They were human beings, with goals and dreams like everyone else. There had to be a solution. She allowed herself a quick internal smile, knowing Nancy obviously felt the same way.

She stepped out of the cave and into the night. From above somewhere in the distance, a helicopter whirred. She shaded her eyes and scanned the sky but saw nothing. Was Dalton up there?

Twenty yards away, the rear end of Nancy's car protruded, half hidden by trees and rocks. She rushed forward, stopping cold when she saw the accordion-pleated hood. She didn't need to get any closer. They weren't going anywhere.

Dalton crouched behind a rock outcropping about fifty meters from the house, where chaparral thinned and desert terrain gently merged with the rugged foothills.

"I'm on point," Hotshot said. He jogged into the darkness.

"Manny is waiting. Half a klick northwest," Fozzie said.

"Roger that," Hotshot said.

From his headset, Dalton listened to the exchange, visualizing everyone's positions. He checked his weapon once more as Ryan lay on his belly beside him, setting up. Dalton lost Hotshot after ten seconds. The moon had dipped behind the mountains, cutting visibility in the pre-dawn darkness to the hand-in-front-of-your-face variety.

"Night vision?"

"Pack," Ryan said.

Dalton unzipped the canvas carryall and found the goggles. He slipped them on, mentally mapping his surroundings in the eerie green glow. "Sorry you got called away—twice." First from R&R, then back-to-back ops, leaving his girlfriend behind. "Been able to check in with Frankie?"

"Yeah. Everything's cool." Ryan wriggled into the dirt, shifting some rocks out from underneath him. "You had to leave Miri. It's not like you had a choice." His tone was matter-of-fact, almost emotionless. Almost.

Since when could Ryan read him like that? Hearing the unspoken, ferreting out the nuances had always been Dalton's specialty. People opened up to him, not the other way around. He lowered the goggles, letting them dangle from the strap around his neck.

Ryan adjusted his rifle's sights. "That hideaway is well below ground. She'll be safe."

"They *all* should be safe," Dalton said.

"They will be. That's what we're here for. And since you're not officially on this op, as soon as we're done, you and Miri can get back to whatever you were doing."

"What are you talking about?" Dalton said.

"Don't kid yourself. You're hung up on her. More than hung up, I'd say."

"You've been here what? Twenty minutes? And you're telling me how I feel? You're full of crap."

"Yeah, right," Ryan said. He squinted through the scope.

Dalton dug through the pack for another magazine and stuffed it in his pocket. Ryan was nuts. He wasn't in *love* with Miri. He didn't do love. She was—Miri. Special, maybe, but not *love* material.

Fozzie's voice came over the headset before Dalton could think of an appropriate retort—or wonder why his chest ached.

"Later, pard," he said to Ryan, relieved at the diversion. "Company's coming."

"Eight bodies, three o'clock, ETA less than one," Fozzie said.

"Friendlies or hostiles?" Dalton asked.

"ID unknown," Fozzie said. "Manny, Hotshot, suggest you intercept, herd them toward Dalton's position. Harper, provide cover."

"Roger that," echoed from all four men on the ground.

Dalton raised the goggles, heading in the direction Fozzie

indicated, moving from rock to shrub, taking advantage of any available cover. At the report of a single gunshot in the distance, he yanked the goggles from his eyes. Muzzle-flash would be enough to blind him. Moving by instincts honed over countless missions, he approached the sound.

"Talk to me, Fozzie," he said. Silence. "Fozzie, come in."

"Sorry, mate. Some radio troubles. Hotshot is twenty meters northwest. In the rocks."

Dalton took a quick peek through the goggles. Hotshot crouched at the base of a large rock formation. With a target in sight, Dalton ran. "In position," he said when he joined his teammate. "What do we have?"

Hotshot cocked his head to the left. "Other side of these rocks. One guy with a gun threatening seven others. Could be a trap. They could all be armed."

Dalton keyed his mic. "Fozzie, give us a situation report." From above, with his surveillance equipment, Fozzie could pinpoint a flea on a squirrel's balls. Silence. Dalton tapped his headset. "Fozzie, do you copy? Repeat. SitRep, please."

"I've got bodies approaching from the tree line. Two from northwest, one northeast. And three more unidentified heat signatures."

"What are they? Deer? Bears? And what about Octavio? Where is he?"

"Give me a tick. I'm solo up here."

"Grinch isn't with you?" Dalton asked. "Who's flying?"

"Yours truly," Fozzie said. "Grinch was overdue for downtime, and this was supposed to be a cakewalk. I can pilot this bird and do recon. No sweat."

"No sweat," Manny said. "Four of us, fourteen of them. They don't stand a chance."

"Hey, let's find out who they are first, okay?" Dalton said.

"Shit, Cowboy, you think I'm going to walk up and shoot

everybody? Maybe the boss was right and you *have* been in the field too long."

Fozzie cut in. "Two more unknowns coming up on your six, Cowboy. Heads up."

Dalton spun around, weapon raised. Nothing. He slowed his breathing. Waited. He reached for his goggles right before he saw the light. It moved up and down, back and forth. Had to be the worst stealth approach in history. Or, more likely, they were unaware they were walking into danger. Crap. Who'd be out here at this hour?

"Cover me," he said to Hotshot. "Let's get these two out of harm's way before anything hits the fan."

Too late. A barrage of gunfire exploded in the distance. The light crashed to the ground. Dalton lowered his head and ran toward it. "Take cover," he shouted. "Down! Rocks!" he added in Spanish.

CHAPTER 30

Disoriented, Miri struggled to remember where she was. Her head throbbed, and she waited for her memory to clear.

Loud noises. A man shouting. Paco throwing her to the ground.

That explained the weight pinning her down. She wriggled out from underneath him. He pressed against her back, keeping her facedown in the dirt.

"Do not stand," he said in a hush. He rubbed his arm.

"Are you hurt?"

"No."

She lifted herself onto her elbows and peeked around the rocks. Nothing but vague shapes and shadows. "What's out there?"

"Coyote, I think. But I do not expect new arrivals for three days yet."

"That was gunfire, wasn't it?"

"*Sí.*"

So, why were they hanging around out here? "Let's get back into the tunnel."

His arm pressed her down again. "No. We wait. Nobody must find it." He cocked his head. "Somebody comes. Hide. Like so."

He folded his arms and buried his face. She'd always been good at making herself invisible, but that was in the city. Here, she followed his lead, trying not to inhale any dirt. Given she was breathing ten times faster than normal, that was challenge enough.

"Don't move," someone said in a stage whisper. The voice came from above, and nearby. "Stay low."

So much for hiding. Miri lifted her head enough to see a pair of black boots. Her gaze moved upward over dark camouflage pants, then stopped at the gun barrel hanging alongside the pants.

"I said, don't move." The gun lifted and pointed at her head.

Dalton's voice. Thank God.

"It's me. Miri. And Paco. We're on your side."

He dropped beside them. "What the hell are you doing here? I told you to stay put, damn it."

Even his whisper couldn't disguise the anger in his voice.

"Don't talk to me that way. Nancy needs to get to the hospital, and you weren't doing anything about it. We seem to have different priorities."

Gunfire cut their reunion short. She flinched. "Are they shooting at *us?*"

Paco belly-crawled to the shelter of a larger rock.

Dalton motioned her silent, and she realized he was listening to his headset. After a moment, he nodded. "Roger." He laid a hand on her arm. "How did you get here?"

"There's a back exit. Through a tunnel."

"Anyone else out here with you two?" he asked.

She shook her head. Dalton inched closer, his body heat radiating through the denim of her jeans.

She edged away, away from the temptation to burrow into his warmth. To sleep, and wake up from this impossible nightmare, to be in the motel room bed the way they'd planned. Which was *not* going to happen. Not tonight, and probably not ever. This was a world she wanted no part of, and this man had abandoned her. The way everyone else had.

He leaned closer, his breath warm against her cheek. "You should get back. Take the old man with you."

"He said no. Nobody's supposed to know about the tunnel."

Dalton slid a pair of goggles over his eyes, raised himself on his elbows and looked around. He sighed, apparently convinced it wasn't secure to cross the open space to reach the entrance. He spoke into his mic. "I need a diversion away from my position. Two civilians to move to safety." He did his listening thing, then said, "Roger."

"Are you going to tell me what the hell is going on?" Miri demanded. "My sister needs help and you're out here playing soldier. It's clear enough you're no private investigator."

"It's complicated." His gaze moved constantly, from her to Paco, then out into the distance and back again.

"Yeah, well, try me." Her voice rose above a whisper. "I might be a little slow on the uptake, given I'm not usually in the middle of the OK Corral, but I'm not stupid."

"Will you be quiet? We need three minutes." He clamped his hand over her mouth. "They'll hear you."

She resisted the temptation to bite his hand. There had to be some way for him to deal with his problem, whatever it turned out to be, and let her get Nancy out of this fiasco.

She squirmed, extricating her mouth from his grip. "Are you going to tell me who *they* are?"

"Damn it, darlin', I said quiet." He covered her mouth with his, pulled her against him. They grappled. She struggled, her hands all over him, seeking enough leverage to escape. On the ground the way they lay, his sheer size and weight overpowered her. She went limp, melting into him, succumbing to his strength. His tongue probed, and she opened her mouth to him, reaching behind him, clutching his buttocks, teasing, exploring. Wriggling against him.

Noise came over his headset and he rolled away. In the

distance, explosions filled the sky. "Okay. You and the old man get to your tunnel. Now. Like the devil is on your tail."

She scrambled to her feet and ran to Paco's hiding place. "Quick. To the tunnel while Dalton's men keep everyone busy." At least that's what she assumed was going on. She grabbed his hand and helped him to his feet.

They used her penlight instead of the lantern, but Paco seemed familiar with the terrain, and she hurried to keep up.

Barely missing a stride, they slipped through the entrance and hastily threw the branches back to disguise it. Paco leaned forward, breathing hard.

"I need you to help me," Miri said. "For Nancy. Can you make it to the community center by yourself?"

"*Sí.*" He straightened. "But the danger? The guns? Will not be safe to bring her this way."

"We don't have a choice."

"This entrance. This place. Even *los coyotes* do not know of it."

"I told Dalton the tunnel was a secret. He'll make sure nobody finds it. I trust him." Almost surprised to hear the words, she stopped for a heartbeat. She did trust him. She just didn't *like* him a whole lot right now.

"Very well." Paco moved along the path, setting a brisk pace.

"Wait," she said, catching his arm. "This is what I want you to do."

Satisfied Miri was safe, Dalton focused his attention on Fozzie and away from the annoying distraction below his belt. Kissing her had to be the stupidest thing he'd done since he brought a garter snake to the church dance to impress Cindy Mae. He could have shut Miri up a dozen different ways.

Yeah, but they wouldn't have felt that good.

Damn it, he couldn't fall in love in the middle of an op, for

God's sake. Ryan was nuts, that was all. Emotions always went into overdrive when the adrenaline kicked in. He tried to convince himself the rush he felt was no different than any other op. That a quick rendezvous with Debbie would get him back on an even keel. But all he saw was Miri. Damn Ryan for messing with his head. And double damn the man for being right. He, Ambrose G. Dalton, the lock-up-your-heart king, was ass-over-teakettle in love. "Fuck."

"You clear, mate?"

Dalton adjusted his headset, as if that would dislodge the emotions flooding over him. He took a steadying breath and activated the mic. "Ten-four."

"Mind joining the party?"

Shit. Plenty of time to deal with this after the op. He made the necessary adjustment to his pants and circled to join the team.

From above, the helo whined. A spotlight illuminated a clear patch of desert ground. Four men stood in the center, hands on their heads, scowls on their faces, and an assortment of weapons on the ground. Hotshot pointed his assault rifle at them. Dalton took in the pock-marked clearing and the smoldering shrubs. An excellent demonstration of Blackthorne's superior air support.

Dalton smiled and collected the dropped weapons. "Doesn't look like you needed me."

"You get your two tucked away?"

"Yeah. What about these folks?" He nodded toward the circle. "Do we know who's who?"

"Allow me to introduce you," Hotshot said, "to Moe, Larry, Curly, and Shemp. Moe, on the left, is a coyote for gullible immigrants, promising them a land of milk and honey, streets paved with gold."

"Can it, Hotshot. Cut the crap."

Hotshot's eyebrows bunched. "Lose your sense of humor, Cowboy?"

"Shut up. Let's get this over with."

"Fine. Moe was leading a small party of immigrants across the border. For a fee, which is every peso they owned, most of it converted to the now-regulated cold and allergy meds, he promises not to ditch them as soon as they hit U.S. soil but to guide them to a halfway house."

"Right. Which ends up being a meth lab."

"True." Hotshot waved his weapon at one of the men who dared to lower his hands. "Hands back on your head, Curly."

"Wait a minute," Dalton said. "We had a total of fourteen unknowns. Where's everyone else?"

"I was getting to that."

"Get there faster."

"Moe—who speaks damn good English, so watch your step—contracted with seven immigrants. At the last minute, three more—that would be Larry, Curly and Shemp—joined the group. Since they were willing to pay triple his usual cash fee, he waived the drug portion."

"And the original seven?"

"Scattered at the first gunshot."

"Wait a minute." Dalton did some quick math. "We're three short."

"Manny is on them."

Dalton rubbed the back of his neck, trying to stave off the impending headache. "These Stooges seem rather well armed for poor immigrants."

"Yeah, that's where things get interesting. How about if you go frisk 'em?"

"Gee, thanks." Dalton stepped into the spotlight. A gaunt faced man eyed him warily. He wore torn jeans and a bulky parka over who knew what. Damn, he didn't have time for this.

He raised his Glock.

"All of you. Strip. Now."

The men exchanged confused glances.

Dalton applied the Glock to the first man's head. "Take your damn clothes off. I'm not in the mood for touchy-feely tonight. At least not with the likes of you."

Muffled laughter came from Hotshot's position. More from his headset. Dalton shrugged. "I'm tired. You got a problem with my methods?"

"Whatever floats your boat, Cowboy."

Keeping a watchful eye out for concealed weapons as the men reluctantly undressed, Dalton kicked shed jackets and shirts toward Hotshot. "Don't stop," he said when the men bared their torsos. "You're getting to the good part. But shoes first. Makes it easier to get the pants off."

"Bingo," Hotshot said.

"What did you find?" Dalton asked. "More guns?"

"A small fortune in crystal meth. None of this start-from-scratch stuff. This is ready to hit the streets. Enough to supply a small city."

Dalton's gut twisted. Blood pounded in his ears. He jammed his rifle into the belly of the nearest man. "Get the rest of your damn clothes off. Now!" The man doubled over. The second man wore an assortment of thick gold chains around his neck. Dalton yanked them off.

Hotshot rushed up and pulled him back. "Easy, Cowboy."

"Slimeballs like these shouldn't be allowed to live. What's a little gold or one sucker punch?"

"Fine. You go through the rest of the clothes. I'll supervise."

Dalton caught the confusion in Hotshot's eyes. "I'm okay. Told you, I'm tired." He trudged over to the pile of discarded clothing and shook out pockets, checking for needles or other paraphernalia before digging with his fingers. He added the packets of drugs he found to Hotshot's collection. These folks were sellers, not users. The sort to prey on young innocents. How many had they pushed along the road to death?

Hotshot tossed four pairs of jeans his way. The men stood, shivering in their underwear.

"Think we need to go any further?" Hotshot asked. "It's cold out here."

Nothing like cold and nerves to shrivel the old family jewels. "I don't know. Maybe we should take pictures of their diminishing privates. Put them on the Internet or something."

From the wide-eyed reaction, apparently all four men understood English.

"Fozzie, come in." Manny's voice came over the headset. "My guys have gone to ground. Can you locate?"

"You blokes got things under control?" Fozzie asked.

"Go," both Dalton and Hotshot said.

"Harper, you napping?" Dalton asked.

"You hear that?" Hotshot said.

Dalton thumbed off his headset and peered in the direction Hotshot pointed. Nothing but darkness. "What should I be hearing?"

"Sounded like a car starting."

Dalton closed his eyes, zoning in on the sound. Definitely a vehicle coming toward them. His lids snapped open. He clutched his flashlight and grabbed his rifle.

CHAPTER 31

Miri slotted the key she'd lifted from Dalton's pocket into the ignition of his car. With a quick prayer her plan would work, she twisted the key. The engine hummed. So far, so good.

She slid the car into gear, then wiped her hands on her jeans. She flashed the headlights one time, long enough to get her bearings, and drew a mental map of the terrain from the community center to the tunnel entrance. By the time she got there, Nancy and Hunt would be waiting. She hoped. They'd get Nancy and have her at the hospital in no time.

She repeated that to herself as she bumped over ruts and rubble, avoiding boulders and brush. Ahead, the rock formation that marked her destination grew larger. She resisted the urge to punch the accelerator.

Hang in there, Sis. Another few minutes.

The car jolted and jarred over the uneven surface. Rocks clunked against the undercarriage. She slowed, then decided to brave another quick flash of the lights to make sure she wasn't going to hit something or end up in a ditch. Before she could twist the knob, a bright light almost blinded her. Closing her eyes, she slammed on the brakes.

The car stopped. She opened her eyes. All she could see was a flashlight beam and a shadowy form behind it. What now? She clicked on the high beams.

Try to blind me, will you? Take that, idiot!

"Get out of my car, dirtbag."

She started at the voice. Not again. She rolled down the window. "Dalton, damn it. Get out of the way. I've got to get Nancy to the hospital."

He stepped forward and ducked to window level. "Are you crazy? You're driving my car through a combat zone."

"What do you mean combat zone? The shooting's way over there." She pointed at the flashes coming from the distant trees. "It's not safe."

"Well, I'll take my chances. Nancy needs me. In about three minutes, we'll be out of here and you can go play soldier again."

"Did you hot wire . . . ?" Anger coated his tone. He stuck his head inside, then backed out and patted his pockets. He shook his head, and his lip curved in a cynical smile. His expression softened. "I didn't mean to snap. Move over. I'll drive."

"I don't think so. Let me get by and pick Nancy up, and we'll be gone."

He stepped away. She put the car in gear and started to move when he appeared at the passenger side and pulled the door open. "Then I'll ride shotgun."

Having an armed man aboard might not be such a bad idea.

He climbed in. "You're shivering." He reached behind the backseat and grabbed his parka. "Put this on."

"Later." She tossed it at his feet.

"All right. Go." He held his flashlight out the window, illuminating the ground. He patted her thigh, and she relaxed. This was going to work.

She drove faster, able to avoid obvious potholes and larger rocks. She glanced his way, and he smiled. Then his face went blank. Someone was talking to him over the damn headset again.

"Here? Now?" Dalton said. A pause. "Damn it to hell." His expression wasn't blank anymore. He was stone-cold furious. "Stop the car."

"What? No way."

"I said stop. Turn back."

"You have *got* to be kidding." She slowed, but if he thought she was going to stop, he was certifiably nuts.

He gazed at her, the same mix of sadness and determination as when he'd left the hideaway. "I've got to do this," he said. "I'll be back." He popped the door open and jumped.

Yeah, right.

She watched him run for several heartbeats, then drove on. With lights. At this point, the benefits outweighed the risk. She reached the clearing and positioned the car as close to the tunnel as she could. With the motor running, she bounded out and ran to the entrance.

"Hunt? I'm here."

Brush rustled, branches moved and Hunt appeared, holding one corner of the cot's mattress. Paco and two more men held the other three.

"Let's get her in the car," Hunt said.

"How's she doing?" Miri asked.

The strain around his mouth answered her question before he spoke. He clawed his fingers through his hair. "Drifting in and out."

She opened the back door and helped the men load her sister inside. Once they'd settled Nancy, her head cradled on Hunt's lap, Miri raced back to the driver's seat and threw the car in gear. Torn between the desire to drive at breakneck speed and the need to keep from jostling Nancy, she stuck to the semblance of a road, clearing her mind of everything but getting to the hospital.

Ahead, a silhouetted figure planted himself in her path, hands above his head, waving like a semaphore. Dalton? She couldn't tell, and she didn't care.

"No way, buster," she muttered, gritting her teeth and plotting a course around him. "You had your chance. This is the hospital express. Non-stop. No riders." She glanced in the rear-view mirror. Hunt bowed his head over Nancy. He murmured soft, soothing sounds.

The car hit a deep rut, and she struggled with the steering wheel, trying to get back on a more level stretch of ground while avoiding the man, whoever he was.

A bright flash of orange almost blinded her. The car shook. An explosive *crack* made her duck.

"What was that?" Hunt asked.

She blinked. "Damn. Something hit the windshield." A spiderweb pattern spread over the glass.

"Don't stop," Hunt said, his voice rising with urgency. "They're shooting at us."

"At *us?* We're the good guys." She found a spot clear enough to see through and stomped on the gas. A blast rocked the car. Dust flew in a giant cloud. She swerved. The wheel jerked and she fought to maintain control.

"Blown tire," Hunt said.

"I think there's more," she said, gaping at the crater beneath the settling dust. The one the car teetered over. This was *not* happening. "Paco said there were tunnels underground. I think one caved in."

"Crap," Hunt said.

"What now?"

A man stood beside her window, a cigar clamped between his teeth, a rifle pointed at her. A big rifle. What was it with these boys and their toys?

"We do what he tells us," Hunt said.

Dalton's heart stopped when he heard the explosion. He spun around and saw headlights disappear behind a cloud of dust. His car? Miri? He lowered his rifle, trying to see through the debris.

Static, then, "Northwest," came from his headset.

Without thinking if the call was meant for him, he thumbed his mic and pivoted in the direction Fozzie indicated. "Damnation, man, how many more?"

"Three I can find, mate. Keep your knickers on. Stick to business."

Business. Right. "What the hell are those asswipes doing here?" Not that it mattered. They were here; they were loaded for bear, but they were *not* going to get away from him this time. Stick to business. He took an intercept position, willing whoever was rustling in the shadows to come forward two steps so he could get a shot. Ops worked because everyone did his job. He'd take out his assignment, then get back to Nancy's rescue.

"Where's Miri?" No response. He mashed the talk button. "Damn it, Fozzie, what's with the fucking headset? You're in and out."

"I know, mate." More static. ". . . flush these fellows out."

Not that many moments ago—or was it a lifetime?—back at the meth lab, when Fozzie had radioed that they'd spotted Octavio, one of Rafael's major henchmen, in the woods, Dalton had answered the call along with the team. Simply picked up and left, ignoring Miri's pain-filled eyes. Again.

He pushed those images—along with the one of the disappearing car—from his mind. He took a calming breath. If Fozzie said he'd identified Octavio, then Octavio was out there. But where?

And Octavio wasn't alone. At least two more goons accompanied him, and although it was too much to hope that Rafael had left his secluded fortress in the mountains of Colombia, Dalton hadn't been able to resist the chance to eliminate one of his top generals. If they'd discovered a major drug conduit, he couldn't pass up a once-in-a-lifetime opportunity to destroy it.

At what cost? He was used to putting his life on the line. But Miri? And what about Nancy?

Distracted, he didn't hear footfalls until he smelled sweat. He revised his first thought, that a teammate approached, when he got a whiff of cigar smoke. No Blackthorne operative advertised his presence by smoking. He thought about the aftershave he'd splashed on a lifetime ago when a night in Miri's company was his only objective. Masked by his own sweat and meth chemicals, he assumed.

His brain processed these details at lightning speed, more in his subconscious than in any deliberate thought patterns. At the same time, he listened for any updates through his headset. Which was annoyingly silent.

"Do not move, *Señor*. Raise your hands. Do not turn around."

A deep, gravely voice, roughened by too many cigars. One Dalton recognized. One that brought back too many unpleasant memories.

He obeyed, all senses sizing up the situation. Were Octavio's goons with him? Dalton thought he detected at least one other person's breathing.

"Ah, Octavio. We meet again. A little out of your territory, aren't you? Surely you didn't come by just to see me. To what do I owe the honor of the visit?"

"You were always one with the words. Words, words, words. Too many words. You will not speak without permission. Perhaps I will remove your tongue. Before I kill you."

"You're not still holding a grudge, are you?" Where was the rest of his team, damn it. With his hands up, he couldn't reactivate his mic, assuming it was working.

"Three of my cousins are dead because of you," Octavio said.

"And your cousins killed seven innocent bystanders. In my

book, we're not even."

"You will drop your weapon. You will tell your friends to leave me alone."

"Oh, I don't think so, *amigo.*"

"Perhaps you will when I tell you I have something you want. Three somethings, perhaps. Two beautiful women, although one is not well. The other—I can imagine what I will do with her later. Is that not right, *mi amor?*"

Vulgar kissing sounds twisted Dalton's gut, but he knew better than to react.

"Let go of me, you creep." Miri. Sounding strong and defiant. He breathed easier.

"A wild one, she is. I like that. She will be fun. Maybe you will enjoy watching, no, *Señor* Dalton?"

"He'll enjoy watching me punch your lights out, creep."

Miri's voice, followed by the sound of a hand slapping against flesh and then a sharp intake of breath tightened the knots in Dalton's stomach. He spun around to see Miri rubbing her cheek. "Leave her alone." He did a quick scan. No goons. All he needed was an opening.

"I'm all right," she said. "I've dealt with scumbags like this one before. Guys who hit women do it because they've got no dicks."

Octavio's eyes narrowed to slits, his lips flattened, but he didn't take his gaze from Dalton. "Your woman has some mouth as well. She needs a lesson."

"I'm not his woman," Miri said. "So if you think he's going to defend me, forget it. He doesn't give a damn about me."

Her tone sent a painful chill through Dalton, as if she'd stabbed him in the heart with an icicle. There wasn't a hint that she didn't mean what she said. No glance his way to say she was bluffing. That she did care.

You're wrong. I love you. He longed to say the words.

But he couldn't let Octavio see his feelings, much less hear them. Keep the guy off guard. He steeled himself, ready for the explosion when Octavio's temper blew.

Instead, a genuine explosion came from the distance, where he'd seen what he'd assumed was his car disappearing in a dust cloud. Octavio's head tilted toward the sound, and Dalton lunged forward. Before he reached his target, Miri elbowed Octavio in the gut and stomped his instep.

"How about we let Dalton watch while I smash your tiny family jewels, creep?" She stepped back, poised to knee the man, who clutched his middle.

Above, helo rotors whirred. The area around them lit up. Fozzie's voice came through Dalton's headset. "You think you blokes can handle things while Hotshot and I run a med-evac mercy mission?"

"Roger that. Hold one second." Dalton pressed his rifle against Octavio's temple. "Miri, Fozzie's going to get Nancy to the hospital. Get to the helo. I've got this dirtbag." He grabbed Octavio's rifle and tossed it out of reach.

"First, I owe him." She followed through with a deft knee to Ocatavio's groin. The man collapsed at their feet.

"Go," Dalton said. "Fozzie's waiting. I'll meet you at the hospital. I . . . I'd like to talk."

She glanced over her shoulder toward the helo, then back at him. All his years reading people, and to him, she was a blank page. "Hurry."

"Thanks. I guess we have things to discuss." She lowered her eyes, her head, and ran.

Dalton automatically reached into his back pocket for flex cuffs before realizing he wasn't outfitted for an op. Instead, he shoved his boot onto Octavio's back, pinning him. Miri bolted toward the helo, hovering near a hole where his car balanced half in, half out. Arms reached from the open helo door and hoisted her inside. The helo lifted off and his car teetered for several long seconds, then disappeared.

"My insurance company is *not* going to like this," he said, increasing the pressure of his boot.

"Can't breathe," Octavio wheezed.

"Tough shit. Where are the rest of your buddies?"

A salvo of automatic weapon fire answered his question. Crap. He tapped his silent headset. "Manny? Harper? What the fuck's going on?"

Nothing but gunfire. Getting closer. He kicked Octavio in the ribs, grabbed the man's rifle, and hightailed it for cover. Not that there was anything for fifty yards. "God damn sitting duck," he mumbled.

Two muzzle flashes sparked from the distant trees to his left. Another to his right. "Shit." He dove. Unless Rafael's men came equipped with night goggles, darkness was his best hope. He hugged the earth, trying to look like a rock. His mind raced through possibilities.

Other than his own, Rafael considered life expendable and went through underlings like a drunk wolfing peanuts at a bar. Why was Octavio here on what seemed a chump-change operation? Had he been demoted? Or had Rafael sent him to supervise this conduit? If so, they were dealing with more than a few illegal aliens smuggling dope and cooking meth.

Another thought wormed its way through. Was Octavio branching out on his own? Instead of being one of Rafael's tentacles, was Octavio creating a new drug monster?

With an ear to the ground—literally—he strained to detect any signs of approaching danger.

Explosions vibrated the earth beneath him. He lifted his head a fraction. His headset crackled with static. "Cowb . . . six."

Gunfire grew closer. His heart jumped to his throat as his stomach plummeted.

Dalton did something he hadn't done in years.

He prayed.

CHAPTER 32

Miri twisted in the helicopter's seat, alternating between watching Hotshot minister to Nancy and checking the time, willing the seconds to tick by faster. One minute he'd been fully armed, a soldier ready to kill, and now he worked to save a life. While Hunter held Nancy's hand, Hotshot inserted an IV into her other arm. Although Miri couldn't hear his words, his compassion permeated the aircraft.

Fozzie's voice came through the headphones he'd given her. "ETA, twenty minutes." She checked her watch again. His voice came back, dead serious, definitely not directed at her. "Roger, Riverside. Have a medical team standing by, please. Hold for our medic."

Then silence. Fozzie had switched channels. She twisted around. Hotshot, his fingers on Nancy's wrist, said something into his mic. Hunt's shoulders stiffened. His eyes widened, his gaze focused on Hotshot.

"What's going on?" she asked.

Fozzie's voice returned. "No worries. Hotshot's coordinating with the medical team." His lip set into a grim line. "Nothing but the best for Hotshot's patients."

"Riverside?"

"Good trauma center, and it's closer. Less busy tonight, too."

She nodded, turning to look out the window. Up here, in the cloud-filled darkness, without landmarks or mile markers, she had no clue how fast they were going, but if they'd been in a car, she'd have sworn he floored the accelerator.

She clutched the buckle of her harness, her damp palms slipping on the metal. She huddled deeper into Dalton's parka. "Fozzie?" She hoped he'd attribute the way her voice trembled to the sound quality of the headsets.

"Almost there."

"Nancy. She's . . . Should I . . . I mean . . . do I have to say . . . I should be with her when . . . if . . ." she choked on the words.

"What?" Fozzie raised the face shield on his helmet, leaned over and squeezed her hand. "Of course not, sunshine. Hotshot's the best, and we'll be there in a tick. No sweat. She'll be apples."

Miri tried to believe him.

Fozzie twisted some dials, pushed some buttons, and flipped some switches. Her headset went silent.

"Damn it," she shouted. "Don't leave me out of this."

Hiding behind his face shield, he tapped her headphones, shook his head, then shrugged. "Sorry. Not working," he mouthed. He pointed toward the window.

She followed his gesture and saw city lights below. Growing closer. She reminded herself to breathe. "Hang in there, Sis."

Minutes later, the painted circle of the landing pad rose to meet them.

"Last stop," Fozzie said. "Riverside General. Everyone out."

Three people wearing medical scrubs waited alongside a gurney. When the helicopter set down, Hotshot threw the door open, and two of them rushed the gurney to them. With Hotshot's assistance, they transferred Nancy. Hunter leaped to the ground.

Miri clambered out of the helicopter, racing to catch up. At the open elevator door, a man in scrubs held his hand up. "Sorry. Not enough room. Two of you will have to wait."

"I've done all I can," Hotshot said. "I'll stay."

"Hunter, you go." She questioned a man in scrubs. "Where?"

"First floor. Emergency-Trauma. Can't miss it." And then the doors closed and they were gone.

"How is she?" Miri asked Hotshot.

He rested a hand on her shoulder. "Doing fine. Don't worry."

Don't worry. Right. Like that was a possibility. She pressed the call button for the elevator. She pulled Dalton's huge parka over her face, inhaling his scent. He said he'd be here. Confused as she was about her feelings toward him, she wanted—needed his strength. Someone to hold her, to tell her everything would be fine, and maybe, just maybe, she'd believe it.

She punched the button again. Three times.

"Take it easy, Miri," Hotshot said. "I got fluids into her, her pulse is steady, and she was awake for a lot of the flight."

Her knees wobbled, and she locked them. "Thanks. For everything."

"She's a fighter. Like her sister." He gripped her shoulders, and she accepted the comfort he offered.

Fozzie ran up behind her. "Sorry, mates. We have to go. This was a non-scheduled stop, and we're needed to help clean up the mess."

Hotshot released her. The men hesitated.

She punched the button again. Five times. "Go on. Save the world. I'm more concerned about Nancy."

The men walked toward the helicopter. She shoved her hands in the pockets.

"Fozzie, wait!" She ran after them.

Both men pivoted, polite but impatient expressions on their faces.

"Here," she said. "I forgot. You might be able to do something with this."

"A cell phone?" Fozzie's shaggy eyebrows arched like furry caterpillars.

"I lifted it from one of the creeps who tried to get friendly. I think Dalton called him Octavio."

Fozzie burst out laughing. He swept her up in a bear hug and swung her around. "Miri, you little ripper!"

She lowered the parka over her shoulders. "Here. This is Dalton's."

Fozzie held up his hands. "Keep it, sunshine. You can give it back when you see him."

Her step lightened as she ran to the open elevator doors.

Dalton sensed someone's approach.

"Do not move, *Señor*." A new voice.

Without turning, Dalton knew there was a gun pointed at him. His own rifle lay under his belly. All that stuff about your life flashing in front of your eyes when you faced death was bullshit. Somewhere deep in the recesses of his brain, there must have been a few cells dedicated to searching for a way out of his personal clusterfuck, but Dalton couldn't find them. His universe held two thoughts. *I screwed up. I'm dead.*

The voice droned on. "I would shoot you right now, but Octavio has claimed that honor. However, I strongly suggest you do not move, or I will have to disappoint him."

Was there a chance? Dalton dug for a possible plan.

"Ah, my *amigo*." Octavio's voice cut through Dalton's swirling thoughts. "Excellent work."

"You're going to shoot me in the back, Octavio?"

"Back of the head, I think. It is efficient, no?"

Dalton heard the shot. When he heard a second one, he figured he wasn't dead yet. He rolled, his hands and fingers operating on reflex, to get his rifle into position. If he was going to die, it wouldn't be with a bullet in the back of his head. Not today.

Two men lay on the ground. One bled from his chest. The other had a neat red circle in his forehead, a pool of blood spreading beneath his skull like a Rorschach inkblot.

Dalton's vision tunneled. He swallowed huge gulps of air. Seconds—or minutes—later, a familiar voice connected.

"It's over, Cowboy. Let's not shoot the good guy who saved your ass, okay?" A shape moved into his field of vision. A hand reached down.

Harper. Dalton lowered his rifle. "Guess I owe you, pard."

"I don't keep score." He stepped back half a pace. "Need another minute?"

"Anyone else looking to kill me?"

Harper gave what passed for a chuckle. "Not at the moment."

"Then I think I'll lie here until the world stops spinning so fast." Above, streaks of pink-tinged dawn filled the sky. "Might as well enjoy the sunrise."

Harper lowered himself to the ground beside Dalton, his back to the two corpses. Dalton knew Harper's aversion to killing, even though he was team sharpshooter. Shit, they *were* corpses, weren't they? "You check the bodies, pard?"

"First thing. You were napping." He took a swig of water from his canteen and wiped his mouth. "Want some?"

Not sure he dared lift himself even to his elbows, Dalton shook it off. "Crap. You telling me I actually passed out?"

"First time for everything." Harper left the canteen within reach.

"How long?"

"Minute maybe. Who's counting?"

Dalton took a modicum of comfort knowing Harper wouldn't be one to speak of this display of weakness, the same way no one paid attention to the way Harper did the Technicolor yawn after a kill. "Fill me in." He yanked his headset off. "This piece of crap's been fucking useless."

"Sorry. Your regular gear's at the compound. That was an extra on the helo."

"Yeah, well next time make sure I'm not working with second-rate equipment."

"Hey, your weapons were functional."

"Thank God for small favors." He propped himself on his elbows, glad the dizziness had passed. He found the canteen and took a gulp of water, then passed it to Harper. "Seriously, this was *not* fun."

"Yeah." Harper's eyes went blank. He lifted a finger signaling he was receiving a communication. "Roger that," he said, rising to his feet. "You ready to travel? Fozzie's got an ETA about ten minutes, half a klick away."

Dalton sat, accepting Harper's outstretched hand, then stood. "What about those two? And wasn't there a third?"

"Manny took care of him. Authorities will be here, and Blackthorne's got his PR specialists on it."

"Blackie can spin anything, can't he?"

"Like a top. He took care of twelve corpses in Montana—a few drug smugglers in this part of the country should be a piece of cake." Harper started off at a brisk walk.

"Shit. You go ahead," Dalton said. "Tell Fozzie I'll be there ASAP."

Harper spun around, concern on his face. "What's the matter? You all right?"

"Fine. Something I gotta do."

"Dalt. Wait. I'll come with you."

"Not needed. I'll be a few minutes behind you, that's all."

"You're going to warn them, aren't you? The people in the underground hideaway."

When had Harper picked up that damn clairvoyant streak?

Trying to BS his way out of this one wasn't worth the effort—or the time. "Yeah. You got a problem with that?"

Harper's reply was instantaneous. "None. Nobody on the team's said anything about them. If they stay put for a day or so, they should be clear. The drugs are the bigger picture here."

Dalton settled alongside Harper as they loped toward the house. "Makes you an accessory, or something, you know."

"And this would bother me because—?"

Dalton punched Harper's arm. "Right. Somehow, I can't get worked up about a few more tomato pickers minus green cards. We gotta figure out how to eliminate the meth part of this equation."

"We will."

Harper tapped his headset. "Fozzie, come in. Change in our pickup spot."

CHAPTER 33

Miri sat, paced, sat, and paced in the surgery waiting room with Hunter. It was nicer up here than in the emergency waiting room, but the underlying panic when the ER doctor rushed out with surgical consent forms for Hunt to sign wouldn't go away. So much for their initial diagnosis of minor injuries from the car accident. Couched in vague medical legalese, it said the doctors were going to open her up and would do what they needed in order to preserve the life of the patient.

Sunlight streamed in from the narrow windows near the ceiling. In the corner, a wall-mounted television played to the morning news. No stories about drug smuggling or illegal immigrants. Too small for the national news, too far away for the local news. Or not worthy of air time. Nothing new or different. Normal, everyday occurrences. The time display on the set said they'd been here three hours. Still no Dalton. She'd left her name at the ER desk, so he should be able to find her. She refused to dwell on the possible reasons he hadn't shown yet.

Hunter yawned, not bothering to cover his mouth.

"More coffee?" she asked.

He shook his head. She dumped her third cardboard cup into the wastebasket. "I know what you mean." She sat beside him and gave him a hug. "Nancy's going to be fine. She's a fighter."

"It's been too long. Something's wrong." He stood, trudged toward the desk where a grey-haired woman in a blue smock read a magazine. She glanced up at his approach and shook her head. He backtracked. Collapsed into the chair. "If anything happens—"

"Stop it. You have to be strong."

"She's . . . she's done so much for me. Without Nancy, I'd be another stuck-up, social-climbing, shallow—"

"I said stop. You're not. And you won't ever be. Nancy has a way of finding the best in people and bringing it to the surface." Her voice trembled. She clenched her fists, digging her nails into her palms. She could *not* break down.

"Mr. Sanderson?" A young woman wearing a white lab coat and holding a metal clipboard stood in the doorway.

Hunt leaped to his feet. "Yes. Is it about Nancy, my wife?"

The woman, who appeared barely out of her teens, stepped to his side. "Let's sit down. Dr. Groveland wanted me to give you an update."

"How is she?" Miri asked, afraid her legs wouldn't support her if she stood. She gripped the arms of the chair. "I'm Nancy's sister."

The woman gently guided Hunter to a seat, sitting down herself as if he needed someone to demonstrate. She smiled, but there was a sadness behind it. Not a teenager, Miri amended when she saw her in better light. Probably late twenties. A young face, but old eyes.

"What happened?" Miri asked. The woman sat on the other side of Hunt, and Miri leaned forward. "They said things were fine and then all of a sudden nobody would talk to us."

Cynthia Mason, patient advocate, according to her nametag, studied her clipboard. "Yes, I understand how you must have felt. That happens sometimes, but the patient is the number one concern. Mrs. Sanderson went into shock, and the ultrasound revealed an ectopic pregnancy."

"Oh my God," Hunt whispered. "Is she all right?"

Cynthia Mason studied her clipboard once again and spoke words she must have recited countless times.

"Mrs. Sanderson came through the surgery very well, but it will probably be two hours at the very least before she's admitted to a room and you can see her. They have her on antibiotics."

"I want to talk to the doctor," Hunter said. "Why isn't he here?"

"Dr. Groveland's team was called to another emergency surgery. I'm sure he'll be available by the time your wife is situated. He'll be happy to answer your questions."

"What aren't you telling me, Ms. Mason?" Hunt said. He sounded more like the Hunt Miri thought she'd known before tonight. Formal, in charge—almost cold and demanding under a veneer of politeness. What Nancy always called his "Don't mess with me" voice.

Once more, Ms. Mason consulted her clipboard. Hiding, Miri thought. The woman knew exactly what was written there. She flipped a couple of pages, sighed, and met Hunt's gaze.

"Mrs. Sanderson should follow up with her own gynecologist."

"Which she most certainly will," Hunt said. "But I'm asking you."

Another sigh. Ms. Mason set the clipboard on her lap and folded her hands atop it. "The ectopic pregnancy ruptured the Fallopian tube. In these cases, it's standard to remove both the tube and the ovary."

"But she's got two," Miri said. "She can still have children."

Ms. Mason addressed Hunt. "They found adhesions, scarring and endometriosis. While it's not impossible to have children under these conditions, it's highly unlikely. The fact that she got pregnant at all was very much against the odds. The important thing is that she's all right."

"I understand," Hunt said, his lips barely moving. His Adam's apple bobbed. "Thank you for explaining."

Ms. Mason stood. "I'll be back once you can see your wife. There's a cafeteria on the first floor if you'd like something to eat."

Miri couldn't imagine anything squeezing into the tight knot of her stomach, much less staying there. The young face with the old eyes blurred, and Miri dropped her gaze. "Thanks," she whispered.

Hunt stood. He shook her hand and walked with her to the door. He stood there, apparently watching her walk away. Then he swung around, stumbled, and staggered. Miri raced to his side and threw her arms around him in support. Sobs wracked his body. She guided him to a chair and held him as he wept. Whether they were tears of relief or sorrow, Miri wasn't sure. It didn't matter.

She wept with him.

Dalton buckled into a seat in the helo.

"That's some *sheila* you've got, Cowboy," Fozzie said.

Some sheila was right. Whether she was *his* sheila remained to be seen. Fozzie tossed something into his lap.

"What's this," he said, turning a cell phone over in his hands. "Am I supposed to call someone?"

"Maybe. Your little pickpocket lifted it from Ocatavio."

"What?" Dalton woke as if someone had doused him with a bucket of ice. "Have you checked it out?"

"Working on it." The pitch of the turbines rose, and the bird lifted off. "The guy was a message freak. Text, e-mail, an address book a mile long. It's a gold mine."

Dalton's adrenaline surged. "We've got to get this to our intel folks."

"We'll have to mobilize fast," Manny said. "As soon as Rafael gets word that Octavio's dead, he'll go to ground."

"Rafael's always in the wind," Hotshot said. "But I agree, this is an opportunity. If Blackie will go for it. No client, remember."

"Yeah. Listen to us," Manny said. "Since when did we start planning our own missions?"

"What about Homeland Security? The DEA? We've worked with them before, and this ties in with the local angle. They can't send US troops in. But that's why we work for Blackthorne, right?" Dalton said. "He can find a way. The Mexican drug connection is getting bigger every day—if Rafael's hooking up, there's a logical reason for us to go after him in Colombia."

"Speaking of the Mexican connection," Fozzie said. "What did you find out about Andrew Patterson? Is he connected?"

Dalton groaned. He'd totally forgotten Patterson. "I don't know. Blackie can put his investigators on it."

"I'm sure the cops will take care of it," Hotshot said.

Dalton wondered. Rich, powerful people like Patterson made bad stuff disappear. Would Blackie keep probing on his own? Maybe, if Grace pushed. This whole thing started because Grace, a former spy, had a bad feeling about Patterson. Or was *former* spy an accurate term? He stretched out his legs and closed his eyes. Another thought tiptoed in. Blackie and Grace? That was a picture he didn't need in his head. "Punch it, Fozzie. Take us home."

"No can do, mates."

Dalton's eyes popped open. "What's going on?"

"We got a 9-1-1," Fozzie said. "As of this minute, we're on deployment."

Everyone's attention snapped to Fozzie.

"Details?" Hotshot said.

"Quincy's daughter."

"Tracy? Again?" Cooper said. "Another wild goose chase?"

"Apparently not," Fozzie said. "Quincy got a ransom note.

He's got thirty-six hours to come up with three mil, or his daughter is toast. No cops, no feds, no nobody. Tracy's in Colombia."

"So our last lead was right?" Manny said. "She *was* in Colombia."

Fozzie nodded. "We missed her in Cali. Tracy's botanical research and Rafael's shadier botanical endeavors crossed paths. His deal is, he lets her go if Quincy gives him three mil *and* pulls whatever strings so Rafael's packages cross the border without question."

"How can Quincy do that?" Dalton asked. "We know he's got the bucks, but are his government connections that strong?"

"It doesn't matter," Fozzie said. "We have our orders. While Uncle Sam's minions are dicking around, we've got to get in and pull her out. Total communications blackout as of ten minutes ago. Nobody knows where we are. We'll be at the compound for briefing and additional personnel in under two hours."

Dalton thought of Miri. And of a chance to do something about Rafael. A battle raged in his belly.

Ten hours later, Dalton sat at the conference table in Blackthorne's private jet, eyeing Quincy's pale green complexion. "Relax, sir," he said. "It's what we do."

The man gripped the armrest, his knuckles whitening. "You're sure this will work?"

"If she's there, we'll get her out," Manny said.

"One more time, mates," Fozzie said. He looked to his left. "Harper?"

"I'll be on the roof of the old factory." He tapped an X on the diagram spread in the center of the table. "I'll have a clean line of sight into the room where they're holding Tracy."

Assuming their intel got it right this time. But Dalton didn't say anything that might sever Quincy's fragile hold on his self-control.

"Manny?" Fozzie continued.

"I'm Quincy's locally hired driver-translator-bodyguard-assistant."

Manny's Hispanic heritage made his assignment a natural choice. Normally, Dalton would've played the role, but he'd deferred to the team's argument that since Rafael assumed he was dead, he'd be more useful in a less conspicuous capacity. Like invisible.

Harper must have read his thoughts. He nudged his leg under the table. "Chill, Cowboy. Eye on the prize."

Dalton begrudgingly admitted Harper was right. Tracy was the goal. But he would *not* leave without dealing with Rafael.

Fozzie continued the recap. "Cooper?"

"I'm on point. The rest of us—" he glanced around the table "—follow SOP and clear the back room while Quincy and Manny stall the negotiations. We bring the target to the rendezvous point where Grinch will be waiting to haul our collective asses out and head for home."

"And I, as usual, will be covering those collective asses," Fozzie said.

"And the damn radios will function this time, right?" Dalton said.

Quincy stiffened.

"Five by five," Fozzie said, glowering at Dalton.

"How do you know your plan will work?" Quincy asked. He wiped beads of sweat from his brow with a soggy white handkerchief. One Dalton remembered being pristine when they'd departed.

"Because you're going to insist on dealing with Rafael, not an underling, which our money says is who's going to be negotiating," Cooper said. "Rafael doesn't like to show his face, so demanding to deal only with him buys us the time we need. You've got to stand firm on that one."

"I'll see to it," Manny said.

None of the men liked that Quincy would be there at all, but the man insisted, and even Blackie hadn't been able to convince him otherwise. A loose cannon. Exchanged glances around the table showed that opinions hadn't changed during the flight. If Dalton had his way, he'd have sedated the man until the op was over.

"Dalton?" Fozzie said.

"Covering the rear in case Rafael tries to make a run for it." *Please let the scumbag make a run for it.*

"I'll have that backed up, too," Harper said.

"All right, mates. ETA is two hours. Get some shut-eye."

The men dispersed to their seats, reclining into the plush leather. Dalton closed his eyes, but sleep wasn't on the agenda. Not until he was home with Miri. Would she have him back?

Dalton wriggled into the jungle undergrowth, eyes trained on the rear yard of Rafael's hacienda. Fozzie's voice in his headset tied him to the team. Quincy and Manny pulled up in the rental car, only a few minutes behind schedule due to several stops so Quincy could puke. Damn, they should never have let him get this far. He should be sequestered in a five-star hotel suite waiting for the tearful reunion with Tracy.

Around him, familiar jungle noises provided background to Fozzie's commentary. Birds, monkeys, insects. Rustling leaves. *Déjà vu* all over again. And then a hush descended as if someone unplugged a stereo.

"Fozzie?"

"Relax, mate." Fozzie's calm voice reassured him. "Looks like a jaguar scared the local critters."

Jaguar? So much for reassurance. Involuntarily, Dalton

tensed. Fighting the urge to get up and look around, he remained motionless.

"You're clear," Fozzie said. "He's found his tucker. Guess you're not on the menu today. But if you want snake for supper, there's one approaching from your right."

Crap. *If you're not a threat, it'll leave you alone.* Dalton played that mantra over and over, not daring to move, barely daring to breathe as he felt the snake slither over his right thigh, then over his ass and down on his other side. Had to be sixty feet long judging from the time it took to continue on its way. Or did he still feel it? It couldn't still be there.

Fozzie's voice came through, laughing. Guffawing was more like it. "You should have seen the expression on your face."

"Gone?" Dalton asked.

"Yep. Must have been a two-footer if it was an inch. Hang tight." All humor left his voice. "We're a go."

Gunfire erupted from the hacienda. In his mind's eye, Dalton saw his teammates burst into the room, each covering his assigned quadrant, taking out anyone who wasn't Tracy. Separating hostiles from hostages. Sweat pooled in his armpits and his stomach clenched. Those split-second decisions decided who lived and who died. Surveillance showed three goons in the room with her, one outside, but the unexpected had a way of happening no matter how good the preparation.

He focused on his target area. If Rafael behaved true to form, he'd leave the fighting to his henchmen and hightail it for cover. Dalton's finger poised over the trigger.

Make my day, asshole.

A cluster of people raced from the building. He squinted, trying to locate Rafael in the milling crowd. Full of women and children. Damn the man.

Fozzie's voice interrupted. "Get to the rendezvous, Cowboy. Now. Target is in need of medical attention. Stat."

Target. Tracy. The mission's target, not his. Once he pinpointed Rafael, he'd need fifteen seconds, tops.

"I'll catch up, Fozzie."

"No can wait this time. Plan B if you're not aboard, mate. Secondary point in eighteen hours."

"I'll be aboard."

"See you there."

Dalton switched off his radio, not wanting the distraction. The jungle noises were enough. He slowed his breathing. He waited. Above, a helo whupped.

"Come on, asshole. Show yourself. One shot's all I need."

"Well, amigo. Reports of your death seem to have been grossly overstated." Rafael's voice reverberated from behind him. "I look forward to remedying that. Slowly. Painfully. But not here. Somewhere nobody will find you. And don't try anything foolish. I am not alone. Right, men?"

Four new voices replied to Rafael. Four gunshots exploded above his head. Four men rushed toward him.

Dalton raised his hands.

A boot on his ass. A kick in his ribs. Rafael's cohorts manhandled him, blindfolded him, and slammed a rifle stock against the back of his head. As consciousness floated away, he clung to one thought. Blackthorne never left anyone behind.

Chapter 34

Miri settled into a rocker in Elsie's nursery and snuggled Amanda close to her chest. "Sleep, little one." The doctors had fixed a hole in the infant's heart. Miri wished someone could do the same for hers. She toed the floor, setting the chair in motion.

Six weeks since Dalton sent her off, promising to meet her. Six weeks since she'd heard a word. All right. Five weeks, five days and an undetermined number of hours and minutes. Which she refused to calculate. Like she refused to cry over one more person who didn't keep his word. At the three week mark, she'd drawn a thick red line through his name in her mental friends list. Between Galloway House and Elsie's infants, she had plenty of people who needed her.

Amanda stirred, wriggled and found her thumb. To the accompaniment of quiet slurping, Miri hummed "My Favorite Things."

Light from the hallway spilled into the dimly lit nursery. Miri glanced over her shoulder toward the open door. Elsie shuffled in. "You go sit in the other rocker, and I'll bring you a baby," she said to someone behind her. She smiled at Miri. "Brought a new volunteer. Thought you'd like company for a change."

No, I wouldn't. "Fine," she said, returning her attention to Amanda. "Yolanda's down for the count, but I haven't cuddled Jimmy yet." She went back to her humming, paying little heed to the familiar cooing sounds behind her as Elsie took the baby from his crib.

Miri heard the rocker creak and glanced up at a gowned, capped, and masked newcomer. Male, judging from his size. A quick peek of a beard curling from behind his mask confirmed it. Tall and slender, judging by his legs. Elsie settled him with his charge and left, closing the door behind her.

More squirming and red-faced grunts from Amanda pulled Miri from her seat. "You are one stinky little girl," she whispered. "Let's get you clean and sweet."

Even with her back to the man, she felt his gaze boring through her as she ministered to Amanda. Miri hoped Elsie wouldn't mind if she cut her session short. She didn't want company, and definitely not male company. If Amanda fussed, the new guy could rock her after he finished with Jimmy.

She fastened the diaper tapes, threw the used one in the diaper pail, and snapped Amanda's sleeper. "There you go, little pumpkin. All snug and ready for nighty-night." Carrying Amanda to the rocker, Miri buried her nose in the baby scent.

Amanda stared at her with wide baby-blue eyes, as if to say, "You're not getting out of here early." Miri set the rocker going with more force than necessary. Amanda whimpered.

"Oh, baby, I'm sorry. Not fair to take things out on you." Miri hummed her lullaby again. "Someday I'll bring my Coltrane CD and you can hear the song at its best."

"Don't listen to her, Jimmy, my man. Pasty Cline's the way to go," the man whispered.

Although the words were barely audible, the hint of Texas buried in the whisper sent goose bumps crawling over her. *Oh, God. It can't be.* She tightened her hold on Amanda, afraid she'd drop her. *Not now. Not here.* Unable to lift her gaze, she studied the cherubic face in her lap. She couldn't avoid noticing the sandalwood teasing her nostrils. How had she missed it?

Her eyes burned. Her throat tightened around a golf ball-sized lump. Kissing Amanda's forehead, Miri carried her to her crib. She settled the infant and flipped on the mobile dangling above. Assorted sea creatures swam in a circle to a music-box rendition of "Octopus's Garden."

She spun on her heel to leave, almost bumping into Dalton. Only the fact that he held Jimmy kept her from shouting—or slapping him. The soft glow of the nearby lamp reflected the pain in his eyes. She blinked back tears. What did he see in hers? Anger? Hurt? Betrayal? Didn't matter. She was out of here. She reached for the tie of her gown.

"Miri. Please. I can explain." He looked at the baby, then at her. Jimmy's face screwed into a knot.

Damn it. She took Jimmy, whose cry rivaled an air raid siren, and whisked him out the door. Before she took three steps, Elsie was there, hands outstretched. Great. Had she orchestrated this whole reunion scene?

Dalton was behind her as she handed off the infant. "Miri."

Ignoring him, she marched to the hamper and stripped off her gown. Dalton did the same.

"Miri, please."

"We've established you know my name," she said. "And I'm sure you have an explanation. The issue is, do I give a damn what it is? I think not."

I think not? Talk about lame. She pushed past him, careful to avoid any contact, knowing if she touched him, she'd lose it.

He didn't say anything as she stormed through the living room, across the porch and down to the Galloway House van parked in front. She got in and cranked the ignition. Nothing. Shit. She twisted the key again. Silence. Damn, damn, damn. She slapped the steering wheel, jiggled the gearshift, and tried once more. Zilch.

She dug through her purse for her cell phone. At least Galloway House belonged to the Auto Club. If only they'd get here right away.

Before she found the number, Dalton tapped on the window. She held up the useless key. "Can't," she said. "Windows won't open."

He crossed to the other side of the car and pulled open the passenger door. Why hadn't she locked it?

"Can we talk?" he said.

"After I call Triple-A. I'm sure there will be plenty of time."

"Don't bother. I can fix it."

"You can? And I suppose you know what's wrong?"

"Since I'm the one who disabled it, yeah, I know." He shrugged and lifted his hands in an apologetic gesture.

"You did what?"

He climbed into the passenger seat and closed the door. In the confines of the van, his scent swamped her. She fought the rising tide of emotional overload, sorting through the flood and hanging on to anger.

"I had a feeling you wouldn't stay and talk to me. I want to explain."

"You could have parked behind me."

"I thought of that. But the last car at the rental counter was that little thing." He pointed to a red sub-compact next to the van. "I was afraid you'd back right over it."

A smile escaped before she could stop it. "You're probably right."

"So, can we talk?"

"Should I believe whatever you're going to say? So far, everything's been one lie after another."

"Not lies. Things I couldn't tell you."

"And you can tell me now?"

"Some of it." He reached for her, and she drew back. His hand dropped as if she'd slapped him. "Let me try. Ask me questions. I promise to answer what I can. Over coffee?"

She'd played and replayed what she'd do if she ever saw him again. Walk away? She'd tried that. Cut him down with scathing remarks? She'd barely been able to get past lame. Scathing was out of reach. Slap him? Pound his chest? Knee him? She'd envisioned them all.

All except talking like two adults. The pain in his eyes cut through her like a phaser on kill. He looked as bone-weary as she felt. And thinner. Too much thinner. Purple hollows under red-rimmed eyes. "Fix my car first."

He hesitated.

"We go in two cars, or in my van," she said.

"Pop the hood."

Dalton eased into a booth at Denny's. As if taking him literally when he'd said they could talk over coffee, she'd turned on the radio and didn't utter a word on the drive from Elsie's. The waitress brought coffee as soon as they sat, filling their mugs and setting the carafe in the middle of the table.

"Apple pie," he told her.

Miri perused the menu, ordered a dish of plain vanilla ice cream.

All the things he wanted to say, all the things he'd rehearsed, stayed locked inside. "How's Galloway House?" he managed.

"Fine. Busy."

"Do you hear from Jillian and Will? Are they still with Grace?"

"I talked to them a month or so ago." She emphasized the "month," clearly driving home how long he'd been gone. "They were fine."

The waitress appeared with their food, giving an excuse for another stretch of awkward silence. Miri avoided his gaze, and he couldn't blame her. He poked at the pie, more to keep his hands occupied than because he wanted to eat it. He'd dreamed of apple pie while Rafael held him captive. Now, he was afraid he wouldn't keep it down.

He clutched the thick white mug in his hands and tried again. "How's your sister?"

"Okay. Fozzie got her to the hospital in time. Ectopic pregnancy. Ruptured."

And they'd thought the car crash had caused her pain. "I'm sorry about that but glad she's all right."

"She and Hunt moved back home. They're regrouping, but Hunt's got a job with Habitat for Humanity now. He's happy."

"That's good." More brilliant repartee. He spun the coffee mug, then lifted it to his lips, pretending to drink.

A waiter approached the booth behind her, his order pad poised. "What will it be?" he asked, his Hispanic accent slicing through Dalton's ears.

He froze. Coffee sloshed over the rim of his mug. With trembling hands, he set it on the table.

"What will it be today, Señor Dalton?" A beam of light burned through the darkened cell.

Dalton covered his eyes, bringing back the blessed darkness.

"Fists perhaps?" A blow to his solar plexus knocked the wind out of him. "Or maybe I practice my football kicks, I think." Steel-toed boots slammed into his rib cage. "No, perhaps it is time to end it all." The spin of a revolver cylinder, the cock of a hammer. Cold steel against his temple.

His team would be back. Get through another session. Hang on another day. Miri. Think of Miri.

Sweat drenched him. He shivered. Hot, then cold, then nothing.

"Dalton? Dalton? Are you all right?"

Miri's voice floated over him. Her scent filled his nostrils. He blinked until the restaurant reappeared. Miri sat across from him, concern carved into her features. He sucked air, struggling to grasp the here and now.

"I'm fine. Spaced out a minute." He released his death grip on the coffee mug. Brought his breathing under control.

"Let's go," she said. "We'll finish at my place. Your car's fine at Elsie's awhile longer. You look awful, and you're obviously not hungry."

Did she care? He looked like hell, which wasn't surprising considering he'd been there and back. Or was she embarrassed to be seen with him after his freak-out? Or was it simply because that's what she did? Took care of people, even creeps like him. It didn't matter. He'd take what he could get.

"Long day," he said. When she reached for her purse, he stopped her. "I'll get the check."

She hesitated, as if she didn't want to be in debt even for a cup of coffee. She nodded and slid out of the booth. He left a few bills on the table and followed her to the van.

"I noticed the babies were different tonight," he said as they drove. More small talk to fill the expanding cloud of uncomfortable awkwardness. "What happened to Xavier and Zoey?"

"Nancy and Hunt are adopting them."

She gave him a sidelong glance, as if to judge his reaction. She'd seen his surprise. Her grin was fleeting, but it was there. It felt good to see it.

"Yeah, I know," she said. "I mean, I know Nancy'll be a great mom, but I didn't expect something like that from Hunt. I totally misjudged him. But the doctors said it would be nothing short of a miracle if Nancy conceived and carried to term, so they decided to take two babies who needed a good home."

"And Hunt's parents?" He couldn't imagine the senior Sandersons gurgling over adopted babies to begin with, much less conspicuously adopted ones, their chocolate brown skin and curly black hair in such contrast to the blond Sandersons. Not to mention their medical problems.

"Horrified at first, of course, but Mrs. Sanderson's putting a positive spin on it. Charitable good works and all. Once she held them, she came around. A little. I'm not sure she's ready to take them to the country club yet."

Relieved that the tension had eased, he tried to find a topic to talk about without losing the ground he'd made. Nothing came to mind. He folded his arms across his chest and leaned his head back. After almost six weeks in Colombia's heat, the damp San Francisco night air chilled him, even though it was August.

"You cold?" she asked. "Your parka's in the back."

He twisted and saw it spread on the backseat. He reached around, stifling a wince as sore muscles, reminders of Rafael's handiwork, protested. "You kept it. Thanks."

"I hope you don't mind that I let residents use it."

"Not at all. Glad it came in handy." He recognized Miri's street. Once they were inside her apartment, he'd come clean. She'd either accept him or she wouldn't. Why did it scare him to think she might not? Too much time alone with nothing but his thoughts.

She parked in the lot behind the building. He followed her upstairs, clinging to the rail, breathing too heavily. Hotshot had put him on fluids from Colombia to Miami, but he'd refused to go to the hospital once they were stateside.

All he could think of was getting back to Miri. Some rest, some regular meals and he'd be fine. He made it to the couch and sat, toeing off his shoes while he waited for the dizziness to pass.

Miri brought him a glass of orange juice. "Drink." She hovered over him, waiting.

His hand shook and he almost spilled the drink before he got it to his mouth. He sucked down half. She took the glass and set it on the coffee table. Still waiting. He couldn't stand the silence.

"What about the migrant project?" he asked.

She stared at him like he'd been on the moon. "I take it you haven't seen the news lately. Or the papers."

"I've been out of touch." A Colombian hellhole wasn't the moon. The moon would have been easy.

"Patterson swears he was duped by his secretary and her sister. The sister, Wendy, was using her gift shops as a cover for smuggling drugs, but it was getting too hard to get the stuff in with all the new border security. Patterson's secretary—"

"Belinda," he said.

"Right. Belinda had access to everything regarding the project. Wanda had the Mexican connections, and she conspired with Belinda to set up a place where they could produce meth. Patterson claims he had no knowledge of her scheming with the contractors to modify the plans for the migrant worker community center and swears he wasn't involved in drugs. Since no houses were built yet, there was no way to prove he was or wasn't going to be smuggling workers in, or even turning a blind eye to whether or not they were legal. He's still promoting the project. Insists it's squeaky clean and promises full access to anyone who doubts it. It's in the hands of the legal system. Patterson's got a team of high-priced lawyers working to clear his name."

Something didn't track. "What about the files you took from Patterson? You got those from his home computer, right?"

"I did. I didn't know what to do with them."

"Let me see."

She shot him a quizzical glance but powered on her laptop. "What are you looking for?"

"Not sure. Maybe something will pop. But unless there was a darn good reason for Belinda to be working from Patterson's home office, I'd say anything in these files might implicate him."

She clicked the document open. "If anyone can tie the files to the migrant community project."

"Let's have a look-see."

She handed him the mouse. "You have the con, captain."

He smiled. It felt good. "Hobart Construction. I'm not an architect, but I'd say these plans are a good match for the room we saw at the community center site."

Miri leaned over his shoulder. Her scent teased, tantalized. He gritted his teeth. *Slow down.*

"Wait," she said. "Move over." She all but pushed him out of the chair. She clicked a few times. "Here it is."

He stood behind her. "That's the meth house explosion, right?"

"Yes. This was in the paper. Look." She tapped the picture. "The Dumpster. See it?"

He squeezed her shoulders. "Hobart Construction. Doesn't prove anything, though. They're a big company."

"Maybe so, but if we tell Detective Braddock about this, can't he trace the records and see if there's a connection between the meth lab here and the one in the migrant place? And if Patterson's hooked in somehow?"

He rubbed his neck. He thought for several moments. "Give the files to me. Then delete them."

"On your say-so?"

"Please, Miri. Trust me. I'll deal with it." Another time.

"Trust you? You hurt me. You're exactly like everyone else who broke promises or abandoned me. I tried to hate you. But I can't. Tell me who you are, what you really do. And why you lied to me. Then I'll decide if I can forgive you for disappearing for six weeks without a word."

"Five weeks, six days—" he checked his watch "—three hours,

seventeen minutes and twenty-three seconds. But who's counting?"

She dropped to her knees. "Oh, God, Dalton what happened? It was something bad, wasn't it? First, I was furious. Then I was scared because I thought you'd died back there with all the shooting, but if you had, I knew Mr. Blackthorne's secretary would have told me when I called. So I was furious again."

"Come here, darlin'. Please." He patted the couch.

She kicked off her loafers, then sat beside him. He ached to put his arms around her, for what he hoped wouldn't be the last time. Instead, he leaned forward for the juice glass. She met his hands halfway. He swallowed a groan at the contact.

"Let's start with an easy one," Miri said. "You're not a private investigator. Why did you lie?"

"I didn't. I never said I was a private investigator."

"But you didn't deny it."

He finished the juice. "What I do, Miri, isn't something I can advertise. I think you know there's more to Blackthorne than what you see in their offices. We go places the government can't. Officially, that part of the agency doesn't really exist. You saw something of what we do, and you can't tell anyone. I can't tell anyone. As far as you're concerned, I'm a private investigator. I know you'll respect that."

She nodded. "I understand."

"All I can tell you is we had an emergency assignment. We left the country. I got back this afternoon and had a hell of a time finding you. Galloway House said you weren't there, but wouldn't tell me anything. Nobody answered at your apartment and your cell number was cancelled."

"Galloway House got new ones." She toyed with the collar of his polo. "But you found me, super-sleuth."

He smiled. "I might not be a real PI, but I know how to follow the occasional clue. I had this scrap of paper with a phone number on it. You gave it to me. I called it."

"Elsie's. At the time, I thought rocking babies would be good for you. I didn't know your history or I'd never have done it."

"No matter. Elsie told me you've been there every night. She promised not to let you leave until I got there. I was stuck at Blackthorne for a debriefing, but I bugged out as soon as I could."

She was quiet for several heartbeats. "You smell good. Like you."

"I did take a couple of minutes to shower."

"Your parka. I didn't let the residents use it right away. Not as long as I could smell you in it."

She leaned into him. He put his arm around her, and Rafael was forgotten. "You smell like you, too. With a little baby thrown in."

Another long, uncomfortable silence, but with Miri in his arms, he could bear it. This time, she spoke first.

"Something bad happened, didn't it?"

He stroked her hair. "Yeah. But it's over. I'm back."

"Until you go away again."

"It's my job."

"Was it worth it?"

"If I didn't think so, I'd quit."

She quieted, and he pulled her closer. Wanting her. Needing her. Afraid to move. Afraid to close his eyes. Afraid he'd wake up back in the dark, alone, wondering when someone would come to give him his next beating. That she'd disappear, be another dream.

"We can have tonight," she whispered. Her hand brushed his erection through his jeans. "I'm not sure about anything else. But I want you tonight."

She found his lips with hers. Soft. Gentle. Feather light. He pressed his hips into her hand. Through the denim barrier, her fingers stroked his cock.

One night would never be enough. But if it was, the memory would have to last a lifetime. "Let me take you to bed."

Miri refused to move. She rubbed her lips, then her cheek against his chin. He tilted her chin. "Does the beard bother you? I can shave." He'd yank each hair by the roots if he had to.

"No. I've never kissed a man with a beard before. It's softer than stubble." She kissed him, a quick and gentle caress of lips. "Tickles. I might like it."

"Darlin', feel free to keep testing." He pressed his mouth firmly against hers. Her tongue teased. She shifted, and her elbow dug into his chest.

He gasped. "Please, darlin'. A bed." He wrapped his arm around her waist and inched himself to a seated position, dragging her with him.

She kissed him again. "Mmmh. Bed. Like we go to the bedroom? Get up and walk?"

"Unless you can call Scotty and have him beam us there. Or the bed out here."

Somehow, they rose to a standing position, her hand still stroking him.

He steered her to the bedroom. Without breaking stride, he flipped the light switch turning on the bedside lamp, backing her up until her knees encountered the bed. She sank onto the mattress. He stumbled, knocking her down, his body poised above hers.

CHAPTER 35

She wrapped her arms around his neck and pulled him into a kiss. A deep, probing, desperate kiss. The one she'd saved in her kiss bank, accruing interest for the last six weeks.

"Darlin'," he panted. "Slow down." He tugged her hands from his neck and climbed to the middle of the bed. "Come here. We've got the night."

She didn't want to slow down. She wanted him, every piece, every inch, every molecule of him. All at once. Now. She wanted to lose herself in his being. To entwine her molecules with his. She crawled to his side and tugged at his shirt. "Off."

He raised his arms. "Help yourself."

As she wrested the shirt up and over his head, he sucked air through his teeth. She tossed the shirt to the floor and leaned over, fumbling in the nightstand drawer for the condoms she'd bought six weeks ago. She dropped two on the table.

She stopped at his bare torso. Beneath the mat of coarse brown hair, he was pale. Except for an array of yellow, green and purple bruises.

"My God, Dalton, what happened to you?"

"Got banged up a bit. Nothing's broken. I'm fine." He grinned, but there was no accompanying twinkle in his eyes. "Where were we?"

"Are you sure you're okay?"

"Darlin' if there's one thing I'm sure about, it's that I want this. You. Now."

She nodded and reached to turn off the lamp. "Let me get the light."

"No." He grabbed her wrist. "Leave it. I want to see you." A disquieting tremble crept into his tone. Something flashed in his eyes. Fear?

She lay on her side beside him, propped on an elbow. "You'll tell me if I'm hurting you, right?"

He laughed, and this time, his eyes twinkled. "The only thing that will hurt is if you stop." He fingered the hem of her shirt. "Your turn."

She slipped the cotton tee over her head, her nipples tightening beneath her bra as the air reached them. Straddling him, she leaned forward, luring his tongue with her breasts. He took the bait, nibbling through the sheer fabric of her bra. Pleasure shot through her. She positioned herself above his erection and lowered her hips, grinding against him.

"Oh, God," he groaned. He thrust upward, at the same time finding the clasp to her bra. "So much for slow." He yanked the garment down and off. He raised his head, his lips straining to meet her pebbled nipples, and winced.

"Wait," she said. She moved to his side and got on her hands and knees. "You lie still." She started at the top of his head, caressing, kissing. Inch by inch she worked down, past his forehead, his eyebrows. One eyelid, then the other. The super-economy sized pillows under his eyes. She traced the edges of his beard, his lips, first with a forefinger, then her lips. His breathing quickened, and he moaned softly.

"God, that feels good."

"I'm glad." She continued down his body. Neck, shoulders, the hollows of his collarbones. She scraped her teeth along his nipples, and her own ached.

She unfastened his belt, then popped the button at his waist. She thrust her hand inside, found his sac and cupped it. It puckered beneath her touch. Something was different. She lowered his zipper, then his jeans. No underwear, but that didn't surprise her.

"Um . . . did you get confused about where you're supposed to shave?" She gave a playful tug to his whiskers.

"Take too long to explain," he said.

Intrigued, she fondled him. Ridged, but smooth. His erection twitched.

"Lift," she whispered, tugging on his waistband. He raised his hips enough for her to tug his jeans off. She lowered her face to his groin, swirling her tongue over his balls. His hips bucked.

She grasped his erection, sliding her thumb over its slick tip. "I want to taste you," she said. "Is it . . . are you . . . did anyone . . . ?"

"I'm clean, but—"

"Shh. You relax and let me do everything."

"Too far to relax, darlin'. Oh my God." He gripped her head, pressing her into his rhythm as her mouth captured him. "Oh my God."

His pleasure aroused her as much as his touch would have. She hummed softly.

"Sweet lord. Stop."

Unrelenting, she shook her head, sliding her mouth along his length as she did.

"Miri! Please. Inside. Now."

She released him. "You sure?"

"God, yes." His breathing came in labored pants.

"Are you in pain?"

"The good kind."

Her own desire made it easy to believe him. She tore open a condom packet and handed it to him. "You do it."

★ ★ ★ ★ ★

Dalton slid the condom on while Miri kicked off her pants and peeled her underwear down her legs. He watched her, afraid if he took his eyes off her, she'd disappear like a mirage. No. He was home. In her apartment. In her bed. She was very, very real.

When she straddled him again, he concentrated on her pleasure. She guided him inside. She was hot, wet, and ready, but he was readier.

Slow down.

He fondled her breasts, thumbing a nipple with one hand while his other searched between her thighs for her nub. He found it, wet and swollen.

She whimpered. Moved faster against him, which carried him to the edge of the point of no return. The combination of pain and pressure built low in his back and spread through his groin. He battled to control the inevitable.

"Miri," he gasped. "I'm too close. Can't wait."

She reached behind her, between his legs, and stroked his balls again. "Come. Come for me."

He lost it. Or had he found it? A soft voice whispered in his ear. "Come with me."

His universe exploded like a dozen flash-bangs. He thrust into Miri, faster and faster, aware of nothing, aware of everything. Pleasure, pain, colors, sounds, and a tiny voice in his ear.

She shuddered, then collapsed on him. Almost immediately, she pulled herself upright. "Are you okay?"

"Never better." She rolled off, but he snaked out an arm and snuggled her to his side. "Stay."

She slid the used condom from his half-erect cock. "I'll be back." For a heart-stopping moment, while she was in the bathroom, his universe emptied and he fought despair, however irrational.

She's here. She's real.

She climbed back into bed, resting her head in the crook of his shoulder. He exhaled a shaky breath. She fingered the hair on his chest. "Tell me what happened to you."

"You don't want to know."

"I have to know you're not protecting me from what you think I can't handle. Not knowing is worse. Guessing. Wondering. Like why you need the light on."

"Maybe I like to look at you."

"Maybe you have to be honest with me."

"Maybe I don't want to say it out loud." His voice broke, and he squeezed her tighter.

"So you keep it bottled up inside until it festers, and cut me out of another part of your life. If we're going to have anything, you have to share. Not the classified stuff. I understand that. But people have lied to me my entire life. They've gone off and left me and never come back. If you can't be honest, we have nothing."

"You're the reason I'd always come back. I'm in love with you, Miri. You saved my life."

"What? How?"

"I had to tell you I loved you. And since I didn't have the balls to do it before I left, I had to come back to tell you in person. No matter what they did."

"Tell me."

He clutched her closer, stroked her hair. "The usual captive stuff. Dark cell. Dirt floor, filthy mattress. Lousy food, what there was of it. Daily beatings. Someone holding a gun to your head, laughing while you wondered if this time, there would be a bullet in the chamber."

"God, Dalton, it's not funny."

"No," he whispered. "It's not. But remembering hurts too much."

"You were there the whole time?"

"Most of it. But Blackthorne never leaves a man behind. I knew they'd be back."

"Did they get the people who captured you?" Her voice held a tinge of anger.

"Some of them." *Not the one who counted, though. Rafael disappeared. Again.* "But you were with me. Every minute of every day." He kept his voice steady, at least at first, as he told her how he'd seen her in the dark, talked to her, imagined holding her, making love to her. How he hated his captors for coming in, not because they'd beat him, but because they'd shine a light in his cell, and he'd know he was alone.

Before he finished, tears streamed down both their faces. She wiped her eyes on a corner of the sheet, then wiped his.

He kissed her palm. "If you're here for me, it's all worth it. I'll never abandon you. I love you. We have something special."

"I love you, too, Just Dalton."

"Turn off the light," he said.

She gave him one lingering kiss before switching off the lamp. She curled into him. "I'm not going anywhere. I'm here now, and I'll be here when you wake up. Always."

He lay there in the dark, holding her close, inhaling her scent, hearing her breathe until she slept. He closed his eyes, following her down. Tomorrow, he'd decide what to do about Patterson. Tomorrow, he'd be able to eat again. There would still be drug dealers, hostage takers, and your basic scum of the earth bad guys, but tomorrow, he'd wake up and Miri would be lying beside him, solid and real. And for many tomorrows to come.

371

ABOUT THE AUTHOR

Terry Odell began writing by mistake when her son mentioned a television show and she thought she'd watch it so they'd have common ground for discussions. Little did she know she would enter the world of writing, first via fan fiction, then through Internet groups, and finally in groups with real, live partners. Her first publications were short stories, but she found more freedom in longer works and began writing mysteries. Her daughters told her the books were as much romance as mystery, so she joined Romance Writers of America and began learning more about the genre and craft. Now a member of Mystery Writers of America as well, she blends romance and mystery into her novels. Terry resides with her husband in the mountains of Colorado. Visit her at www.terryodell.com.